I had no such qualms. If
worn away by the grindstone

Diana took the doctored passport. "Aramji? That's funny! In Gujarati it means Mister Relaxed, Mister At Ease!" Eyes gleaming, she spun around. "But Jim, Adel is a girl's name!"

I said, "Remember Abigail, in Chicago? For days I hadn't a clue that Martin and she were the same person. You've plenty of clothes, yes? Enough to travel with your sister, Adel?"

Adi's face flushed. "As a *woman*? You want me to dress as a girl?"

I chuckled at his scowl. "Beats returning in custody, don't you think?"

"I . . . you think . . . how can I . . ." He took in Diana's boyish figure and blinked.

Diana grinned. "I'll see Mama and Papa again! We're going back to Bombay!"

My beater gave a hop and banged away under the beam of her glee. "People do, my dear. If the ship is watertight and takes on sufficient coal, we'll taste your mother's curry before the month is out."

She whirled around the room, passport held on high like a holy chalice, while Adi shook his head in dismay.

* * *

Next morning, I contributed little to the conversation. I wasn't sure Diana's aunt and uncle were aware that Adi was a wanted man. But when we told them of our intended departure, I caught their quick glance at each other. Of course! Adi would not shelter under their roof without making a clean breast of it. It was like him to be honest and upstanding about every little thing. But Burjor had been worried enough to send him from the country. A tight kernel of dread took root inside me.

Tradition required that Diana wed only a Parsi. By marrying me, she had broken the rules of her clannish Parsi society. These descendants of medieval Persian refugees were an insular, influential group. Diana and I had left Bombay in 1892 to avoid the ruckus caused by our union. Now, we were going back. It had been two years, but that would not matter.

Out of sight and far away, our transgression was a distant slight. Our return would place it squarely under society's gaze. Just what might we walk into?

* * *

The sour-faced clerk at the shipping office said the next departure for Bombay was on a P&O ship, far smaller than our liner from New York, the RMS *Etruria*. That troubled me. It would have been easier for Adi to escape notice among the *Etruria*'s eight hundred passengers.

The shipping clerk tucked a pencil behind his protruding ear and squinted at me. "*Arcadia* calls at Gibraltar, Marseilles, Port Said, and Aden. Reaches Bombay on a Friday."

"I'm traveling with my wife and her sister," I said and forked over £55 for each first-class berth, a princely sum, but thanks to Dupree, within our means.

The agent took his time gazing at the wall beside the ticket window. Shouldn't he know the timetable by now? With a start I realized that he was probably checking the wall of offenders for my likeness!

His mustache twitching, he handed over my change, saying, "Two persons per cabin, sir. Ladies together, single gentlemen will have a male companion."

"Companion?"

"A suitable gentleman," he assured me and jotted our names in his ledger.

I left, a fresh worry brushing my skin like the tickle of ants. Adi could not remain in his cabin the entire voyage. Could he maintain the pretense for almost two weeks?

Next, I cabled Diana's father from the telegraph office: THREE ARRIVING ARCADIA OCT 10. My spirits lifted, seeing Burjor in my mind's eye, his jowly smile as he understood my missive. He'd sent Adi to get help; he'd known I would offer it.

Here was my chance, then, to justify the trust he'd shown when he gave me Diana's hand in marriage. Yet if I failed, it would not only bludgeon the delicate bloom of that confidence. God, if I failed—the thought burned through me—Adi's reputation, his future, his very life would be forfeit.

CHAPTER 4

SHIPMATES

Adi took one look at the garments spread out over our bed and said, "*All* that? You expect me to wear *all* of it?"

"Start with this," said Diana, picking up a petticoat. "Over your drawers, 'course. Right. Take this off." She flicked at his sleeve. "You can keep your *sudreh* on."

Grumbling, Adi climbed out of his trousers and shirt, to stand before us in his underpants and thin, snowy-white muslin undershirt, a sacred garment for Parsis. With a sigh he untied a yellow twine from around his waist, and asked, "Di, you don't wear your *kusti* anymore?"

"Of course I do!" she retorted. "Jim can attest to it. I say the prayers each morning! Here, let's get the petticoat on."

She gathered up a mass of fabric and dropped it over Adi's head. He stood like a morose tailor's dummy while she reached around him. A few expert tugs moved the flounced skirt into place, then she tied the drawstring.

"Too short!" Diana tut-tutted. Although the siblings were alike in build, the skirt hung above Adi's narrow ankles. "We'll have to add a ruffle. Aunt Dinbai will have some fabric."

At the mention of ruffles, Adi looked pained.

"Now a corset," she went on. "We won't lace you tight, but it will give you some shape."

Chuckling at Adi's horrified expression, I picked up one of Diana's lace gloves. It was soft, the fingers neat, seams invisible. "So small," I said, tempted to try my hand through the narrow tube. "Will it stretch?"

Wrapping the corset around Adi, Diana slapped away his fingers, then hooked it up and tugged at the rigging. As though squeezed by an invisible claw, the waist contracted into a thick-necked hourglass.

Adi's face scrunched like a child eating pomegranate seeds. When Diana loosened the folds, he huffed and grimaced at his reflection.

Diana leaned back to survey his pale, hairy chest above the blue, satin-trimmed garment. "Yes, Thomson's sateen, long waist is all right. Now a high-neck blouse, I think," said Diana, pulling out more pastel fabrics. "Or would you prefer a sari?"

At Adi's shocked intake of breath, she giggled, her chuckles tumbling over us. "Come now, Adi, I didn't mean it. Here. A blouse that a nun would be proud to wear."

She offered it, smiling when he thrust an arm through the sleeve. "No-o! It buttons up behind, so you put both arms forward."

Alas, the blouse gaped at his back. Though Diana tugged the sides together, they remained inches apart.

"Di, it's hopeless," said Adi, groaning.

Diana tapped her chin, then brought out a blue jacket with white trim. "Let's leave it open and cover it with this. It's very loose for me, so might just fit you."

Adi tried. He put one arm in, then flailed about with the other. Diana helped him, but he could not get it on. Pulling out of the garment, he dropped it on the bed.

His lips quirked in mock despair as he peeled off the blouse as well. "I'd have to wear this for days onboard. Could you alter a couple?"

That gave me an idea. From my own wardrobe I pulled out a grey jacket. "Diana, your jacket isn't that different from this. What if you added some . . . uh . . ." I pointed at her waist.

She raised her eyebrows and passed a hand across her chest. "These? Jim, that would take rather more skill than I have."

"Ah, no," I fumbled, feeling my face warm.

Adi chuckled. Diana's eyes twinkled as she said, "Goodness, Jim, I've never seen you blush before! It's very becoming."

"Dash it. *These*—can you add these?" I picked up her blue serge jacket and pointed at the seams in front.

"Oh! Darts! Why yes! Adi, put this on. Let me measure you."

My jacket went on easily. It hung off his shoulders, making him look like a child.

Grinning, he shook his head and took it off. "It's the Goldilocks problem. Too small, too large. But this one"—he put on his own jacket over his undershirt—"is just right!"

"Now we're getting somewhere!" Diana rummaged in her sewing basket for a box of pins. These she tucked here and there, fitting Adi's coat to the shape of the corset. Touching his crisp linen shirt, she toyed with the collar, which was still buttoned on.

"This isn't bad. If I add some ribbons and trim the collar in pink, then you could wear your own clothes onboard."

I gave the pair a considering look and said, "Not quite. Look in the mirror."

They turned to stand side by side before the glass, the genuine article and our make-believe woman. Adi's short, cropped hair wouldn't pass muster.

"Oh, that's easily fixed," said Diana. From a hat box she extracted an enormous confection of ribbons and feathers. This descended on Adi's head and was fixed with a pin. When she donned her own hat, my skin tingled. A startling pair of elegant beauties stood before me with dark eyes and neat figures—one diminutive, the other lean and straight.

"You won't be able to take off your hat," I told Adi. "What about the dining room?"

Diana pulled in her lips, then caught his chin and turned him to right and left. "You have nice eyes, Adel," she said. "We could do you up a bit, what d'you say?"

"Why thank you, ma'am." Adi's stage whisper had a strangely pleasant sound.

Pulling out some bottles, Diana went on, "Why don't we ask Aunt Dinbai for a wig? She wears one every day."

When I jerked in surprise, she smiled. "Her own hair is sparse, so she's worn them for years. The only time I saw her without was in her bedroom. Jim, ask her if she can spare one?"

"Now?"

"Mm-hmm."

"Righto." I took myself off to find our hostess.

Aunt Dinbai and Uncle Shapur were in the reading room. I declined Shapur's offer of a whiskey, and posed my bizarre request. "Ma'am, could I ask you for a hairpiece, if it's not too much trouble?"

She blinked. "A hairpiece? Did you say—"

Face warm, I explained, "Adi's got to return to Bombay. Safer if he travels as a woman."

"Oh! Like Charley's aunt in the play! He's dressing up!" she cried, turning to her husband. "On stage, Lord Fancourt Babberley pretends to be Donna Lucia, the dowager aunt! We saw it at the Royalty Theatre last year. Penley played Babbs, simply hilarious as Charley's aunt!"

Beaming, she hurried from the room, leaving me to explain the matter.

"As a woman?" her bemused husband repeated.

When I returned carrying my prize, the door was opened by a composed young woman with creamy skin who offered her gloved fingers. "Pleased to meet you."

"Ma'am," I said automatically as Diana took the wig from me, grinning.

The siblings shared a glance then burst into laughter.

"His face!" chortled Adi. He took tiny steps to the window seat, sank into it gracefully and arranged his skirt.

"It *will* work! Mr. Agnihotri, may I present you to a new woman!" cried Diana. A tendril of hope curled inside me, winding around the worry rooted in my chest.

***

Two days passed in a flurry of activity as I wrapped up my London assignment. What with outfitting and preparing Adi for his new role, we had little time to explore the heart of the Empire. Seeing the dome of St. Paul's Cathedral rise above the fog, I sighed. I dearly wanted to visit Baker Street where Doyle had situated Holmes's quarters, but gave it up as hopeless.

On the eve of our voyage, in a bookstore window on Piccadilly, I spotted *The Memoirs of Sherlock Holmes*. Diana bought it over my objections. Smoothing the leather cover, I anticipated long sunny days stretched out on a deck chair when I'd dive into it.

Then I remembered. At the Dupree Agency in Boston, most blokes had heard of the famous detective. One had a subscription to *The Strand Magazine*, so we borrowed his dog-eared copies. Just before we left, I recalled him saying, "Holmes's last adventure! I mean, can you believe it? His *last* adventure."

I frowned, turning over the crisp binding. Holmes couldn't die, could he? Although we scoffed at the ease with which he came to his miraculous conclusions, he was our hero, a detective nonpareil. Conan Doyle wouldn't do a thing like that?

* * *

At dawn, the "girls" preceded me as Adi wobbled up the gangplank clutching his skirts and reticule. Since he lacked Diana's coifed hair, his hat teetered frequently. From the ship's railing we watched the flutter of kerchiefs on the overcast wharf and made our way toward our staterooms.

In the corridor, sharp voices broke the hum of excited conversation. Mustache bristling, a flushed Englishman glared at a tall, emaciated young man whose dark complexion and high forehead marked him as a fellow Indian.

"But this *is* my cabin," the youth insisted, holding out his ticket. "Number seventeen. That's what it says." He fell silent as we approached.

"Where's that damned purser?" The older man snorted and strode away.

The dark lad gazed after him, a morose matador, determined to stand his ground but fearful he would not prevail. Catching my glance, he retreated to his cabin.

Diana had spotted her cabin number, so I knocked on my own, next door. When no one answered, I keyed it open and stopped in surprise.

A plump, mature gentleman inside said in a pronounced accent, "*Guten Morgen!* You must be my cabinmate?" Wobbling, the whiskered gent came up to shake my hand.

"Jim?" At the door, Diana glanced back, biting her lip.

An irate voice rose behind us, familiar in its protest. In the corridor, the perspiring purser was shaking his head. "We have no vacant berths until Port Said."

The Briton cried, "I was told I would share with a *suitable gentleman!*"

The Indian youth winced, holding himself against the wall as though facing a firing squad. His glance searched the carpet but found no comfort there.

Adi strode over to the red-faced Briton. "Excuse me. Would you prefer to switch cabins?"

Diana sucked in a sharp breath because Adi had forgotten to disguise his voice!

I hurried over. "What she means is, I'll switch," I said, slicing Adi a look.

Grabbing his elbow, I propelled him toward Diana. "Well done, *Adel!*"

Adi acknowledged my reminder with a wry twist to his lips. Dash it all, I'd make a sleuth of him yet.

The Briton examined my curious German cabinmate hovering at the door, and the matter was settled. While the sweating purser directed a steward to move the Englishman's luggage, the lamppost-like Indian shook my hand. He was John Raman, he said, a musician returning to Bombay. His eyes kept darting to Adi, sashaying down the corridor toward Diana.

Our purser returned to express undying gratitude and bestowed a fervent look at Adi that matched young Raman's. I hid a grin. We'd barely left dockside and already Adi had acquired a pair of followers. At this rate, by the time we made Bombay he'd leave a slew of broken hearts in his wake.

* * *

Since none of Diana's shoes would fit, Adi still wore his Oxfords under his copious skirts. Well-equipped with enormous hats, the siblings garnered companions for games, and generally went about as young people do.

On a ship the size of a teacup, one constantly brushed elbows with other passengers, so we'd decided not to discuss Adi's troubles onboard. There would be time enough when we got to Bombay, or so I hoped. Gazing over the calm sea, I settled down to write my employer a full account of my London assignment. Hours later, as I stuffed my report into an envelope to be mailed at our next port of call, I thought Dupree would be relieved that Petersmith's matter was settled. He might even grin at how I'd managed it.*

That afternoon we passed the crowded Alexandria harbor, our ship signaling others with streams of fluttering pennants. With the sun beating down and little to do, we entertained each other by attempting to "read" the signal flags.

My cabinmate John Raman guessed first. "We're low on beer, send supplies."

When Diana gave a delighted chuckle, he flushed with pleasure.

Adi pointed at a passing steamer, flags aloft. "Dancers onboard. Need one?"

Raman gasped. Diana smacked Adi's arm with her fan, then chuckled. At least he'd remembered to use Adel's whispery voice.

Content that at least for the moment Adi remembered his role, I picked up *The Memoirs of Sherlock Holmes* and turned to "The Adventure of Silver Blaze." However, some part of my mind resisted, as though warning me not to continue. At the end of this book, my hero would no longer be immortal, no longer be solving puzzles with deft complacency. The book's allure was strong, but I set it aside.

* * *

Our ship crept along like driftwood in a lazy stream as we approached Port Said, then stopped to join a convoy. Since the Suez Canal could not fit two steamships passing, we waited to allow oncoming vessels through. Over the next day, a ribbon of liners trailed behind our stern.

Bright sunlight scorched the deck. The hot air buffeted my temples, my shirt adhered to my sweat-soaked back as I shifted in a deck chair. Adi hid his downcast face in the shade of a veiled hat, his abundance of coverings giving the impression of a trussed-up turkey.

Not so Diana. She wore a light cotton sari that flapped in the slightest breeze. Pale-yellow fabric sheltered her face as she pointed at a dhow piled high with bales.

"Look! Beyond it!" she cried, her eyes aglow.

---

* This case is described in the short story "A Disgraceful Embrace."

Along the shore, youngsters leapt and splashed in the shallow estuaries between the ridges of the docks. Ever since we embarked, Diana wore an expectant look. She was returning to the bosom of her family. Did she still think of it as home?

I contemplated that word. *Home.* It conjured an image of our little apartment in Boston: our threadbare rug, Diana's tablecloth with trailing roses, a dented couch covered with a paisley print fabric. Her mother's yellow drapes warmed the winter light and the battered old stove, the bane of Diana's cooking ambitions. With assignments taking me away, I'd spent barely a year in that tiny place, but it was our own.

At four bells, Diana said, "Presents for Mama and the little ones," and wafted away to change clothes.

The thought of seeing her parents again brought an unaccustomed flutter to the pit of my stomach. Given enough time, our memories tend to extremes: happy times are bejeweled with glorious moments as though they were exclusively so; times of trouble painted unreservedly dark. Since I'd grown up sans parents, I had adopted Diana's. Her father Burjor had embraced me in Simla—that was real enough. But was it a momentary enthusiasm? While I recuperated in Diana's home after the rigors of my ride to Pathankot, her mother had taken particular pains over my care. She had sent up trays of food and servants to tend me. Was that just the great lady's nature?

At first, the Framjis had disapproved of my interest in Diana. Her father had warned me off, saying, "Please understand, she's not for you!" Despite that initial reluctance, they'd accepted me as Diana's choice. A half-breed without social standing or fortune, a man without claim to status or parentage, the illegitimate castoff of some nameless Englishman, yet they'd given *me* their daughter—their glorious girl, the center of their home, their being. Would they have done that if they had no feeling for me?

Before we left, Burjor had wheedled the Parsi elders' compliance by setting up a Widows' and Orphans' Trust. By marrying outside the faith, Diana could no longer inherit, he was told, and our children would not be accepted as Parsis. We'd had no choice but to agree. Our return might break that gentlemen's agreement. Dread flickered in my chest as I gripped my book, unread. Would all Burjor's careful diplomacy come to naught?

Beyond the ship's railing, dusk had descended over the dunes. Perhaps Diana was looking forward to our return, but I knew better. We'd come to fight Adi's battles. But we'd also need to face our own.

Digging into his reticule, Adi pulled out a ship's brochure. "Look here. We stop in Aden for a day. I'm going ashore, if that's all right."

I frowned. "You'll remember, yes?"

His quizzical look told me he'd quite forgotten. When I tapped the brim of his flounced hat, he gave a muffled groan, and said, "I want to buy a watch. A Waltham pocket watch—American. Couldn't shop in London, you see?"

I shrugged. "It's a port city. You're more likely to be robbed than spotted."

Adi's brow cleared. Without his mustache he resembled an earnest choirboy. He said, "Then I'll have to be on the lookout, won't I?"

* * *

Eventually I went along to guard the "ladies." If Adi wanted a lighthearted foray before the ruckus in Bombay, I could hardly blame him. But I was damned if I'd see him fall prey to a slimy pickpocket.

The crowd flowed and pushed against us in the bazaar as I kept the ladies close. Meat simmered on open grills, baskets of spices were piled high with aromatic herbs, and bright colored scarves streamed above the stalls. It was almost too much to absorb, mounds of fabrics, statuettes, kabobs, rounds of bread, tokens to ward off the evil eye. Vendors hollered, black-draped women haggled, little turbaned boys hawked everything from tobacco to handmade toys—the street was a circus gone mad.

Adi's slim elegance attracted a wave of eager vendors whom I was hard-pressed to dissuade. Then one of them had the nerve to draw Adi's attention by yanking on his hat. It wobbled, almost toppling off.

Before I could intervene, Adi pulled back a fist and laid the bloke out flat.

The fellow gawped up at us from the dust, his pride in shreds, while I waggled a finger at him, admonishing him to leave the ladies alone.

"Manhandle women, will he?" Diana said, as I bustled the ladies away. "Won't make that mistake again." She laughed all the way back to the ship.

CHAPTER 5

THE PRODIGAL RETURNS

With a girl on either arm, I searched the welcoming crowds at Bombay's Victoria pier for Burjor's wide girth. There was no sign of him at the dock, nor of Mrs. Framji's petite sari-clad figure. My insides clenched, as though expecting a blow. Was someone unwell? A sense of dread filtered through me. Why hadn't they come to receive us?

While Diana's eyes scoured the festive throng, Adi gestured. "There's Soli Wadia. God, I hope he doesn't see me!"

Diana frowned. "Wonder why he's here. None of his relatives were onboard."

Soli Wadia. Why did I know that name? Ah—he'd been one of Diana's beaus!

"Diana! There you are!" he called, a lean young man with dark eyebrows. As he approached, dapper in a white linen suit and beige solar hat, Adi slid behind me.

Wadia bent to kiss Diana's cheek but she caught his sleeve. "Are my parents well?"

"Yes, yes, they asked me to fetch you," he assured her, then reached a hand toward me. "I'm Soli. You may not remember, we met at Diana's birthday ball in '92."

Smoothly done, I thought, liking his open smile and firm grip. "Jim Agnihotri."

That name came easily to my lips, although we had not used it in America. When we left Bombay, a ship's officer had recorded my name as James Agney-O'Trey, so that was the moniker I adopted, using O'Trey for work, and Agney or some variation of it on assignment. Now back in Bombay, my old name dropped over me like a comfortable, well-worn coat.

Diana was saying, ". . . my—cousin Adel, from London."

Wadia shook hands with a startled look. He burst into a laugh. "Come, come, *Adel,* Diana," he said, leading us to a waiting coach.

Thank heavens the bloke had a sense of humor, I thought in relief.

In the carriage he spoke with my companions in rapid Gujarati. Diana replied in English, so I followed the gist well enough: Adi's absence had given rise to a great deal of gossip. His return would likely engender more. When Diana enjoined Wadia to silence about the manner of our return, he promised readily. He said Chief Superintendent McIntyre and his cohort had visited Adi's factory and home but had made no arrests.

* * *

To ride through Bombay's sleepy streets was to step back in time. A warm breeze blew through the carriage, lifting Diana's hat, so she took it off and leaned to peer through the window. From the P&O Company dockyard we rode past a round building, the Mazagaon Ice Manufactory, which exuded the ripe odor of fish. Brown sawdust carpeted the road. Bullock carts lined the roadside, loaded with ice blocks sheathed in sawdust and jute against the heat.

Sleepy houses with terra-cotta roofs clustered along the road. I spotted a Zoroastrian fire temple flanked by winged bulls carved onto pillars, and the brick-front of St. Peter's Church. Adorned with cawing crows, a large sign proudly proclaimed the squat building as St. Peter's School. Curving past warehouses on Mazagaon road, we passed the vast edifice of Jamshidji's Hospital, with a long row of windows and wings reaching out around a central pond. Next came the pointed Islamic archways of Grant Medical College, which sported spires and a crenellated roof like a medieval fortress. Obelisk Road led onto crowded Grant Road, where barking stray dogs accompanied us partway. The road climbed through a busy market, each cart surrounded with milling customers.

Temples. We passed small roadside shrines, just marigolds piled around a statue at the foot of a tree and also tall pagoda-like spires heavy with stone ornamentation. The chime of temple bells grew louder as we passed, then faded into the distance. Strange how I'd forgotten that sound. To me Bombay meant birds, tongas, street vendors, and the rumble of trains. However, almost every street boasted a temple, mosque, or church, and often, all three. At Frere Bridge we crossed Tardeo Road running north to Black Town, as it was called.

The street was clogged with handcarts laden with gunnysacks or produce, and cyclists of all ages. Diana pointed out a pair of young women industriously pedaling in divided skirts. Once through, my spirits rose as we clipped past swaying carts and sweating boys plying bicycle rickshaws. At last we rode to Malabar Hill along a coastal road lined with palm trees which bent and swished in the tropical breeze as though greeting us with a lazy wave.

Framji Mansion was draped in dappled shade under a canopy of gulmohur trees. Pink bougainvillea danced in the warm, fragrant breeze. As our carriage neared, Burjor and Mrs. Framji hurried down the great sweep of stairs.

Our welcome at Framji Mansion was exuberant. However, in just two years, Burjor had aged ten. His neck had disappeared and his shoulders bowed under the weight of his head which bent forward. Never sturdy to begin with, Mrs. Framji had grown thinner, her face a tapestry of wrinkles. Surely she was only fifty? She garlanded us with fragrant white tuberoses and embraced Diana, her eyes closed tight.

When it was my turn I tucked a careful arm around her, then slanted toward Adi.

"And who is this young lady?" she asked, smiling.

"Mama," said Adi, pulling off his hat, his cheeks flushed. "I'm in disguise," he explained, as Burjor's eyes bulged in amazement.

Mumbling apologies, Adi dashed from the room in an unladylike gallop.

In the commotion I returned greetings and gave instructions to the startled Gurkha bearers about our luggage. Soli Wadia engaged Burjor in an earnest conversation, then took his leave.

Calling for refreshments, Burjòr ushered us to the morning room where Jiji-bai, the family's cook, had gathered the children. How the little ones had grown! Twelve-year-old Fali was taller and had shed his childhood roundness to resemble a spectacled, younger Adi. Wearing a brocade vest and trousers, hair neatly smoothed back, he had the fresh-faced manner of a junior clerk in a bank.

The two younger children had been babies when we left. After clinging to their mother, they ran to Diana to be picked up. She hoisted the youngest and sat, so the other climbed aboard her knees as well.

Charmed by this tableau, I approached and squatted before the trio.

"This is Shirin," said Diana, nodding to the older girl. "Do you remember Captain Jim? He lived here with us before we went to America."

Shirin offered her hand like a grand duchess receiving a serf.

I took her tiny fingers and bowed over them. "Honored, madam princess!"

She giggled, then informed me, "I'm five!"

I agreed that was a very respectable age, then was presented to three-year-old Tehmina, who shook her abundance of riotous curls, gave me a doubtful look, and buried her face in Diana's neck. Someday, would we have a daughter like her? I felt winded at the thought, as though I was flying through the air without a tether.

While Burjor and I lounged in long chairs, Adi returned wearing male attire and dropped into the couch. His recounting of our shipboard adventures had his mother shaking with mirth, while Burjor rolled his eyes.

Soon electric fans whirred overhead, and the family's bearers Gurung and Ganju arrived with trays of cool sherbet, grinning their namaskars. Years ago, I'd taken charge of securing the house and come to know them quite well. Quizzing them about local happenings gave me a chance to practice my Gurkhali.

"*Kasto samachar?*" I asked Gurung, the older of the pair, seeking news.

He replied eagerly, briefing me military style, as though we'd only been away a week instead of two years.

On the settee opposite us, Mrs. Framji leaned against a pile of pillows. Her fingers worried at the folds of her sari, pleating them incessantly. Looking around the room, she said, "We are complete again. How good it feels. We are almost an army!"

Adi gave a wry smile. "Yes, now that I've brought the cavalry!"

Chuckles rang out. I hooted at this allusion to my army career then said, "Adi's right, though. To clear his name, we'll need all the help we can get."

Adi sobered. "I can't keep hiding, not here."

"You don't need to. Behave as usual, but keep a low profile." I glanced at Burjor. Did he have reason to send Adi away or was it just his general distrust of the law?

Mrs. Framji patted Diana's arm. "When you left, the house was so quiet. As though someone had died."

Diana gave baby Tehmina a hug, set her carefully aside, and dropped to her knees on the carpet. Laying her cheek against her mother's knee, Diana said, "I'm sorry, Mama. I didn't want to leave you."

I knew this. Had she not refused my first proposal in order to avoid the scandalous union with a *parjaat*? The word meant "outsider," but within it were other echoes: pariah, outcast. Yet Diana had persuaded her parents to relent.

I had no parents to help or hinder. I'd never known either my Indian mother's family or my English father. That thought got a familiar heat bubbling inside me: someday I'd meet that dratted man who'd taken his pleasure of a sixteen-year-old and abandoned her, friendless, and with child. If I could have one moment with him, I'd teach the blighter a thing or two.

My fists uncurled as I thought of Shanti, my mother. Fragile and consumptive, she'd had the presence of mind to take refuge at a Christian mission in Poona. There, tended by Anglican nuns, she'd died, leaving me to be raised by them and old Father Thomas.

Diana murmured softly in Gujarati, to which her mother replied in kind.

Mrs. Framji went on, "Even the children knew something was amiss. They kept asking for you each morning. As soon as she was dressed, Shirin would run to your door and knock and knock, asking you to come out."

"Oh, Mama." Diana patted her hand. "We are here now."

"Our family was like a banyan tree with branches hacked off. I knew I would miss you, just as when you went to England for school, but not how much. We had saved up for your wedding . . ."

Diana flicked a glance at me. "Papa gave me the cheque."

"Did you buy a house?"

"No," Diana replied softly.

In fact, my wife had spent part of our nest egg rescuing me in Chicago. To spare her blushes, I said, "We bought a bakery in Boston; our friends run it."

Diana's look thanked me for that tactful phrasing, for she'd made the purchase in my absence. She added, "And an old copper mine, but Papa, we don't yet know if it's worth much."

Adi knew this from conversations onboard. He sat up, the lawyer in him roused. "Do you have contracts for these ventures?"

"What do you think?" Diana grinned. "Properly signed and witnessed! I've learned a bit or two from you."

Burjor grunted his approval. "Two enterprises. In less than a year!"

I grinned at his raised eyebrows. "Your daughter is as sharp as any *bania* shopkeeper!"

He harrumphed, unable to mask his delight, then asked, "And the detective business, is it steady work?"

I nodded, preparing to broach Adi's legal troubles, but Mrs. Framji preempted me. "Son, can anything be done for Adi?"

We spent the better part of an hour discussing the case. Gradually a more complete picture emerged. Adi denied seeing anyone leave the factory when he entered, just before noon. Two employees had been dining on the other side of the building. They'd returned together and found Adi bending over Satya as he drew his last breath.

Adi and Satya had been alone. Adi's clothes were spattered with Satya's blood. His bloodied finger marks were on the murder weapon.

I asked, "Did anyone see you arrive?"

He grimaced. "Our old *chowkidar* said he was at the gate. Claims he didn't see me enter just moments before the ruckus."

His phrasing puzzled me. "Did you see *him*?"

Adi clicked his tongue. "I wasn't paying attention when I arrived."

I frowned. "Did he see anyone leave?"

"He insists that no one left the building. He claims I got there earlier, at eleven thirty."

Taken aback I asked, "Can he read time? Does he own a pocket watch?"

Burjor replied, his voice uneven. "Said he heard the clock tower. Bloody fool."

I glanced at Adi. "But . . . where were you that morning?"

"Later, Jim." Pulling in his lips, Adi looked away.

Perplexed, I frowned. Why did McIntyre think Adi would kill his partner—was it just the lack of alibi, or something more? What possible motive did he imagine Adi had?

CHAPTER 6

A WELCOME AND A WARNING

Diana sat on the bed, smoothing her fingernails with an ivory-handled nail file, watching me go through my morning drill. Our voyages had disrupted my usual regimen, so I closed my eyes to maintain form through my aches. Inhale-push-exhale.

She said, "How many do you do? Are you counting?"

Puffing in rhythm, I grunted through my push-ups. "No."

Droplets of sweat tickled as they rolled down my arms.

To my surprise, she dropped down on the carpet beside me and copied my stance. Lying prone, I grinned as she set her hands by her shoulders and wobbled upward.

"Put your knees down," I suggested.

She did, and tried another push-up, then flopped onto her belly.

"Pull forward," I said softly, resisting an urge to catch the ringlet that tumbled over her forehead. She tried again and went down with a thump.

"How do you do it?" she cried, crinkling up her face.

I smiled. "Started at fourteen, copying the sepoys. We drilled daily, in the army."

My reasonable tone made her frown. "So it's easier for you?"

"Precisely." I watched her wheeze upward. She did two more that weren't bad.

"Men are stronger, sweet," I said, "but you could build some strength too."

She flipped over. "Poppycock! Women's minds are stronger. We have to be. To bear children."

I sat up and mopped my face with a towel, remembering how she'd disappeared while investigating her sisters' deaths. She'd had a companion in Chicago, but still got into a soup. "Won't argue with that. But . . . you won't travel alone, yes?"

She pushed her curls away and glowered at me, her face pink with exertion. "Can you promise the same? Not to get into danger?"

I tossed the towel over my shoulder and contemplated her. "Things that are dangerous for you may not be, for me."

"Oh!" She scoffed. "Your skin repels bullets? You're impervious to knives? Then what's this?" She poked at a scar on my neck, not gently.

"And this?" She put her hand flat on my back, then traced over my skin.

Why wouldn't she look at me? "Di?"

She blinked hard, trying to be stern, but tears shone in her eyes. I pulled her close.

"You stink," she said softly, but she didn't pull away.

Her skin was soft and warm. She smelled so good that I pulled her atop me and forgot what I was going to say.

✳ ✳ ✳

Most officers arrived at the Bombay constabulary after nine in the morning. Knowing Chief Superintendent McIntyre's penchant for an early start, I arrived at eight—after his breakfast, but before he went on rounds of the bullpen and jail. I timed it well—the morning air was still fresh, sparrows chittered, and palm trees swished outside his window.

Seeing me at his door, McIntyre barked, "By God, it's Agnihotri!"

This effusive welcome caught me flat-footed. "Good to see you again, sir," I managed, taking off my felt hat. For a moment, it was as though I had never left Bombay, but continued in my post at the constabulary. Two years ago, the local havildars had grown accustomed to my comings and goings at all hours, and I'd come to know McIntyre well over the course of my brief tenure. In private, Smith and I called him Mac.

Despite his initial distrust, he'd been a good superior, assigning me a slew of old case files to learn my craft. He'd been surprised at how many I'd resolved.

"Returned from America, is it? Bloody Yanks not treating you right?" His growl held an almost affectionate tone that made me blink.

Dressed in a crisp khaki uniform, he stepped around his table to offer his viselike grip, blue eyes keen above his walrus mustache. Exchanging the usual preambles, we sat.

McIntyre's fifty-pound gaze had not diminished in the two years since we'd met. As it pressed down upon me, I pretended to be unaware of it and maintained a pleasant expression. I liked him, but only a fool would forget that he was English to the bone. I'd found him a fair man, as long as one did not question the unspoken authority of British Rule. After a long moment, he leaned back in his chair, looking satisfied.

His eyes glinted. "So, what can I do for you? Ah, it's the Framji mess, isn't it? Who'd have imagined. Fine family like that."

I spread my palms. "The Satya Rastogi case. You can't really suspect Adi Framji."

He gave me a look I could not decipher. "Wouldn't be the first time for young Framji."

"The first time for?"

McIntyre watched me closely. "This friend of yours, he's killed a man before."

I drew back. "Adi? What're you talking about?"

The superintendent's eyes bored into me. "You *can't* have forgotten."

Adi, a killer? When I just stared at McIntyre, he coughed and touched his neck.

I pulled in a breath, remembering. Two years ago, I'd been up against a formidable foe, the heir to a native princedom. Furious that I'd ruined his plans, Prince Akbar had lured Adi to the Bombay University tower—as bait for me.

Swapping blow for blow, I'd grappled with the princeling on the tower gallery. Then a blow rendered my arm useless—the memory was vivid: his knife at my throat as I held him off, his weight tilting me backward, the edge of the parapet slicing into my hip. Adi had crawled toward the door, hands bound, searching for my handgun.

McIntyre said, "Prince Akbar of Ranjpoot was shot and killed."

"That was different!" I blurted. Diana had arrived just in time. She'd picked up my revolver from the mosaiced floor.

McIntyre squinted as he sorted through my words, adding, subtracting, making deductions.

"Yes," he agreed. "That wasn't young Framji at all." The skin around his eyes crinkled. "Let me see. Who else was up on that gallery? Why, the charming Miss Framji." There was no question in his tone.

Instead of refuting it, I said, "Self-defense. Akbar was out of his mind. Said he'd kill us. You were at the inquest."

He leaned back and toyed with his pipe. "Which was sympathetic, since you had that wound..." He tapped his throat again. "Young Framji said he fired the revolver." Eyes gleaming, his smile broadened. "And how is the fierce Miss Framji? Ah! Mrs. Agnihotri now."

Damn the man. During the raucous inquest, Adi and I had chosen to keep Diana out of the report, but McIntyre had sniffed out our subterfuge.

"She's well, sir. But Adi, you know his sort. Intellectual, a lawyer, a responsible bloke. Can you really see him cutting his partner's throat? If they had a disagreement, he'd simply buy Satya out. Then, he'd probably take him to a club for dinner!"

"So why'd he run, hmm? Looks bad. Looks guilty."

"He had business in London, but he came back," I reminded him.

"He panicked. Innocent men don't, usually."

"If he's guilty, why would he return?"

McIntyre's eyes narrowed. "Because you made him."

"He had a choice," I said.

Thinking back, I wondered, was this true? With Diana demanding Adi clear his name, and me espousing his innocence, what choice did he have, really?

McIntyre huffed. "If Rastogi had mucked up their sterling reputation? All that planning, months of work all ground to dust. His name destroyed, dragged through the mud. What then? Think he'd just take Rastogi to court?"

Blast it, he made a good point. If Satya had sacrificed months of hard work, it would hit Adi hard.

Content that he'd flummoxed me, McIntyre dug at his pipe with a sixteen-penny nail. I recalled that he carried it for that exact purpose. Knocking the bowl's contents out over a wastebasket, he said, "It's the quiet blokes whose feelings run deep. Quiet blokes with strong ambitions, passions reined in tight. Young Framji, I'd say he learned of Rastogi's betrayal and snapped."

Dread crawled over my skin. "Betrayal?"

Packing the bowl of his pipe, McIntyre paused. "Your client," he said slowly, "hasn't told you, then."

Drat the man, he was giving me palpitations. "What d'you mean?"

Tilting his head, he gave me a look, then struck a match to his refilled pipe and exhaled a puff of smoke. That damn pipe! It gave him time to mull things over, set up his play. He's enjoying the moment, I thought, my skin itching with a need to refute his complacent deductions, but I held back. Silence often won more results than questions.

In a low growl, he said, "Before he died, young Framji's partner cleaned out their bank account. Took it all. Two thousand rupees."

That was more than a year's pay! I grappled with the significance of such a sum.

Keeping my tone level, I asked, "Have you found the cash?"

McIntyre made no answer, so I went on, "There's motive then, for an intruder. Burglary gone wrong."

McIntyre's burr gentled. "Young Framji was heard arguing with Rastogi, just before noon. Just before he was found covered in Rastogi's blood." He sighed, pushing back in his chair. "Don't take Framji on, not as a client. You're married into the family, lad. Look to yourself! And the little missus. Hire someone else."

His implication pulsed into me with painful pricks. If Adi was convicted, he was saying Diana might consider it *my* failure. I took my leave with a neutral manner, but the sapling of worry within me was sprouting fast. I'd brought Adi back. I'd damn well better make good on my promise to exonerate him.

Now I understood why Burjor had been so eager for Adi to leave Bombay. The case against him was ominous.

CHAPTER 7

RIPPLES OF THE PANIC

The monsoon had pummeled Bombay on its way north, leaving the hot October air heavy and moist. My shirt blotched with sweat, I climbed the restful, dark stairwell to our quarters upstairs to change.

Diana stood at a window, looking out from under a bamboo *chattai*. Neatly rolled up, it would be soaked with water to cool the bedroom. In a sari, a light peach confection that seemed spun from early morning cloud, Diana looked fragile, barely there, like a bird that is all downy feathers. Her cotton blouse was sprinkled with lace.

She seemed absorbed. I said, "Diana?"

Her smile brightened the room. "You're back. Did you find the superintendent?"

"I did." I shrugged out of my jacket. "Everything all right?"

She took my coat. "I was watching Bhim, the new *sais,* bringing hay to the stables. Their lives are driven by such routine, such . . . clarity. He cares for the horses, feeds, cleans, and tends them. Everyone has their role. You"—she glanced up and saw my smile—"you recover people—the missing woman in Boston, the lost children, the boy from Pathankot. And—if someone's dead, you help their loved ones learn what happened, to set things right. But . . . what do *I* do?"

Her fingers clutched my garment, one hand rubbing the knuckles of the other.

I touched her cheek. "You bring color and joy to the world. It would be mighty dull without you."

A rueful smile lifted the corners of her mouth. "That's kind, but . . . is it enough?"

Thinking about this, I peeled off my soaked shirt and took fresh clothes from the dresser. Her look inward, she went out with the used clothes and left me to bathe in the white tiled bathroom, where gleaming faucets hovered over a wide, porcelain sink.

Several years ago, her father Burjor had installed modern commodes at Framji Mansion—not the usual water closet at the end of the hall, but a washroom for each bedroom, a shocking luxury. A faucet over the snowy-white scalloped sink was matched by another against the wall. Someone had decided these humid chambers were really hothouses, so a curtain of greenery cascaded from pots by the window. Undressing, I stepped into a porcelain claw-footed tub and reached for the nearby bucket of water. A metal *lota* lay upside down nearby. Using it, I poured cool water over myself. Bombay had not yet discovered American shower baths.

When I'd worked for Adi two years ago, Diana had been keen to join my investigation. At the time I thought she wanted justice for her sister and sister-in-law, but now I realized it was more. Diana needed a purpose. On our voyage to Liverpool, I learned that she'd been with child, but had lost it while I was away. She bore it bravely, but now and then sorrow flickered across her features like clouds lit by silent lightning.

I washed and dressed quickly, mulling over McIntyre's unpleasant revelation as I knotted my tie. Where was the missing cash? With Adi? If he'd secured it, I could not imagine why he would have hidden such an important detail.

Diana returned, her lips tight as she dropped a letter on her dresser. "I don't believe it! Mrs. Sureewala says her party has had to be postponed. Indefinitely, she says! I wonder . . ." She stared at me. "Mama told her we'd arrived. Is this her way of—*disinviting* us?"

"The Sureewalas, your neighbors?"

She scowled at the letter. "The tone, it's so—offhand. It's not even an apology. Oh dear." She huffed. "Jim, I think we're being snubbed!"

I chuckled, sliding up my suspenders. "Since our livelihood does not depend upon it, I daresay we shall survive."

Diana turned to me, her brown eyes wide. "How *can* you be so calm!? Don't you see? What one does, the others will do as well. The Jeejeebhoys, the Petits, Readymoneys, Tatas! Once that happens, not even the Mehtas or Wadias will oppose the current. What about Mama and Papa, then? Jim, this is bad."

I had no reply, so I opened my arms instead.

"Oh you!" She hummed, stepping in. Long moments of comfort followed. This, I thought, *this* was peace and quiet contentment. Diana stirred and frowned against my skin, fretting over the damage to her parents' social station, damage we were likely to cause, might already have caused by our presence.

Shortly after, when we went down to lunch, I heard Adi speaking with his father in Gujarati. Switching to English, Burjor asked, "I kept it going as you wanted, but now, don't you think it's time?"

"To wind it up?" Adi replied. "I'll have to. The rent alone is . . ." He shook his head.

"Your factory?" I guessed.

He nodded, his face glum. "With all this—chaos, we've sold nothing," he said, disgusted. "So why keep the place, what's the point? It was a dream, a fool's errand."

His partner's death had drowned Adi's efforts, his hopes. Just when he'd found something worth building, Satya's murder had quashed it and put a pall over the future. I needed to show him progress on the case, but had barely begun.

Ganju, the bearer, came to tell us luncheon was ready. Entering the dining room, Diana turned on the overhead fan and directed him to draw the jalousie windows.

"Right," I said, as we followed. "About the chaos. The case. Did Satya tell you he was withdrawing funds? From your business account, I mean."

"I knew about the missing cash, two thousand fifty rupees," said Adi, straight away.

I sighed. "How? How'd you know?"

Adi shifted his weight from one foot to the other, then admitted, "I went to Lloyd's bank, where we have our account, that morning."

I dropped into a chair. "*That's* where you found out? Satya didn't tell you?"

He seated himself across the table and rearranged the cutlery with close attention. "Satya was responsible for purchases. I oversaw sales. That morning, the bank manager called me on the telephone and asked me to visit."

"Dammit, Adi," I grumbled. "You've got to tell me these things. Is this why McIntyre's set his sights on you? If Satya stole the cash, the police can claim you dashed back to stop him from skipping town. They could say he was cleaning out funds at the factory, and you caught him in the act."

He frowned. "That's nonsense. We don't keep cash there."

I groaned at his naïveté. "Don't you see? It's a motive. What I was counting on was that you had none. Now they could make a case for it: Satya stealing from you, leaving you and your employees high and dry."

"They can't believe I'd *kill* him over that?"

"It's a lot of cash. Livelihoods destroyed. Enough to rile a man, even a peaceable one."

I watched Adi fidget. Even on his worst days, when his wife's death was being called a suicide and he was suspected of having driven her to it, he'd kept an even keel. Now he tugged at his cuffs and wound his watch chain through his narrow fingers, his motions jerky, unconscious.

Damn it all to hell. "Adi," I said, "what else aren't you telling me?"

He gave me a quick smile. "Nothing important, Captain. Nothing that matters."

I probed, but he had regained his balance, and I did not want to jar it. Yet worry was gnawing at my insides because Adi's clear eyes radiated a calm light, the sort of light that must have shone from the eyes of Rome's martyrs.

I needed a plan to investigate Adi's case, but so far, I had no clue who else could be involved. I suggested, "Can we invite your friend Tom Byram? I'd like a word with him." We'd need his access to information, I thought, remembering the elegant, erudite man who ran the *Chronicle*.

Burjor had just joined us. His eyebrows shot up. "The editor?"

"Is there another?"

He dropped his chin to his considerable chest and considered it.

"This business, I wouldn't want it in the papers," he said, eyes narrow in his broad face.

"No," I agreed. "But we could use his sources. Someone must know something about Satya's murder, and people talk. A servant, a groom, a rickshaw driver. We need an ear to the ground."

He grunted. "And you think Byram can help? All right, I'll call him."

After he left, I asked Adi, "Is all well between them? He didn't like the idea overmuch."

Adi pulled in his lips, then said, "Things have changed since you left, Jim. We're not, ah, so close to Byram these days."

Two years ago, Byram had been a veritable member of the family! "Why ever not?"

Adi looked uncomfortable. "Because of you, actually."

I felt as though he'd socked me with a hammer.

He explained, "Byram championed you. It put Papa's back up." He spread his hands, grimacing. "Don't mistake me, Jim. Papa likes you. He's quite reconciled to your marriage now. But I suppose . . . he resented being pushed into it."

I protested. "He created a charitable trust so the Parsis wouldn't object!"

Adi fiddled with the spoons. "The elders drove a hard bargain. In good times it would be no problem. But lately, things haven't been as good for business. So many banks crashed last year . . . we had funds at two of them, you know. Lost quite a packet. Papa has little liquidity, now. What's earned each week is spent in wages."

Heavens. The paint peeling in the humid bathroom, the pile of dried palm leaves against the building. I'd imagined Burjor's empire was vast enough to be impervious to the usual swings of fortune. I'd been mistaken.

I said, "In the States they're calling it The 'Panic of '93.' Columbia National Bank, then others. Berkeley's Bank folded, thousands of businesses, several railroads. People starving."

He winced. "What about Boston?"

What about you, he was asking. *What about my sister?*

I sent him a half smile. "We bought a bakery, remember? When she was in Chicago, your sister bought a thousand dollars' worth of wheat.

She sent it to Boston and rented a warehouse for it. Even bought three cats for the place!"

His eyebrows shot up. "Cats!"

I laughed. "Good mousers, so she said. Wouldn't let our neighbors the Lins feed them. 'Make them catch their dinners,' she said! Ran the bakery every day. Long lines every morning. She kept it going, your sister, handled purchases herself."

We had returned from Chicago that summer to find Boston in a panic.

I told Adi, "Loans were called in. Farms went bankrupt, people lost their jobs—Diana priced our loaves low, and gave away 'stale' batches to the 'rear door line.' She told them that the dough had not risen right or not enough salt. Starving folk don't care a hoot, but she kept it up for months, handing out free bread. We still made money. It was the volume, she said."

Adi's pale face glowed.

Those days, Diana and Mrs. Lin sold bread in the morning, while I worked evenings after getting back from Dupree's, hauling sacks and mixing dough with old man Lin. When Adi's cable arrived, I grasped the chance to give Diana a holiday and booked us on the steamer to Liverpool.

But now we'd got back, Adi seemed determined *not* to let me help. I watched him with concern. Did he not realize that unless we solved his silversmith's puzzle, he was facing the noose?

CHAPTER 8

NOBODIES

Byram agreed to meet us that evening, so after a quiet lunch Adi and his father withdrew to their rooms for a nap. It was the practical thing to do in the tropics while the noonday sun blazed overhead, but I had not picked up the habit. In my army days, afternoons were for study, reading every book my commander, Colonel Sutton, could procure—history, biographies of Nelson and such greats, Shakespeare, and sentimental old Dickens.

So, I went in search of Diana and found her upstairs with her mother.

"Captain!" Mrs. Framji's lined face creased in a welcome that lifted my spirits. Her brown eyes glowed, shockingly youthful in a tired face. Her sari *palloo* had slipped from her hair. Seeing the threads of silver pulled back in her bun gave me a curious sensation, a surge of protectiveness, of gratitude for her trust.

She pointed at a black, iron contraption. "Our new sewing machine. Such a troublesome thing. The thread breaks constantly, but Diana made it work!"

Deftly folding children's clothes, she smiled at Diana, who had positioned a large swath of material in the machine.

"Mmm." Frowning in concentration, Diana ran thread from a spool over and through the machine's metal entrails, her dark eyes almost crossed with the effort.

I left them to it, saying I would be back by dinnertime.

Adi's reticence had caused a churning in my gut. He knew something, blast him. But what? No, this was Adi, quiet, honorable Adi, who wouldn't lie to save his life! He *could not* have a hand in anything so vile as murder.

Unable to settle on any plan, I walked around the house. My steps took me to the kitchen.

Here I paused, remembering that Chutki would not be inside. The young girl I'd found on the way from Lahore—the teenaged waif who'd called me brother, who had grinned and huffed and cooked rotis—was dead. For an instant I had forgotten, and the remembering brought a weight down on me, an ache of loss. I would never again hear the proud tinkle of her *payals* as she hurried to set the dinner table.

"Captain sahib!" said a female voice.

Jiji-bai, the old cook, came from the dark interior with a toothless smile. Befuddled with memories, I could not answer but only ducked my head.

She folded her hands, then brought a metal tumbler of water from the earthen pot, assuming in some unspoken fashion that this was what I'd come for. Perhaps the children came to her for water, and she was accustomed to it.

"Come inside, sahib. Don't stand on the *umbhar*," she said in Gujarati, handing me the container.

Thus bid, I stepped over the doorstop into the restful dark kitchen, feeling as though we'd never left Bombay. The cool metal felt smooth and reassuring in my hands, the water sweet and refreshing. Grateful, I returned the tumbler and asked after her family. Framji Mansion had opened once again to encompass me. In the kitchen garden stood the urn of tulsi and mint where I had given Chutki a blue-green sari, the first gift she'd ever received. A few weeks later, she was gone. I exhaled slowly, remembering her shy resolve, her devotion. She'd been cremated wearing her new sari.

Past the row of banana trees, the cool, shady mango orchard beckoned. Where were the guards I had trained? Had Burjor dismissed them? The grassy maidan behind the house seemed deserted as I reached the overgrown back lane. Brambles snatched at my trousers, and the rear gate was padlocked with a rusty chain. Creepers and bushes straggled over the stone wall.

The financial crisis had been harder on the Framjis than they let on. My stomach plummeted. Had their finances shrunk because I, a half-breed Eurasian, married their daughter? The theft of two thousand rupees from Adi's account took on a new significance.

I crossed the irrigation trenches to the row of shady banyan trees, then followed the curved driveway to the front gate, my boots crunching on the gravel. I'd walked this path innumerable times as a bachelor.

That dire morning six weeks ago, Adi had probably taken a tonga. I headed down to the crossroads to trace his steps to Lloyd's bank at the Esplanade, Fort. As the blazing sun crept overhead, the heat beat down on my head like a fist.

A canopy of banyan trees offered some shade where lines of one-horse tongas, closed Victorias, and narrow bicycle rickshaws stood at the Teen-batti crossroads, named for a large three-pronged lamppost nearby.

Climbing into a tonga, I accepted the driver's salaam and directed him down through the crowded streets of the old Bombay fort to Lloyd's bank.

Wide stone buildings established the area as Bombay's financial district, with molded cornices and carved heraldry over the doorways. The paved sidewalks had been so recently washed that a haze of steam rose from the pavers. A pair of dogs lay panting in the shade. Turbaned men hurried by, squinting from the glare. A water carrier bearing a leather sack over his back poured into a metal bowl for some passersby. In the heavy quiet of afternoon, the splash brought to mind Kipling's army water boy: *Of all them blackfaced crew, the finest man I knew, was our regimental bhisti, Gunga Din.* I'd known his like, a dozen-fold.

At the bank, a blue-and-white-uniformed guard salaamed and pulled open the heavy teak door. Stepping into the old marble portico, I asked for the manager.

A young Indian man in a smart suit came up at a brisk clip and invited me into a quiet chamber where we sat across a fine carved desk.

"I am Bisvas Gupta," said the Bengali banker, his high forehead shining. "May I help? Your name, sir?"

He looked startled to learn it. Ah, he'd been told an Englishman was waiting.

No matter. "I'd like to open an account," I said. Pulling out Dupree's cheque for my last wages, I laid it on the glossy rosewood table.

Gupta hurried away and returned with a clerk carrying a large ledger. There I entered my particulars, giving my address as Framji Mansion, and handed over the cheque.

He mentioned international currency exchanges. Consulting another ledger, he said, "The rupee is strong, sir. But foreign currency is much in demand, so we will give you a special rate." He entered a modest sum against my moniker. Since we had left no funds in Boston, and our friends the Lins lived off the bakery we owned together, a little over fifteen hundred rupees was all we had to our name.

Gupta went on, merrily describing financial transfers between continents, the collection of taxes due to Her Majesty, and more. Apparently content that he had established his bona fides as a wise old owl, he wrote out a series of notes that I might use to avail myself of funds, reminding me, "Each transaction is confirmed with a phone call. I will remind you that we met today, the hot, sunny afternoon of October eleventh. You will know me when I call?"

"I will," I said, noting his Indian intonation. "Will you? I was with the Fourteenth Light Cavalry, on the northwest frontier."

"Dragoons," he said, in a hushed tone. "Yes, sir, I will be happy to assist you. Will that be all?"

"Not quite," I said. "My wife was Miss Framji. If she requires funds, you will oblige without objections?"

His eyebrows climbed that noble forehead as he made some notations, saying, "Mrs. James Agnihotri will be most welcome."

This brought me to my main purpose. "Do you know Mr. Framji? Adi Framji?"

He interlocked his fingers over his middle. "Of course."

In a few moments he confirmed Adi's statement about the morning of the murder. Mr. Rastogi had indeed withdrawn a large sum, and he, as manager, had thought it prudent to inform the other account holder. Young Mr. Framji had arrived, learned of the transaction, and departed shortly after.

I asked, "How did he seem, when he heard about the cheque?" After all, this was McIntyre's entire case, that Adi was enraged at an embezzlement.

The manager gazed at me. "Seem, sir?"

"Was he calm, or agitated?"

He shrugged. "He seemed surprised, but not unduly so."

I jotted it down exactly. "Now, mind, if anyone asks you to change that statement, you will let me know, yes?" I wrote the Framjis' telephone number on a page and tore it out.

Handing it to the astonished banker, I asked, "What time did Mr. Framji leave?"

He scratched his eyebrow. "Uh. You are a captain in the army, sir?"

"Retired. What time?"

"I cannot exactly say. About eleven thirty? Perhaps later?"

"Good." I wrote it down word for word, puzzled at the spike of fear I'd seen in his eyes. A suspicious man would wonder if Gupta had something to hide.

We said goodbye in the foyer. As I stepped out into the street, a voice hailed me, "Jim! Good Lord, it's Agnihotri!"

My old friend, Major Stephen Smith, stood before a carriage, solar topi in hand, gazing at me in delight. He paid off the fellow, who watched, amused, as Smith shook my hand vigorously.

Smith cried, "What luck to find you! We're back, did you know? Nine months in godawful Africa and even this hellhole looks like heaven! Where're you billeted?"

He didn't know. I slapped his back and grinned. "Married her, old chap."

He gawked at me. "Miss Framji? Bloody hell! What d'you do that for?" Then he guffawed and punched my arm. "Can't say I blame you, lad. Found a 'soft spot,' have you? Married old moneybags' daughter!"

Soft spot? Was that what my comrades believed, that I'd married Diana for her money? Thus reminded why, in younger days, I'd often been tempted to sock Smith a good 'un, I chuckled and asked where he'd put up. He was in Esplanade House by Victoria pier, so, agreeing to meet up with the lads soon, we said our goodbyes.

I left Smith standing by the bank, looking after me, and remembered that he had almost always been in debt. Had he come to collect funds remitted by his aging pater, or to try to wheedle a loan?

* * *

Framji Mansion was quiet when I returned. Ganju admitted me, the knees fraying on his uniform. Of Burjor's considerable staff only Gurung, Ganju, and a new youth remained. What of Jiji-bai's son and daughter? What of the Bengali cook and her husband, and the gap-toothed boy who'd served the family two years ago? Had they been pensioned off or sent away?

I recalled Smith's gleeful laugh. He'd cheerfully assigned me the role of money-grubber. It made me want a long, cleansing bath.

The household was not yet astir, so I sat down in the morning room with my notebook and my musings. Much had changed in two years. We'd left a prosperous bustling household. Though recovering from the tragic deaths of two beloved young women, they'd given the impression of forging ahead with promise and energy. Now the home seemed depleted, troubled, and burdened with secrets.

Thrusting away these dismal thoughts, I began to construct the steps of my investigation. I needed to see the place where Satya was killed and meet the factory staff, the witnesses.

Sona—that meant gold. *Na becho* . . . don't sell it. No, I thought, that wasn't it. *Na beych-ney doh*. Don't let them sell it. Don't let *who*? And what gold?

I recalled banker Gupta discussing the impending transfer of India's gold to Britain—a great deal of gold, to secure India's "home charges against British administrative services"—a pretty euphemism for the taxes India paid to the royal exchequer. Ever since the mutiny of 1857, the Crown had taken charge of the Indian subcontinent from the erstwhile East India Company, so funds went directly to the British treasury through the India Office.

My company sepoys had been sons of laborers and tradesmen, and much given to cursing their local zamindars and landowners. But weren't those the very folk paying taxes? When the crown demanded its due, landowners in turn squeezed their dependents. The bullion accumulated at the British treasury paid for all Her Majesty's Government desired: New ships? Why not! British officers' salaries and pensions, upkeep of Her Majesty's several palaces and the war in Africa, all funded by tradesmen like the Framjis and sweating Indian farmers.

Gupta had mentioned transfers of gold—could there be a connection to my case? The possibility seemed remote. I returned to the matter at hand. Who else would know what Satya was up to? His parents, siblings? Was he married? I examined my page, surprised. Except that he was Adi's schoolfriend and came from a family of jewelers, I knew nothing about the victim.

Shortly after this, Diana entered carrying a wad of notes.

Waving these at me, she said, "Seems we're not good enough for Mrs. Mehta! She's declined my invitation. The Petits, and the Sureewalas! They are 'otherwise engaged'! I wanted to introduce your pianist from the ship, John Raman, to Bombay society. He's brilliant, dear, but we can't help him. We're back, Jim, and nobody wants us. We're nobodies. And Adi—they're staying away, as though they think he's guilty!"

She blinked, trying to hide the hurt in her eyes, but I saw. And could find nothing to reassure her.

CHAPTER 9

THE SILVERSMITH

Adi's factory was a large shed, once part of an old bungalow that had fallen into ruin. Much of it was demolished, leaving a dismal footprint and assorted walls to show it had once been a home. The unattended gate hung open.

I followed Adi's quick steps into a long building and glanced around at partially stocked crates, stacks of boxes, and packing materials in neat rows. Somewhere inside, a machine made a whirring noise.

Surprised, I asked, "You kept the firm running?"

"How would the men feed their families? But . . ." Lips compressed, he sighed.

I motioned at his inventory. "The loan you'd taken. Was that cash with Lloyd's?"

Adi nodded, his mouth morose.

"So." I swung an arm to encompass the room. "How are you paying salaries?"

A smile twitched over Adi's face. "I'd put by some savings. Not much. I have to tell them it's over, close up shop."

He went to a table where instruments were laid out for packing. "I suppose I'm hoping for a miracle. Something's got to sell, else it's all scrap, every bit. They put their hearts into it, you see . . . we all did."

Per my request, we'd driven the carriage past Lloyd's bank. The factory was less than half an hour from there. I frowned. The timing of that morning still felt out of whack. "That morning, why d'you stay so long at Lloyd's? It would take only a few minutes to tell you 'bout Satya, surely?"

Adi clicked his tongue as we walked through the hall. "Gupta kept me waiting. Well over an hour. Something about the quarterly reckoning, Jim. He'd said it was important, so I read newspapers and waited."

The whirring had ceased while we spoke. I searched the empty hall. "All right, so where are they?"

We found his desultory employees under a banyan tree. A call from Adi roused the pair, who clambered to their feet and salaamed. Adi introduced Faisal, who had the look of a tired bulldog in the way he hung his head, with grey hair that spiked up and then drooped over his ears. The young accountant, Vishal Das, had a thin, sparse beard just coming in, and spectacles that enlarged his dark, curious eyes.

I asked to speak with them separately. Adi offered his office, saying he needed to inventory the supply room. "Shall we go inside?" I asked Faisal Khan, the older man who wore his worry like a cloak.

Settled across Adi's desk, he told me he'd been at lunch with Vishal when Satya was attacked. When Adi called out, he rushed back into the factory. "With Vishal," he insisted. "We entered together."

"What did you see?"

Faisal's face puckered like a frightened child's. "Blood, sahib. A lot of blood." He clutched the hair over his ears. Shaking as though he had a palsy, he repeated much of what I knew from Adi. I took down his particulars and he left in slow plodding steps, holding his elbows as though he was cold. Could he have stabbed Satya and then dashed back to the others without drawing attention? Unlikely. Or was that just the impression he wanted to give me?

On his turn, Vishal wiped his spectacles, insisting, "We both together, we found Adi-ji and Satya-ji. I told the police this already, sahib." I recalled that Indians often added the suffix *ji* or sahib to denote respect, just as Mr. was used in England.

"Tell me too. Was there anything different about that morning?"

Frowning in thought, his head swayed, no.

To loosen him up, I tried a broader question. "What about your work, anything amiss?"

His head wobbled. "The accounts are in good order. I can vouch for that. But the business? There is no income. Only outgoings."

"Did you hear an argument?" I asked. McIntyre had mentioned raised voices.

He grimaced, nodding. "I heard Satya-ji. No one else."

Neither man inspired much confidence, each eager to know what the other had said. They clung together, holding their alibi as a shield, insisting they had returned to the workshop at the same time. Neither admitted being first to enter the room. Something about this troubled me, but I could not quite account for it.

They seemed . . . scared. Was it that simple? Was it only reluctance born from a natural fear of being questioned, of making a mistake? Or was there more to it? Why in blazes were they so united? Surely two men could not spend every second together? That morning, had neither seen or heard anything that could explain what had occurred? Or was there some agreement between them?

When Adi returned, they ducked their heads and answered without meeting his eyes, as though Adi had an incurable illness.

I understood. They thought him guilty, the shadow of the noose already over him. Yet they owed him some loyalty, for he was paying their wages, sums they knew he could ill afford. It put them in an awkward spot.

Later that evening, I visited the home of Faisal Khan, the elderly Mohammedan, and learned that he was married and with a family of four.

Seeing me on his doorstep, he started, then recovered and led me to a small parlor. It was furnished in the Indian style, with carpets, bolsters, and cushions around the sides. On a low table at the center, an incense holder held a pair of smoking joss sticks. Smoke wisped upward, scenting the room with the fragrant tones of sandalwood and attar.

His hair stuck out under his prayer cap, curling over his ears. Seating me near a window, he hurried away and returned, carefully bearing a cup of tea. He remained standing until I invited him to sit.

The cup and saucer did not match, but they were scalloped porcelain, perhaps purchased at different times from Chor bazaar, the well-known market of thieves. Blowing on the tea to cool it, I asked again about the day Satya died.

Sitting crisscross, he said, "I could not find a tonga that morning, so I walked to work. Around eleven thirty when I arrived, I saw the carriage leave."

That puzzled me, Adi had been at the bank until that time. "Did you see Adi?"

"Not in the workshop. But he is often working with machines in his office."

I raised an eyebrow. "You thought he was in the building?"

Faisal's eyebrows shot up. "Yes. I do."

But Adi claimed he had entered the factory at noon, only seconds before Satya died. I sipped the dark aromatic tea and considered my host.

Outside, a pack of stray dogs set up a howling protest. Perhaps the bread-walla or postman had cycled past, escaping the horde who snapped at his feet. The barking of strays was a common nuisance during hot afternoons. Outside the window, sunset rays twinkled on trembling leaves.

As though uncomfortable with the silence, Faisal said, "The watchman also said Adi sahib came in the carriage."

"Really? Why tell you?"

"Not me, sahib. I heard him telling the *Angrez* policeman."

The gateman must be mistaken, I thought. I knew from prior investigations that people often confuse the sequence of disjointed events. In the quiet chamber, Faisal gazed at me expectantly, one hand gripping the other. Why was he so anxious?

"Tell me," I prompted, "when you arrived, did you see the watchman?"

"Yes. A *bhisti* was giving him water."

"And you are certain it was Adi Framji's carriage?"

He reared back. "Of course! I know it well."

His insistence was curious. McIntyre would believe him because he had no apparent reason to lie. I gestured for him to continue.

He said, "I had to sharpen and pack thirty pieces that day. But Satya-ji did not find the forceps satisfactory. He asked me to reset all the hinges."

"Is this common?"

He shrugged. "I've worked there only three months. What's common, not common, I don't know. Each day Adi sahib, Satya-ji, they assigned my tasks."

"Did you see both that morning?"

"I am telling you. Only Satya-ji. He came and went from the supply room, the workshop, his office."

"What about Vishal?"

"He was in the supply room."

"Hmm?"

"He does accounts, sahib. Some coal was delivered, so he went outside to the cart. I could hear him."

"What time was that?"

Faisal frowned, thinking. "After I had just reached there."

Since all this was well before noon, I did not really care, but I wanted to know how closely the employees noted each other's movements.

"After eleven thirty," I prodded, "the cart approached—did Satya go to it?"

He spread his hands. "Don't know, sahib." His face took on a troubled look.

"But he should have been there?"

He wobbled his head in agreement. "They are the owners. Must have been busy, sahib."

I checked my notes, then asked, "Was he with someone at the time?"

No answer. I caught Faisal's perplexed gaze.

"I did not see anyone enter," he said demurely.

"Did you hear anyone?"

He winced. "The machine, it is very loud. The sharpening machine."

"You were using it?"

He nodded, hands folded. I'd heard a scraping hiss when Adi and I entered the factory. Instead of joining Adi and myself, Faisal had gone out to the garden with the accountant Vishal. Perhaps the machine obscured distant voices.

"What happened then?"

"We worked till almost noon. From the workshop I called to Vishal. He brought his tiffin and we ate in the *bagicha*."

"The garden?"

"The bungalow once had a fine garden. Our factory used to be the adjoining stable."

"And then?"

"We heard cries. Someone crying out. We rushed back and—*hai baba!* What a sight. Adi sahib holding Satya-ji. So much blood on him. Adi sahib kept talking to Satya-ji, but he was choking." He grimaced and swiped at his eyes.

He'd been barely able to speak about it that morning. I waited, assessing him.

Faisal said, "We tried to stop the bleeding, but Satya-ji . . . it was no use. After some time, the doctor arrived. Vishal brought the police."

"Did someone ask Vishal to do so?"

"Yes. Adi sahib."

I wrote quickly. It was a fairly clear account, but that troubled look in Faisal's soulful eyes held me like glimpsing the barrel of a gun in the bushes.

"There's something you haven't told me. What is it?" I said quietly and waited.

He fidgeted. It was something he did not want to share or wasn't sure about.

Secrets are like balloons. Silence pumps air into them. The more one wants to shy away, the bigger they loom. Now Faisal had waited too long to fob me off.

"It's nothing, sir," he mumbled.

I raised an eyebrow. Sir, not sahib, as before.

"Tell me anyway," I said, in an informal tone.

His eyes darted around as though seeking an escape, so I cleared my throat to prompt him. Diffident, barely audible, he said, "His family, sir, you should ask them."

"Why?"

He looked ambivalent. "Sometimes Satya did not go home. After work. Many times, he stayed in the factory. He asked the gate man to buy food."

"Didn't Adi also work late? They were inventors, no?"

"Yes. Yes sir, you are right," Faisal said gratefully, swinging his head in agreement. He seemed relieved to have unburdened himself and eager to have his concerns dismissed. Curious, I thought. He'd pointed me toward Satya's family, but it seemed that he had not wanted to.

I asked him if there was anything else, but he insisted there was not.

I departed, heartened to know that it was Adi who'd summoned the police. It further strengthened the case for his innocence.

But Faisal's testimony also indicated that someone else was speaking with Satya when the supplies were delivered. Was that Adi, or another visitor? Why did Adi insist that he had only just arrived at noon, when two witnesses, the watchman and Faisal, claimed to see his carriage leave earlier that morning? His denial put him in an awkward spot.

Faisal's testimony echoed what Adi had said about the gateman's. I searched my memory of the morning's visit, but could not recall seeing anyone at the gate. Had he been dismissed? Strange that Adi had not mentioned it.

* * *

On my return, I discharged my huffing bicycle-rickshawala at the base of Malabar Hill and walked up to Framji Mansion. Dusk had dropped over Bombay while I traveled, and purple twilight filtered through trees. Here and there lamps glowed, announcing gated driveways, their great houses hidden behind tall yew hedges or stone fences. An orchestra of crickets followed me, a chorus of frogs rounding out the bass.

At Framji Mansion, a pair of guards sat smoking before the gate. I smelled the acrid scent of native *beedees* as I approached.

Then one asked the other, "What of the *gora* sahib, the *ghar jamai*?"

Hearing the slur, I paused. The servants thought I had returned broke, to mooch off my in-laws! My face felt warm, though I wondered, why should I care? Yet I did. Dammit, I was no longer the penniless soldier whom Burjor had taken under his wing.

"Gurung," I called to the older man, my tone sharp. "Why is the gate open?"

He leapt to his feet and saluted, then hauled the gates shut. While he was occupied, I quizzed the younger man. "Your name? What's your job here?"

"Bhim, sahib. I'm the new *sais*," he said, shifting nervously on his feet.

"You drive the carriage? What about the day Satya Rastogi died? Do you remember it?"

Eyebrows drawn together, he nodded. Gurung must have grasped that these were no idle questions, for he stood at a distance, watching. I asked the new groom, "What time did you drive Adi sahib from this house?"

His mouth dropped open. Then he said, "Sahib, I did not take him. I drive Burjor sahib every morning."

I squinted at him. Adi could not have taken the carriage. Was Faisal lying, as well as the factory watchman? Or had someone else visited that morning in a carriage that both men mistook for Adi's?

CHAPTER 10

SATYA'S FAMILY

Next morning at breakfast, I mulled over Adi's problem. I had to treat it as an ordinary investigation, explore it as I usually did and find facts upon which to build my case. It didn't feel at all "usual" because I fretted over each bit of testimony, doubted and questioned everything, so that nothing seemed steady or reliable. I was too close to it. By now the famous Holmes would have sifted out which evidence was of consequence, but I was still gathering the pieces.

Tamping down my frustration, I told Diana, "One usually begins an investigation by speaking with the victim's family. But if I present myself as Adi's representative, I doubt I'd get past the gate. I need a pretext."

Dressed today in a pale blue sari, she heard me out, her dark eyes amused. "You want to enter Satya Rastogi's home incognito?"

Back in India, it felt strange not to wear my usual army attire, khaki shirt and shorts. I glanced down at my linen trousers and white shirt, de rigueur in the tropics. "At Lloyd's they took me for an Englishman. I wonder . . . could I use that to my advantage?"

She set down the teapot. "Jim, I believe Satya's people are hereditary goldsmiths."

Diana was reminding me this was a traditional Hindu family. In the army I'd met traditional Bengali tradesmen and Sikh farmers who signed up for better prospects but I could recall no sepoy from a gold-smith clan. In such closed communities, one needed a personal or familial connection to enter.

She said, "Can't imagine they'd speak freely to an Englishman. Can you pretend some official capacity?"

I scratched my forehead. "No one tells the police more than they absolutely must." My experience at the constabulary had taught me that. "I could go as a newspaperman, but that won't serve. Satya's parents would hardly speak with the press."

"You want them to trust you, volunteer information?"

I accepted a second cup of tea. "I need to question them, examine where he lived, discover what his parents are like, his friends, his siblings—"

"But who are they, the Rastogis? Have you asked Adi about them?"

I shook my head. "Leave him out of this, sweet." I struggled to articulate what had kept me up most of the night, and said only, "He's . . . being obstinate."

At that, her glance caught fire. I rushed to preempt the conflagration. "No—don't lay into him. Let me poke around first. There's something . . . peculiar about all this. Two witnesses who cling together like burrs on a saddlebag, and a gateman I've yet to meet."

Diana blinked at me, so I narrated Faisal's comments that apparently matched the factory watchman's statement.

She grew thoughtful. "So, what will you do now?"

I finished the last bite of my omelet and picked up my solar hat. "I'll drop in on McIntyre again. Need to know what he's got against Adi."

* * *

I walked in on McIntyre and Stephen Smith in the middle of an argument, or as close to one as I could make out.

Smith sputtered, "I do! But I can't manage their accents, blast it! Send someone else."

"You've been in India twelve years," McIntyre began, his tone cold. "Sending a local chap would just—" He caught sight of me and stopped, eyes narrowed.

"Morning," I said from the door. "I'm interrupting. I'll come back."

As I turned to leave, he called, "Agnihotri! Here, I've got a use for you."

I shook hands with Smith, whose usually ruddy face seemed pinched. "So you're my replacement, eh?"

I had intended it as a jest, but both men looked at me with close attention. "Is there a problem?" I said, lightly.

"What'd you want?" asked McIntyre, waving me to a chair. "Your old job back?"

My eyebrows shot up. "Hadn't thought of that." Judging it best to keep my questions for a more private moment, I invented quickly. "Is Dr. Jameson still around?"

"He is." Reminded of my close connection to his friend, he brushed his mustache and said, "Look here, go with Smith, will you? He needs an interpreter."

I considered that. It wouldn't hurt to have Mac owe me a favor. "On one condition. Could I see the Rastogi file when I get back?"

He barked a laugh. "Or what? You'll return with his solicitor?" Getting to his feet he said, "Oh, all right. But I wager you'll be interested in Smith's investigation."

As we left, I smiled at my old comrade. "You joined the force! Congratulations."

He grimaced. "Don't know how you stood it. The bloody heat, for one. He expects me to go round in this frightful blaze! But you don't mind, you're half—" He cut short, with an apologetic glance.

Ignoring the tired assumption that natives were so hardened that we did not feel the heat, I greeted an old acquaintance. "Sub-inspector Sabrimal, good morning!"

"Welcome back, sir!" He saluted, grinning, his round head dancing on his neck. He'd grown more rotund in the intervening years. The friendly fellow's stripes told me he was still awaiting his promotion to inspector.

As we stepped down the outer stairs, I asked, "So, where are we going?"

"The Rastogi residence," Smith muttered, hailing a nearby Victoria driver. "Third time. They can't speak English, and my Hindustani only goes so far."

This was a piece of luck! He gave directions to Satya's home, then I asked, "What have you learned so far?"

"Not much." He mopped his crumpled brow, already pink from gusts of October heat. "They're a large family, cousins and uncles all over the place. When we broke the news, there were a score or more! That's without counting the women. Couldn't tell who was his father or brother."

"He has a brother?"

"No idea. Place was a circus!"

The Rastogis lived on crowded Sonapur Lane near Lohar Chawl, where they occupied an entire building. Through a padlocked gate we spoke to a man chewing tobacco. He summoned another, a thin bloke with shrewd eyes wearing a banded topi.

"You are the *khansama*?" I asked. The cook is often a large family's steward.

"The *mistri*," he corrected me, folding his hands. Clasping his long fingers together, the craftsman heard my polite request.

He motioned to the tobacco-chewing *darwan* to unlock the gate, said, "Wait here," and left us in the courtyard.

Smith stalked over to a large stone by a tree and perched there gingerly. I glanced around at the neatly tended shrubbery and white-rimmed well, catching sight of figures peering from a higher floor. The barred windows brought an odd sensation to the pit of my stomach, like I was looking up at a prison.

When Smith pulled out his official book, I said, "Let me speak with them. We can compare notes afterward."

He chewed his pencil and agreed. A few minutes later the thin *mistri* returned and bid us follow. He led us around the side, through a garden thickly treed with peepul and jacaranda. Like most homes, the kitchen was in a separate structure to protect the main house from kitchen fires.

A verandah abutted the kitchen shed from which wafted the aroma of spice and garlic. Here a large woman in an orange and yellow sari sat sideways on a swing suspended from the ceiling. A metal plate was propped on one bent knee, while she deftly wielded a small knife, shelling a mound of small vegetables with unconscious efficiency.

"*Pranam,*" I greeted her, folding my hands. Beside me, Smith blinked as though unsure whether to follow my lead, then took off his hat instead and fanned himself.

I explained that we were seeking Satya's family, and asked where they were.

She made a wide motion with the knife. "Here. All around. We are all family."

"His parents?"

She pointed at herself with the blade.

"Your name?"

She gave an amused sniff. "My parents named me Meera."

"Thank you Meera-ji," I said, adding the appellation. "And his father?"

The blade curved around toward the top floors. "Working."

"He is a craftsman?" I asked, using the vernacular word, *karigar*.

"They all are."

"And Satya?"

Her look dimmed. "What do you want to ask?"

Feeling my way, I asked, "Did Satya work here, earlier? Was he trained?"

"All are trained."

Speaking of Satya had made her coldly angry, so I sought another direction.

"Do you train others too? Outside your family?"

She flicked her head, saying, "We are Daivadnya Brahmins. Only family members can become goldsmiths. You see that girl?" She pointed at a child working in the garden. "She is from another caste, a low caste. Do you think just anyone can handle gold?" She scoffed and returned to shelling her peas.

I asked, "Your husband. What's his name?"

She showed teeth reddened with betel leaf. "Tansen. You met him just now."

"The *mistri*?"

"All are *karigars*, workmen. We make *kundan*, *Kolhapuri saaj*, beautiful styles of jewelry. It takes years to learn!" Her hands worked automatically, plucking, cutting, shelling the green orbs.

"Why didn't Satya work with his father?"

At this, she stared at me. "Ask him! Ask my son who is dead! How much we told him, begged him, shouted! But he wanted to work in a factory!" She spat the word, pronouncing it phac-ta-ry. I had touched a nerve.

The woman occupying the swing was unlike any mother I'd seen. Here was no kindly matron, but a matriarch. As a teen, I'd been invited by army comrades to visit their village homes. Curious about civilians, I'd accepted, but found myself confounded by a maze of unspoken rules. By custom, outsiders did not speak with the women whose faces were hidden under the edge of their saris. Satya's mother showed no such modesty. Did she run the clan? Or was she deputized to turn us *gora* officers away?

I asked, "What did Satya do, at the factory?"

She turned a disgusted look on me. "He made spoons, knives of silver! Ugly, base things! After teaching him to spin gold into royal ornaments, the craft of the gods!"

She saw his choice as a betrayal. I asked, "Was he unhappy here?"

"Unhappy?" She reared as though such a thing was unheard of. "He had food, a place to sleep, clean clothes, a respectable craft. What more did he want?"

Smith cleared his throat and mumbled to me, "Did he have enemies?"

When I translated his question, the woman grimaced in surprise. "What enemies? We are all kin! Whoever killed him, they are from outside."

No need to remind her of the countless princes, both English and Indian, who'd murdered brothers and fathers. I asked a few more questions, but her curt tone suggested the interview was at an end. No, her husband could not speak with us. No, Satya had no siblings. We departed, returning to the bustling gully with a sense of relief, even of reprieve.

As a boy I had fondly imagined coming home to find a hot meal awaiting me, to have a loved one place a cool hand upon my brow and fuss over me, checking for coughs or fever. No fear of that here.

One night onboard, Adi had mentioned that Satya had been a classmate. "At school," he'd said, "what mad boys we were." Although intensely traditional, Meera and Tansen Rastogi had educated their only son in the ways of the West, and possibly lost him to that life. What recriminations, what regrets did they feel? Yet in that brief, strained visit I had not sensed any familial affection—rather, it felt like a foray into an alien fortification.

* * *

I was writing my impressions in the morning room when Diana and her mother returned, laden with brown paper-wrapped packages and baskets.

"I cannot decide," said Diana, tossing her hat and parcels on the table, "whether British rule is a blessing or a curse!"

Mrs. Framji slipped off her shoes at the door near the morning room, saying, "Imagine! Pears at eight annas a dozen. And custard apples."

Smiling, she tucked her feet into a pair of slippers and went to the kitchen. Since shoes were never worn indoors, I usually padded around in my stockings. The Nepalese bearer Ganju bowed a salaam as he followed her, bearing more produce.

Diana dropped into a seat and fanned herself with my newspaper.

I set down my pen. "British rule?"

"It's odd. Some are lovely people, like Emily Jane and your friend Superintendent McIntyre, but then, there are all these stupid rules . . ."

I chuckled at this. "Your friend Miss Channing might qualify as lovely people, but I doubt that my old boss has ever been called that." Mac was as stiff as an Englishman could be, but his integrity was beyond question.

"Oh, you know," she said, tugging the bellpull and laying her head back against the chair. "Take Jameson then, what a darling man he is."

I hid a smile at the thought of what Dr. Jameson would think of such a fond characterization, then recalled his hand in our own union. Two years ago, when Diana had gone to him to inquire about my injuries, the old codger had guessed the nature of her affection. So, he'd sent me to the Framjis with a gift—a ruse, I now knew. Without his canny intervention I would have had little opportunity to declare myself to Diana.

Darling man, then—I allowed the epithet to pass unchallenged—

and asked, "What stupid rules?" To her puzzled look, I added, "Something's upset you. You said, a blessing or a curse?"

"Oh!" she huffed. "Emily Jane cannot visit me without a chaperone. How was it all right before I was married? We went everywhere together. But now she writes that her mother 'thinks it's unwise'!"

Her dark eyes held an astonished, injured look that turned irate. "Unwise! And I cannot borrow books from the Asiatic—I must be proposed to the board and seconded by two members who've been there two years already! The clerk sneered at my sari and acted as though I wasn't standing right there. I felt quite . . . awkward . . . humiliated." Her mouth mutinous, she ended, "In America they have the decency to be courteous to a lady."

I chuckled at her tousled hair and outraged pout. "You always say you wish women were treated as men are. So, you cannot fault the boor—he cut you just as he would a man!"

The scrawny lad Bhim came in with a carafe of some pale liquid I took to be coconut water. Diana downed the glass with unladylike speed and handed it back to be refilled. When she'd finished this too, she sent the awed boy away with a smile that had him bouncing on his feet.

Her face grew serious. "It's not that, Jim," she said. "I like Europeans, individually. They're usually pleasant to speak with and have interesting things to say. But collectively, the rules they insist upon are quite ridiculous and unfair! They say Indians are quite capable but won't give us positions of responsibility. Take Adi, for example."

I stiffened. "What about him?"

She flung out a hand. "His business. If his surgical tools would sell, they'd see how good they were and wouldn't need to buy expensive stuff from abroad. But for months, Adi couldn't get the permit to build his factory! And when he finally persuaded the governor and got the enterprise underway, the Englishmen in charge of Bombay Hospital wouldn't believe Indian scalpels are any good! They still won't!" Her eyes narrowed. "I wonder whether there's a rotten British manufacturer who's put the word out against Adi's knives."

Put the word out? I set aside the question of individual versus collective character of the British people and focused on the possibility of a new suspect.

Hoisting myself from my chair I dropped a kiss on her still-flushed cheek, saying, "You've given me an idea."

As I dragged on my boots and fetched my hat from the stand, she called, "Where are you going? Mama bought fresh drumsticks for our curry."

"Wouldn't miss it," I assured her, tapping on the broad-brimmed solar, a mainstay for gents in the tropics. "Going to chat with the darling man. He buys surgical supplies."

"Oh!" She sat up, all eyes. "To get him to buy Adi's scalpels?"

"No." I grinned. "To find out whose profits are threatened by Adi's business!"

CHAPTER 11

DARLING MAN

Jameson spotted me at the door and snorted as he choked on his afternoon toddy.

"Agnihotri! Back, are you?" He chortled, setting down his glass.

I grinned and shook his hand. "Like a bad penny. How are you?"

A bit more silver glimmered in his brown hair. He'd parted it on the side and slicked it back—to cover a bald spot? I would not have thought him in any way vain. His clothing was more formal than in previous years—a grey vest over buttoned-down shirt. In my memory he was almost always rumpled, collar open at the neck, sleeves rolled to his elbows.

He waved me to a chair. "How is the charming Miss Framji? Ah! Pardon me, the missus."

"Glad to be back with her family," I replied, then waved at his attire. "You're mighty fine today. So, who is she?"

"Me?" He scoffed. "Who'd have an old sawbones like me?" He spoke lightly, but his pink cheeks told another story. He chuckled, leaning back. "Matrimony's not so bad, eh? You've filled out a tad." His eyes narrowed. "Broken any bones lately?"

I shook my head, but my hand covered the scar on my forearm, a deep gouge I'd won in Chicago that had taken a while to heal.

"Show me."

Taking off my coat, I snapped off a cuff and pushed up my sleeve.

He put on a pair of wire-rims and hummed over my forearm, poking and pressing. "Neat job of sewing. Lucky, though, missed the brachial artery by a hair. Cut some of the *extensor carpi ulnaris*. Any closer and you wouldn't grip anything for a while!"

"My aim's shot," I said, showing him a fist. "Old days, we boxed without gloves."

He tut-tutted over my hand, pulling and twisting like a happy Torquemada. Taking in his snappy attire, I had an idea. Diana had been miserable over those declined invitations. She'd called the medico "darling man" . . . and I had never really thanked him for playing Cupid.

"Jameson, you wouldn't care to visit Framji Mansion?" I asked. "Small do, next weekend. They put on a nice spread."

"They must do! Since you're looking well-fed," he said. "Moneybags having a soiree? I'd be happy to! When d'you want me?"

I gave him the day and time, then came down to brass tacks. "This business about Adi, you know about it?"

"'Course!" He tapped my arm. "No more knives, yes? You were in the army, the constabulary, and now . . . what d'you call it?"

"Operative."

"She lets you fight fellows with knives? Can't you find another job? One that doesn't risk dismemberment?"

I grinned, sorely tempted to tell him Diana's sobriquet for him, but that would have ruined his earnest scolding, so I said, "She's got a flair for it, too. Gets the sense of people quicker than anyone I know. Likes to poke around, makes deductive leaps with almost nothing to go on. And not above getting into the fray." I grumbled as I restored my cuff and buttoned it, "Followed me to Chicago and into a real brawl, she did."

Remembering my panic when I'd been unable to find her, a chill still dripped down my back.

He chuckled, looking smugly satisfied. "That's a novel method. Canny little thing." He steadied his gaze upon me. "About young Mr. Framji. What'd you need?"

I gave him a grateful look. "He's innocent, of course. You know the type. Won't tell a lie to save his skin. But . . . someone did kill Satya Rastogi, and I aim to bring him in. Any idea who'd do it?"

His eyebrows shot up. "Suspects? That's your department. Seen McIntyre? He's dead set on your man. You know, young Framji came to me, couple months ago, showed me his scalpels. Nice tools. I sent him over to medical ordnance, but you know how it is, fellow'd already got someone for the job. Now if young Framji was selling blankets, we'd have taken a thousand—new hospital in Madras."

I let him run his course, then asked, "Who? Who was he buying from, your army chap?"

His bushy eyebrows twitched. "Fellow by the name of Howard Banner." He rummaged in a drawer and passed me a card. "That's him. Been around almost a year, I think."

* * *

Howard Banner lived on Ash Lane, off Esplanade Road, a quiet tree-lined neighborhood of modest homes. It surprised me that he'd already acquired property, since by Jameson's account he was a fairly recent arrival. A shrewd operator? Or did he come from the bosom of landed gentry in Great Britain?

A tall native servant took my card with alacrity—It gave my name as *James O'Trey, Dupree Detective Agency, Boston.* Although in India I preferred to use my original name Agnihotri, as yet I had no calling cards proclaiming it. O'Trey would have to do, for now.

"Please to wait, sahib," he said, then hurried away, his feet skimming across the tile. His swishing footsteps ceased. Some words were spoken, then silence. I waited, watching a lamplighter set up on the street outside. Banner must be finishing up a letter, that would explain the silence, but where was his man, then?

The door swung open, startling me. A young man approached on white rubber-shod feet, hand extended. "Tennis, yes? Capital! Did we say tomorrow, at the club?"

I shook his hand, trying to gain the measure of the man. Was this young dandy capable of killing off a rival for his business? Sandy hair drooped across his brow giving him a careless elegance. His white shirt was unwrinkled, despite the heat, sleeves rolled to bare muscular forearms. His fingers were stained with ink. Tennis? He'd mistaken me for someone else.

When I did not reply, he tried to extricate his hand. After a second, I let go, saying, "I'm not here about tennis."

His bearer reappeared with a tray and glasses. Setting it down, he picked up my card from the tray and offered it to Banner, who read it and blinked as though he'd just been awakened. "Detective agency. Boston?"

"I'm investigating the death of Satya Rastogi. Did you ever meet him?"

His eyes steadied the moment I said Satya's name. He said slowly, "Yes, I have."

"When?"

He pulled in his lips and reached for a decanter. Pouring a peg without much thought, he glanced at me.

I shook my head to decline. The silence lengthened, grew heavier.

"Some weeks ago," he said, at last. "But I don't know what that has to do with—anything."

That was his prudence emerging. When in doubt, withhold information, I thought. He'd dashed out, expecting a fellow sportsman. So he liked tennis, played at an Englishman's club, and was looking for a partner or a fourth to make up the match.

He picked up my card again, eyebrows startled. Did I look so much older, then? I practiced McIntyre's stare, keeping my face neutral.

"What's this about?" he asked weakly. "I met Rastogi a couple of times. Wasn't a friend or anything."

"What did you speak about?"

He shrugged. "Just . . . London. He'd been to Oxford, studied science—chemistry."

"That takes five minutes. Yet you met him again."

"Umm." He spread his hands, waved his fingers about, then apparently noticed his drink and clutched it. He took a sip, liked it, took another, and set down the glass. He might have wanted to down it, but perchance thought that would give away his anxiety.

"What's this about?" he asked again.

"You met him at least twice. What was your business with him?"

I was reaching, but it seemed to shake Banner. Perhaps it sounded as though I knew something more. His lips opened a few times, then he said, "Look. We met in a hospital waiting room . . . it was purely accidental. We got to talking, just social, it was. That's all."

By his tone, I knew it wasn't all.

"Met at his residence?" I could imagine the to-do that would have caused.

"No, here."

Banner's innocuous answer meant he had no idea what Rastogi's home was like.

I asked, "Why?"

"Told you. Just chewing the cud. Downed a couple. Bachelors, y'know."

I scoffed. "You invited him over for drinks. To play cards?"

He blinked, apparently assessing whether to admit to it. Fraternizing with Indians and all that. I would have liked him better if he'd thrown it in my face, saying, "Any law against that?" but he only shook his head.

"What, then?"

He blushed, like a schoolboy abruptly facing the headmaster. "Just— reminiscing, y'know? College men. Swapping stories."

"So you were friendly with Rastogi."

"No!" He backed away as though I'd accused him of something indecent. "Just polite, is all. Nothing more."

Three denials—too much? Could Rastogi have been more than a brief acquaintance?

"He had no head for drink, see?" He tried a chuckle that didn't convince me.

After a pause, I asked, "So what did you discuss?"

Sweat beaded on his forehead. "He was entering the game, see? Trying to sell to hospitals and such. I'm a medical salesman, so ah . . ." He spread a hand aimlessly, then went to a bureau and brought me his card: HOWARD E BANNER, MEDICAL REPRESENTATIVE, EVANS & WORMULL, SURGICAL INSTRUMENTS, LONDON.

"He came to you for business advice?" I let my question sound skeptical.

"Something like that. 'Cause we'd swapped a few stories and such."

I asked, "Did he play tennis?"

This gave Banner a footing, which he grasped like a man who'd been slipping into a bog. "He knew the game, tennis, I mean. He'd played, but the clubs—well, you know how they are."

"Hmm?"

"Won't let in a darkie. Rastogi didn't mind. Didn't make out like he minded, see? He was a quiet bloke, respectful, yes?"

Immobile, I said, "You liked him."

"We were polite. Cordial," he retorted, taking another swig.

"He was a competitor. He made equipment like yours. And you gave him a hand?" I raised an eyebrow.

"I . . . just. He was a college man," Banner mumbled, his eyes dashing about like ponies.

I glanced around the room. "So you've been here six months—"

"Nine," he said.

"Nine months, selling to hospitals, army, clinics, surgeons. What's the rent for this place?"

He reddened, swallowed, then went quite pale. "What're you accusing me of?"

His rough tone surprised me. "One might say you're worried about something, Mr. Banner. I haven't accused you of anything. But something's on your mind, isn't it?"

He groaned and dropped into a chair. He could have asked me to leave, but perhaps he thought that would look guilty. He poured himself another tot and spilt some golden liquid on the tray.

"Dash it," he cried, looking up. "I haven't done anything to be ashamed of!"

"All right," I said, and took the chair opposite him. "So what's rattled you?"

"*Rattled* me? Nothing. I'm not . . . rattled."

I suppose, living in the States, some of its language had rubbed off on me. I'd worked with some tough blokes who wouldn't give a bite of their apple to a starving grandma.

Gentling my tone, I said, "Mr. Banner, something's troubled you. It's best to tell me now, before things get, ah, complicated."

He abruptly made up his mind. "All right, here it is. Rastogi asked me for a loan. I declined. Had to. I don't have—I'm not made of money, all right? I told him so. My old man gave me a start," he said, waving at the molded ceiling, the white cornices over the window.

"How much?" Seeing his startled look, I added, "How much did Rastogi want?"

"A thousand rupees! A thousand. Madness!"

That was six months' wages as an inspector of police, my old job. Almost a year's wages in the army. Banner tugged at an invisible thread in the tapestried chair. I could have left it there, but some instinct demanded I push further. "You refused. Said you didn't have it? The sole agent for medical equipment and supplies. The sole agent."

He went beet red, then slumped. "All right, I could have raised it. But he wasn't my brother, see. He was a pal, not blood."

"Just a friend."

He nodded, looking glum.

"There's more, yes?"

Looking sick, he said, "I, ah, I didn't know what he wanted it for. He wouldn't say. Kept on about paying suppliers, just a temporary problem, he said."

"But you didn't think he could pay it back."

"Yes! Yes, that's it. I wasn't sure!"

He'd grabbed my answer so readily it made me pause. "No . . . something else. What was the trouble?"

"I told you. His business might not . . . it might not fly—then where would I be?"

"Having funded a competitor, you mean? In fact, you hoped it would not succeed. Why would you help him?"

Color ebbed from his face as he sat up, angry again. "That's not true. I'd help a fellow in a spot, if I could. Even a chap that's selling against me."

I believed him. It was the sort of mad thing an Englishman would do, the honorable thing, even against his own interest.

"So, why'd you refuse?"

"Because"—he winced—"not to speak ill of the dead, Rastogi, he just seemed—odd. It isn't done. To borrow a thousand rupees off a bloke his own age. And not say why."

I understood. His caution had prevented it. "It reeked."

"Yes," he admitted unwillingly. "I don't know what he was up to, I swear it. Just . . . that he *was* up to—something."

"All right," I said. "How did he seem, when he asked for the funds?"

Banner frowned. "Agitated. He kept talking. Went on and on."

"Desperate?"

He agreed with that assessment, his eyes worried and sad.

I asked a few more questions, then gestured toward my card on the table. "Right. If you learn anything, remember anything, would you call me?"

He agreed, so I pulled out a fountain pen and jotted down the number for the Framji residence. Then, picking up my hat, I shook hands with the mystified young man and left.

Satya Rastogi had tried to borrow a large sum from the young Englishman. He'd been desperate. Why? Having been refused, he'd emptied Adi's account without telling him. But for what purpose? And where was the cash? Banner was right. It reeked.

CHAPTER 12

INCONSISTENT EVIDENCE

When I returned, the family was at dinner. I popped my head in to say hello before heading to the kitchen to wash up. There, the servants were sitting in a circle for their own meal.

Seeing me, Gurung jumped up. Jiji-bai too, climbed slowly to her feet.

"*Baithey raho,*" I reassured them and went to the *mori,* a tiled-off area separated by a ledge. Leaning over it, I ran the tap and soaped my hands while asking after Jiji-bai's health.

Gurung handed me a cloth. Drying off, I realized Jiji-bai had not answered. The others would not meet my gaze. Out of respect they did not eat in front of me, but only ducked their heads.

Jiji-bai wiped her eyes with a corner of her sari and said in Hindustani, "Sahib, I remember the little one, Chutki. She was so young, too young. Her memory comes to me, sahib."

I recalled Chutki's large, dark eyes, which rarely looked up, and the tinkle of her *payals,* how they sounded when she limped and their joyful rhythm as she recovered. A tiny teenager, she'd joined the kitchen crew at the Framjis, winding her hair in a bun to appear grown-up. I'd called her my sister, if only for a few months. Her spirit, her loss still had me in its grip.

My throat felt tight as I touched Jiji-bai's shoulder. It was enough. She mumbled to Gurung to set another place in the dining room for me.

When we entered there, conversation ceased. Had I interrupted some disagreement? Burjor looked unhappy, Adi was frowning.

Draped in fabric the color of moss in a shady well, Diana held her youngest sister on her lap and kept her little fingers busy shredding a roti. Offering greetings around the table, I took my place. Mrs. Framji passed the rice and directed the other dishes to my attention. The silence thickened as I served myself, but Diana's lips held the glimmer of a smile.

Nothing too bad, then. I said, "Apologies for my tardiness, Mrs. Framji, sir. Can I help with the present difficulty?"

Adi gave a wan smile. "He's caught you out, Papa. One second in the room and he knows there's a problem."

"No problem, *beta*," said Burjor, picking up his spoon. "I decided to sell our hotel in Simla, and Byram has found a buyer. That's all there is to it. Now come on, don't spoil dinner."

Ah! So I'd missed Byram's visit. He'd arrived while I was out quizzing Banner.

Adi protested. "Sell? After all the work you've done, importing French tablecloths, towels, chefs from the south. The craftsmen, designing archways, tables, monogrammed bowls, silver cutlery! Why should we sell?"

Burjor chewed.

Adi went on, "You've never mentioned this before. We were going there this summer. So why sell? And to whom?"

Burjor burped, raised a hand in apology. "Let's discuss it later. Now, Captain, have you found anything?"

Adi clearly did not like the change of subject but I said, "Yes, something, but I'm not sure what to make of it." I turned to Adi. "Satya Rastogi—he went to Oxford with you?"

"And Cathedral—boys' school."

The Framjis had almost finished their meals. Hurrying to consume mine, I said, "Describe Satya—his nature," then closed my eyes as the first flavorful mouthful blossomed in my mouth.

Adi leaned back and considered. As usual, when he spoke, it was succinct. "Satya was bright. Brilliant, even. After Cathedral, we both chose Oxford. I suppose his choice of subject was natural—being brought up around jewelers and craftsmen. What astonished other students was his ease with complicated terms. He said it was pie, compared to memorizing Sanskrit *shlokas*! He'd mastered the essence of chemistry, I think. Could tell you at fifty paces what a smell was, look at a bit of stone and tell you what minerals it contained. Yet he was humble. Friendly, in an unobtrusive way."

"A charmer?"

"God, no." Grinning, Adi picked up his utensils. "Frightfully shy around the ladies. He'd barely look up! But he played a mean game of whist."

"Did he drink? Smoke?"

Adi's brow puckered. "No. He was a high-caste Brahmin, you know. Vegetarian, even in England. Ate potatoes endlessly, poor sod. No vices, really. He liked music but was terrified of attending a do. I made him go to the opera once. Despite the expense, I mean. Ten minutes in, he wanted to leave! I wouldn't hear of it, so he sat back down. Said he couldn't believe the noise at first, but then became entranced."

"Was Satya crooked?"

My bald question sounded like a day-old cod going splat on the rosewood table. Finally, Diana said, "What d'you mean, Jim? What have you found?"

When I told them about Howard Banner and the loan that Satya had pleaded for, Adi's mouth dropped open. "But we *had* money. Two thousand in the bank! Why would he borrow from Banner? Without saying a word?"

"You had not discussed another loan?"

Adi shook his head. "I wouldn't have accepted it from Banner. That much? Why on earth . . . ? We had enough for six months—I'd have got some orders by then. If the Brits ganged up on me, I'd sell in Rangoon or Hong Kong!"

"So why did Satya need the cash?"

Just then baby Tehmina reached out. Diana gave a cry as the little hand knocked over her glass. Water splashed over the tablecloth. Instantly the others offered napkins and helped mop up.

When we settled down again, Adi shook his head at me. "Satya, crooked?" he said. "I wouldn't have believed it. He was quiet, though, rarely spoke of his parents or childhood. As though he was ashamed of it."

"If he needed cash, why wouldn't he ask his parents? He's the only son in a goldsmiths' clan," I said, spooning mutton and potatoes reddened with spice onto my plate, "among a lot of cousins."

Adi's eyebrows shot up. "He's the only son?"

"You saw him as bright, friendly but quiet. Your workman Faisal said he didn't want to go home, and his mother said—"

"You met Satya's mother?" Adi asked.

I smiled. "A tough lady. She was . . ." I gave it some thought, then said, "furious with Satya. They gave him an expensive education. Perhaps he was expected to settle to the yoke, after that. But he didn't. He worked 'in a phac-ta-ry.' She didn't know he was your partner."

Adi looked stumped. "He didn't tell them?"

I shrugged, savoring spicy chickpeas and lentils. "Same reason he didn't ask them for money. Or perhaps he did, and was denied. Kept things close to his vest, young Satya."

The Framjis had finished their meals, so Gurung brought in finger bowls. Starting at the head of the table he bathed Burjor's hands from a thin-spouted silver jug.

Burjor grunted his thanks and dried his fingers on an embroidered napkin, saying, "This Mr. Banner, the medical salesman . . . is he a suspect?"

I handed my empty plate to Ganju and complimented Mrs. Framji on the meal, then replied, "Everyone's a suspect until I find the culprit, sir." Then recalling the invitation I'd made, I turned to Diana. "My dear, you wanted to have a party this weekend, didn't you?"

"Well, yes," she said, her eyes on baby Tehmina, who was splashing in her finger bowl. She tapped the child's hands together to shake off the droplets, then enveloped them in a napkin and gave Gurung a smile. This signaled him to whisk away her bowl and attend Mrs. Framji.

Diana went on, "I had almost given up, but I met my old friend Mary Fenton—the actress. Her father was Irish—he was in the army, Jim. Anyway, we attended a talk at Wilson College, and she introduced me to two charming sisters. Rata Vakil teaches French there and her sister Mehr studies medicine at Grant Medical College." Her calm voice held a note of suppressed excitement.

Diana had recently been keen to study medicine. She asked, "Shall I invite them for dinner on Saturday, Mama?"

Her mother demurred. "Diana, I have heard of Mary Fenton. She's married to Kavasji Khatau, the playwright—you know she has left him?"

Diana countered, "She learned Gujarati so she could act in his plays. She made him famous."

After a pause, Mrs. Framji said, "So three guests?"

"Four," I said. "If it's all right, I've invited Jameson, the army medico."

Diana beamed. "I like him. But we need two more young men to balance out. There's Adi, 'course. Who else can we have?"

Who did I want at our table? I considered the bachelors I knew in Bombay. Smith would rejoice to be invited, but since he'd joined the constabulary, that would be awkward.

Mrs. Framji cast an anxious look at me. Two of the ladies invited were Parsi, so I said, "What about Soli Wadia, who fetched us from the pier?"

Mrs. Framji sighed. "His mother sent me such a nice decline. She feels awful, she said, but now isn't 'the right time.'"

Seeing Diana's shoulders slump, I asked, "Why not let him make up his own mind?"

There were nods around the table. Diana said, "All right, I'll write out the invitations. Will you give Dr. Jameson his, or shall I send Ganju?"

How Jameson would guffaw if he got our missive through a bearer. He'd never let me live it down. "I'll take it, sweet."

At my words, Diana's parents glanced at each other, and some communication seemed to pass between them. The family got up, Mrs. Framji hoisting the youngest, who burped loudly and fussed. Since the younger son Fali and little Shirin were at school, three-year-old Tehmina was the center of adult adulation. Now she cooed at me, "Carry! Carry me. I'm big now!"

Taking her carefully from Mrs. Framji I assured her that she was indeed very grown-up.

"Up, up!" she demanded, with the authority of a sergeant major.

"Captain," said Burjor, clearing his throat.

"Sir?" His formal opening after our pleasant meal surprised me. Then recalling the argument I had interrupted, I expected he would invite Adi and me into his study. Instead, he said, "It is Mama's birthday tomorrow, so we plan to go to the *agiyari* in the morning."

That was the Zoroastrian fire temple, I recalled. "Of course."

"I'm sorry," he said. "You can't come. Only Parsis are permitted inside."

Diana put a hand on my arm. "It's one of those silly rules, Jim."

So Diana was going, too. Dropping my voice, I asked, "Will they let *you* in?"

From the door, Adi snorted. "I'd like to see someone object! I did pass the bar, you know. I'll sue the blackguard!"

Sometimes I didn't think Adi understood just how much trouble he was in. I said, "Right. Tomorrow's Thursday, so I take it I'm on my own."

Diana grimaced. "Only until lunch. We should be back then. Or earlier, even." *If they throw me out,* said her mocking look.

"I'm seeing McIntyre. To take a look at the file."

Adi's file? her eyes asked.

As I replied with a nod, a rush of gratitude washed over me. *This,* I thought, this was being married. Having someone who understood, who knew the meaning behind what was said, the implication. Diana's glow told me she knew I'd made inroads with McIntyre, gained Jameson's public support with my invitation, and begun beating the bushes for Satya's killer.

It was progress, although Banner's intelligence could mean that Satya was doing something illicit. I had a whole lot more searching in store.

The toddler in my arms yelped and squirmed. Remorseful, I loosened my hold.

"I'll take her," said Burjor, so I handed Tehmina into his arms where she perched like a pudgy miniature Queen Victoria surveying her empire. If Diana and I ever had a child, I thought, she'd look just like that. The thought made my chest tight.

* * *

McIntyre wasn't in that morning, but he'd left instructions with Sub-inspector Sabrimal to seat me in his office. True to his word, there on his blotter lay a discreet brown manila folder. I felt a rush of gratitude, then tempered it with caution. McIntyre was an ally, but I'd be a fool to trust him blindly. His true allegiance was to the crown.

"Chai, sahib?" asked Sabrimal, his round face beaming.

"Thank you," I said, and waited until he'd left before I flicked open the file. It was laid out pro forma, with photographs. Satya, hair cropped short, lying on a slab, a small wound in his neck, barely an inch long. He'd worn a thin mustache, and . . . what was that, sprawled off center, on his face? A Brahmin mark? Scanning the page, I read: strawberry birthmark on forehead.

Then came the statement from investigating officer Stephen J. Smith, the witness statements from Adi's employees and medical examination reports. I set aside Adi's written statement. The bank manager swore he'd handed over two thousand rupees in banknotes to Satya Rastogi; a conversation with one Bala Mali was transcribed verbatim.

This last was damning. Bala was Adi's watchman, stationed at his factory gate. The employees had arrived between nine and eleven fifteen. He said Adi had arrived in a carriage around eleven thirty. A coal cart had then arrived and the carriage left soon afterward.

Vishal, the accountant, had overseen the unloading of sacks, paid, and sent off the cart. I frowned at the page, an ache throbbing at my forehead. Adi had insisted that he arrived at noon.

The rest matched what I already knew—just after the clocktower struck twelve, the watchman heard a hue and cry, and rushed to the factory building. Satya was on the floor, bleeding, etc. He saw blood on Adi's shirt and hands. Adi sent Bala to summon a local havildar, so he ran to the police *chowki* at Grant Road. He returned, riding behind a mounted officer.

I frowned—hadn't Faisal said that Vishal brought the constable? If the gateman rode behind the havildar, what was the staff doing during the ruckus? Perhaps I was making too much of it, I thought. If they arrived together, would Faisal really remember who brought whom?

I tapped the pages, puzzled at the minor inconsistency, then spotted a cup of tea at my elbow. Sabrimal had discreetly withdrawn, leaving me to my cogitations.

Based on the gateman's statement, McIntyre had placed Adi in the factory at eleven thirty, and therefore earlier than noon, as Adi claimed. Was this why he was set against Adi? When Adi fled the country, it must have seemed like an admission.

Adi's testimony was concise. When he arrived at noon, he hadn't noticed anyone at the gate. He was the sort who'd nod and acknowledge his man, even a lowly sweeper, but mightn't remember it if he was preoccupied with missing funds. Or Bala Mali was not at his post just before noon when Adi arrived. If he'd stepped away, then someone else could have entered, had an altercation with Satya, and stabbed him just as Adi entered the building. Or perhaps Bala Mali was with Satya himself. That made him a suspect, too.

I closed my eyes, recalling the factory—the gate was about thirty yards from the structure, which had once been a stable. Large archways along the side were now boarded up, leaving doors on the narrow ends. When we visited, the rear egress had been open "to get some fresh air." The front of the workshop connected to a small passage with doors leading to the supply room, accounting office, and other rooms. Adi could have been walking through that hallway when Satya was attacked. He could have approached just as the killer ducked out the rear. I frowned— was I trying to force the facts to fit my theory?

The property was densely treed with chickoo, palms, and banana trees, banyan heavy with vines, ample shrubbery where one might secret oneself. All a killer need do was wait for Bala to be called from the gate, then dash out.

Bala Mali—was that his last name, or his occupation? A mali is a gardener, so possibly he was employed as both. An ordinary morning, he'd said. He gave his position as "gate man" whereas McIntyre's slanted hand denoted him as "watchman" at the top of the page, which indicated his role was that of a guard.

Mali's address was listed as Plot 12 Dady Lane. Adi's factory was on that same street, wasn't it? Closing the file, I returned it to McIntyre's blotter, feeling grim. Time to see the watchman.

CHAPTER 13

A GRIEVOUS MISTAKE

A hot breeze blew dust into my face as I rode a one-horse ekka toward Adi's factory. This cart had been called "a tea tray on wheels" because every rut in the road jarred one's spine. Europeans sat in the shape of an N hugging their knees, as the elder Kipling's book described. Instead, squatting brought a brief relief. Hanging onto struts that supported the cloth roof, I urged the driver onward. If Bala Mali was not dismissed, ostensibly he still worked for Adi. He had not been at the gate when I visited with Adi, yet no one had mentioned him. Was he such a nonentity that his absence went unnoticed?

Bells jingling, my conveyance headed east toward Babula Tank and Bombay Jail. To my left rose the spires of Grant Medical College, the swath of Jamshidji's Hospital and behind it, the daunting façade of the Hospital for Incurables. Nearing the turn for Dady Lane, I hollered to the driver. He took it without slowing, the cart wildly atilt, but I clutched my hat and kept my seat.

Adi's factory looked bereft as though mourning its lost usefulness. At the open gate I got down and paid the sweating *ekkawala* as he watered his horse. Patting the short mare's neck, I glanced around. Where was that inconspicuous gateman?

My footsteps crunched on gravel, muted where grass and weeds poked through. The roots of great banyan trees hung like sinewy pythons over a stone wall at the perimeter, while tall jambul trees sheltered the silent building. I tried the door, hammered on it, but no one opened. Had Adi given his employees leave for the day? I did not recall any such mention, so I walked around the compound, stepping through the high foliage.

Overhanging vines descended in cascades to screen dense thickets. If one wanted to hide, he would not lack cover in waist-high brush, though most would avoid it for fear of snakes.

Specks of white adorned the flower beds to my right; behind, a row of mighty teak bloomed with spiral candles. Yet violent death had visited this tropical splendor.

Coming around the side I entered a formal garden, row upon row of glossy bushes and shrubs crowded with petals. At the back, overgrown stones showed what had been part of the home's foundation. The thoroughfare beyond walled off Girgaon Back Road, so the tree-lined path had once been the main entrance. Here Adi's employees claimed to have taken lunch together. Glancing around the cool, shady perimeter, I could not fault their choice. At the center, a rubber pipe lay near a hand pump and its wide stone vessel.

Spotting someone crouched in the bushes, I hailed him. "Bala Mali?"

An older man in a rumpled brown dhoti got to his feet and joined his hands in greeting over his scrawny chest, still holding a forklike implement. Small in stature, with thin arms and muddy hands, he stood barefooted near a pile of weeds. He ducked his head, a toothless smile on his lined face.

Since he had continued work when recompense was uncertain, the garden must be dear to him. Around him a jumble of red hibiscus crowned a bush, while stephanotis, jasmine, heliotrope crowded adjacent beds. The scent of honeysuckle descended from the vine-covered wall. Behind us, great bell-shaped elephant-creeper and lilac flowers grew over the iron trellis of the dilapidated front porch.

"You like flowers," I said.

He showed his gums and pointed with his gardening fork. "Champak, sahib. Hibiscus. Chameli over there, and Aparajita." He gave their Indian names in an affectionate tone.

I said, "Your employer was killed, some weeks ago. I'm looking into the case."

He wobbled his head, turning serious. I motioned him to the shade nearby, sat on a stump, and took off my solar topi. "Tell me what happened, that morning."

He rattled off the sequence as though accustomed to repeating it.

Once he ended, I asked, "When the carriage arrived—did you see Adi sahib in it?"

He had not.

"Did you see him get out?" I watched closely, for this question could trip him up. From the gate, the carriage would stand between him and anyone descending toward the foyer.

When he shook his head, I pointed at some protruding roots. "Sit—it is a hot day."

He jerked. "Sahib, I am a poor gardener. I am not *kursi-nashin.*"

That was a term I'd almost forgotten. Natives were required to purchase a certificate that entitled them to sit in the presence of an Englishman. "Tsk," I said. *"Betho!"*

He squatted, folding his hands before him.

"How do you know it was Adi sahib's carriage?" I asked.

Surprised, he shrugged, so I pressed on. "Who was driving it? Did you recognize him?"

The hapless mali shook his head, so I tried a series of questions: Was the driver young, or old? What was he wearing? What color were the horses? Was there anything unique about the carriage? He could answer none of these.

"So how do you know it was his carriage? Could it have been someone else's?"

He gave this some thought, then said, "It is possible," but without conviction.

Next, I asked whether he had left the gate that morning. He admitted freely that it was unlocked all morning. He had watered the plants, opened the gate for the early arrivals, and returned to tending the beds. He could place no time on this.

A simple explanation. Adi had likely arrived during that interval.

"Why didn't you say this to the police?" I asked.

He looked surprised. "They didn't ask me."

From where we sat, I could see the path to the building, so I asked, "Did you see anyone come in on foot?"

Now he stared, then dropped his gaze. He had remembered something.

"What is it? Who did you see?"

As I became more insistent, the fellow fumbled, and turned pale. He held out trembling hands to me, saying, "I am just a mali sahib. I open the gate. I don't know anything."

"Where do you live?" I asked.

He indicated a dilapidated garden shed leaning against the distant wall.

"Family?"

He signaled that he had none. By now he was fairly weeping, repeating over and over that he had seen no one. And that's why I knew he had.

Who had he seen? Something was afoot, yet I could not tell what. However, knowing the methods of police havildars, I asked, "Did anyone beat you?"

He shook his head, his chin buried in his chest.

"Bala, I will not hurt you. Tell me what troubles you?"

When he raised his face, I was appalled. Tears ran down his sallow cheeks, but his eyes! They held such sorrow, helpless fear, pleading, a weary dullness that tugged at me deep within.

"Has someone harmed you? Threatened you? One of the workmen?"

He only shook his head.

Out of desperation, I asked, "Was it Adi sahib?"

This drew a sharp reaction. "No, sahib! No!"

Then it came to me. "Satya. Satya did something."

He covered his face and wept like a child, silent sobs shaking his thin shoulders.

I gazed at him, unable to console and caught in a dilemma. Could such a mild creature really stab his employer in the neck? Ridiculous. But his torment begged explanation. Did he imagine he would be made a scapegoat? He knew something and was deathly afraid. However, until he was reassured and trusted me, I would get nothing from him.

"Get up," I said, rising to my feet. "You can't stay here. Come with me."

He tucked the gardening implement carefully into the crook of a tree and followed meekly. I went to the nearby hand pump and worked the lever. He stood back as the water gushed, then realized it was for his benefit and leaped forward to drink and clean his face and hands. I pumped the lever as he washed his feet and backed away with folded hands.

I booked him into Bombay Jail near Nowroji Hill, giving instructions that he was to be fed, have a cell to himself and remain unmolested. Recognizing me from my previous stint in the constabulary, the havildar on duty did not question my authority.

When he took hold of Bala's arm, the mali turned astonished eyes on me.

"You will be safe here," I assured him. "No harm will come to you."

"How long?" he gasped.

"A few days. Rest here. You are not under arrest."

I repeated my instructions for good measure, then, unable to do any more to comfort the fellow, I left.

It was a mistake I will always regret.

* * *

At Framji Mansion, lunch had already been served and the house was suspiciously quiet. In the kitchen Jiji-bai got up from a low *charpoy*.

"Where is everyone?" I asked.

She raised folded hands to her ear, mimicking sleep, and asked whether I'd lunched. When I replied I had not, she uncovered a series of bronze and copper vessels. The heady aroma of spice and fried onions filled my senses. I pointed to a few pots and soon a plate was prepared.

Rather than sup in an empty dining room, I sat cross-legged on the cool kitchen tiles. In the army, officers dined on tables with white linen, but sepoys held out their metal plates to the company messmancook, then sat on the green to eat. Somewhere in the formal rooms a grandfather clock chimed a mellow call. Smiling, Jiji-bai brought me a spoon and a glass of water, then sat beside me, fanning herself with a corner of her sari.

In the slow silence of that afternoon, we spoke of Chutki and the other children I had found in Punjab. Jiji-bai had no news of the two little brothers we'd returned to their parents in Jalandhar, but the youngest, Baadal, who'd been adopted by the Bengali cook and her husband, was now three. They had returned to their ancestral home in Calcutta some months ago; the child was growing well, she assured me.

That quiet moment ended when young Fali came stamping into the kitchen with five-year-old Shirin in the middle of a high-pitched quarrel. My presence shocked them into silence.

"Sit," I said, pointing at the floor beside me.

All eyes, they gazed at me, then obeyed.

"Did you go to the *agiyari*?" I asked, to make conversation.

Alas, my topic was ill chosen, for both began hurling furious accusations. When I could make sense of it, I realized that the visit had gone terribly awry.

"So you entered the temple, then left? Is that it?"

"I wanted to go in!" cried Shirin. "But they didn't let me!"

Fali snorted. "You and Mama could have gone in. Papa and I were going home with Diana." The shadow of a mustache darkened his upper lip. Was he ten when we left Bombay two years ago? I could not remember.

Additional questions elicited a clearer recounting. They had alighted at the temple when a deputation of elders surrounded Burjor.

From the children's outrage I deduced that some insult was offered—it was unclear to whom. However, Burjor had then proposed returning home with Diana, while Mrs. Framji and the children made the offering to the holy fire. Diana wanted to return alone, whereupon everyone protested. Perhaps the hullaballoo so distressed Mrs. Framji that she insisted they cancel the visit. She had then dispatched the two children to school for the afternoon session, from which they had only just returned.

I exhaled, feeling a weight press down upon me. As I'd feared, my union with Diana had disrupted the even keel of the Framjis' lives.

Ignoring their mutinous faces, Jiji-bai served the bickering children a platter of boiled egg sandwiches that had been set aside.

Depositing my plate in the *mori*, I washed my hands and went up to Diana.

A tap on the door brought no response. I knocked. Could she have fallen asleep? I tried the knob and found it locked. My insides jerked. Had Diana locked me out?

Footsteps pattered on the tile, Diana opened the door, her face blotched and wan.

"Ah sweet," I said, helpless against her distress. "How do I fix this?"

"You can't," she mumbled, tucked against me, her arms tight around my waist.

I enveloped her tiny frame and held her close, regret burning through me. I had known Diana was expected to wed a Parsi, and only a Parsi. Yet somehow, she'd captured my affections, and I could no more turn away than slice off an arm. She'd become integral to me. Our difference mattered less in the States, or even in Britain—but now, faced with expulsion from her place of worship, she must feel diminished, even rejected.

"I'm sorry," I said, against her hair.

I could not see her face, but I felt her tense. "Sorry?" Her voice held a strange tinge, an edge of anger.

She pulled back and gazed up, eyes blazing. "Those small-minded nincompoops! Those rotten hypocrites! They talk of good deeds, then blindly rebuff me just because I disobeyed their dictates? Who gave them that power? And who needs them? Why should I give a whit what they think?"

"Whoa!" I said, "Slow down. Tell me what happened."

As she went on, I realized that the matter was more serious and far-reaching. Because it was some holy day, many members of the community were present when the Framjis arrived. Some had sided with the temple priests, while others hotly opposed them. Harsh words had been spoken.

"Soli defended us, so someone taunted him about his uncle—Curset Rustomji, an engineer who'd married his own aunt, Lowji Annie, a half-Parsi Englishwoman. The things they said! It was awful."

Adi had reminded the priests of their earlier compromise, citing the legal agreement they'd entered into. Byram insisted that if they refused to hold up their side, they must return funds that the Framjis had secured for the Widows' and Orphans' Trust.

Heavens. Adi and Byram had gone to the temple prepared with legal ammunition! I shook my head in amazement. "Quite a to-do."

Diana looked glum. "Trouble is, both Mr. Banaji and Mr. Jussawalla were there and they agreed with the priests. Jim, these people do business with Papa, and now they're upset with us. I don't know if they will break off or refuse to deal with him."

"Adi would have made sure Burjor's contracts are solid," I reminded her.

"But if we take it to court, it will make things worse," she said. "There's no coming back from that. Others will be leery. And no future business from them."

I sighed, holding her troubled gaze. "Will you still have your soiree tomorrow?"

Her chin rose. "Absolutely. Here's Jameson's invitation." She opened the lid of her secretary and handed me a monogrammed ivory envelope.

As I slid it into an inner pocket, another fear beckoned from the shadows. What impact would this have on Adi's case? If McIntyre was holding back out of respect for native sentiments, now nothing prevented him acting on his suspicions. How long would he wait?

Dressed in a fresh linen suit, that evening I returned to police headquarters. Jameson wasn't in, so I left the invitation propped up against a bottle of castor oil on his desk. He'd get a chuckle out of that, I thought, and went to the cells to find Bala Mali.

The native officer with whom I'd spoken had gone off shift. The English sergeant in charge ran his finger down the ledger and said, "No one here by that name."

I snapped. "He's not arrested. I had him held for Superintendent McIntyre only this morning."

He shrugged, then checked another file.

"Well?" I demanded.

"You're . . . ?"

"Captain Agnihotri, Fourteenth Light, retired."

"Army," he said. "You can't just park your fellow here. Take him down to the barracks, next time. No one of that name here. Can't help you."

Frowning, I went to see McIntyre, but found him occupied. He spotted me over the heads of three formally dressed gents and said, "I sent him home, Agnihotri. Chap's useless. Can't hold him without a reason."

I *had* a reason, dammit! The mali was terrified of someone. Given McIntyre's present company I only bowed from the door. It drew a wry chuckle from him, then he turned his attention back to his guests, saying, "Once the ship arrives, send me word and you'll have your escort."

An armed police escort could mean some bigwig arriving. There'd been nothing in the newspapers, so I put it from my mind. I toyed with the idea of fetching the mali again, but where would I stash him? He'd fare no better in an army clink, and I could think of no credible explanation that would serve.

It was Mrs. Framji's birthday, and the fracas at the fire temple must have been unpleasant. Since the sun headed toward the horizon, I returned to Framji Mansion, determined not to be late for supper, for once.

As it turned out, that was my second mistake.

CHAPTER 14

YOU CAN'T

That evening, a few guests had been invited to celebrate Mrs. Framji's birthday. Adi and I entered the drawing room together, spiffy in our dinner jackets. Bombay folk held to the traditions of earlier decades in a motley mix of native and English garb. Burjor usually wore traditional garments: a white suit tied at one side called a Parsi *dugli*, or a loose, embroidered oriental jacket. Tonight Adi and I had adopted English formalwear—black coattails with white vest and bow tie. In America these would be hopelessly old-fashioned; young men had taken to wearing lounge suits and black tie for dinners. One rarely saw a frock coat these days.

Since we were alone, I asked Adi the question that was haunting me. "You've taken the carriage to work before, haven't you?"

Adi nodded. "When Papa was in Simla, or down south, I had it every day."

I watched him closely. "So Bala Mali would recognize it?"

"Of course."

"Certain 'bout that?"

Adi shrugged. "One time, Soli Wadia dropped me off in his coach, the mali refused to open the gate! I had to get down and reassure him. He's stubborn about supply carts too, won't let them in. Insists that Vishal attend to them." He paused, then asked, "Why d'you ask?"

Diana came in just then, and sat down quietly beside Adi. Her choice was deliberate. Women always seem to know who needs them more—perhaps they can sense it, without words, and are moved to offer sympathy. Or was it instinct—did she see something under Adi's calm demeanor I could not? Was there some undetectable clue she knew from a childhood spent together? I had no wish to cause Adi anxiety, but I had to address this. To do less would be to shirk my duty to him, and that I would not do.

I huffed a breath, then said, "You didn't take your carriage, but the mali and Faisal say they saw it the morning Satya died. I thought they were mistaken or confused. One, perhaps, could be wrong, but both?"

Behind his glasses, Adi's eyes were too wide, too dark.

I explained, "It's in McIntyre's file. Your *sais* Bhim will remember where he drove the carriage that morning . . ."

Adi pushed back his chair and jerked to his feet like a jack-in-the-box. "Don't say any more, Jim . . . I think we have to stop. Drop the investigation."

I felt a jolt through my spine. "*Drop* it? Why? What are you afraid of?"

"Stop, Jim." His eyes were black pools.

If there was evidence against him, we had to stare it in the face and reckon with it. I plowed on. "Faisal and Bala saw it leaving the factory. Both thought you had arrived in it. The coachman said it was an ordinary day. That means your father took the carriage as usual."

Adi cried, "Enough. I'm—you can't!"

Diana's hand went to her mouth, shaking her head. "No, you must be—"

"I'm not, sweet. Your father visited Satya that morning."

Adi turned from us in a panic, his hands fluttering.

I said to Diana, "I've suspected all along that Adi wasn't telling me everything. Why wouldn't he speak, even to save himself? Only one reason, sweet. To spare one of your family."

Adi stopped at the door, breathing as though he'd just run uphill. "I'm sorry, Jim. I'm releasing you from the investigation."

My pulse hammered my ears, but I felt oddly calm. "So, I'm fired?"

Diana made a sound of protest as she hurried to him.

"You don't understand," Adi whispered, his fist clenched. "You can't accuse Papa!"

I kept my voice even. "Have a little faith, Adi. In your father."

Adi looked up, his face twisted with hope.

I went on, "If you fire me, Diana will hire me back. Or I'll hire myself."

Diana clutched his wrist, "Adi, I consulted Miss Sorabji in confidence, for her legal opinion. Gave her a retainer, so I'm a client. Here's what she said: If you confess to inadvertently killing Satya, you could get life imprisonment, or worse. Have you been worrying that it was Papa? You can't take the blame because of that!"

"God, Diana! Don't you see? If you accuse Papa, he'll say he did it! He'll say that to save me!"

That made me pause. It was just possible.

Confronted with evidence he'd met Satya that morning, would Burjor snatch at the chance to spare his son? Surely he would not confuse things with a false confession?

Even as the thought formed, I wondered, could he really have done it? Could Burjor have discovered something untoward, and rebuked Satya? Had Satya laughed, mocked Burjor, threatened to scapegoat Adi? Such insolence, it could outrage a father, drive him wild. Had Burjor plunged that blade into Satya's neck?

Or, could it have been an accident? He's showing Burjor his work. One wrong step, Satya lunges, trips or falls onto the blade. Was that what really happened?

I said, "We have to speak with your father."

Adi's plea tore at me. "No! Keep our parents out of it!" He swung around. "Tell him, Diana. Ma's already upset because her sister's shunned us. Don't make it worse!"

Speaking in Gujarati, she calmed him, then turned to me, her eyes shooting a command. "Jim, please. Our guests will soon be here. Leave this be tonight."

Adi looked so distraught, I feared he'd rush off and confess to McIntyre within the hour.

"I'll wait," I said. "But we have to sort this out before one of us has apoplexy."

Miss Fenton had declined, but Diana's lawyer friend Miss Sorabji arrived in a grey sari with a shirtwaist and sleeves that extended modestly to her wrists. It bore neither frills nor lace. I caught Diana tucking her embroidered collar under her sari. She need not have feared the comparison, because her sweetly proportioned face and cheerful manner lit up the company. Her brave effort convinced the others, but not me. The lilac stain under her eyes was more pronounced, and she'd wept in her sleep last night.

When I volunteered to fetch the whiskey, Diana followed me to the morning room to carry glasses. There, she whispered, "Miss Sorabji is a Christian. Her father is Parsi, but he converted to Christianity thirty years ago—a huge to-do at the time. Now Cornelia and her sisters are each making their mark. Her sister's in Glasgow, studying medicine. Cornelia's studied law, at Oxford." She made a moue with her mouth. "But women aren't permitted to take the bar."

"She works for a living? Clerking for a barrister?"

"She's advising the ruler of Baroda, the Gaekwad himself, on education in his state. It's a temporary appointment." Her doubtful glance conveyed that her friend's future was uncertain.

Soli Wadia arrived with a massive bouquet of flowers, then ruined his entrance by gazing around the ladies as though wondering who to hand it to.

When Diana stepped up, saying, "I'll take these to Mama, shall I?" Soli handed them off in relief, then looked at Miss Sorabji in admiration.

Diana's parents arrived together, Mrs. Framji's diminutive frame dwarfed by Burjor's girth. Though pale and slight in a sea-green silk sari, Mrs. Framji welcomed her guests with warm embraces. Nor did the children's formal clothes dampen their excitement, as the littlest ones bounced about in frills. Ever the expansive host, Burjor too rose to the occasion, telling anecdotes in his deep, rumbling voice.

Dinner began well enough, with pakoras and spicy prawns. Berry pilaf and lamb curry followed, with salmon soufflé on a bed of greens. Through it all, I studied my father-in-law discreetly. What the devil could he be hiding?

Continuing the conversation, Diana said, "Europeans puzzle me. As a group they are stuffy, sometimes, even unfair! But I have dear friends among them. In England, Emily Jane and her mother Mrs. Channing were so kind. There's Dr. Jameson, even Superintendent McIntyre. You've met some good ones, Jim?"

I nodded. "Father Thomas who raised me. An elderly couple I met in Ranjpoot, Sir Peter Gary and Lady Mary. Felt a sort of affinity with them." I savored a spoonful of savory salmon, and added, "Army officers—I owe some a great deal. Colonel Sutton taught me to box when I was a lanky, ragged boy. Bought me books when I won."

Diana wrinkled her nose. "But British rule hasn't helped most Indians, has it? The endless famines and epidemics. Just walk through a bazaar. The children—I can often count their ribs. And why can't Indians hold top positions in civil service or banks?"

Miss Sorabji stiffened. "You wouldn't say that if you knew what the princely states were like! Individually a European may be petty or biased against Indians and deprive us of our due, but you cannot deny India is the better for them in whole! They brought us law and order, railways and . . . indoor plumbing!"

"The pinnacle of human achievement!" said Soli.

The group erupted into relieved laughter as the peace was rescued.

Then Burjor growled. "British law and order? Where was it when my children were murdered?"

Silence froze the company and held us captive. Hearing again that Burjor did not trust British law, I felt the ground sliding under my feet. Did his distrust run so deep that he would take the law into his own hands?

Mrs. Framji clapped her hands together. "Oh! We have caramel custard for dessert. Come, Diana, let's turn it over."

Revived by dessert, the conversation veered to safer topics—the warm October, and Mrs. Framji's ailing sister, who lived in the rural suburb of Bandera. The meal had been surprisingly fraught, but I thought the awkwardness was behind us.

Then, after the ladies returned with the promised confection, Soli Wadia said, "I say, Diana, I read a startling bit in *The Times*. It was about you! In Chicago."

"Me? Heavens!" Diana cried, rushing to bring the newspaper from her father's study.

She flung it open, shook out the pages, then groaned. "That dashed petticoat picture!" She held it up. "How ever did they connect it with me!"

Chaos broke out. Burjor barked an order. Children protested. Taking the paper, I scanned the column under a grainy photograph of Diana turned toward the camera with her mouth agape.

The din ceased as I read aloud, "Indian Princess Saves Man on Ferris Wheel. Last year in Chicago, Bombay's Lady Diana made a splash at the World's Fair."

Diana grimaced. "Oh no! The Vakil sisters will have another reason to cut me, I suppose. And your parents, Soli! Jim, we're already rather scandalous, and now this!"

"Let me see." Adi took the sheet and read out the rest, "Indian sage Swami Vivekananda was lauded for his speech at the Parliament of World's Religions. But Bombay's Miss Framji was found in a state of undress. Her skirt was used to restrain a madman who panicked on Mr. Ferris's wheel—a mammoth wheel which raised a set of railcars two hundred feet in the air. Miss Framji (dubbed Lady Diana by the adoring press) was perhaps confused with the Spanish princess, the Infanta Eulalia. The incident caused much excitement among fairgoers."

Diana buried her face in her hands.

"It won't bother Jameson," I offered. "He'll come, on Saturday."

"Nor me," said Miss Sorabji. "If you'd still like me to attend?"

"Of course!" Diana's head rose, revealing flushed cheeks. "Thank you, Nelia. I think it will be a quiet dinner. Jim, we must give up any hope of redemption. It's all over. I'm a scarlet woman!" Diana attempted a laugh, which failed dismally.

Burjor glowered at the newspaper, while Mrs. Framji patted her daughter's hand.

I said, "We're not invited to the governor's Christmas ball, then? Oh good!"

My heartfelt tone drew laughs around the table, though Diana's cheeks remained pink.

She'd held such high hopes of returning to Bombay, yet all we'd received were brickbats and slurs. I reconciled myself to it—if this was the cost of defending the Framjis, I'd take it as long as Diana could. If it sapped her generous spirit, we could go back "home."

But where would that leave Adi? I couldn't whisk Diana away amid his turmoil. Would she even go? No, that settled it. We had to sort out this mess before we could think of getting back to Boston.

CHAPTER 15

THE KEY

Just then, Gurung entered on silent feet and bent to whisper into Burjor's ear.

Sitting near him, Adi frowned. "Papa?" he said, his voice low. "Why is Jussawalla here?"

Burjor's great chest heaved as he lumbered to his feet. "Let me deal with him."

Making his goodbyes to the guests, he hurried away. Shortly after this, our visitors took their leave. In the foyer, Diana embraced her friend, while I shook hands with Soli Wadia.

When they'd gone, Mrs. Framji gave her son a stern look. "What is this about, Adi? Papa looked upset."

From the doorway, Jiji-bai drew her attention. "Mai-ji, the children won't come to bed. They want to stay at the party."

"The party's over," said Mrs. Framji, her tired eyes resting on Adi. "Coming, coming. They'll be climbing the walls in a minute."

Diana, Adi, and I returned to the morning room and sat across from each other much as we had two years ago. Yet Adi kept gazing at the door, his clever fingers tapping on his knee.

"Adi, what have you done?" asked Diana.

The remaining color left his cheeks. "Done?"

"Why is Jussawalla here?"

"Don't know."

"Then you suspect why. What is it?"

Sounding defeated, Adi said, "Papa is selling him the Simla hotel."

She flinched. "But I thought Byram found a buyer. He'd never suggest Jussawalla. At the temple, he called me a traitor, a slut!"

I hauled in a sharp breath. "Perhaps he came to apologize?"

Adi shook his head. "He's a tight bloke. Old-fashioned, crass. We used to buy silver from him to plate our instruments."

I pulled out my pencil and notebook. "Start at the beginning. How do you know him?"

Adi placed his hands on his knees and met my gaze. "Satya found a way to plate scalpels with silver, using electricity. Ingenious, really. The process required silver ingots, so Satya bought them from Percy Jussawalla. His store sells silver vessels and things."

Writing, I asked, "Percy Jussawalla. He's also Parsi?"

"He is. He sells things made of German silver for religious ceremonies. That's an alloy of copper, nickel, and zinc. No real silver in it. However, aunts and uncles often gift silver spoons and cups to newborns, or silver rattles, Lakshmi coins. It's tradition."

Diana added, "On Deepavali, a Hindu family pools their savings to buy gold or silver coins. When they have a wedding, they melt these down for jewelry or to pay expenses. It's how many people save."

I tapped my pencil. "How does Jussawalla know your father?"

Adi shrugged. "He heard that Papa was selling a hotel. Some days ago, he came to Papa's warehouse at the dock."

"He had no other business with Burjor?"

Adi squinted, tilting his head. "They had some venture together, years ago—sending India ink to Britain. But nothing recently."

I asked other questions, but Adi seemed absorbed, distracted by some inner calculations. He made as though to speak, then looked away.

As Burjor's slippers sounded in the corridor, he blurted out, "Remember, Jim? Don't let him confess to save me. I won't have it. I'll go to McIntyre straightaway!"

I could do no more than nod before Burjor entered, looking as though someone had stolen his best horse. Seeing us, he said, "Still here? Adi, you could have offered them some liqueurs."

He wanted to play the host, but it was time for a reckoning.

"Sir," I said, "may we discuss the case?"

"Humph." He dropped into a chair. "You can call me Papa, you know."

Call him Father? It took me by surprise. I said, "Thank you, sir."

He chuckled, a wry smile lifting his worn face. "Now, what's happened?"

Would my questions wound him? If I could avoid it, I would. But nothing good comes from hiding from truth.

I said, "The morning of Satya's death both Faisal and the mali recognized your carriage. But Adi had gone to Lloyd's bank. So it must have been you."

Burjor did not dissemble for a moment. "Yes. I met Satya that morning."

Diana flinched. Adi blurted, "You never said. Why?"

"Why did I meet him? Or why did I not say?"

I interjected, "Both."

Burjor slumped, his eyes squeezed shut. Exhaling, he said, "All right. Satya . . . he stole from us. I felt that bringing it up would look worse for you, Adi." He noticed our stillness. "What's the matter—you think *I* killed him?"

Adi said, "No."

I said, "Not deliberately. But perhaps, he tripped or slipped on something while you were . . . expostulating."

Burjor pulled back, affronted. "You think I'd skulk away and let my son take the blame?"

Adi gave a surprised laugh. "Papa, I've been terrified you would confess to something because you feared it was me!"

"Ah!" Father and son locked gazes, which were not unkind. They were more alike than they'd realized, I thought. Pulling in a long breath, I asked, "Satya stole from you, how?"

Burjor mopped his forehead. "Months ago, in July, he asked me for a loan."

Adi cried, "Papa!"

Burjor spread his hands. "Well, you wouldn't let me help!"

Satya had been murdered at the end of August. I asked, "What was the loan for?"

Burjor shrugged. "Plating equipment, nickel, copper, I don't know."
I frowned. "Would you invest in a business you did not understand?"
"I was investing in my son!" Burjor grated.
I said, "You agreed to the loan?"
He sighed. "One thousand rupees."
Adi stiffened. "That much?"
Burjor dropped his gaze. "That's what he wanted. I gave him a promissory note in exchange for his IOU." He turned to me to explain. "It's like this. He could use my note to purchase something, and I would owe his vendor. Mind you, that vendor could use the note like cash for a small amount of time."

He cleared his throat, then said in his deep baritone, "But when the note came due, *this* is what I received." He took a page from his pocket and unfolded it on the table, framing it with his hands.

Adi glanced at the page and yelped. "Papa! This is for five thousand!" He looked like he'd taken a blow to the head. "That's why you sold the hotel. But this is a forgery!"

Burjor shook his head. "It will be difficult to make that case. It is my signature."

Adi held it to the light. "But for a larger amount! Satya changed it. Damn him!"

Burjor said simply, "Yes."

A pretty piece of thievery indeed. My head spun with the implications. I asked, "When it comes due, you must pay up, is that it? When did it come due?"

"The day before Satya was killed," Burjor said.

I squinted at him. "But Banner said Satya wanted a loan two weeks before. At that point Satya already had your note. Why did he need more funds?" Silence answered, as I took stock. "So on the day he died, he had two thousand in banknotes, and also something he bought from Jussawalla for five thousand."

Diana covered her mouth. Throat dry, I asked, "Sir, why did you go to see Satya?"

Burjor said, "To remonstrate. He had spent five thousand rupees but his IOU was for one thousand!"

"So you argued. Did he get violent?"

Burjor leaned back in his chair. "Nothing like that. He offered to sell me his share in Adi's business. Then he changed his mind and said, 'You want collateral? Here, take it.'"

Burjor placed a small silver key on the glossy wood table. "He pressed this in my hand and hurried me away, saying he would explain later."

I squinted at him. "Satya was killed on the twenty-fifth of August. We met Adi in Liverpool on the sixteenth of September, and he'd been there a week. The ship takes thirteen days, so you dispatched him two days after the murder. Was this why you sent Adi abroad? Because Satya stole from you?"

He shook his head dolefully. "No, Captain. Someone killed Satya, perhaps for that." He gestured at the key with his chin. "I was afraid for my boy!"

I picked up the neat, shiny object, two inches long and curiously modern in design. Passing it to Adi, I asked, "Does this look familiar?"

He fingered it, turned it to and fro. "Never seen it before."

"Satya suggested selling his share, then changed his mind," I said. "Was he expecting someone else?"

Burjor's brows clumped in thought, while the grandfather clock ticked a slow dirge. "I don't know. He was . . . distracted. He looked past me, but the door was empty. That's when he changed his mind."

"What time was this?"

Burjor's brows knit. Rubbing his jowly chin, he said, "About ten minutes before noon."

That was later than the other witnesses had claimed seeing his carriage leave. I felt a chill cut through my veins. "I think someone was standing at the door behind you. Perhaps, the killer."

CHAPTER 16

THE FACTORY

Satya's key was now my main lead, but I had no idea what it unlocked. He had something worth seven thousand rupees, or maybe more, stashed somewhere. It had to be accessible, else why give Burjor the key as collateral? I'd been toying with this oddly shaped bit of metal at breakfast. Placing it beside my plate, I scoffed down eggs and toast.

Adi pointed with the butter knife. "That key, it's unusual. It's not the sort for trunks, almirahs, and such. Latchkeys that open doors are heavier. That's too small."

His rumpled weariness sent a pulse of sympathy through me. "I'm going back to your factory," I said. "Got to be something there, some clue to what's going on."

Adi wanted to come along, but I said, "Best not. If I find evidence, your presence could call it into question, at least in Superintendent McIntyre's view. He's already suspicious, and by now probably skeptical of my role too."

"My staff has stopped work. Place is closed now. I've got to return this to the landlord soon." Adi took a long iron key off his bunch and slid it over.

His eyes drooped above the disappointed twist of his lips. I slapped his shoulder in sympathy, then asked, "Your mali—did you dismiss him? He still weeds the garden."

"Bala lives there, Jim, in a shed. I suppose he has nowhere to go. Now I've got to dispose of the inventory. It might bring in some cash . . ."

I begged him to wait. "I've got to figure out what Satya was doing, examine his office, see if there's some hint of, ah, illicit activities."

And I needed to know why Bala was so afraid. Who had he seen, that morning?

In addition, since Adi's staff was no longer employed, I intended to watch them in turns. Anyone possessing seven thousand rupees would be hard-pressed not to spend some. If I saw evidence of new purchases, I might find the culprit. But posing questions as Adi's brother-in-law would get me nowhere.

To that end, dressed as a journalist in long kurta and vest over loose trousers, I headed once more to my old haunt on Dockyard Road. In my penniless bachelor days, I'd slept among sacks of grain in that bakery warehouse, jute dust and sawdust clogging my breath and making my eyes itch. Later, I'd used it as a waystation for my disguises.

A half hour later, my old landlord, the baker, uttered a shout, wiped his floured hands on the front of his apron, and hurried around the counter to embrace me.

"*Ma-shalla!* I thought you were dead! You have returned to us?"

I chuckled and asked whether he had rented out his warehouse.

He turned serious. "Janab, such a place is not for you. The gunny sacks, they have much dust. To sleep there is no good for the health."

When I assured him I only wanted to store some goods, he bargained for a higher rent than before. Grumbling, I paid for a month.

Next, I flagged down a Victoria and directed it to Adi's factory. In my pocket I fingered Satya's silver key, hoping it would fit a chest or safe. Stopping the carriage at the gate, I handed the driver a coin and descended. The gate was closed, but it creaked open with a loud metal protest.

"Bala?" I called, searching the lush vista. The air was heavy with floral scents, of which one distinguished itself, a deep romantic note.

The wide-boughed saptaparni tree was in bloom, each aromatic white bulb clasped within seven wide leaves, which gave the tree its name—"seven leafed." The tree flowered only in October, seeding the air with a distinctive, exotic scent.

As I unlocked the factory door, my body tensed. The place already smelled dusty and abandoned. In the still air, dust motes floated in beams of sunlight from a high window. I stepped softly through the building, checking nooks and crannies. The windows were secure, but the rear door hung ajar.

Because Adi would not have left it gaping, I approached with caution. The metal latch was torn apart, a paltry lock dangling from the jamb. I glanced around, treading as silently as my boots would allow.

I compared the untidy space with my memory of it. A row of crates lined one side of the long room, stacks of boxes and sacks interrupted the other. One gunny sack had been disemboweled, spilling hay. Three days ago it had not been so. I stepped around it, now wishing I'd locked the front door behind me. Someone could be here. And I wanted them trapped.

Something deep and malicious was taking shape. Here Satya had been set upon. A hand had grabbed the very instrument he'd worked to perfect, and thrust it into his gullet. He'd flung his arms back, swiveling perhaps, like a demented semaphore—was that what Adi saw when he bolted forward to break Satya's fall?

Had that murderer now returned? And if so, why?

I skirted the spilled packing material, my footfalls softly crunching hay. The intruder could ambush me as I turned into the vestibule connecting Satya's office with the accountant's. I stopped before the corner, crouched, then burst forward, intending to ram my assailant into a wall.

But there was no one. The dark hallway lay empty, holding its secrets. Sliding my hand along the wall, I flicked a switch. A naked bulb overhead shed a dim, sickly yellow light.

Hearing nothing, I entered the accounting office, where files lay tumbled on the floor. Whatever the thief had sought, it was not written, for no care had been taken in this disgorging of shelves. Crouching, I picked up invoices for chemicals and equipment, bills of lading and letters from other cities. Adi had been trying hard to interest the medical community in his products.

The desk drawers hung wide, contents askew. An earthenware penholder had been emptied on the table. What on earth was the thief looking for? I examined the filing cabinets, the floorboards, the windows, and the beams across the ceiling, but found only a crumbling bird's nest.

The supply room seemed untouched, until I tugged the top off a crate. There, the straw packing had been yanked out. A box of leather strips lay on its side. Picking up a swath, I brushed a finger across the pockets sewn along its length. These would be filled with individual implements and rolled up. The searcher had examined one box and left the rest.

In Adi's office, the air was soft with the scent of leather and machine oil. It felt peaceful, as though the chamber awaited his return. One shelf contained rolled leather cases, instruments neatly buckled into the supple binding. Beside these lay a stack of medical brochures from Britain and the United States.

A collection of models and machines cluttered Adi's room, many with wheels and gears, others that vaguely resembled sewing machines. Some bore dials; a strap showed another might be worn over a shoulder. Leaving them untouched, I worked through Adi's desk.

Paperweights, pens, pencils, drawing instruments, gloves. Stacks of paper, calling cards, a pair of broken wire-rims, scraps with phone numbers and scribbles. A few rupee notes, some change and a spare pair of trousers were stuffed into the lowest drawer.

Next door was Satya's office—that was a misnomer, for it was a laboratory. What gave it that sharp stench? Was some bottle open, the chemical evaporating? Such a dizzying array of urns, tubs, bins, and wire racks—Did the plating process require multiple steps? Perhaps Satya had also been an inventor.

In a drawer I found a paper twist of peanuts—saved for his dinner?

A man's possessions draw a picture of his inner self, I thought. My own possessions were few—a medal I could not bring myself to wear. A loose orange braid from a *rakhee* ceremony—with it, little Chutki had claimed me as her brother. My dress uniform with frayed cuffs; a handful of books; a knife that fit in my army boot; and a gold watch, engraved with the name of my grandfather—*I Agnihotri*—my mother's only gift. Then there was the Webley revolver Adi had given me two years ago, and old Father Thomas's Bible, worn, with broken binding, its yellowed pages dog-eared.

Satya owned two shirts and three kurtas, a narrow pair of trousers—could a grown man possess such a small waist?—an unironed vest and a grimy white dinner jacket made in Soho. He had books about chemistry in tiny typeface, assorted coins, and that single packet of peanuts. Diana would have wept at this sad collection. Had he lived here, rather than at home?

The chemical smell was strong as I poked around his shelf, disturbing ants, roaches, and spiders. What the devil was that stench? Lizards scuttled up the wall as I moved bottles. An object rattled behind them, so I reached through, grunting as my fingers closed around something cold. Grimacing, I pulled out a shiny silver briquette.

Satya plated instruments in silver. Seeking the rest of his supply, I moved objects around and uncovered a cloth bag with two small, heavy ingots at the bottom. They'd been almost out.

A ring of dust on a shelf showed where a heavy barrel-shaped bottle had recently been moved. I paused, eyes adjusting to the light. I touched the cold surface of the jar, pushed it back into place. It slid an inch. My quarry was strong—*or he had brought help.*

Empty tanks littered the cluttered laboratory, wires spooling to some apparatus like an ungainly octopus. Then, in the cramped space, my boot caught on something, tripping me off balance. Machinery stabbed my thigh as I grabbed at air and crashed onto one knee.

Pain speared my injured joint. Swearing internally, I'd just dusted myself off, when a faint metallic noise came from outside.

The outer gate. A jolt ran through me like current. Aches and gouges forgotten, I took a wide step over the mess and slammed through the vestibule. Someone *had* been here.

Even as I charged toward the lane, I spotted something on the path. A pile of cloth? A garment? No. Large saptaparni blooms lay scattered beside it.

Bala Mali was curled on the ground, his dhoti askew, his knees drawn to his chin. Blood still seeped from a head wound. I knelt, cursing. Had he heard me in the workshop and come to see who it was? He'd blundered into someone's path—the thief, the killer stealing away?

Blast the bugger, why did he strike Bala? The mali was so puny he could scarcely swat a butterfly. Calling myself a dozen kinds of fool, I lowered my ear to his chest. Nothing. I searched his wrist for a pulse, looking out, unseeing, through the gate. I was too late, too bloody late.

Everything changes in the presence of death; our concerns shrink in comparison; time is more scarce and thereby more precious. A clank sounded in the road beyond, an everyday sound. The jingle of carriages mingled with the whir of bicycles.

Then, Bala sniffed.

It galvanized me. Relief, hope, and something more. Hurry, hurry. Might have a chance—God, I needed a chance to set this right.

I yanked off my vest and wrapped it around his head in an overdone turban. Gently, oh, so carefully I eased him into my arms and hurried outside. One angry shout brought the nearest Victoria to heel. I climbed in carrying Bala, for the old man weighed scarcely more than a child.

Settled in my arms, mouth open, he slept, while I cringed over every rut in the road that jarred our jolting ride. When the Victoria stopped before police headquarters, I raced to the infirmary, with Bala's scrawny legs dangling in a pendulum at my side.

Ignoring the hubbub, I turned the scrawny mali over to Jameson. To his credit, the medico never asked how the old man came into my care, nor his connection to the constabulary. Snapping upright, he rapped out orders left and right. Then, pointing to a gurney, he flicked his thumb toward the door.

I placed Bala carefully on the canvas, told Jameson his name, and stood back as the apparatus of the clinic took over. A group of sturdy orderlies hoisted the gurney like a bier and carried Bala from my sight.

CHAPTER 17

BUT WHY?

What now? I did not want to leave, but could do no more for Bala, so I steered toward McIntyre's office. My progress through the building generated stares, which I ignored. Yes, I was dressed in native garb, but they'd seen me come and go as such before and should be accustomed to it.

"Hoy!" A burly havildar stood before McIntyre's door, blocking me.

"Out of my way before you do yourself an injury," I snapped, without thinking.

His eyes bulged. He turned, facing me as I strode past.

At the wide mahogany desk, McIntyre's gaze jerked up from his file. In a moment he'd grasped the situation and said, "I'll get Jameson."

"I've just come from him," I said, then glanced down at my kurta where the old mali's bleeding had soaked through. My heart squeezed like a clenched fist. How could he survive such blood loss?

"Adi's factory gatekeeper," I said, my tone bitter as I dropped into a chair. "He was assaulted while I was inside the factory. Some blighter had just been rifling around."

My forearms were trembling. I leaned them on the desk, pressed my forehead to them, and closed my eyes. The darkness seemed to help.

McIntyre said something over my head, then told me, "Patrick's a good surgeon, the best. Here, take this."

"The mali was bringing me flowers," I said, then drained the glass he handed me. It burned going down. Why was he wasting good liquor?

Forgetting to moderate my tone, I demanded, "Why did you release him? I left him here because he was afraid. He knew something. He'd have told me, in time."

Something in McIntyre's blue gaze shifted. "You don't work here, you know," he said mildly.

"Had nowhere else to stash him," I mumbled, gazing at the empty glass.

"Could have taken him home with you," said the boss, "but that would be interfering with a witness."

I winced. "Someone's interfered with him now."

"Any witnesses?"

I frowned. "The blasted killer, I suppose. Or someone who searched the factory. The assault—I didn't see it. Bala was lying near the gate."

"You've just brought in the key witness against your brother-in-law. An injured witness who may die?"

I stared, astonished at his dry tone. "What? You think I'd—? You think—"

He sucked his teeth, then said, "He did say something, when he was here. No"—he held up a hand—"no one pressured him. He was fed, given a separate cell and a bedroll. No one molested him. They seemed to think the captain sahib would be irate."

Why was he so jolly about it? "What did he say?" I asked.

"Bicycle. Or basket. Couldn't make heads nor tails of it. Make any sense to you?"

I stiffened, hearing the whir of wheels just outside the gate, crunching as they pushed through gravel. That clank—was it from a metal kickstand being thrown up? I searched my memory. Had there been a bicycle leaning on the wall beside the gate? I'd been occupied with opening the gate itself.

"No," I said, "if a bicycle was against the wall, I'd have noticed it. But there're bushes too. I didn't look between them." I frowned. "Heard one outside the gate. Didn't see the rider."

He sat, rummaged in his drawer and pulled out his pipe. Tapping it meditatively, he asked, "Why'd you go to the factory?"

I paused. How much should I tell him? Would it work against Adi?

His fingers stilled and his eyes grew steely. "Well?"

"There could be more going on," I said and told him about Banner's reluctant admission.

McIntyre's mouth tightened. "So. Satya Rastogi needed money—you're sure?"

"It's what Banner said. That's a couple of weeks before Rastogi took off with Adi's funds. An old debt? Gambling? He played a mean game of cards."

A native voice spoke from behind me. "Sir?"

In accented Hindustani, McIntyre told a heavyset havildar, "Leave it here."

After the fellow placed a garment on the table, saluted, and left, McIntyre said, "Go on. It's for you. You can't walk around like that. People will call out ambulances."

Restored to good humor, he fussed about his pipe while I stripped off my sodden kurta and donned a clean khaki shirt that had been sized for a hippopotamus. Straightening the collar, I turned to thank him and found his narrow gaze intent upon me.

He pointed his pipe at my midsection. "Where'd you pick those up?"

My scars. I extracted my billfold and notebook from my ruined garment, saying, "Gifts from army days."

Where was Satya's key? I rummaged in the pockets, but found only my pencil stub and the heavy iron key for the factory. Damn, I'd lost the little silver one.

"Twelve years on the frontier," he said. "And Burma." His tone was reflective, and he hadn't lit his pipe.

That missing key was crucial to Adi's case. Rising to leave, I thanked him for the shirt.

"Hmm-mmm," he said. "Walking around unarmed, again."

I tried a smile. It didn't hurt. "I'll be all right. If Bala wakes, give me a shout, will you?"

"Mmm," he said, returning his attention to the file before him.

* * *

On the way back to Adi's factory, I bought a screwdriver and padlock. Then I retraced my steps to Satya's office and scoured the floor.

Something gleamed by the ledge where I'd tripped. Bending, I scooped up the missing key with a sigh of relief. If only these walls could talk! But they remained stubbornly silent, and I had no Holmes along to spot the logical reason for the mali's tragic assault.

Hammering the rear door latch into place with the screwdriver's handle, I muscled in a pair of screws, then added the new lock and surveyed my handiwork. The latch dangled crookedly. Pathetic. It would not keep out a determined schoolboy, let alone a violent killer.

What had the thief taken from Adi's factory? What had he been looking for? It was something fairly small, since he'd searched inside a pen stand.

I looked at Satya's key, then tucked it into my wallet.

A weight settled on my shoulders as I thought of the old mali seeing me enter the factory, and deciding perhaps to gift some fragrant blooms for Adi's home. A kind thought. It had earned him a blow to the head from which he might not recover. But why?

Someone had searched the factory, probably looking for Satya's key. The thief had come armed. He hadn't needed to use a scalpel on Bala Mali. If I'd accosted him in the factory, that weapon would have been for me. Feeling grim, I stalked through Crawford Market making a series of purchases which I carted to my Dockyard Road hideaway.

* * *

I returned in time to clean up for Diana's dinner party and found her in our bedroom, in tears.

She said, "They say they've been called away. To decline an invitation just a few hours before the event—it's the height of bad manners." She sounded sad, rather than angry, as she flicked at the too-short sleeve of my billowing borrowed shirt.

"Who, sweet?"

"Miss Vakil's father is a reputed barrister," she said, and showed me the note from Miss Rata Vakil, which, while polite enough, looked to be hastily dashed off.

"Probably just as well. Doubt that Jameson will come," I said, then told her of the assault on Bala, Adi's aged gateman. She listened, lips parted, as I described his injury and the flowers that fell from his hands, blooms he'd likely gathered for me to bring to the house.

"Oh, the poor man! Who'd do a thing like that?"

It made me pause. "He told McIntyre, 'Bicycle, basket.' Fellow doesn't speak English. He'd be too intimidated by the constables to say much. But McIntyre set him free, so he tried to tell him something. Di, I think . . . perhaps he can identify Satya's killer."

"Oh?"

I explained, "That could be what he meant. I'd asked if he saw someone walking up the drive the morning Satya was killed. Bala was watering plants or weeding, when perhaps someone wheeled in a bicycle."

Hope shone in Diana's deep brown eyes. "It's a lead, isn't it? Could it get Adi off the hook?"

"There are thousands of bicycles in Bombay. Many with baskets attached, or hanging from the handlebars. Not enough to go on."

Sighing, Diana pulled the bell. When Gurung arrived, she asked him to bring me bathwater. Apparently, we were going to dress for the evening, regardless. When he returned, I hurried to wash and don suitable attire, then went down to find Adi.

He was in the hall, so I handed him two keys to his factory and told him about the new padlock. Then I narrated what had befallen the mali.

He stared, unmoving, his dark eyes wounded. "He's alive?"

"He's with Jameson."

Deep hollows curved at his Adi's temples. On our shipboard adventure, he'd been both appalled and delighted at his subterfuge. Now the waiting, the inactivity must be intolerable.

I asked, "All those months, Satya must have confided in someone. Adi, think back to when he was most relaxed, most at ease. Who did you see him with?"

Addie frowned at the window, his look inward. Rubbing his forehead, he said, "Satya wasn't the sort to kick back after work. He was always the same—quiet, diligent. I'd seen him speak with Bala, the gardener, about plants . . . the weather, rainy season, oh, I don't know."

Just now, when I'd told him about the attack on the gardener, his first question had been one of concern, hadn't it? But—wait. He'd actually asked, was the mali alive? A logical question, but one that the assailant might also ask. I felt as though a tremor passed through the earth below me.

So I watched Adi closely as we followed Gurung into the foyer. I asked, "Bala Mali—where did he come from? Did you find him, or did Satya?"

Adi inspected the doorway and gazed out at the curved path.

"Satya hired him for the garden," he said. "The old chap came from Satya's home, I think. Maybe a family retainer?"

A piece of the puzzle clicked into place. "He knows Satya's plan, even if he does not realize it. The killer is afraid he knows enough."

CHAPTER 18

STRAY DOGS AND BANKERS

Soli Wadia arrived just before Miss Sorabji. Diana's friends, the Vakil sisters, had sent a polite, if somewhat incoherent, apology and Jameson's orderly brought Mrs. Framji a note with his regrets. Our dinner discussion centered around a local magistrate who had deemed stray canines a public nuisance and hazard. Dogcatchers had been hired to round up "pariah dogs" in the streets, and a number of the animals had been slaughtered. Worrying over the mali and what he might have seen, I contributed little to the conversation.

"It will be quieter at night," said Soli, without enthusiasm.

Miss Sorabji protested. "But to *kill* them! They cannot help barking, can they?"

Mrs. Framji said, "My sister feeds the poor creatures on the sea-face road. She said the dogcatchers lure the mutts with the scent of food, then trap and shoot them. She and her friends were appalled—wagons carting away dozens of carcasses. If this goes on, there will be a riot!"

The soiree was a subdued affair, though Miss Sorabji and Diana both played piano. In two years of marriage, I'd not heard my wife play before and now found myself entranced. As the melody flowed over me, rising and falling like ocean waves, Adi winked at me and smiled.

Later, when the guests had departed, Diana helped her mother put the little ones to bed. I changed into pajamas but felt too restless to lie down.

Hoisting Diana's gift, *The Memoirs of Sherlock Holmes*, at last, I began reading. In "The Adventure of Silver Blaze" I paused, rereading a line. "See the value of imagination," said Holmes. "We imagined what might have happened, acted upon the supposition, and find ourselves justified."

Imagination—was that how it should be done? I read on. However, before I could finish the story, Diana returned with tales of the children. Little Tehmina had a fever, so Mrs. Framji would stay up with her tonight, placing cloths soaked in eau de cologne on the child's forehead. The child, the key, the injured mali. I faded into sleep to the low sound of her voice.

*　*　*

I got to Lloyd's bank early the next day and held out the troublesome silver object that haunted my dreams. "Mr. Gupta, can you identify this key? What might it unlock?"

He took it with delicate fingers, turned it and passed it back. "I'm sorry, Mr. Agnihotri. It's not one of ours."

"Is there an expert you could ask?"

Shrugging, he summoned an old clerk with white eyebrows on a face like a gnarled oak who examined my key and swiveled his head from side to side.

"If there's nothing else," said Gupta, his tone hinting it was churlish of me to waste his time. I left, pondering where to try my luck next.

When stumped, as I now was, I'd found it helpful to walk. *A turn or two I'll walk to still my beating mind*—Shakespeare's *Tempest*, I thought, as I traced my way toward the sea face. God knows, I was facing a storm. In a black mood I strode the cluttered length of Queen's Road, a shore drive that curved along the western edge of Black Town, where most Indians lived.

Satya had been furiously gathering funds. In August, he'd borrowed and altered Burjor's promissory note to make it five thousand. Two weeks before he was killed, he'd begged Banner to lend him a thousand. Then he'd taken two thousand rupees from Adi's bank.

Yet no money was found on him. So he must have locked it some-where with that silver key. Where?

He hid things from his family; if he was in trouble, it was not likely he would seek their help. He hadn't taken Adi into his confidence. After bilking Burjor, it would be a brazen man who could meet Adi daily, work with him, speak with him, make plans. Yet giving Burjor the key was not the act of a cheat, but one who intends to make a clean breast of it.

It all came back to why he needed so much cash in the first place. If I knew that, I could unravel the rest. Yet for the moment I had no means to uncover it.

One by one, I examined the individuals in my case. Adi—so upright that he could not believe Satya would deceive him and remain right un-der his nose. In recent days Adi had seemed exhausted, even hopeless. Yet his priority was clear: keeping his parents out of his mess. In that he was mistaken. His father was very much a part of the case. I considered Burjor—determined to aid his son, to bankroll or railroad the path to his success, despite his own financial problems.

Then there was Satya's suffocating family—a proud, dominant mother, clever, watchful father, and generations of cousins, living together.

What of young Howard Banner—charming, athletic, prim? He'd ad-mitted to being friendly with Satya, yet unwillingly, as though it were an unpleasant admission.

Adi's two employees—I knew too little of them, and yet there was some story there, something out of place. Why did they cling to their joint narrative so firmly? Surely one or the other must have had a closer rapport with Satya?

The old mali was afraid of someone, and now unable to say whom. What did he mean—basket, or bicycle? He'd said that to McIntyre, the highest-ranking man he'd met, so it must be important. If he ever gained consciousness, I would ask him.

Who else?

The thief, who'd felled the shriveled mali with a single blow. I frowned. What had he been struck with?

Again I went over the scene Burjor had described: Satya, glancing past Burjor's shoulder, sees someone who alarms him. He recognizes the person, knows he has come for something . . . the key. He has it on him, in his very pocket. Does he fear the man will search him? This would mean it was someone stronger, more vital, someone he knows capable of violence. His mind races—how to get rid of the key quickly, without drawing attention to it? Burjor stands before him, upset, belligerent, his carriage waiting. He palms it to Burjor, tells him he will explain later.

But after Burjor leaves, Satya is killed, and there *is* no later.

Adi comes in, sees Satya stagger like a puppet without strings, lowers him to the floor, and cries out to the staff. Satya knows he has but little time. He's desperate to say something—struggles, chokes, sputters.

When Adi moves the blade, fingers trembling, Satya knows he has one chance. "Sona," he says. Gold. "Don't let them sell it."

Had he been amassing the precious metal? Was that what he'd secured with his key? Had he passed it to Burjor because it led to the gold, in coins, perhaps? Sovereigns were easily secreted, though heavy. Hundred-rupee banknotes would be lighter and more portable. I scratched my itching forehead, feeling that this was significant. A savvy businessman might accumulate Bank of England notes. So why had Satya mentioned gold?

What did the key open? A letterbox? No, *dak*-carriers would intrude to stack new mail. Where else could one lock something of value?

Well past luncheon I visited Churchgate Station and pretended I had forgotten the number of my locker, but again, the effort was futile. Victoria Terminus Station was a bust too.

Sweaty and crumpled, my gut churning, I returned to Framji Mansion wiping perspiration off my forehead. I was missing something, a vital link. Until I found it, Satya's key would be useless. I was at an impasse, out of leads.

Holmes had noted, "It is of the first importance not to allow your judgment to be biased by personal qualities." McIntyre would say, "Look at the obvious! The simplest explanation is best." But he didn't know Adi. if Adi had done it, he'd be the first to own up. That was his nature, as it is the nature of water to flow.

There was no help for it, I'd have to look closer at Adi's employees.

CHAPTER 19

TOOLS OF THE TRADE

Two years ago when we emigrated to America, I'd boxed up my disguises and supplies. In the chaos of leaving Bombay, I'd told Adi about them as Diana and I boarded our ship. Now, I asked Mrs. Framji about my motley collection.

She smiled and set aside her sewing.

"I put your crates in a godown. Come," she said, including Diana in her glance. Nonplussed, we followed her to the kitchen, where she piled fruit in our hands, then she bustled outside toward the servants' quarters.

This row of connected rooms, fronted by a joint verandah, lay thirty yards behind the main house. Gulmohur trees spread their branches like open arms over the squat building, their canopy a giant umbrella. In the shade, the new houseboy mended a *char-poi,* literally a four-legged bed meshed with woven jute. A Nepalese woman, Gurung or Ganju's wife, was hanging clothes on a line. Tossing wet garments over her shoulder, she joined her hands in a *pranam.*

Our arrival caused a cheerful tumult in the yard. Gurung and Ganju's children ran up and surrounded Mrs. Framji. Smiling, Diana handed out chikoos and apples to the gaggle of grinning toddlers who bit into them immediately. Their dark eyes shone as juice ran down sunburned cheeks and dripped from their little chins. They giggled and chattered, tugging at Diana's sari to command her attention.

Meanwhile Mrs. Framji tried keys from her bunch at a sturdy lock on the door. "It is one of these, *beta*. We didn't expect you would come back . . . it is quite a mess inside."

A string of dried flowers drooped over the door. "Who lived here?" I asked.

Silence answered. I caught Diana's sideways gaze and knew. "Chutki. It was her room."

* * *

Later, I sat on our bed and asked Diana, "D'you want to live in Bombay, sweet?"

"Not with these daily slights and bruises!" she retorted, opening a trunk of clothing.

I saw the morose downturn of her lips. "Why do you care so much what they think? Can your papa not manage without the Parsi businessmen? If the Wadias refuse to ship his tea, why not hire Sassoon Shipping? Why not English companies, or other Indians? The Parsis cannot have a chokehold on everything?"

"They do seem to manage most of it," said Diana, shaking out a skirt. "Papa sells tea and coffee using *hundis*—bearer notes. To get paid, he must have access to money changers and banks. Most are run by Parsis."

While Diana floated to and fro putting away laundry, I wondered whether they'd blackballed her father because she'd broken their rules or because Burjor broke ranks to forge a connection with me. I leaned my forearms on my knees. "Do these people matter to *you*?"

She made a face. "It is nice to be admired, but the world outside these windows matters in itself."

As she went by, I swung out an arm and hooked her tiny waist. "All I need is here."

She chuckled. "But we cannot live without others. You'd become . . . too accustomed to me." Her voice turned teasing as she set the clothes down and touched my hair. "It's gone too long, again. Without others, you'd no longer be enamored of me!"

I snorted, pressing my lips to her chin.

She kissed me, then pulled back, her brown eyes liquid chocolate. "And what of our someday children? How will they learn a trade? Or find spouses? If they believe all families are like ours, won't they be dismayed when they venture out? How will they earn their livelihoods, find adventure, like you? We need the world, Jim."

I closed my arms around her and there was considerable room to spare. "Sweet, I have to be away some days."

She arched back to see my face. "Days? Where will you sleep?"

I paused to consider that. "In my godown near the dockyard, or . . . on the street."

Her intake of breath hissed near my ear. "In disguise. Why?"

"I must watch to find the culprit."

"No!" Her narrow arms clung. Then she pulled away so I could see her face. "Come late, come in the morning, come by noon! But come home, Jim. Don't stay away. I can't . . . do that again."

I remembered her panic when I'd had to leave her in Boston. "I'll find a way to send word. Maybe Gurung and Ganju can take messages . . ."

* * *

I hired an ekka to cart crates bearing the tools of my trade to my rental warehouse behind the bakery, then took a tram to Adi's factory. The gate was as I had left it, and my new lock still dangled on the paltry latch. Tugging it, I sighed. Anyone could lever it open. Its only purpose was to let me know whether the thief who'd assaulted the mali had returned. Reluctant to leave, I walked the perimeter of the compound, pondering the mali's plight.

Dead blooms littered the flower beds where brown leaves curled, so I unwound the rubber hose and worked the pump to spray down the rows. Soon droplets showered the foliage, scenting the breeze that cooled my skin.

Trees rustled as sparrows chittered to each other, bringing tranquility I had not known in months. With regret I turned off the faucet and gathered up the hose. Bala's gentle presence was everywhere. Would he die, then? My limbs felt heavy. Such senseless waste of life: first Satya and now his gardener, whom McIntyre believed to be a watchman, a guard. Having met the gentle mali such an idea was laughable.

I started down the path to the gate, pausing at the spot where I'd found Bala. In the shrubbery, a dark object caught my eye. Bala's hand-tilling fork, the tool of his trade. He'd held it constantly, even when he pressed palms together in greeting.

Shaking open my kerchief, I picked it up, feeling bleak. Brown-black stains smeared the white linen. Here was the weapon that had struck the old mali. Wrapping it securely, I lodged it inside a pocket and pulled the gate closed behind me.

I searched the dry scrub around the entrance for signs of a bicycle, but the pebbles and dirt kept their secrets. Handcarts and tongas rolled past. A vegetable vendor pushed a laden handcart. A carriage rolled by, then teenagers in school uniforms cycled past. A woman balanced pots on her head, calling, "*Topli-wali, topli nu paneer!*" hawking fresh curds and cheese.

Uncertain, I circled the block. Diana would know in an instant what was wrong, but I could not pin it down. Here was the old formal entrance to the property, now closed and barricaded. I caught glimpses of the factory as I strode around the stone perimeter. Through it, the mali's verdant garden was a lush paradise.

Across the street, a peanut vendor sat on his haunches. When I hailed him, he scrambled over with his basket and began to prepare a twist of paper. Recalling the packet in Satya's desk, I asked the *chanawala* whether he'd sold peanuts to a young man at the factory.

"Yes," he said. "In the evening, he would often buy."

I asked a few questions, and learned that he had not known Satya except as a customer. As I handed him a coin, an idea took shape. "Would you like to earn a bit more?"

He was willing. I said, "Sit on this street, each day, or at the corner. Watch this gate, and tell me if someone comes in. I want to know how long they stay."

He blinked a few times, then asked what I would pay. After some haggling, we settled on twelve annas a day. "This is a good lane for business," he said. "Schoolchildren come, people pass. When will you pay me?"

We agreed upon a plan: If anyone visited the factory, he must remember them; it would earn him an extra four annas.

Having planted the *chanawala* in place, my spirits lifted. The case had to break soon. The mali's tool still weighed down my jacket—a murder weapon, perhaps. Would anyone care if he died? As yet no one had investigated his assault. I went to police headquarters and left it on McIntyre's desk with a short note written on his own stationery.

CHAPTER 20

INTERROGATION

Diana and I were dressing the next morning as I described the steps I'd taken when a knock sounded on the door. I reached for my trousers, while Diana deftly pleated her sari and tucked it in at her waist. Tossing her pallu over a shoulder, she opened the door.

"Captain sahib, Papa-ji requests you downstairs," Gurung said. "Not you, Bibi-ji."

Diana frowned. "Not me? He specifically said that?"

Gurung nodded, downcast. I straightened my cuffs and reassured her. "Probably about the case. Tell him I'm coming."

"Oh!" Diana said. "I remember. That row at the temple upset Papa terribly. He's asked Dastoor Kukadaru to visit this morning, our family priest at the Mazagaon fire temple. Jim, everyone listens to him. Perhaps he will intercede for us. Get the other families to see I've done nothing wrong."

The house was hushed as I went through to the study, where two men awaited me. Burjor's family priest was a short man with a squarish face. Greying mustache, beard neatly trimmed; small wire-rimmed glasses hid his eyes. He wore a close-fitting white hat, loose white robe over white trousers, and closed Indian slippers, which tapped on the tile floor as he approached, his hand outstretched.

Burjor introduced us awkwardly, without meeting my gaze. "Ervad, this is my son-in-law, Captain Agnihotri. And this is our respected priest, Ervad Kukadaru."

To break the silence, I said, "Ervad is your given name?"

"Only a title," the priest said with a thick Gujarati accent, each syllable weighted down with lead. "Let us speak privately, Captain. Join me for a walk?"

His curved shoulders stooped, Burjor let us out. As I caught his gaze, his face squeezed in an unspoken plea. So that was it. Before the priest lent the weight of his influence to our cause, he'd want to ascertain what kind of man I was.

We went down the wide front stairs under boughs of pink bougainvillea while I sought about for a suitable opening. What could I say, I who sorely wanted him in my corner, not for my own sake but for Diana's? She'd lost so much from our union. How could I make amends? Yet this was unnatural territory for me, the complex terrain of social customs. How to proceed?

The short, sturdy priest glanced around the verdant yard and said, "Come. I will say a prayer as we walk around this home." Stretching out his arms, palms upward, he intoned a prayer in a language unknown to me.

As he walked in slow measured steps, his deep voice filled the air with a strange melody, half spoken, half sung. I kept pace, puzzled as he headed straight for the trunk of a coconut palm. Only then did I notice that his eyes were closed!

Reluctant to interrupt his chanting, I caught his elbow and steered him around the obstacle. This was apparently satisfactory—he neither slowed nor changed his attitude. In this way we walked down the row of palms to the stable. Sunlight twinkled the fluttering leaves above us. Tiny red petals of gulmohar floated through the scented air.

Our path was up to me. I calculated to save his slippered feet and white trousers, taking us around the grassy perimeter and through the trellised garden. I thought perhaps to guide the priest along the treed side of the house. However, before we reached it, his chanting ceased.

He stood, gazing around at beds of fragrant herbs. Bees hummed past us in the quiet green as he eased onto a nearby stone bench.

"Come," he said, patting the seat.

I sat beside him. He said, "I can help Burjor-ji. Would you want me to?"

"Of course."

"Hmm. But first, I need an assurance. Will you tell me the truth?"

Why the emphasis on truth? Some presentiment warned me to caution. "If I can."

"If you can?" He frowned. "You wed Diana far away from us, so I will ask you now. Will you be a good husband to her?"

"As long as I live," I said lightly.

"This is a serious matter, young man," the priest snapped.

It was a curious habit I must have picked up from Englishmen—the more important the matter, the more flippant we got. I gave him a half smile in apology.

Clearing his throat, he said, "Two years ago when you examined the deaths of Adi's wife and the child Pilloo—"

I interrupted him. "What does that have to do with it?"

"Who was responsible?"

"You can't be serious."

"I am. Very serious."

I pulled back, discomfited at this change of subject. "Why d'you need to know?"

"What if I say—the man who was accused has asked if I will bless his home with a Zoroastrian prayer. Should I do it?"

Two years ago, Manek Aslaji had been tried for causing the deaths of Adi's wife and his cousin. He'd been acquitted, and I had brought the perpetrators to justice. Now the priest was asking whether Manek was responsible. He was innocent, but I'd promised Adi my silence.

I said, "Only you can decide that."

"So you did not exonerate him."

I spread my hands, feeling a flame in the pit of my belly. "I cannot speak of it."

"Why?"

"I gave my word."

His dark gaze narrowed on me. "And this word of honor, it cannot be broken?"

I wanted to say, that's right, it is absolute! But was it, really?

I sighed. "If there was good reason I suppose, I would break it."

"Yes?"

"If it were life or death," I snapped. "My word is not worth some-one's life."

He absorbed this. "What about, to save the Framji family much pain? Would you do it?"

Drat the man. He'd put me in a fix. I said, "I'll ask them. If they agree, I'll tell you."

"No, no," he tut-tutted. "If they are responsible, that wouldn't work. Tell me now."

I shook my head, my gut knotted. "Can't do that."

"Would you not like to help?"

"'Course I would. They're my family! They took me in, gave me—everything."

"And it costs them a great deal. But you can easily solve that."

I searched his face. Light reflecting on his thick lenses obscured his eyes. "How?"

He spread his hands. "Leave. Walk away. It will take a while, but eventually things will go back to how they were."

His matter-of-fact tone stabbed me. "Leave Diana? Live without her?"

A fire flared inside me, consuming the tissue around it. My throat closed. Could I survive without Diana? With dismal clarity I knew that in fact, I could. I could return to the States or go to Canada, Australia even. It would not matter where I went.

"She'd be furious. After all she's done so we can be together, all she's given up?" I remembered Diana's crumpled face two years ago, when she'd admitted to lies of omission. Drooping, her eyes dull, lips pale, shaking. God no.

I said, "Can't do it. We'll sink or swim together."

He swayed, rocking in his seat. I pulled a breath into my starving lungs, wanting to rail, to call him out as a coward. Could he not restrain his flock? He was shilly-shallying, an excuse to avoid intervening.

Instead, I tried once more. "They are good people. Good Zoroastrians. If it is in your power to help, then do so. Ask me a price that I can give, and I will pay it."

"Hmm." He sat back, a hand tapping his white robe, then said, "We are building an *Atash Behram*, a cathedral, you might say."

"I'll contribute all I can."

"Tsk." He waved aside my interruption and went on, "Would you, ah, break the law if I asked you to?"

I felt as though he had plowed a fist into me. *This* was Burjor's holy man, the revered high priest? I said grudgingly, "I've bent some laws in my time. But no, I would not commit a crime for you."

"But you withhold information when it pleases you," he said in an easy, reasonable tone. "Have you told the police everything about the tower deaths?"

I looked away. Adi and I had decided to keep some matters between us.

He smiled. "So, you have a code of your own."

Now he became amiable, saying, "All right, Captain, listen. I have already told Burjor that I will help. The family will come to Mazagaon tomorrow and attend a *boi* ceremony at my fire temple. On Saturday I will perform a *jashan* here, a blessing. This shows I favor the Framji family. It is decided."

"Already decided?" I remembered Burjor's pained look as we had left the room. I'd thought he was pleading with me to help. Had he been asking my pardon? "So what was this for, your questions, demands?"

He patted my knee, then clutched the bench to push himself to his feet. We made our way back to the house without conversation.

At the entrance, he said, "When I send for you, come alone to Mazagaon fire temple. At ten o'clock that night. Now goodbye."

Mazagaon was to the east of town, near the dockyards I knew well. I'd borrow Gurung's bicycle, I thought, then remembered Diana's cautioning words.

"But I cannot enter," I blurted.

He chuckled. "Who said anything about entering? Now, mind, not a word to anyone. I may have a job for you. A discreet one."

Damn, I thought. *That* was what he wanted. He'd been assessing me for some doubtful task of his own.

CHAPTER 21

SILVER, LOST AND FOUND

A week had passed since we arrived in Bombay. I made arrangements to spy on Adi's employees, then rode back to Framji Mansion in the deep indigo dusk. Haloed gas lamps glowed to either side of the entrance. Amid the rapid chirp of crickets, Gurung swung open the gate to admit my tonga. Ganju salaamed as I ran up the front stairway. Hearing the children's chatter in the dining room, I hurried to clean up, taking the stairs two at a time, heartened to know that my knee could stand it.

Hands scrubbed, I ran a palm over my hair and went down to a boisterous Framji welcome. Adi and Diana were going at something hammer and tongs, but dishes laden with savory delights claimed my attention. Devoting myself to them, I won Mrs. Framji's smile by serving the children and passing tureens of yoghurt raita and biryani around them.

When Diana's fresh-cheeked smile turned to me, the gap of age between us yawned. Her grin, her laughter fed something within me, a chord resonating, like a harp plucked in a great cathedral. I wanted to guard the innocence of that look, lock it in a fortress and set sentries, because I knew, deep down, that it would not last. I feared it would fade or explode into disappointment. But not yet. Let her be a girl yet, smiling at boats bobbing in the harbor, teasing kittens out from corners. Early in our marriage she'd nestled in my arms, weary from the day's excitement, and blurted out, "Jim, you won't be angry if I tell you something?"

I could barely make out her face through the tangles of her curls, but knew she was biting her lip in worry. I'd said no, I would not, no matter what it was.

"I'm not ready to be a mother," she'd whispered.

I'd hugged her. "In time, yes?" She'd nodded and cuddled closer. We'd had our ups and downs in the following months, so when she trusted me completely, I thought my heart so full it might truly burst. And we'd come close to parenthood, though I didn't know it at the time. The inexplicable loss of her pregnancy had caused a long malaise which gouged me to the core.

Beside me now, Diana tilted her face for a kiss. Encouraged, I brushed her cheek with my lips. God, I could swear her skin grew softer each day! Inhaling her creamy, floral scent, I asked, "What have I missed, sweet?"

"Well," she began, "Adi says Satya must have been pressured but I—"

"Sahib!" Gurung interrupted. "There is a visitor . . ."

From the entrance came a harsh voice. An angry visitor! Ganju was holding him off.

Pushing back our chairs, Burjor, Adi, and I headed to the door, leaving Mrs. Framji protesting, "But the food is hot, my *jaan*! It will all get cold!"

In the foyer, the silver merchant's nose flared, his mouth grim. Without greeting us, Jussawalla stabbed a finger toward Burjor. "I let you persuade me! But no one wants it! How will I sell it?"

"Percy," Burjor said, "shall we sit here?" Without waiting for a reply, he opened the morning room doors and entered. Adi followed, so Jussawalla had no choice but to do the same. I brought up the rear, noting he'd dressed hastily, his white Parsi coat caught in the waistband of his trousers. His hat was askew, and patches of sweat yellowed the fabric under his armpits.

"Bring water," I signaled to Ganju, who gave me a military nod and strode away.

Adi and Burjor had taken the couch, leaving tall chairs for our irate guest and me.

Jussawalla began again, his tone ugly. "Did you think I would not find out it was worthless? All this will not work. I won't tolerate it!"

"I'm James Agnihotri," I said. "Diana's husband. Could you explain what this is about?"

My tone put a damper on his outpourings. Frowning, he glanced back and forth. "I don't know if you are part of this, but you should know what kind of people you have married into!"

"I'm entirely aware of my good fortune," I assured him.

Taken aback, he cracked his knuckles. Ganju entered with a tray which he set down on the dumbwaiter behind us. Rising, I poured out glasses and handed them around.

"Please."

He grudgingly took the delicate container and drank down the cool liquid.

As his glass descended, I said, "How can we help?"

Ganju leaned forward, holding the engraved silver tray. As Jussawalla carefully set the glass on it, I swallowed a smile. The Framjis' courteous manner would surely win over the hardest critic. Yet their elegant presentation could enrage those who envied them. Which was he, then, this merchant of silver?

"You cannot help me," he said flatly.

"What's the trouble? Can you explain?"

"These two"—he pointed at Burjor and Adi and snarled—"they owe me cash."

Burjor waved a calming hand but Adi said, "I don't know what you mean! What cash?"

Jussawalla snapped, "Your partner bought silver. A lot of it. And now you won't pay?"

"Wait," said Adi, his gaze intent. "We needed silver ingots to plate scalpels and forceps so they won't rust. We paid you in January!"

Jussawalla snorted. "You bought forty kilograms in August!"

Adi's mouth opened and closed. Ingots, I thought. Like those I'd found in Satya's room.

Adi choked out, "That's what Satya bought with Papa's promissory note."

Satya had spent the forged note on silver ingots? Burjor met my glance and nodded.

Jussawalla spread his hands. "Burjor, I don't want some hotel in Simla. How do I know what it's like? It could be a rubbish heap! I need cash, hard cash!"

So saying, he thrust a wad of papers at Burjor. Adi took them and uncurled the pages. Recognition lit his face. "The deed to our hotel!"

I questioned Jussawalla, "Satya bought silver worth five thousand rupees?"

"He knows"—he jabbed a finger at Burjor—"I was to be paid months ago!"

Before his vitriol overflowed, Adi said. "Look, I don't know what Satya did or didn't do, but we had no more silver. We ran out weeks ago."

Jussawalla cried, "I trusted your partner because of you! There is your hotel deed. Give me my cash. If you cannot pay, I will tell everyone you are both cheats!"

With a face like thunder, Burjor strode to his office. He returned with a heavy tread and wrote out a cheque for two thousand rupees, likely all the liquid cash he could muster.

Jussawalla snatched it up and demanded the remaining amount.

It took an hour to persuade him to wait until month's end for his payment. His lips compressed, Burjor penned a new IOU for three thousand rupees.

This was a new piece to my puzzle. I fingered Satya's slim key, still nestled in my vest pocket. When Satya gave it to Burjor, had he meant to offer his stash of silver as collateral? In that case, who was he keeping it from?

Satya must have another associate, one that Adi was unaware of. Hadn't he speculated only an hour ago that Satya had been pressured into doing something illicit?

CHAPTER 22

INCOGNITO

I dreamed of a hoard of coins, ingots piled high like Aladdin's cave. Forty kilograms? That was a lot of silver. Surely one of the staff had known about Satya's schemes? I played out a sequence in my mind: Satya's office was full of strange chemicals. If he was doing something illicit there, he might have been interrupted and seen. He'd then have to bribe the busybody to keep it from Adi. But why should that cause his death?

Had he been blackmailed, fought back, and lost? If Vishal the young accountant or Faisal the distressed tooler was the killer, then the other man had given him an alibi—out of fear?

To explore this, I borrowed Gurung's bicycle and headed to my dingy warehouse in Dockyard Road.

How different it was from being up on a horse! A mare could sense the terrain, her gait telling me she liked turf, sand, or brush. Gripping with knees and thighs, I could let her go on, or hold. Seated on her broad back, I could see far. A nudge, a flick of the reins and we gained ground. Now perched on the tiny seat of a wobbling bicycle, I worked the pedals to gain speed.

* * *

At the storeroom, doors and windows wide to admit light and air, I opened my crates and set out mirror, clothing, and bottles to assemble my disguises from two years ago.

To re-create the persona of an old army pal, I donned loose trousers secured with drawstring at the waist, then a dark grey kaftan that went to my knees. Rumpled and stale-smelling, it was perfect. Over that went a vest that was too small and hung open. I wound a strip of cloth around my head for a turban—it took several attempts to get this right—and draped another around my neck.

I glanced in the mirror and frowned. Ah! There was my error: I was clean-shaved.

Crafting a beard that looks natural is no easy task. On a plank of wood, I poured out a strip of collodion. Though contained in a sealed bottle, the liquid had thickened to a spongy stickiness. Measuring my jaw with outstretched little finger and thumb, I created not a full beard, but a scraggly one. Threads stripped from the tattered end of a dark cloth I pressed to the collodion, arranging them in untidy lengths. Two patches I left bare, to resemble the shape my own beard had once taken, and left it to dry.

An hour later, lifting the mess in one piece posed a challenge, because it stretched and tore. Yet this too was fortunate, for I added more threads and teased the smaller part into an unkempt mustache. Donning this made all the difference. Rashid Khan's rascally grin blazed back from the looking glass.

Later that day I hunkered at the crossroads by Faisal's house and posed as a loafer who occasionally sought work but was never satisfied with the wage.

At noon, Faisal returned carrying vegetables and stayed home the rest of the day. I inquired at his residence if there was work, but his wife said they had no need of a laborer. Then a dhobi dismounted from his bicycle and took his load inside.

When he returned, I begged a match of him. "Do they pay well?" I asked, jabbing a thumb toward Faisal's door. "They have some work for me."

The dhobi shrugged. "They pay all right."

"Now, yes? But not before?"

He frowned. "I have not had trouble with them yet."

Just past ten, the lamps indoors were extinguished. Dark deeds often wait for darkness, I thought, I should stay. Having eaten only peanuts and an apple got off a passing fruit cart, my stomach protested. And Diana would fret, for I had not told her of my plan.

At eleven, a lamplighter passed on his way home. He cast me a look.

"Still here?"

"They owe me money," I invented.

Eventually I trudged back to Dockyard Road and cleaned up. No, this would not do. I needed to get closer to study the two employees, Faisal and Vishal. Chased by crickets whispering in the moonlight, the road seemed long as I pedaled back to Framji Mansion.

A gaslight glowed in Burjor's study, drawing me near. The great man bent over his desk, his ledger before him, pen in hand as he strove to make up the sum he'd promised Jussawalla. His lined countenance told a painful tale.

"How much short?" I asked, from the door.

"Too much," he said, unsurprised, then blinked to see me there. His glance traveled to the tall clock in the corner. "You are very late. Any news?"

Any success, any hope? Anything positive at all, his pointed eyebrows asked.

I shook my head. "But there's more to learn about this fellow named truth."

"Satya, humph." Burjor tried a weak smile at my pun, then gave up the effort. "What can we do, Captain? The superintendent won't wait much longer. I cannot see the boy go to . . ."

Go to the gallows; to say it aloud was unbearable.

"I brought fifteen hundred from the States. Will it help?"

His face lifted as he locked gazes with me. "Your savings, my boy."

"You gave us five thousand, two years ago."

His hand rose, palm showing. "That was Diana's inheritance!"

"But if you need it . . ." Opening my pocketbook, I laid a cheque form on his blotter.

He tried some sums, pen flying over his page, then shook his head. "Still need fifteen hundred more, in two weeks. And three hundred for the staff's wages."

"Anything we can sell quickly?"

His breast swelled with a ponderous breath. "Mama's jewels. But—"

"Hold off, then. I'll try something else. If you give Jussawalla all that"—I gestured at his math—"would he not wait another month for his pound of flesh?"

Burjor's pen dropped from his fingers; his head swiveled in a hopeless rhythm. "He would talk, and it would be the end of us. Talk is worse, because rumor has wings beyond the fact of things."

He was losing hope, losing faith in me. God give him courage, give me speed! I was working too slowly to help Adi.

* * *

The following day, I returned to my storehouse and disguised myself as a banana seller to continue shadowing Adi's staff. I spent the morning near the Lohar Chawl area, speaking to shopkeepers and such to learn the habits of the accountant, Vishal. I saw pickpockets, a woman begging while an infant suckled at her breast, old men with open sores slumped against broken-down walls, children too weary to shoo flies from their lips, but made little headway on my case.

My summons came that evening. Breaking my rule about delivering messages only at my warehouse hideout, Gurung found me in front of Vishal's tenement. Although Diana had warned him that I would be dressed in disguise, my appearance as a vendor of bananas seemed to distress him. His captain sahib, fallen so low!

His voice husky with awkwardness, he dropped his gaze and said, "Diana Memsahib says a phone call came for you. She sends this message. Tonight at ten o'clock."

Delivering the priest's missive, he left. I watched Vishal's street until the bell tower chimed nine o'clock. Then I offered bananas to a pair of passing urchins who took them with eyes full of questions. They peered doubtfully at me, unaccustomed perhaps to receiving something so easily.

Then it was time I made for the fire temple. Mazagaon was near my haunt on Dockyard Road, where I hurried to discard my guise. My task: to see a holy priest who'd asked whether I cared to break British law.

CHAPTER 23

A CLIENT IN THE DARK

I was reluctant to take a carriage of any sort. The priest's assignment felt somewhat underhand, and I wanted no witnesses. I would have preferred to ride, but hitching a horse on a city street would offer no anonymity. Few Indians could afford one. So, I hauled out Gurung's bicycle, which I'd stashed in my warehouse, and pedaled east along Grant Road to Obelisk Road.

In the red-light area at Cammattipoora, barely clad women leaned from upstairs windows to offer themselves. Grimy, bearded men sat on the stairs to collect their respective fees. Some peered at me as I passed, for I was dressed Indian-style in kurta and baggy trousers, with a length of dark cloth wrapped about my head and the lower part of my face. Soon I turned north on Mazagaon road.

The Zoroastrian fire temple was just past the wood-fronted edifice of St. Peter's Church and walled off from the street. A lantern at the temple gate shone on twin statues of bulls at either side of the entrance. Attached to the temple, widely-spaced pillars gleamed ivory white, but the archways between were cloaked in darkness. The distant chime of the university clock tower struck as I pedaled up and dismounted at the gate. A figure moved in the dimly lit garden.

The middle-aged priest, Ervad Kukadaru, called, "Who is it?"

When I replied, "You asked me to come at ten," he motioned me around the back.

In the light of a streetlamp, a workman pushed his handcart, eyes squinting against his perspiration. Glancing this way and that, I walked the bicycle through shadows around the temple's stone wall.

"Leave the cycle here," said the priest, exiting a narrow grated gate. "We'll go this way."

Wearing a pale, baggy shirt of limp fabric over baggy trousers, he led me down the lane. About halfway, he turned into a dark, wooded green and headed toward a dim light in the middle of a field. Puzzled, I followed a few steps behind until we reached a gazebo.

Two men rose to their feet, their shapes moving through the lantern's light. A third remained seated. A voice called, "Ervad?"

My companion answered in Gujarati. I'd learned enough from hearing Adi and Diana talk so I gathered the gist. *He's with me. He is alone.* The priest said to me, in English, "This is Boman Padamji," indicating a short man whose white shirt gleamed in the dim light.

Padamji put out a hand, his grip steady and strong. He introduced the next, a lean, younger man as "Dorab, my son. He is an expert shot."

Since I knew nothing of the task, this did not reassure. Still seated, the third man was bowed with age. His voice cracked as he said, briefly, "I'm Jeejeebhoy."

Since the others gave him such deference, I took him to be the author of our present endeavor and asked, "How can I help, sir?"

Instead of answering, this doyen asked the priest in Gujarati, "You said he was Indian."

"*Fauj-wala hatoh,*" my companion answered—he was in the army. He turned to me. "I have told them how we spoke. You would not tell me how you solved the tower mystery, even though I pressed you. So you know how to be silent."

"But is he trustworthy?" the young man asked his father in Gujarati, sotto voce.

"Offer enough money and you could buy off most men," I replied in English. "But I would not shame the Framjis for anything."

I'd understood their vernacular. One of them gasped. The priest chuckled. "Good one," he said, clapping me on the arm. "He is Burjor's son-in-law, Diana's husband. I can vouch for him. Tell him about your . . . conundrum."

Bidding me to sit, the older man spoke in faintly accented English.

"You are kin to Burjor-ji, so we asked you to come. We need your help. You understand this is in the strictest confidence?"

When I acknowledged this, he motioned to Padamji. "Tell him."

Before Padamji could speak, his son put out a cautioning hand. "Papa, wait. Captain, what will you charge?"

I considered that. This priest was Burjor's most trusted man. By the look of it, the elders were taking a risk that sat heavily upon them. "Cover any expenses I incur."

"And your fee?"

That was difficult to answer without knowing more about the case. I addressed the patriarch. "I leave it to you. If you are satisfied, pay what you will."

"Boman-ji," the old fellow said, stroking his beard. "Tell him the problem."

The older Padamji drew an audible breath, his lined cheeks sinking inward, and began. "For over twenty years I have worked at the Royal Mint. I manage the forge, melting coins paid as tax into imperial bullion. I have given faithful service all my life. But now, there is a thief among my staff."

In a heavy voice, he said, "Someone has stolen a bar of gold. And I will be held responsible."

A theft, right under the nose of Her Majesty's Government! "Do they know, your employers . . . or the police?"

He shook his head. "I discovered it last week. Each batch is examined by a Parakh—it is a hereditary skill, you see, to test gold for purity. He examines the bars before they are secured in the vault. There is a large stock, so the Parakh does not handle each piece. But on Monday, when he picked up one, he was upset. He completed his round, then handed it to me. He certified the batch as usual, but afterward, when we were alone, he said, 'The one I gave you. It is fake.'

"Can you imagine my horror? I asked him, 'You signed for the lot! Why didn't you say something?' He shook his head, pitying me. 'Because you are in charge, my friend. This falls on your head.' Captain, his silence gives me a chance! Please help.

"Find out how it was done, and by whom! I cannot sleep or eat until I uncover the culprit! When this load of bullion reaches the Bank of

England, the fake will surely be discovered. My name, my reputation will be dust. Worse than dust. To a Parsi, to be known as a thief, a criminal . . . you cannot imagine what this means. My life will be over, but that matters not. My wife and children will be pariahs! Beggars will spit on them!" The diminutive Parsi clutched his hair in desperation.

Was this how Adi saw his disgrace? I stared at Padamji. "How long do you have?"

"The bullion is escorted by a man-of-war and other gunships. It will be shipped to England in a week or so. They do not say exactly when."

"Could he have made a mistake, this gold tester? All we have is his word. Perhaps he just wants a bribe?"

A sharp intake of breath answered me. Padamji said, "He is honest, Captain. He is my sister's brother-in-law. If he says the bar is fake, then it is."

I asked, "Can you get me into the mint, after hours?"

After a moment's consideration, he said, "It is a risk. But yes, I run the forge, so I can admit you. What reason shall I give?"

"Could I be presented as another Parakh? One in training, perhaps? Then your friend could indicate the fake as though he were teaching me."

He pulled back. "No false names, please. That bar was identical, numbered properly. But it was too light to be gold. Too light by far."

That piqued my curiosity. "How large are these bars?"

"Seven inches long, two inches wide and about an inch thick. Two and a half kilograms."

That was small enough to slip into a pocket! I said, "I'll take the case, on one condition. When it's done, you will provide me with letters of introduction to the top bankers in the city."

Padamji pulled back. "Introductions? That would make our association public, Captain Agnihotri. I cannot afford that."

"You need not provide a personal reference. Say it is for the son-in-law of an upstanding Parsi, Mr. Burjor Framji. Would that serve?"

"And I have your word that . . . ah, you have only honest motives?"

I pulled back. "You have to ask? Are you sure you want me for your problem?"

The priest touched my elbow. "Sir Jamsetji could give you those letters."

The stooped old man peered at me, then motioned me closer. I stepped up and held still under his rheumy gaze. What did he see? An Englishman wearing dirty Indian garb? My stubble itched. How I wished I'd dressed in a light linen suit or well-pressed trousers. Burjor's good reputation and perhaps my manner of speaking weighed in my favor. Was it enough?

Jeejeebhoy's gaze scoured me. The moment stretched, twisting the hope inside me to a frail thread. Voice creaking, he said, "Help him, Captain. Our honor, our reputation is at stake."

He nodded slowly. "You shall have your letters."

CHAPTER 24

THE IMPERIAL MINT

Wearing a formal dark suit, I rode a Victoria down Breach Candy road and across to the Bombay mint enclosure. There I gave my name because we had agreed to keep clear of aliases.

A short gent greeted me, hair slicked back neatly, wearing an impeccable white jacket and trousers—the mark of an elite Parsi in a country where simply keeping the grime off was a challenge. "I am Dara Parakh. Let's go to Padamji. You want to know how I test the gold?"

His voice ended in a question, but I made no answer, only thanked him and started down the corridor. My new client, Padamji, was playing it close to the vest. He had not included Dara Parakh in our plan, although Parakh had bought him time to find the culprit.

Troubled, I recalled his weary tone as he said, "My life is over, but that matters not."

We went through a series of heavy, guarded doors. Each time our names were recorded.

An armed British guard accompanied us to a long room lit by electric lights where along one side, metal tables were piled with short stacks of gold bars. At the end glowed a furnace, surrounded by urns of different shapes. Wisps of smoke smelled of some pungent chemical.

The guard indicated a mark on the floor. "Don't cross this line."

Padamji came from the far corner to reassure him, then shook hands with me, radiating relief at my new appearance. He said, "The forge is not operating today. There are usually two workers, one to cast the metal, and another to stamp the numbers. Here—" He plucked a bar off a stack and showed me the crest incised on it. Below that lay a long series of numbers.

He explained, "As they enter each morning, workers strip off their street clothes under guard. They wear white overalls to work here. In the evening, they must drop their overalls and walk unclothed down a corridor to a shower. Only then are their clothes returned and they're allowed to leave."

He pushed open the metal door to an adjacent chamber, where gold bars were ordered into flat wooden boxes. The guard followed. He had not taken his eyes off me.

Although this room was larger, I felt as though a hand clamped my nostrils. The air was laden with that same sharp smell. Electric lights glowed over metal walls without windows. It was a prison.

"... the weight is uniform," Parakh was saying. "I sample each stack. My systematic method has worked for decades." He began to lift and replace bars in a curious sequence. Taking a metal ruler from his pocket, he drew the bar across it and showed me the resulting stripe.

"What of that specific one," I asked. "Is it still here?"

Padamji cast a glance at the door where the guard watched, his face inscrutable, then went to a distant stack and selected one from the middle. This he brought and placed in my hand. For something so small, it felt quite heavy.

Picking up another bar nearby, Padamji said, "Now hold this." It was even heavier.

He set it on a nearby scale. Tipping small weights on to the balance, he said quietly, "Two point five kilos. Now the other one."

When he placed it on the scale it sank. He removed two smaller weights, which returned the scale to balance and handed them to me. Since each was stamped with a number, I calculated the fake was a little over 1.8 kilos. Parakh took each in turn and struck them across his gauge.

"Identical," he said, in a low voice. "It's gold all right, but the weight is wrong. After I found this one, I went back and examined them all. Took me nine hours, but all are clean."

Parakh replaced both bars in their previous location.

In an undertone, I asked, "If I had such a bar, how would I know to number it just so?"

Padamji shrugged. "The gold standard means that one can ask for their bank deposit to be delivered in specie, but in India banks do not have to comply. I have checked the number inscribed on that . . . bar." Discomfited, he avoided calling it a fake. "It was minted decades ago. An old number."

"All right. Say I acquire a gold bar, get the number, and manage to craft a replica. Could that replica show up here?"

"There *is* no way to bring it in or take one out," said Padamji quietly.

Pitching my voice low, I said, "Then you have an extra bar?"

"No."

"Could it just be flawed? Perhaps nothing was taken."

He shook his head. "Each one is weighed after etching. And counted precisely. In twenty-seven years, the number has always been accounted for. It is exact, even now."

"So, if that one came in, then one did leave this room. Could someone switch them?"

"Impossible. The workers are watched constantly. Guards view us from there." He tilted his head toward the corners, where glass panes were inset in the walls.

We traced the workers' route from the rear entrance to the forge, examining where their clothes were stored before they were checked and returned. Deep in the heart of the stone building, each room was secure in itself. The ceilings were metal sheeting, air vents shielded by grilles only inches across—not wide enough for a child to fit through.

Throughout, our English guard watched closely. And yet, someone had brought in a fake bar and perhaps, walked out with a five-and-a-half-pound weight in his pocket.

"The guards don't enter?" I asked.

"No. I have the only keys to the forge and this vault. I lock them behind me."

That was why the axe hovered over his neck—no one would believe such a theft could be conducted without his compliance.

"The two men who work here—I need their names, addresses."

He consulted a ledger and wrote them down.

I asked, "How long d'you think this has been going on?"

Padamji sucked in a breath. "You think . . . it's been done before?"

"Why not? Now we think there are no other—ah—bad ones. But some could have passed through earlier batches."

Padamji looked as though he might drop in a faint. Touching his arm, Parakh murmured, "From now on, I will check every single bar."

Next, I explored the chamber walls, while the guard glowered at us. An hour later, after the two Parsis escorted me back toward the main vestibule, he motioned me to a wall.

He patted me down thoroughly, asked a few questions which I answered, then jerked his chin at the door. We proceeded to the final gate.

While Parakh went up to complete our formalities, Padamji whispered, "Did our Ervad tell you how little time we have? A steamer has come for the bullion. The warships will arrive soon."

I had no time to dive into this case before the gold was handed into the crown's custody. Would the fake be discovered? That was the real question behind the man's fright.

I said, "Proceed as normal. Let me think it through. If the gunships arrive, call the Framji residence." It went against the grain, but there was no help for it. I'd have to study the forge workers before returning to Adi's case.

He nodded, his mouth sour, his eyes sorrowful. "A man makes his reputation over years, decades of honest service." Now, all he'd built over a lifetime could go up in smoke.

Shaking hands, I stepped out from the heavy, carved mahogany doors, then stopped as though I'd run into a wall. I was standing face-to-face with Chief Superintendent McIntyre of the Bombay constabulary. He wore a white regimental solar, his face red in the harsh sunlight. A group of white officers clustered behind him.

"Bloody hell, Agnihotri!" he said, by way of greeting. "What're you doing here?"

His sharp tone drew his colleagues' attention. One touched the service revolver at his belt. Others stilled, watchful and grim.

"Pleasure to see you, sir," I said mildly as steam rose from the pavement. "Fine day, isn't it?"

He brushed aside my pleasantries. "You're on the Rastogi case. Why're you here?"

"That's not my only assignment," I said. "These gentlemen were assisting me in another matter."

"What matter?" McIntyre demanded with all the grace of a bulldog chomping on an errant leg. Padamji swallowed, his cheeks collapsing inward. Even sturdy Parakh looked daunted, the whites of his eyes gleaming.

Bringing out Satya's key, I held it up at eye level. "Identifying this. Could *you* take a look, sir?"

He took it, turned it over and gave it a cursory glance. "What's it from?"

"That's what I need to know. It was given to my client as collateral. I'm looking for the object it unlocks. A personal vault, perhaps."

McIntyre returned the key and sent a suspicious glance at my escort.

Turning, I formally presented them to his attention. By this point, his companions had lost interest and passed behind us. Courtesy required that McIntyre shake hands after the introduction, which he did with little grace.

"Gentlemen," he said, then narrowed his eyes at me. "You, come see me tomorrow."

He stomped into the vestibule without a backward glance. When McIntyre was gruff, it usually meant he was worried. As his stiff shoulders receded, I wondered what irked the honorable chief superintendent.

Parakh's sigh of relief made me smile in sympathy. Gripping my hand with both his, Padamji thanked me in a heartfelt tone as he said goodbye.

Since we were still in earshot, I returned the niceties. "Gracious of you to see me. Good day, sirs." Touching my hat to them, I headed down the street.

Then I remembered. Those officials I'd seen sitting in McIntyre's office could have been from the Imperial Mint, requesting a police escort for the transport of bullion. The semiannual transfer of India's taxes to the British crown would soon be underway.

CHAPTER 25

OLD FRIENDS

Who should I be today? I fingered the linen suits Diana had assembled for me, white, tan, grey, brown. Beside my formals hung a blue serge suit and two in dark wool.

The *chanawala* I'd set to watch Adi's factory had nothing to report. The previous week I'd watched Adi's employees and spoken to their neighbors, but still didn't know whether they'd been involved in Satya's plans. Then there was that disconnect about who'd gone for the police, the mali or one of the staff. Was there something to this or was it just the jumbled confusion from what they'd witnessed?

I chose a tan suit to work on my new case: to determine how someone had stolen bullion from the mint, one I needed to solve without attracting official attention. How would the redoubtable Mr. Sherlock Holmes do it?

No doubt he'd smoke a pipe or play his violin at odd hours of the night to produce a flash of inspiration. When explained to the modest Dr. Watson, his observations and deductions seemed reasonable, even obvious. Cause and effect. Everyday occurrences developed special significance when placed in the framework of human motives.

Trouble was, I was awash in minutiae, with a threadbare theory to sew together the scraps. I had to identify Satya's key and discover what he'd stashed, because it was likely someone had murdered him for it.

Perhaps the killer intended to search Satya's person, but Adi's arrival prevented it. So, who was he?

The dining room was empty when I served myself from tureens on the sideboard. A glance at the grandfather clock showed it was ten, so the family had already breakfasted. How had I slept so late?

I slathered spicy mango preserve called *amba-kalyo* on my toast and polished it off with soft curds of scrambled eggs. Steepling fingertips over my plate, I considered Padamji's domain at the mint. With eyes closed, I mentally walked through the vestibule and corridors to the forge. Besides the foundry employees and guards, who else entered that chamber? The forge had to be fed periodically with gold, therefore whoever brought supplies also had access. Padamji had not mentioned this part of his process.

Cooled, the gold bars were transferred to the vault next door and stacked into crates—according to Padamji, a task performed by those selfsame foundry workers. Once sealed, there would be little chance to extract a bar. Lastly, the boxes would be wheeled down the ramp to load well-guarded carriages. So how was a five-and-a-half-pound bar removed from the mint? All the rest might be managed, the fake hollowed out in something like Satya's laboratory, to be assembled into a new piece by an expert forger. But to leave the mint with a seven-inch gold bar undetected was no easy matter. Only Padamji walked in and out in his street clothes. He'd just hung up his jacket and donned an apron over his vest.

Could he have been an unknowing courier, a bar slipped into his coat pocket unnoticed? Impossible, I thought, touching my linen jacket where the lump of a kerchief disturbed its neat lines. No, Padamji could not be oblivious to such a weight dragging down his clothes. And then, how was a fake bar replaced inside the vault?

The air vents high in the walls were grilled. My pulse jerked as an idea took form. No one could enter, but . . . could a bar be slipped through? But then, how would it be collected?

Voices sounded at the door. Gurung, and someone else. Visitors?

"I'm coming!" cried Mrs. Framji, hurrying from the kitchen. She bore a tray in one hand, scooping up folds of pale blue sari with the other. "Are they here?"

Diana twinkled a smile from the doorway. "It's Allie and Manek, come to visit." Dressed in pink cotton today, she was impossibly pristine, a morning cloud gone astray. "Mama, you're doing *aachu meechu*? They were married months ago!"

Curious, I headed toward the ladies, so different in age yet so alike in their excitement.

Mrs. Framji said, "It's their first time here. Allie is a bride! How will you keep our customs in America?"

Ah. Parsi traditions and ceremonies, I thought, and began my retreat.

However, Mrs. Framji said, "Wait, Captain! Please stay. When Diana and you arrived, I was not well . . ."

Bidding Gurung to set the silver tray he carried on a table, she sprinkled water from a tumbler onto the foyer, then mopped it with a white cloth. Next she stooped to tap a small tray on the floor, leaving a design in white powder, saying, "Stamp it three, five, or seven times. Odd numbers for good luck."

We heard voices outside. Diana swept open the door saying, "Manek, how good to see you! And Allie, welcome."

She embraced the couple while I shook hands with Manek. Gone was the deathly pale lad I had once harangued in Matheran. Though his hairline rode farther up his forehead, he was trim in a neat suit and patent-leather shoes. Allie—I'd known her as a grey-garbed matron, his landlady Alice—beamed, looking a decade younger in a svelte yellow dress and large white hat. Greeting them, Diana's mother directed Ganju to place a long flat stepstool over the chalk design ornamenting the tiles.

"Mrs. Framji!" said Manek, taking in the preparations. Face lit with emotion, he turned to his wife. "It's the welcome you should have had at my uncle's house. See the design on the floor, the silver *sesh*. That's taken out for family!"

"Come, stand on the stool," instructed Mrs. Framji, garlanding both with strings of tuberoses from the tray. Handing them a pair of envelopes, she applied a red dot upon each forehead. From the tray she gathered grains of rice in her palm, and pressed them to the couple's foreheads.

All the while she chanted, *"Ghanu-ghanu sukh johjo, sada sukhi sukhyara rehjo, sada hasta ramta rehjo, buddo-doso thajo!"*

Diana translated, sotto voce, "May you see much happiness, always safe and secure, stay laughing and playing, live to be ancient—it means the blessing of a long life!"

Lastly, Mrs. Framji circled a closed fist in the air around the pair, cracked her knuckles to her temples, and tossed a shower of rice to the side.

Near my shoulder, Diana murmured, "That's to be rid of the evil eye."

Mrs. Framji swept the couple into her embrace, then said, "Diana, Captain, your turn!"

Our turn? Manek and Allie stepped off the stool, while Diana tucked an arm through my elbow and propelled me up onto it. Protesting half-heartedly, I complied.

To receive Mrs. Framji's blessing felt as though I'd been given a medal of honor. Smiling, she reached upward to place scented garlands over our necks. I stooped to receive mine, the damp blooms smooth against my neck.

With her thumb, Mrs. Framji applied a ceremonial red smear to my forehead. Palming grains of rice, she pressed them to the red paste. A wave of emotion hit me then, for her touch was familiar, yet I could not recall who might have caressed me so! Throat closed, I ducked my head against the unexpected tug of emotion. Mrs. Framji touched my shoulder, then adorned Diana in like manner.

Taking a gold chain from her own neck, she put it around Diana's, speaking in Gujarati, to which Diana replied, protesting. Then Mrs. Framji pulled a ring off her forefinger and handed it to me. "This was my father's. Will it fit? Go on, try it."

The jewelry slipped over my little finger to sparkle against my skin.

A cherished gift. I swallowed, incapable of speech as Diana and I stepped off the stool. When I bent to touch Mrs. Framji's feet as I'd seen sepoys do, she clucked at me and hugged us both. I doubled over to gather the Framji women in grateful arms.

In this poignant moment I thought of Satya. Had he no one who tethered him this way? Had his mother, that tough martinet, ever held him near when he was a boy? Once he was a grown man, who did he rely on? Divorced from his kin by a Western education, part this, part that like me, had his unreconciled halves repelled each other? A slow fog rolled through my veins. Satya must have lived an achingly lonely life.

Once Burjor arrived, luncheon proceeded with warm chatter. I felt caught in a dream, as though watching myself smile, pass the pilaf, and decline the wine.

Did other men feel they were stepping between multiple worlds? A day ago I'd lived the rough life of a banana seller, making barely enough to purchase *vada-pav*, dependent for my dinner upon a sandwich Mrs. Framji sent with Gurung. Adi's employees evidenced no windfall. Faisal was desperately short of cash, while Vishal earned barely more than a *kelawala* himself.

Diana said, "I've never felt so . . . isolated. Made me think of little Chutki, when she came to us, so alone. Why, last week, Mrs. Sureewala's man said she wasn't in, although I heard her inside. Schoolfriends pass me at the Asiatic Society Library as though they don't know me. I was so miffed, I walked out!"

She sent me an apologetic glance. *People are asses. It's not your fault.*

The hurt in her voice gouged me. I'd long suffered cuts and slights, beginning with childhood fights at the orphanage. Each new injury piled onto the mountain of past disdain: a bastard with no name, family, fortune or skill. Not respectable, immediately suspect, beneath contempt. I'd thought it was what I deserved, until I met Adi and Diana.

Their outrage when I accepted such common abuse had surprised me, moved me. Smirks and scorn once jabbed like tiny needles in my gut. Now they seemed irrelevant.

Perhaps I craved Diana's good opinion more than a husband should. And perhaps I set Burjor and Mrs. Framji too high above other beings as exemplars of saintly goodness. Adi too, with his quick intelligence and calm judgment, was as near to blood as I'd ever had.

Diana had been cosseted and admired all her life. In Boston she'd entered white-only establishments and train cars as though she had every right. If her sun-kissed complexion caused doubt, her fine clothes and manners laid them to rest. Now her own beloved society shunned her, because of our union. I had not realized how much it bruised her and could do nothing to help. Under the ache of her defeated, angry helplessness, I set my face to parade rest and stuffed a forkful into my mouth.

Allie covered Diana's hand. "Forty years ago a Parsi called Shapur Edalji converted to Christianity—after that no Parsi would hire him! He went to England to be a pastor, I think. When we got married, Manek's people wouldn't even see him. He needed work, so he tried the Sassoon docks. There, his pedigree stood in the way."

Diana's brown eyes echoed my incomprehension. "His background? Why?"

Allie shrugged. "Not Jewish. But he was so brave. Tried the railways, Port Trust, Victoria docks and banks. Hopeless, of course, without a reference. Those were hard days—my boardinghouse barely brought in enough to feed us. But Manek's doing well at the bookstore now. Everyone wants to read . . . young people, most of all." She sent her new husband a fond look.

Manek took up the tale with gusto. "They spend hours on window seats thumbing through my books but can't afford them! So, I turned half the inventory into a lending library. Sometimes it earns ten rupees a day!"

"Oh, well done!" said Adi, shaking his hand.

"What about you, Adi?" Diana asked, teasing. "Closeted in your room for days. Last time you did that, you were reading about surgical instruments! What're you up to now?"

Adi shrugged, a grin escaping his modest manner. "It's not ready yet, Di. Like Mr. Holmes here"—he gestured at me—"can't say until I'm ready."

I made a disgusted grunt. "More like plodding old Watson." I dug in my vest pocket and held out Satya's key. "It's this dratted thing. Need to find its partner, the lock, see what's in there. It is, literally, the key to this puzzle."

Adi took it and twirled it in his fingers. "It's funny, really. That's what I've been doing. Seen the newspapers?" He smacked the stack beside his plate. "Every day some burglary or other. Yesterday a cotton warehouse was looted, day before, a shipping office."

Allie said, "Shops at Kolaba have all put up grilles. Feels like a jail when I enter. Three were burgled last month."

Burjor said, "People are hungry. This market is tougher than I've ever seen."

Manek added, "I daren't leave cash at my bookstore. The restaurant next door was robbed a few weeks ago."

"That's it!" Adi cried. "That's what I'm working on. A fireproof safe that can't be broken into or carried away." He spread his hands. "Here's how locks work. When the door, box, or safe is closed, a bolt sticks into the frame. It won't slide back out, because it's stopped by a series of pegs, sometimes in a cylinder. Now the job of the key is to lift the pegs inside, which then allows the bolt to slide out, and open the door."

He ran a finger over the key's serrated edge. "This might open a Yale lock. While back, a chap called Linus Yale came up with the idea of the cylinder. A spring pushes each pin into the bolt, so the ridges of the key much be just so, to raise it to the correct height. Only then will the tumbler rise, the cylinder turn, and the bolt slide away. My lock won't have springs—cheaper that way, but equally strong."

He hadn't been so animated in a while. I asked, "So *what* d'you think this key opens?"

He rubbed it between finger and thumb. "It's new. Modern. Five pins. Could be something quite small, a safe, or a cabinet."

When Allie and Manek departed I returned to our bedroom, sat at Diana's desk, and browsed my notebook. All night it had troubled me, a disconnect, a contradiction, hiding in these pages. Adi had found Satya choking on his own blood, had broken his fall and held him. But there were three other people nearby. Two employees and the mali had rushed to answer his calls.

"Jim?" Diana said, behind me.

"Mmm." I turned another page. Where was it, that first statement? Whose was it?

"Dearest, let me help! Why must you always work alone?"

I looked up, startled at her tone.

She turned away, shaking her head.

"Wait." I got up and pointed to the chair. "You jot it down. I'll find it."

She perched and took up the pencil, waiting as I sat on the bed and flipped pages. I said, "Someone's lied, but I don't know who. Here's what we got from Adi . . ."

I scoured my notes. "Here." I found Diana waiting patiently, and dictated, "Faisal Khan—he said Adi sent Vishal the accountant for the police. Faisal stayed with Adi until the constable arrived."

Over the next half hour, we checked other statements to see which concurred.

Diana jotted them down as I read. Returning to where I'd stuck in my thumb, I said, "The mali said he returned with a mounted police-man, riding behind him."

Her lips tightened. "One of them is lying. Vishal or the mali."

I steepled my fingers, planning my next visit.

"What will you do?" she asked.

I smiled. "Yesterday a fellow came to our kitchen door—he had on a uniform?"

"The gas-walla from Bombay Gas Company. He checks the meter and the stove."

"Think you can rustle up the sort of jacket he wore? And that thin cap?"

She shot to her feet. "And a clipboard. Let me see what I can do. When d'you need it?"

"Tomorrow will do nicely."

She grinned, fingered through my clothes to pick something out, then rushed off to her sewing machine.

Next I went to Adi's room and told him I needed something that looked like a tool that a gas meter man might use.

He closed his book and asked, "Why?"

I glanced at the title—"*The Memoirs!*"

His pale face split in a smile. "You left it in the morning room. Did you read 'The Adventure of the Crooked Man'? What a story! Mentions the Indian Mutiny."

"Haven't got that far," I confessed. "Now, the fellow yesterday had some sort of equipment. I need something small that looks complicated."

His eyes glinted. "Going to impersonate a gas-walla? I've got just the thing."

* * *

I passed the Imperial Mint three times that day, once in the afternoon, and twice in the evening, each time carrying a newspaper or boxes to explain my presence. As far as I could tell, this went unnoticed. On the last pass, I bought a fag and stopped at the crossroad to light it. The smoke assailed my nostrils, so I stuck it between my fingers, and watched the broad grey structure of the mint.

A sweeper brushed leaves off the sidewalk in slow strokes, his back bent to his task. After some time a cart approached the side door, horses' hooves clip-clopping on the cobbles. A turbaned man pushed a trolley down a ramp, loaded bundles of newspapers and trundled them inside. Three empty trolleys stood tucked against the side of the building like sleeping sentries.

An idea sizzled at the back of my mind, like the crackling of kindling catching flame. But when I tried to grasp it, it wafted away like smoke. The carriage left, the doors closed and the side street emptied. I wandered over and had a look at the trolleys, then left with a growing sense of wonder. Satya's last words were about gold. And someone had stolen bullion from the Imperial Mint. That would be worth killing for. Were my two cases linked, somehow?

Was Satya behind it all? If so, he couldn't have been working alone.

CHAPTER 26

DISASTER

Sunlight filtered through the trees, while a morning gust fluttered my clothing. I was putting Gurung and the lads through squats and push-ups, which had been de rigueur for morning drill in the army. The group conducted these exercises with snappy shouts that made me feel I'd stepped back in time.

At nine that morning, disaster came in the shape of a gleaming black carriage. It rolled through the gate, the new houseboy running alongside to announce it.

When the carriage crunched to a halt, Smith stepped out in full police drill. A pair of crisply uniformed constables flanked him. Holding his white solar cap stiffly at his side, he started up the front stairs.

"Stephen!" I called.

He turned and paused for me to catch up. We shook hands without ado.

"You know why I'm here," he said, nodding at the house. "Sorry, old chap."

I felt short of air. "For Adi. To question him again?"

He grimaced. "I'm to arrest him. Here, give us a hand so he don't make a fuss."

Bloody hell.

"Why now?" I demanded. "What's happened?"

"Mac's orders. I'm to get your boy so he don't fly the coop again."

Adi's trial must be near at hand. I was out of time.

Despite the warm breeze, Smith looked pale. He swiped a kerchief across his forehead. "The boss thought this would be easier than showing up himself. Sent me instead." He gave a low grunt.

I nodded, feeling nauseous. "He'll come. Let me get him."

Disregarding Smith, I strode ahead and stamped up the curved staircase to Adi's quarters. I knocked and entered.

"Jim?" Dressed in crisp white shirt and dark trousers, hair slicked back, Adi came from his water closet, wiping his face. He plucked his glasses from a breast pocket and put them on, then hauled up his suspenders.

Breathing hard, I struggled with a grenade-sized lump in my throat.

Adi said, "So. It's come. Will I be handcuffed?"

"No." I forced the word through my swollen gullet.

He smiled slightly, came up and laid a hand on my arm. "It's all right. I've been expecting it. Surprised they waited this long."

I groaned and grabbed his shoulders. "Hold on, all right? We're not done."

"Mmm. Should I pack a few things?" He glanced about, pulled a narrow valise from under his bed, and flipped it open on the counterpane. When I'd helped put in a few clothes, his diary and pencils, he knotted on a tie and rolled down his shirtsleeves to add cuffs.

"Go back to America, Jim," Adi said, as he wore his coat. "Take Diana, and leave."

"God's sake, Adi, why?"

"If I'm going down, can't take you too."

Or was it you *two*? Although my ears buzzed as though I was underwater, I got out the words, "You can't give up." They sounded calm, believable.

Adi straightened his collar, ran his hands down his lapels. "Better this way. The waiting was killing me. Mama and Papa can start over in Rangoon."

"What're you saying?" I snapped. "D'you know who attacked Satya?"

"No, no!" He waved that away, slipping a kerchief into his pocket.

"Who are you protecting?"

He smiled, a twist of lips. "No one, Jim. I don't know who killed Satya."

Once downstairs, Smith was quick about administering the formalities. Burjor and Diana kept their composure, embracing Adi with admonitions as though he were going to university. "Make sure you drink enough water." "Exercise, every day. You need to keep up your strength." "Don't forget to write!"

Burjor enveloped Adi in a bearlike hug. When he stepped back, Burjor's wide face looked sallow and clammy, strands of hair sticking to his perspiring forehead. In his dark eyes was the glitter of desperation, and something I could not quite name. He glanced at me in entreaty, then back to Adi, as though grasping at straws and resolved not to show it.

Mrs. Framji hurried from an inner room. With a wordless cry she clung to Adi, holding him in a close embrace for long moments. Neither spoke. When she released him, her eyes blazed some message I could not decipher. He ducked his head, then nodded.

Adi turned to shake my hand, but I swiped it away and put an arm about him. "I'm coming with you." I did not ask Smith's permission.

Once Adi, Smith, and the two constables were ensconced inside the carriage, I hailed the driver, "Move over!" and clambered up top beside him.

We went down Queens Road to the police court on Chuikshank Road and then on to Bombay Jail on Caskine Road. Dismounting there, Smith escorted Adi through the bullpen and down a hallway I'd known well when I worked at the constabulary. I followed, carrying Adi's valise. Our process drew attention—my old friend Sabrimal met my gaze and flushed. Others stood back in silence to give us way.

While Smith handed over the necessary paperwork, Adi tilted his head to me. "Some of these chaps know you."

"Mr. Framji," McIntyre said, behind us.

"Yes, sir." Adi swung around and stuck out his hand. The gesture stabbed my side, as he said, "We've met. Last year at the Governor's Holiday Gala. And other times." He smiled politely as though this were an ordinary day but his cordial tone pierced me. Adi did not know how to be any other way.

McIntyre shook hands. "Should you require anything, Mr. Framji, please let me know." He glanced at my clenched jaw and back to Adi, saying, "I suppose we'll see Agnihotri every day now. Who's your lawyer?"

Adi said, "Don't have one yet. My father will find someone."

"I'm sure. Brown and Batliwala aren't used to this sort of case. Barrister Dinshaw Daver, now, he's an excellent pleader. Or Pheroze Shaw Mehta."

Superintendent McIntyre recommending defense counsel? His cheeks somewhat ruddier, he nodded a farewell and strode away. However, the conversation had been noted, and Adi would be afforded as much consideration as possible under the circumstances. He was not stripped and forced into the usual stripes of inmates awaiting trial but was escorted to a wing I had not seen before, where most cells were empty.

In the political prisoners' row, each cell contained a low bed and worktable, a chair and washbasin. A ceramic latrine was parked in a corner with a bucket of water. All the amenities of home, then. Adi would be spared the hard methods used on suspected insurgents.

In his cell, Adi's valise was subjected to a cursory examination. He emptied his pockets as asked. The native constable in charge did not demand that he disrobe, but placed striped khaki clothes on his bunk. The British constable stood stiffly, giving instructions in a flat tone, while native constables tightened their lips. A glance confirmed what I suspected. Adi, a respected Indian gentleman, had been arrested; their manner said they had no wish to be his jailors.

Adi held up under the strain, although he flinched when a metal door clanked in the corridor. Smith waited outside while I embraced Adi, feeling the nervous tremor in his thin frame, the bones of his shoulders. His frayed look told me he was close to collapse.

In an undertone, I said, "Don't you give in. I'm not done, hear?"

He pushed me away. "Go now, Jim."

Swearing inwardly, I left, then turned to reinforce my message with a look. Adi attempted a smile that damn near brought me to tears.

Leaving him in that cell was one of the hardest things I ever had to do.

CHAPTER 27

DISGUISED

My chest tight, I dragged in a breath as I plodded back through the jail. As I was already nearby, I went to check on the injured mali.

Jameson grimaced when I told him Adi had been arrested. He patted my shoulder with a fist, then led the way. "I had the old fellow moved to the women's wing—empty, 'course. He had a lucid moment yesterday— was in pain so I put him back under."

An orderly stood as we entered and snapped to attention as though grateful to be remembered by the living. Jameson questioned him while I approached the ward's only occupant. His head buried in bandages, the mali looked like a shrunken child. A bony hand lay atop the bed- clothes like a discarded chicken drumstick. There would be no help from him today.

With Adi arrested I could think of little else, yet I had exhausted my leads and knew I must take a new tack. Dressed as a gas meter man in Diana's costume—a simple modification to one of my oldest brown coats, with a narrow native cap, a battered clipboard, and Adi's instru- ment, I visited the mint workers' modest homes. The guise allowed me to scout the exteriors and look for new construction, bicycles, or water tanks. In each dwelling, multiple generations went about their busi- ness. I found no evidence of recent prosperity.

Desperate for some progress, that afternoon I visited Faisal's neighbors and probed them, even inventing a marriage proposal to his cousin as my ruse. Other than gossip and trivial jealousies, I learned little. Recalling that young Vishal was sharp, ambitious perhaps, and rather observant, once more I traced my way to the accountant's home.

I scouted the street, noting gas pipes protruding from the homes, then squatted under a nearby tree. As I watched, Vishal's family exited their home, dressed in festival finery. A temple visit? I'd lost track of the date, but here and there flowers adorned doors and gates, denoting a festival. Dussehra? Dhanteras? Surely Deepavali was a month away?

Once they'd crammed themselves into a Victoria and departed, I wandered over to the little house and crossed to the rear. The door was cracked open for air, latched on the *kadi*. What was the sentence for breaking and entering, I wondered, as I inserted a pencil through the slot, lifted the latch, and slipped inside.

Vishal's home was furnished much like other traditional homes I'd seen. Low beds, a cloth divider in the bedchamber for the barest privacy. The kitchen was a low table in a corridor under which pots and pans were neatly piled. There was no washroom *mori,* so that must be shared in the common area outside. A living room with cushions and piles of bedding, likely for the children, completed the accommodations. I passed a table stacked with newspapers and plunked myself down on the single chair. How could I get the truth from him? Daylight faded while I waited, turning over the case in my mind.

The door rattled and opened, and a pair of children burst into the room. An older child followed, then Vishal and his wife. He lit a lantern in the corridor.

"Hello," I said from the chair.

Vishal's eyes bulged.

"Go inside!" he shooed his wife, pushing the older child after her.

"Who is it?" she cried.

When the younger children bounced toward me, he yelled, "Inside!"

They paused, their faces pinched. Vishal grabbed their arms and fairly lifted them off their feet as he thrust them at the bedchamber and the querulous protests of his wife.

He showed me his palms, saying in Hindustani, "Please. Don't hurt us. We have nothing. You can see . . ." He gestured at the room.

He didn't recognize me. Of course. I was still wearing the gas man disguise.

I let silence work on him. Squatting, he joined his hands in entreaty.

"You lied," I said quietly. "You were sent to bring the police, but you didn't. The mali brought a constable. What did you do instead?"

"Captain sahib!" he cried, rising. When I didn't move, relief dropped off his face like a wet rag. "Don't be angry, please."

I said nothing. The whites of his eyes shone in the yellow lantern light.

Was this what I'd become, I wondered, watching his hands tremble, his throat work as he swallowed. Childish voices protested from the bedchamber, their mother shushing them. Yet someone had shoved a blade into Satya's gullet, and I needed the truth.

"Answer the question," I said.

"My children—" he began.

"Tell me the truth, and I will leave."

He licked his lips. "I went toward Kennedy Bridge, French Bridge, but there was no havildar. Only tongas, Victorias. So I came back. It is the truth, sahib! I swear it!"

"Where else did you go?"

His mouth dropped open, then he cried, "Nowhere, sahib!"

I cannot tell how I knew he was lying. Yet his panic was real.

"You met someone. Who?"

"No one, sahib! There was no one . . ." He fairly wept. But he'd begun to say a word, and stopped. *There was no one . . . there.* "You expected to see someone. Who?"

"Satya-ji was on the floor, the blood," he fumbled. "I saw no one."

He'd run out looking for the killer? But his manner was one of relief.

I tucked away this curious impression and persisted. "Where did you go?"

"The doctor," he gasped. "I know a vaid nearby, so I begged him to come. It was no use, sahib, Satya-ji was dead."

Ah! Faisal had mentioned a doctor, but I'd forgotten.

Weary and rumpled, I returned to Framji Mansion in the early hours.

"Hoy!" cried a voice from the garden as I entered. Ganju.

"It's all right," I called back. The lads were on guard as I had instructed, but it felt as though the keep was empty.

Upstairs, I stripped off my shirt and drank from the earthenware pitcher in our room. Rather than wake Diana, I dropped a pillow on the carpet of our chamber and lay down. She would see me in the morning and know I had come home as promised.

Home. A distant clanking told me that Ganju had secured a chain around the gate. The rhythm of crickets, the swoosh of palms, the ticking of the grandfather clock somewhere below, and near at hand the swoosh of Diana's sweet breath. She sniffed like a child and turned, pulling the bedclothes with her. After living rough, Framji Mansion was a palace.

Yet sleep eluded me. None of Adi's employees appeared to have an influx of funds. None had left Bombay or made plans to. Faisal was most in need. In the moments after Satya's death, Vishal had searched for someone, but not seen him. Logically that would be the killer—perhaps he had a suspicion, but it was not borne out. I sat up with a jerk. Did that mean—the killer remained nearby?

Was the killer one of those who gathered around Adi that afternoon?

*　*　*

Waiting at a crossroads offers one much opportunity for contemplation. I had gone back and forth over Padamji's problem a hundred times. I'd put myself in his shoes, then Parakh's and each of the foundry workers. Each might have motive to secret away some of the bounty constantly around them.

The fake bar had been identical but for its weight. That needed an expert hand. The two foundry workers were the most likely suspects, since they made bars all day. Yet making one lighter implied premeditation and the connivance of the other, for surely they would handle each other's work. So both, then, were implicated. However, they returned to work each day passing back and forth through the security gates. It took a strong stomach to do that.

My back eased, releasing a cramp. I rolled my shoulders, relishing the ache as they pushed against the carpet. Was this why Diana insisted I return? All day I watched, recording impressions, faces, behaviors, snippets of conversations. Gradually the weight of these fell away, and I made a plan.

CHAPTER 28

SUSPICION

In the morning, I donned fresh clothes to visit the Imperial Mint.

A group of guards solemnly watched me enter in my tan suit and solar hat. I gave my name and waited, fidgeting while Padamji took his time to fetch me.

His face lit up as he spotted me, then he signed the ledger and ushered me through the sets of double doors.

"Find anything?" he whispered when we were scarcely out of earshot.

I waited until the metal door clanged behind us, then asked, "Are both foundry workers here?"

"N-no. One did not show up for work."

As we walked toward the foundry, I asked, "The younger one?"

"Yes."

When you remove the impossible, whatever remains, however improbable, must be the truth. No one could leave with a gold bar, but something carted dozens around.

"Right," I said. "Let's check your forge again."

Once I signed the guard book, he led me back to the workroom and nodded to the guard sitting outside. However, this time I did not enter it, but stooped beside the trolleys at the door.

"You transfer the boxes to the wagon on these?"

"Oh no. Policemen load the wagon," he said. "We seal the boxes and wheel them out."

I examined the first, made of sturdy metal trays at top and bottom riveted to four poles that went down into a set of small wheels. Squatting, I ran my fingers around the edges and along the four legs. To the narrow-eyed guard, I gave the appearance of checking whether the trolleys squeaked or required maintenance.

I checked the second and third, then tilted my head at the door. After rolling the third cart into his forge, I motioned to Padamji, who helped me tip it over.

There. What looked like a torn chocolate wrapper clung to the underside of the bottom tray. I jiggled it, then yanked. It slid out in my palm, strangely heavy for its small size. "Cadbury's" was written in gold lettering. The metal case was colored to look like a crumpled piece of waste. My pulse began a jig, booming away in my eardrums.

A hollow slit was just the size of a gold bar. Marveling, I examined the clever construction, then handed it to Padamji. Two small metal notches had been added to the underside of the trolley. Standing it back on its wheels, I showed him how a bar could be neatly attached below the trolley and wheeled away, invisible.

"After loading the boxes, your worker slides a bar into the chocolate slot wrapper under the trolley. He rolls it outside, unloads boxes, and leaves it there. Soon, someone disguised as a sweeper takes out the chocolate wrapper, makes the switch by setting the fake into the trolley and continues down the road."

"My God," breathed Padamji, palming the wrapper. "It is exactly the right size!" He blinked. "But . . . that fellow still has the stolen bar! What shall I do?"

"That's up to you," I said. "Your absconding worker—I might have alarmed him yesterday. I visited as a gas man, got a close look at his rooms. You could report the theft and make an accounting of the loss. If not . . ." I spread my hands.

"He worked with me for six years," Padamji said, his throat moving rapidly, relief and indecision crowding his face.

Progress at last! I returned to Framji Mansion and sent Ganju with the modified chocolate wrapper and a note to Dastoor Kukadaru:

Padamji problem solved. Will your connection write me the needed letters?

* * *

That very evening, an elderly retainer in a white kippah and black overcoat arrived at Framji Mansion and delivered a thick envelope into my hands. He bowed, saying, "Sir Jamsetji sends his compliments, and hopes that this is satisfactory. If not, you may call on him tomorrow."

"Sir Jamsetji?"

The messenger pushed his glasses up his nose. "Sir Jamsetji Jeejeebhoy is a baronet. Queen Victoria knighted his grandfather in 1842 and awarded him a baronetcy."

So that was the Parsi elder I'd met. As requested, the peer had written six letters of introduction to the leading banks, each with his signature and seal. Also, on ornately edged, satiny cream paper was a cheque on the Commercial Bank of India for two thousand rupees.

I found Burjor before the picture of his prophet, his head bent over folded hands, sparse hair covered by a black velvet skullcap. Reluctant to interrupt his devotions I backed away.

"Wait," he said.

He climbed slowly to his feet, his white muslin undershirt gaping over his white-haired chest. Perhaps he had always worried about Adi's idealism, his outsized grit housed in a lean frame. Burjor had been dreading his son's arrest, and now it was here. He could not bellow in pain, so it had turned inward; it was consuming him.

With a quiet greeting, I handed him the cheque and turned to leave.

His fingers snapped over my wrist.

"What's this?" he gasped. "You borrowed money? No, my boy!"

The regret in his voice! I caught his sorrowful glance, glad that this, at least, I could spare him. "It's a payment—for services rendered."

"Services . . ." he echoed, then comprehension lit his face.

"Two thousand . . . my God! We can do it. We can pay Jussawalla!" Beaming relief, he clutched my shoulders with shaking hands.

"Thank you, *beta*!" he choked, hugging me, his temple pressed to my jaw.

Emotion clogging my throat, I returned his embrace. I'd not yet found a way to spare Adi the noose, nor Diana the stings of her peers, but their father's reputation was salvaged for the moment. And he had called me son.

* * *

Over the next day I visited the institutions where the baronet had provided introductions. I was received cordially and brought to the senior man without delay.

"You are recommended as a man of discretion," said the president of Bombay Chartered Bank, glancing at the seal on Jeejeebhoy's letter.

"Won't take much of your time," I said, and offered Satya's key. "Is this familiar in any way? Would it open one of your vaults, perhaps?"

The bank president summoned other directors. Staff brought forth a set of keys to explain how their security boxes could not be opened with one such as mine. Accessing a vault required personal identification, a known signature or a letter of authorization attested by a governmental signatory. Eager to aid me, they detailed long processes for inheritance, intestate or otherwise. Apparently, Sir Jamsetji Jeejeebhoy's name bought both compliance and unlimited cooperation. Hearing my credentials, the bankers assured me that should they require such assistance, I was just the man. Unfortunately, none of this helped Adi's case. I'd been sure solving Padamji's problem would offer some break in my case. I was running out of time!

My chest tight with disappointment, I returned to find Diana in a dither.

"It's McIntyre. He called for you three times on the telephone. He even sent a constable. Jim, I'm worried. He seemed quite irate when I explained you were not at home and I didn't know when you would be. I felt—like a little dog facing a bear! A dozen bears. Snarling and rumbling."

"I'm sorry, sweet." I scooped her into a hug, where she continued her muffled barrage.

"He demanded, over and over, where you were! Saying it was impossible I should not know. I'm the one person who would always know, he said. Are you in trouble, Jim?"

"No, sweetheart," I spoke into her hair, burying my face in soft curls, the scent of soap and flowers and . . . dessert. She always smelled like petals and strawberries.

". . . just saying that so I don't worry?" she went on.

"What time's dinner?" I asked. Hearing it was two hours hence, I pressed a kiss to her fretful lips and went to see my old boss, the formidable chief superintendent of the Bombay constabulary.

I was too late. Sub-inspector Sabrimal said Mac had already left for the day, so clapping him on the back, I splurged on a Victoria. Arriving in a tonga could bar admission to the homes in elite south Bombay.

A thin, liveried bearer admitted me to a shuttered parlor and disappeared. Left to my own devices, I noted the garden outside and the abutting lane, then glanced around the elegant furnishings, as unlike McIntyre's office as it was possible to be. Draped in ivory damask, tufted couches were paired with eggshell blue striped chairs. A rosewood sideboard stood beside an ornate fireplace. Above this hung a framed mirror which echoed a portrait on the opposite wall, a posh young woman with oval face and clear hazel eyes. I examined these with interest, then sat down with my notebook.

"Blast you, boy!" McIntyre rumbled from the door, yanking it shut behind him. He wore white-tie well; black patent leathers, sharp creases on trousers whose satin stripe matched his lapels. A gemstone gleamed in his tie. The impeccable dark jacket, snowy vest and shirt instantly turned my garb into that of a grubby urchin.

I'd leapt to my feet when he entered. Now I tucked my book into a breast pocket. Under glowering brows, his eyes followed the gesture as I said, "You wanted to see me."

He grunted and went to a sideboard, pulling open the drawer. Not finding what he wanted there, he snapped at me, "What've you been doing?"

"Doing?"

He rummaged in the drawer. "Where've you been? Last three days."

More rummaging. But his head hadn't moved. I caught his glance in the mirror. Giving up the pretense, he turned, skewering me with a glare.

Something was amiss. He was . . . worried? "Three days? Why?"

"I ask the questions," he growled. "You're on thin ice, Agnihotri. Hell, boy, I'm trying to help you! Where were you? And don't give me 'at home.' You were bloody well not home." His brogue thickened when he was agitated, and now it was sludge.

I would say nothing about Padamji's troubles. I also hesitated to mention my disguises, because Englishmen had a horror of wallowing in dirt.

"I was . . . working."

"On what."

"Establishing Adi's innocence."

He snapped, "How? I want every movement for the past week."

I pulled back, feeling rebellious. "As you reminded me, I don't work at the constabulary now."

He blinked, his blue eyes incredulous. I felt like a cad, so I turned away, tasting the sourness of regret.

"Get out," he rumbled, his face tight.

I flinched. Why had he summoned me with such urgency? He was angry, fearful.

"What's happened, sir?" I asked, my tone sincere. "Have I . . . done something to displease?"

He made a sound in his throat and flung himself into a chair. "Sit."

Huffing, he patted his pockets and found a pipe, pulled it out and examined it.

"Christ, lad. You've ruffled some big feathers," he said. "First Imperial Bank, then governor's office looking into you. Sent them your file."

My pulse gave a knock and began to bang about like a frog dumped in hot water. "The *governor* asked about me?"

"Yesterday. Told me to investigate you. What've you done, you silly sod?"

I closed my mouth and swallowed. "I visited six banks in the city today."

"Why?"

I dug in my pocket for Satya's key. "Because of this."

"That again!" he snorted. "What d'you take me for?"

"It's the truth. Satya had withdrawn two thousand rupees when he died. You didn't find the cash on him, did you? But sometime before, he gave this key to someone. I think . . . if I can find what safe this opens, what it holds, it will lead us to his killer."

His brow in deep ridges, his cool gaze measured me. "Still trying to save young Framji. You're missing something, aren't you? Killer's in front of you—blighter who took that key off the body."

I shook my head. "Impossible."

"Why?"

"Why would he give *me* the key?"

"Humph. Who is it?"

I shook my head, sending him a half smile. *Can't tell you.*

He returned a sardonic look, then asked, "Are you armed?"

My eyebrows twitched. "Not at present."

"Christ." He went to the sideboard, poured a shot and tossed it down. Remembering my existence, he turned, tilting the glass in a belated offer.

I got to my feet. "Thank you, no. If there's nothing else?"

He tapped his fingers against the crystal. "Be careful, yes? Stop—ah—traipsing about unarmed, goddamn it."

I smiled at him then, seeing through his marble exterior. He'd got orders to investigate me and called Framji Mansion repeatedly. My absence had worried him. Despite the fact I was not in uniform, I gave him a proper salute. He motioned me down with something akin to a groan.

The door opened and Mrs. McIntyre entered, saying, "Robert, they'll be here any minute . . ." Her low voice held generations of breeding secured in a velvet bow. Dressed in voluminous silks, draped in pearls, silver hair coifed, she paused. "Am I interrupting?"

"You remember Agnihotri, my dear," said McIntyre with a cursory wave. "He's just leaving."

I took the satin-gloved hand she offered so tentatively, bowed and smiled into a sweet pair of hazel eyes, those very eyes that graced the portrait hanging above her.

"Honored, marm," I said, then took my leave.

As the door closed behind me, I heard her say in a wondering tone, "Robert, is *that* the boy?"

CHAPTER 29

THE STATUETTE

After the dishes were cleared away, Diana and I remained at the table with Mrs. Framji. She was describing their plan to get Adi out on bail, when the house phone shrilled in Burjor's office. We heard him answer with a grunt, say a few words. Then his footsteps thumped toward the dining room.

Unshaven and in his dressing gown, Burjor spotted me from the door and said, "McIntyre's called you. Something about the watchman. You're to go right away."

"Wait! I'm coming too," cried Diana, and went to put on shoes.

We headed out with Mrs. Framji's words ringing in my ears. "I hope the poor man's recovered!"

Jameson had his stethoscope on the mali's chest when Diana and I hurried into the ward. When the medico was done, Bala raised a hand and tried to speak, his voice almost inaudible. Another garbled effort was also incomprehensible. Then I understood. He'd asked in Hindustani, "How is my garden, sahib? Does it survive the heat?"

"I watered it myself," I assured him in the same tongue.

Jameson gave me an amused look. Here was my principal witness, and we were discussing his plants.

The mali joined his hands, his fingers so crooked they left a gap. "Why did you put me in jail, sahib? My breath was stopped. The darkness . . .

nothing there. Only memories. Forty years ago, I had a wife and three small ones, but in just one week they sickened and died. Many people died that month. The cremation cart was full. Bodies piled, awaiting the woodcutter's wagons. Why did I live all these years?"

Diana bent and touched his hand. It was a poignant contrast, her delicate fingers against the mali's gnarled palm.

The old man told her, "Now the garden is my family, the trees are mothers, aunts, relatives; the plants my grandchildren." He went on. "Do not take me from there, sahib. There I have lived and there I will die. Bury me there. Do you promise?"

Diana said in a hushed voice, "Adi leases that place. It does not belong to us."

The mali replied, "I have no child to light my pyre. So do not take me to the burning ghat. Bury me in your garden. Plant flowers over me."

Clearing my throat, I asked, "Who struck you, Bala?"

His weary eyes filled, the lines of his face crowded like a topological map. "I am an unlettered man, sahib. How can I tell who to trust?" Hands folded, he begged my pardon.

"You did nothing wrong."

He smiled, showing his gums. "I am a foolish old man. I did not see who came behind me."

Diana grimaced in sympathy.

I frowned. "Bala, you were struck with your own tool—who grabbed it from your hand?"

He blinked rheumy eyes. Was it possible that he could not recall it? In my early boxing days, I'd been knocked out, and come to without remembering anything past the first round.

"Bala," I said, "we think Satya was doing things without telling Adi sahib. Do you know anything about it?"

"I knew him, sahib. From when he was a small boy," said the mali. "Always reading, singing, playing. His father said he would be a fine gentleman! He would run home from school and ride on my shoulders. But then . . . these months, such a piteous sight.

"At night I used to see him through the windows. He would put his face in his hands. Once, I could not bear it. I went and spoke to him. He cried out as though I was a devil. When he saw it was me, he wept like a child. Once again I held his head against my chest and consoled him, just as when he had been whipped as a boy."

"Did he say what troubled him?"

"No, sahib, only that it was hopeless. That it was his own fault. So I helped him."

"How?"

"Just keeping things in my hut. At night a man would come on a bicycle. I waited at the gate and put what was given in his basket."

"The bicycle with a basket! Who is he?"

"I do not know his name. His face was hidden."

"What was inside the parcels?"

"I did not look, sahib."

Another dead end! I groaned in a cloud of despair.

He said, "But one bundle is still in my room, inside a sack of hay."

We rode to Dady Lane posthaste, speaking little on the way. My insides wound tight with anticipation, hardly daring to hope, I urged Gurung to speed, while Diana kept her own counsel.

At Adi's factory, dismounting from the carriage, she said, "Wait, Jim," and took an old lantern from a nail on the factory door. She reached upward, fingers searching the ledge over it, then made a satisfied sound. Moments later, a match flared. As the acrid smell wafted over us, she stooped and lit the wick.

Replacing the glass flute, she handed it to me. "Find it, whatever it is. We've got to solve this."

Bala's hut wasn't locked, and if it had been, it would not have mattered. Slatted timbers had rotted away, leaving gaps in the walls. The door creaked open under my touch.

Diana waited outside while I swung the lantern, spilling light over the mud floor of the mali's shack. A small Primus stove stood in a corner by a pan and some bottles. Along one side lay a bedroll, not unlike my military issue on campaign. The mali's wash drooped from a short clothesline bearing a crumpled dhoti.

Sweeping aside the grey cloth, I ducked under the hemp rope and raised my lamp to the corners. Two sacks lay along the wall, one open at the mouth, spilling coal.

The second was tied. Setting down the lantern, I tried to pry open the knot with shaking fingers. It was no use. Reaching to my boot I yanked out my blade and made quick work of the rope. The earthy smell of hay and jute dust rose as I reached inside. My fingers closed over a lump. I gripped and drew it out.

The shapeless burlap wrapping was tied with raw jute. I tugged it apart, peeling back layers until something gleamed in the weak lamplight. In my shaking hands I held a golden statue of Ganesh, the elephant-headed god, each burnished curve gleaming.

About ten inches tall, the piece felt dense, as heavy as a baby. For this, a young man had died? A life cut short in the midst of some devious and complex plan. Why was it so important, so crucial? What was Satya doing with this?

I'd never met him, but perhaps I knew him better than anyone else. Each person had seen one side of him—he'd persuaded Adi, Burjor, Jussawalla, and the insignificant mali to his ends.

My grip tightened on the golden idol. Satya had forged the promissory note for this? Had he planned to be off before Burjor confronted him? If he was going to flee, emptying Adi's account would be the last step. He would have run—but the killer had preempted him.

Hearing the mali's story, I'd pitied the young man I'd never met. Now I felt as though I was reading a letter, a confession that lacked the last page. One more piece—just one more and I would have it.

Standing in the mali's sad hut, I made Satya a promise. Whatever he wanted so desperately, it was likely why he'd been murdered. If I learned his plan, I'd follow it and see where it took me.

Somewhere along the way I'd find his killer. I only hoped that by then, I would recognize who he was and know what I should do.

CHAPTER 30

THE CHASE

When we returned to Framji Mansion, Diana's parents accosted us in the foyer. "Thank heavens you're safe. You disappeared for so long!"

I uncovered the statue.

Mrs. Framji gasped, taking it from me with both hands. "So heavy! Where did you find it?"

When the excitement died down, we trailed into the morning room where I dropped into a couch. "Satya's leading us on a merry chase. The mali was his go-between to hand over stuff to a bloke on a bicycle. This was stashed in his hut. Who'd think to look there?"

Diana touched the intricate draperies carved into the statuette. "It's Lord Ganesh. D'you know how he got his elephant head?"

I shrugged, so she went on, "Parvati, the wife of Lord Shiva, made herself a child from river soil, a beloved son. One day Parvati asked him to stand guard while she bathed. When Lord Shiva came by, the boy would not let him near, so Shiva beheaded him."

Burjor rolled his eyes at her.

She went on, "When Lord Shiva discovered the boy's identity, he regretted his hasty deed. So he killed a passing elephant, set the head on the boy's shoulders, and revived him."

I chuckled. "He was a god but couldn't identify the boy? Sounds like those Greek myths. Zeus turning maidens into willow trees and such."

It was past eleven, so we deposited the statue in Burjor's safe and turned in. I slept fitfully, my head spinning with wild dreams where a vengeful Ganesh demanded why I had not done something. Gold dripped from his trunk, as though he had a cold.

The next morning, dressed as an Englishman, I retrieved my find, bundled it in a spare tablecloth and took it to a jeweler in Kolaba. His shingle read GHANSHYAM AND SONS.

Seated on a large pillow I awaited the store's proprietor and noticed the festive decorations. Was some festival nearing? Deepavali, the festival of lights, was late October or early November. High on a shelf, I spied a decorative Shiva statuette overlooking the room. It depicted him as a dancing Nataraja, the god's four golden arms outstretched while he balanced on one bent foot.

The owner entered, holding my calling card. After the usual preliminaries I asked him in Hindustani, "Is that statue made of gold?"

"Yes, indeed!" he assured me. "Solid gold, twenty-two carat."

When I asked for it to be weighed, he summoned a pair of scales and a pile of ornate weights. Like a master chef, he orchestrated the business of adding tiny measures to the balance until presto! The Nataraja rose gently and the scales evened.

Once he'd completed his calculations I wrote down the weight and brought out Satya's Ganesh statue from my satchel. It stood as tall as the Nataraja and gleamed as bright.

Saying, "D'you mind?" I placed it on the scale.

Shrugging, he repeated his delicate maneuvers, then said, "Four point one kilograms."

That was just over half the Nataraja's weight. A heavy silence filled the room as I added this to my notebook. Had I broken some convention, I wondered, glancing over the staff. They were too still, too quiet.

The jeweler asked, "Do you wish to sell it?"

Declining, I asked what the idol was worth. As he calculated it, I felt an unnamed tension, a sense that the store folk were passing private messages with their eyes, messages not intended for me.

"Have you seen another like it?" I asked.

"No, indeed! It is remarkable. The detail on the clothing and jewelry is very fine."

"If I want to sell it, I'll return," I assured the perplexed proprietor.

An hour later I was back in Framji Mansion.

Diana's face grew serious as she said, "Jim, you've been working all alone, and it's taking too long. Look, we've got Bhim, Gurung, and Ganju. Papa could help. What about me? And Mama? Put us to work, Jim! Put us *all* to work!"

I sat, excitement pushing through me. Since I could not be in two places at once, her suggestion sparked new avenues to explore. "Call the fellows. Your father too, and your mother if she can be spared."

While Diana assembled the troops, I considered my notes and leads. It was a poor showing: the Ganesh idol, a key that unlocked an unknown vault possibly filled with silver, and a dying message that spoke about *sona*—gold. And the accountant Vishal. Something still wasn't quite right about him.

"Captain, at last," said Burjor, pushing his bulk through the door. "Something I can do?" His sparse, thinning hair stood on end over his bald pate, and his stubble showed grey and silver. Had he not slept since Adi was arrested?

I turned over the statuette. The base was smooth, complete. "This has something to do with Satya's murder. The mali did not know how many parcels he'd handed off. So how many did Satya sell? Where are those funds? Someone around him had to know what he was doing."

Burjor grunted. "How do we find out?"

An hour later we had an agreement. Gurung and Ganju would take turns shadowing Faisal, while the new boy and I would surveil the accountant Vishal. Burjor would make inquiries about Jussawalla's finances, his connections, and any rumors about him. Mrs. Framji and Diana would visit local goldsmiths, pretending an interest in buying jewelry. In fact, they were seeking a gold Ganesh statue like Satya's.

I leafed through my notebook. There it was: the dancing Shiva, about the same size, weighed 7.8 kilograms, while Satya's Ganesh weighed 4.1 kilograms. Though differently shaped, neither was hollow. Why did this feel wrong?

To find an answer, I decided to see Adi in the nick. Upon hearing this, Diana had me lug over a sack of his books.

Adi had been lying on his metal cot. When he sat up, eyes brightening, I felt a shot of chagrin that I'd not visited each day.

I broached the matter directly. "We know that Satya was gathering funds willy-nilly. Why? To gyp you and Jussawalla and leave with his nest egg, walk out on his family, and start over? Here he had you, a partner, a business—even if it was yet to become solvent, it was a start. He seemed an intelligent, promising youth, someone who'd make his mark."

As I spoke, enumerating the details, Adi became more animated. This was what he needed—to be engaged in the intellectual challenge. I'd been wading in solo and had floundered. Together then, we might make sense of this puzzle.

I went on. "He was estranged from his family—a temporary distance? Or worse? Would he really ruin his reputation—and by extension, theirs? What was driving him?"

"Money." Adi shook his head in wonder. "His needs were so sparse, I'd never have guessed it had such a hold on him."

In an undertone I told him about my discoveries at the mint and of the gold statuette. He listened intently as I went on. "Adi—there's something strange about all this." From my notebook, I read out the weights measured at the jewelry store.

Adi frowned. "You're certain?"

I nodded. "The proprietor weighed it in front of me, I wasn't adding up all the bits he put on the scale, but the fellow knew what he was doing." I described the strained atmosphere after we'd weighed the Ganesh statue.

Adi leaned back against the concrete wall, his brow ridged. Unlike my favorite fictional sleuth, no pipe, no violin, no opium aided his faculties.

I counted four breaths. Then he said, "And you're certain the Ganesh wasn't hollow?"

"The bottom is solid. No seams that I could see. It makes no hollow sound."

"Jussawalla's silver," he said, sitting up.

His face was clear and bright. "Jim, the statue must be silver, plated in gold. Silver is about half the weight of gold. That's why the jeweler was silent. He suspected—no, he knew from the color that it was pure—twenty-two carat, from your description, perhaps twenty-four! But the weight didn't match. I've been wondering why Satya paid Jussawalla so much. Forty kilos of silver, why, that should cost about twenty-four hundred rupees. He paid twice that!"

I pondered that. "Jussawalla got a nice profit. But Satya was no fool. He saw a bigger opportunity, with gold. *Sona.* So he buys silver, gets someone to make statues, then plates them and sells them as gold."

Adi's voice rang with urgency. "Jim, Satya wasn't this complicated. He must have had help with this clandestine business. You need to find his accomplices." Then he sobered. "Look at the sequence, the connections! It's a web. And Satya got caught in it. Beware, Jim. They use whatever's at hand. To kill."

* * *

At last, on the third day I hit pay dirt, as the Americans say. It was the Deepavali festival, which Hindus consider a particularly lucky day. Servants watered the streets to tamp the dust. Windows were flung open, clotheslines taken in to set fresh linen upon the cushions. Great quantities of food were prepared, their aromas vying for ascendancy. Families celebrated with visits to temples and then gatherings at home, festooned with music and sweetmeats, their doorways loaded with copious strings of marigolds.

The last of Vishal's guests were departing, men dressed in colorful kurtas and turbans. They thanked him at the door and left, trailing each other. To my surprise, one of them looked familiar. Where had I seen him? I recognized his tall, skinny frame, the uneven slope of his shoulders. Then it struck me. I'd seen him leaving the mint while I pretended to smoke outside. He was the mint worker who'd run off!

My pulse kicked into a canter as I followed, keeping thirty feet behind. Shadows lengthened along dimly lit streets. He did not turn north toward his home in Parel, but headed southward toward the bazaar. Where was he going? I kept pace, then stepped closer as the streets narrowed and became more crowded. He bought a few things in the market, then turned into an isolated stretch near the docks.

When I caught sight of him, he was farther away. Had he sped up? I lengthened my stride. He glanced back, but I marched along without meeting his gaze and he continued on. If he were to disappear into a *mohalla* or tenement, how would I find his bolt-hole?

I drew abreast and said in Hindustani, "We should talk."

He stopped with a cry. "What do you want?"

"You work at the mint," I said calmly, "and you came from the home of Vishal Das. How do you know him?"

He gasped. His breath shuddered as I lowered the shawl to uncover my face.

It did not calm him. "How do you know Vishal?" I repeated.

He choked, "He is my wife's brother."

"You gave him the gold for Satya."

"No!" he cried. "He did not know! Please! He cannot know."

His sudden movement took me by surprise. His hand shot out, not with a plea, but something that glinted in the lamplight. I responded with a reflex, a blow that knocked it from his fist before it was buried in my belly. Clutching his elbow, he backed away, staring from me to the blade reflecting on the cobbles.

I cried, "Stop! You're under arrest!"

A mistake. I had no authority to detain him. Worse, it was the wrong thing to say.

He fled. I leapt after him, but the devil was in his step and he bolted like a startled deer. Damn.

My knee pulsed as I pounded after him. That first spurt gave him a lead of ten feet. Barely keeping up, I struggled to close it, and could not spare the effort even to curse.

I'd lost track of where we were, somewhere near the Pydhonie police station? If we came in sight, I had some vague plan of hollering, "Stop, thief!" A vain hope, but all I had.

Ahead was an intersection. I heard the chug of a tram, the squeak of metal, and gained a yard. My knee no longer whined a protest, but bellowed. If I did not slow, it would buckle.

While I argued this point with my shrieking joint, I felt a gust and yanked away as the tram passed. I staggered, and my knee gave way. I went down hard, caught myself on my palms, and felt the burn of scraped flesh.

Ahead, the tram descended on a dark shape, my quarry. With a cry, he threw up his hands and turned. Did he think I was upon him?

The tram slammed into him, screeching to a halt; people cried out. The electric car jerked and shuddered to a stop. Like an ocean liner, its momentum carried it a full ten yards away. The tram driver climbed down, visibly quaking. Voices in the crowd grew loud and accusing.

Stunned, I searched the street, unable to spot him. Then realization struck a blow that winded me. My quarry lay in a pile across the street. Doubled over, I gasped, my pulse a wild drumbeat in the long moments. Breathing hard, I started toward him, but two other men got there first.

"What happened?" I asked, gaping at the bloodied clump of clothing and hair.

"He ran in front of the tram," said one, shaking his head. "Was he drunk?"

The other rasped, "Maybe a suicide?"

A distant whistle sounded. Collecting my wits, I backed away. Constables would be here soon, asking questions, and I had no answers to give.

I wasn't quick enough. As I trudged away nursing my aching knee, a whistle blew behind me. A voice hollered, "Stop!"

Standing among the milling bystanders, I turned to see what the ruckus was about.

"You!" hollered a white officer, pointing at me. "Is that blood?"

I glanced down at my light grey kameez where I'd wiped my scratched palms. Two constables approached, brows drawn, prepared to give chase if I should make a break.

I said in a thick northern accent, "I fell in the street, *huzoor*."

They were not impressed, but bore me to the officer, who glowered, smacking his baton into his palm as I lumbered over.

"Whose blood is that?" the officer snapped, his face stark white in the lamplight. He'd been one of the blokes in McIntyre's office when I salaamed him. With any luck he would not connect me with that little joke.

"Mine, *huzoor*. See." I offered my scraped palms, where drops were still welling up. "The shouting startled me, so I fell."

He scoured my face with narrowed eyes—good instincts for an Englishman, but hopelessly awash in the myriad dialects and peoples of India. "Did you know this man?" He pointed with his baton at the crumpled mass that someone was covering with a sheet.

"No, *huzoor*." I folded my hands in supplication, then clutched my knee with a gasp I did not need to fake.

"Your name?"

"Rashid Khan."

"Residence?"

"I am a visitor. From Pathankot."

Lips set in a tight line, the officer waved me off. I limped away, disgusted at myself.

✳ ✳ ✳

Back at Framji Mansion, Diana fussed over my scraped hands, sending the houseboy scurrying. "Clean water—bandages, Bhim! Haldi root, grind it to a paste. That's right, turmeric! Yes, now."

I closed my eyes, breathing in the smell of soap, tuberoses, and coconut oil that wafted off her. The snippets of information I'd collected whirled around my mind, snatches of conversation, odd looks that I'd tucked away to examine later.

God, it was a mess. Holmes had said, "It is a capital mistake to theorize before one has data. Insensibly one begins to twist facts to suit theories, instead of theories to suit facts." I had accumulated a kaleidoscope of evidence but had no clear suspect for the murder.

While Diana dabbed and swabbed at me, the bits swirled until they settled, one by one, like puzzle pieces on the floor. Slowly a picture emerged. I hoped it wasn't too late.

CHAPTER 31

THE MYSTERIOUS WITNESS

Before nine the next morning, McIntyre hauled me in with a peremptory phone call, wouldn't say what it was about. Fearful for Adi's well-being, I left my meal untouched, my hair uncombed, and my hat on the handstand.

Puffing little clouds of aromatic smoke, McIntyre stalked about, taking it all in with cynical amusement. And then I had no time to think, for he was flinging questions at me like a firing squad, and I was the blindfolded bloke trussed to the pole.

"Bloody mysterious key! Won't say where you got it."

"It belonged to the victim," I repeated, "Satya Rastogi."

He rapped my knuckles with the stem of his pipe. "How'd you get that?"

"Just a scrape. Tripped and fell."

"So you say." McIntyre gazed down at me with a grimace. "And that key. You got it from young Framji?"

"No." Why did my voice sound so hollow? I frowned, swallowed, and tried again, realizing I had to give him at least part of the truth. "His father Burjor met Satya that morning. Satya gave it to him for safekeeping."

A lie, but a reasonable one. It had been given as collateral.

McIntyre's gaze froze. "My God," he rumbled. "He admitted that? Have we got the wrong Framji?"

"It's not Burjor," I said flatly.

"How d'you know?"

"When Adi entered the factory gate, he would have seen his own carriage waiting there. He didn't. So Burjor had already left."

McIntyre contemplated this, his frame rigid. When he spoke, his voice cracked like reluctant thunder. "Something you're forgetting. Framji senior and junior, they could be in it together."

His words chilled me. This I had not imagined, a devious collusion that defied belief. Now I considered it like a surgeon at an amputation— disliking the task but resolved to it.

Eventually I said, "No, I know these men like I know my own hands. Murder does not leave the killer unscathed. The act changes a person."

Was that why I could no longer aim true? Diana was a superb markswoman, but I could no longer trust my aim. I recalled sepoys in my company trudging past broken bodies, the charnel we'd left along the way to Kandahar. "Some spend hours on their knees, desperate to forget, to return to how they used to be, used to feel. But it's no good. One can't go back. The sooner one accepts it the better. Few do."

McIntyre scoffed. "I've seen blokes ice-cold after killing half a dozen." His eyes had an unusual gleam.

I held his gaze. "I watched both Framjis. Lived with them. I've questioned Adi's staff, Satya's family, even Banner. Adi, he's deeply hurt, grieves his friend and partner. And he's rather stunned by Satya's secrets. He's learning about the mechanism of locks—these recent burglaries, got anywhere with them?"

McIntyre snapped. "What's that got to do with it?"

"Adi's an inventor of sorts. Wants to make a new kind of safe. Might have quite a market now. That's how the lad thinks: problem— opportunity. He won't take the easy way; the crudeness of crime repels him. Burjor, now, he prays in the morning just as much as he did two years ago, when I recuperated here."

He slumped into his chair. "How on earth can you know that?"

I chuckled. "Whole house can hear him. Their Zoroastrian prayers are a singsong chant. I hear Diana most mornings. This market crash has shaken Burjor, but he's busy trying to trade as usual. That's his center, where his energies lie." I said nothing about Burjor's repeated appeals for bail—no sense poking a sleeping bear.

McIntyre leaned his bulk forward, forearms on the table. "So, who else?"

"The two employees—I've watched their homes, followed them, even snooped around inside. Neither has any extra cash. They have their problems, but there's no sign of guilt eating away at them." I said nothing about Vishal's dead brother-in-law.

McIntyre pulled back. "Humph. So, no leads."

I said, "Well, Satya bought a large quantity of silver."

McIntyre picked up his fountain pen as I went on. "So, we have three possibilities. His parents—" I had a flash of memory, his mother Meera, beheading vegetables easily with a little curved knife. "Two, Jussawalla, the craftsman who sold him a pile of ingots. Or three, a customer we haven't met yet, who paid for a *murti* of solid gold. People take religion seriously here. To sell a fake idol is akin to heresy. Worse, because Ganesh is the god of wealth. To cast him in gold would be seen as honor. To cloak him in gold over base silver could be seen as a betrayal of the god himself."

"A betrayal of what? Slow down, man!"

"To us it would feel like being gypped—paid for gold, got silver. To a devout Indian, to a Hindu, it could feel like—like a debasement of his faith." Hadn't the whole mutiny, just thirty-some years ago, been driven by religious outrage? British administrators now avoided disrupting religious practices, no matter how cruel or unfair they might seem.

"What were you doing at the Imperial Mint? And don't give me that hogwash about the key," McIntyre said, dropping his anvil-like stare on me.

Blast. I felt sweat trickle down my armpits, reassembled my face to neutral respect. "That's a separate case, sir."

After what seemed like hours, McIntyre said, without moving, "Boy, you're running out of rope."

I heaved in a breath, felt my aching shoulders ease. McIntyre maintained the cold glare that reminded me of a stuffed tiger.

"I understand," I said, wobbling to my feet. When I ducked my head in farewell, he did not move. "Right," I said, turning to leave.

A pale English officer entered, his sweat-patched uniform indicating the rank of inspector. New to the tropics, then. Unkempt as I was, I did not expect he'd rate me a look. But he met my glance and flinched. His gaze sharpened into a frown. Damn.

I forced myself to keep a steady pace as he watched me exit.

It was the British officer who'd questioned me after the tramway accident yesterday.

* * *

The timing of McIntyre's interrogation puzzled me. Why now? Was he preparing for Adi's trial? I spent the rest of the morning going through my notes to collect material for Adi's defense. After luncheon, Gurung came to tell me I had a phone call.

"Who is it?" I asked Burjor as I entered his office.

Dressed in his linen undershirt and prayer cap, Burjor gave a slow shrug. He hadn't shaved, but his eyes were keen as he handed me the instrument.

"Yes?" I said into the mouthpiece. For a second, I heard only breathing.

"Captain sahib?" asked a low, unsteady voice.

I knew that voice. I had worked with that voice two years ago—the round-bellied sub-inspector who brought me chai whenever he could. I had not once paid for it.

"Sabrimal?"

He spoke quickly. "Sahib, you saved me from poison, remember? So I am thinking, this favor I should do in return, sahib?"

Two years ago, that sentence would have been beyond him. His mastery of English had improved. "That was long ago, Sabrimal. What's the matter?"

He was quiet, then said, "Sahib, don't say I told you, all right? Trial is starting soon. There is a witness. He is saying he heard your brother. He is . . . come and see, sahib! I must go."

The line went silent, then a female voice spoke. "Operator seven nine, do you wish to place a call?"

"No, ma'am," I replied, and lowered the earpiece. I held it for a moment, then gently placed it on its cradle. Heavens. I had a mole inside McIntyre's police force!

Nodding to Burjor, I made for police headquarters without delay.

* * *

When I ambushed Smith in the corridor, he scowled. "How the devil did you know?"

I pulled him aside. "Heard about it. The trial's starting?"

His mouth thinned. "It can't get about, all right? We've got a new witness. Saw your boy arguing with the victim the day before Rastogi was killed."

I flinched. "Did he identify Adi?"

"Official identification's tomorrow."

Taking his uniform hat from under his arm, he stuffed it on his head, a signal for me to leave. Yet a voice in me hollered, no! This was all wrong. Why would Adi have an altercation in the street? He shared premises with Satya, why wouldn't they speak inside?

I followed Smith through the bullpen. "This new witness. Who found him? What's he saying?"

Dropping into his chair, he said, "Name's Pritam Dutta. He's a clerk working on Queens Road. Walked in this morning with information about the death of Satya Rastogi. He has named Adi Framji. Says he heard them clear across the street."

I scowled at this blatant nonsense. "How could he be sure who it was?"

"Says he knows your boy." Smith shifted about in his seat, then read off the damning words from his notebook. "Your chap said, 'You swine! I'll kill you.' No doubt at all about it."

"Where's the report?"

"Being typed up."

Jotting down the witness's name, I mumbled a goodbye.

Reluctant to return to Framji Mansion, I searched the bullpen. If I could just get hold of that new witness's report . . . Pritam Dutta—what community was he from? It was strange, I thought, how one's name immediately gave one a picture of the person, an expectation, however false. My own moniker was a contradiction that should not exist, yet I had no time now for the rage that usually simmered toward my irresponsible English father.

I dithered at a window, trying to decide how best to proceed. The worst hadn't happened yet because Adi's trial was still ahead. I gripped the windowsill, unsure what to do. Seeing the injured mali had brought back disjointed details without cohesion. I felt as though I was chasing a locomotive that would soon be out of sight.

So, it was pure chance that I spotted Sub-inspector Sabrimal leading a man out, a small, compact man in traditional dhoti-kurta and black brogues.

Wait—was that the new witness?

There was no statement in Smith's file, because it was still being typed up! They'd kept Pritam Dutta waiting. My God! Sabrimal had called me on the telephone, while Dutta, the witness, was stashed somewhere in the constabulary. He was leaving, but I could not follow him—dressed in my civvies, I'd be easily spotted.

With no time to waste, I went the other way and charged up to McIntyre's burly sergeant. "Have you a spare *kameez*?"

He blinked in incomprehension while the dratted witness was getting away. I cried, "A chador, a turban. Anything!"

Pulling open a drawer, he gestured at some folded clothes. I squatted, hauled out a dark kurta and a strip of white cloth, then peeled off my coat, vest and shirt, tossing them at his feet.

As shocked gasps hissed behind me, I donned the billowing kurta, wound a tight turban, and wrapped the chador over myself. Damn, I thought, glancing down at my trousers and army boots; they'd have to do.

Ignoring the astonished stares from policemen both native and white, I dashed through the hall and down the outer stairs. Where had Dutta got to?

Right or left? I rushed toward the market, and there spied my quarry. He'd paused watching a large group under a banyan tree where humbly clad civilians clustered around black-coated lawyers who resembled crows among a host of sparrows.

Dutta stepped across the busy street to avoid them, and then crossed back again, for he was headed toward the left.

That maneuver allowed me to catch up. His furtive manner was peculiar, the way he avoided the group, turning his face to the side. I filed it away to consider, lengthening my stride to cover the distance. As I neared, he gave a *tongawala* an address. Sonapur Lane.

My pulse thudded in my ears. Sonapur Lane? Satya's family lived

there. Hailing a Victoria, I leapt in, ignoring the cry of surprise from
the driver. Leaning out of the window I said roughly, "Go! That way!"

The startled driver clicked to his mare and flicked his whip over its
back for good measure. Leaning out of the window, I kept my eyes on
Dutta's tonga. When we were so close as to overtake the three-wheeled
tonga, I called, "Slow down!"

The tonga driver pumped hard, bearing Dutta away. He turned left
and we followed.

Passing Lohar Chawl, we continued on to Sonapur Lane, where Dutta
descended and shook out his dhoti. He climbed up a few stairs, his black
shoes stamping over colorful *rangoli* decorations. Then my Victoria continued and I lost sight of him. At the next intersection I pounded a fist to
halt the carriage, thrust a rupee at the driver, and hurried back.

Why had this blasted bloke popped up just now? Why not earlier?
An ache hammered at my temples as I strode toward his door. I wanted
to choke the truth out of the blighter.

Sounds of welcome came from above the stairway. An urgent question and then "Baba!" A woman and a child, perhaps two. When their
voices dropped, I could no longer distinguish the words. My quarry
was speaking in rapid vernacular. Gujarati? The dialects of India numbered in the hundreds, and I could not make this one out.

Now I knew where he lived, how could I learn more? I leaned against
a wall pretending to assemble a smoke as I considered how this could
be better managed.

Dutta had taken pains to avoid that group at the banyan tree. So
that's where I'd start. I needed a way to question him without giving
away my purpose. Why had he pointed the finger at Adi? If I got the
truth from him, I might just get Adi out of that miserable cell.

CHAPTER 32

BAITING THE TRAP

Just past dawn, it was cool and I'd been waiting an hour already. Dewdrops clung to the glistening banyan leaves and crept down the overhanging roots. My back against the wide, muscular trunk, I sat on a smooth, wide root that stretched twenty feet and thrust the cobbles into undulated stone. Here I'd seen lawyers besieged by potential clients, but as yet it was quiet.

Soon a scrawny *paan* seller carried his basket of betel nut leaves and condiments to the tree. I asked for a sweet *paan* and squatted near him as he applied preparations to the betel leaf.

"*Chuna?*" he offered.

I declined the coating of corrosive white lime and asked in Rashid's guttural tone, "When will they come, the lawyers?"

"Tsk. Today is Sunday," he replied. "Court is closed. They return tomorrow."

To get him talking, I said, "I need money. Some work or . . ."

He glanced over. "Where are you from?"

"Pathankot, near the village of . . ." I named a place he was unlikely to know.

His head wobbled in admiration. "Far away! That is good. The lawyer will like it. Just say whatever he tells you."

So that was it! At the banyan tree market, false testimony was offered for sale.

"How much will they pay?" I asked, handing him a small coin for the *paan*.

"The judge will question you," he warned me. "If you stand your ground, come back and you will get a full rupee. If you are found out, only eight annas."

Was a man's freedom worth so little? A rupee to lie and land some defendant in the clink. How easy it was to dismiss one's part in it—those found giving false testimony paid only a small fine and blamed the lawyer for putting them up to it.

I wobbled my jaw as though weighing his words, then nodded.

"The friend who sent me here—he got a good deal more," I went on. "It is a big case. I hope I can get something like that."

"How much more?" His eyebrows rose, radiating doubt.

"He will not say," I grumbled. "Keeps his windfall to himself. Can't you help?"

"I can point out the big lawyers," he said, handing me the *paan*. "It will cost you."

"To make a tidy sum, it will be worth it," I agreed. A few minutes of haggling and the price was set. I had no fondness for sweet spicy *paan*, but chewed on it until he was out of sight.

Next, I collected supplies from my stash in Dockyard Road and returned to Framji Mansion. Entering Adi's chamber, I rummaged through his clothes. Dash it all, where were they? *There.*

The lawyer's robes that Adi had earned were folded in a drawer. I shook them out, chose the largest, and donned it. Alas, the full-length mirror showed it hung at my knees.

Returning to our bedchamber, I added a woolly astrakhan hat from my collection and frowned at my reflection. Freshly shaved, I looked too young. The straggly mustache in the last of my goopy collodion was still stuck to a corner of the washroom mirror. Applying that and a pair of wire frames gave me an older, more studious look.

As I was trimming the mustache, a cry came from the door. *"Ay Khodai!"*

Dressed in a cream-colored housedress, Diana clung to the door-knob, a hand over her mouth. "It's you! What *are* you doing, Jim?"

"I'm sorry, sweet," I said, swinging my arms out. "A disguise. But the robe's too short."

She pulled in her lips and tapped with a finger. "Have it off and let me see. I'll unpick the hem, iron it out . . ." Grimacing, she tilted her head. "That awful mustache, Jim. Like a mangy terrier!"

A half hour later, she'd altered the legal garb and insisted that I have a meal, so a tray had been summoned. Both Gurung and Ganju brought it, and then Jiji-bai and the other boy ventured into the dining room on assorted excuses to evaluate "captain sahib's new clothes."

They gawked, ducked their eyes, then offered dubious praise. "Captain needs a few good meals, return soon, sahib?" "If you go out in the dark, no one will trouble you."

"What will you do?" Diana asked, her brown eyes worried. "How will this help?"

I scoffed the fried plantains, roasted chicken, and potatoes, then set down my spoon in regret. If I'd been in less of a hurry, I might have tasted them. "Adi was arrested because a new witness came forward. I think he was hired."

She sucked in a breath, her mouth tight. "Paid to frame Adi? Why?"

"Diverts attention from the killer, hmm? If I get him to talk, we might have the culprit."

Excitement rising, I counted out a few rupee notes and stuffed them in the pocket of my newly lengthened robe, then pecked a goodbye on Diana's cheek and went to visit the prosecution's new witness.

* * *

An afternoon gust threw dust and leaves at my face as I descended from the Victoria in the narrow gully where I'd last seen Dutta. Hunching over, I thumped on his door.

An elderly neighbor opened an adjacent door, others came to windows. Perhaps few rode a carriage to this neighborhood.

"Pritam Dutta?" I asked the local busybody.

"First floor," he replied. Stepping through a narrow archway, I climbed the steep flight of stairs. On the landing, my arrival drew more attention. Neighbors peered out, curious and eager. They probably knew when Dutta showered, shone his shiny shoes, or burped. When I said I had an urgent message, they pointed to a door at the end of the *chawl*. Dutta opened to my knock.

"Yes?" he said, identifying me as a lawyer. "Vakil, sahib?"

He bid me enter a dingy room that smelled of old socks, and closed the door.

"I have no time," I said roughly in Hindustani, thrusting three rupees at him. "The plan has changed. We said five rupees?"

His mouth dropped open. Recovering, he took the money. "How can you say that? It was ten! I asked for twelve, but *bada vakil* sahib said ten. I am very reliable, sahib! No one will suspect me."

Bada vakil. Senior lawyer. With a show of nonchalance, I said, "Yes, yes. That's why he sent three rupees in advance. You have the description?"

"Simple, sahib. I will point at the thin man standing in the dock. Adi Framji. I have memorized the name."

"There is a new plan. You will say the same name. But you will point at the Englishman sitting near the lawyer. He will be wearing a grey suit with a blue cloth, here." I patted my breast pocket. "Do you understand? They are going to trick you. So point at the tall *gora*. That is Adi Framji, not the youth."

"Oh!" His eyes wide, he wobbled an agreement.

I said, "Look, why not speak to the *bada vakil* before you go in? Go early and seek him. He sent me with this message, but why not ask him yourself?"

So saying, I cracked the door, peered out, then gave him a nod and departed.

The stage was set. If he did not identify the lawyer who'd set Adi up, I'd have only the dubious testimony of the *paanwala* from the banyan tree. That bloke might keep his end of the bargain and identify Dutta and the mysterious *bada vakil*, but it was not as definitive as catching Dutta with the crook. Satisfied, I headed for the police headquarters to set my trap for Monday morning.

Since I was in disguise, it took a while to persuade the constable to admit me. By then Mac had gone home, but his burly sergeant took me around to my pal Stephen Smith, who went beet red, and then laughed for a quarter of an hour.

Some time later, we'd come up with a neat plan. It was better this way, I thought. McIntyre might not have approved it.

CHAPTER 33

NOT A SHRED

The public had gathered in great numbers at the Court of Justice on Mayo Road. Bombay's high court was a wide, four-storied building near the university, sheathed in stone and embellished with Gothic grillwork. Four turrets surrounded a high central roof, giving it the appearance of a castle. On either end stood staircase towers wearing pointed hats. A notice on the door said that Adi's case would be heard by Chief Justice Charles Sargent.

"What's he like, Justice Sargent?" I asked a Parsi lawyer in a tall shiny hat.

He gave me an assessing look, then said that though elderly, Sargent gave unbiased, incisive judgments. Bystanders chimed in, offering a mix of intelligence and rumor.

Standing with the multitude under the pointed arches, I spotted the tall spike of Rajabai clock tower. There, two years ago, Adi's bride and his cousin had fallen to their deaths. My first case. This time, Adi wasn't the bereaved widower, but the accused. Gut churning, I searched the swarm of civilians and black-robed barristers. *There.*

Wearing a jacket over his dhoti, the witness Pritam Dutta climbed the courthouse steps, peering around. My appearance at his home with altered instructions had disturbed him and now he seemed unsure how to proceed. To accuse an Englishman was a far cry from his earlier task. I hoped he would seek out his employer and beg to be let off. When that did not work, he would demand additional moneys for this, more dangerous job. As he wove through the crowd, I followed, hoping to discover the "lawyer" who'd framed Adi.

Failing that, I needed to discredit Dutta's testimony, but would Smith cooperate?

The first part of my plan went awry immediately. I should have known the perpetrator, the *bada vakil*, would not be around where Dutta could approach him. The heavy court doors swung open. Keeping Dutta in sight, I shuffled through with the throng.

When Adi's case was called, Dutta hurried into a seat, casting anxious glances at the packed mezzanine floor above. At the head of the room, two defense attorneys sat beside Burjor. The older partner in gold-rimmed glasses gazed straight ahead. The younger one consulted his stack of papers and whispered to Burjor at intervals. If he'd been calm, I'd have had more faith in him.

Diana and Mrs. Framji's arrival caused a commotion. Newspapermen lobbed questions from the door. Baton-wielding constables pushed reporters away.

Both ladies were pale, though Diana had worn a cheerful peach sari and her mother was in buttercup yellow. Parsis do not wear black, even in mourning. Mrs. Framji's pale silk would not have looked out of place at the fire temple. I recalled that she'd worn it on her birthday, when the Framjis had been ousted from their place of worship.

Wearing a neat dark blue suit, Adi came in with his guards, his white collar as crisp as the pleat of his trousers. He met Diana's gaze and smiled. She stood and waved her reply, tossing decorum to the winds. Message received, I thought.

Mrs. Framji fluttered a white kerchief, her face encased in smiles. As Adi climbed to the dock, Burjor gave him a nod. I uncurled my fist and tried to breathe.

Adi cast a look about, a line appearing between his eyebrows. He was looking for me, I thought, feeling a spike of remorse stab my chest. I'd had no time to tell him my plan. When at last he spotted me, he flinched. His face fell.

Immobile, I held his gaze and prayed that he understood my message.

A voice hailed our attention. As the courtroom rose to its feet, the judge entered and the court began its formalities at a glacial pace. The clerk droned on in a tone so slurred from repetition that he seemed to be speaking gibberish.

Two British officials led the prosecution. The senior lawyer Burjor had hired accepted statements that were admitted into evidence. The bank manager and medical examiner were told they would testify another day. Although each step of the court's proceedings ran painfully slowly, Adi took a keen interest, as though it were a particularly engaging play. Diana listening attentively, a notebook open on her knee.

Next, Pritam Dutta was called to the witness stand, a seat across from the dock. Licking his lips as he was sworn in, he peered up at the judge's bench.

The lead prosecutor was a dashing Englishman with a thick mustache. He established right away that Dutta had met Satya in the past when he sought to be hired by him. However, the pay did not satisfy, so Dutta had declined and found work as a clerk in a store instead.

I thought the whole thing improbable, since the only man who could verify his words was dead. After some prompting, Dutta described an argument he'd overheard, reciting the damning words in an undertone. He was made to repeat them loudly.

The prosecutor then showed that although it was dark, the two men had been arguing under a streetlamp. That was mighty convenient, I thought.

With a flourish, the prosecutor flung out his hand. "Thank you, Mr. Dutta. You've been very clear. Please point to the man you saw arguing with Satya Rastogi."

At this point it should have been a formality. The prisoner stands in the dock for all to see. Dutta leaned forward and pointed.

Shock held the courtroom still for a moment. Then it erupted into waves of consternation, because Dutta was pointing at me!

* * *

McIntyre had been suspicious, even affronted, when he found me at the prosecution's table, but he'd arrived too late to do anything about it. I had no idea how Smith got the crown's counsel to agree. As I had requested, I sat at the prosecutor's table, wearing a grey suit with a blue kerchief.

An hour later, I faced McIntyre, feeling blood suffuse my face. "But you saw it! Blighter didn't know Adi Framji from a monkey in a banana tree!"

"Control yourself, Mr. Agnihotri," McIntyre barked, his brogue thick as he demoted me to a civilian. "If I'd known you were up to this farce, you'd not 'a got me to let you come. And you!" He stabbed a finger at Smith, sitting stiff as a taxidermist's masterpiece. "You turned the court into a sham! The pair o' you! Visiting a witness, bribing him!"

I protested, "Three rupees, which he accepted as advance payment on a promised sum. He was bought, can't you see? I could buy a dozen witnesses to swear Satya Rastogi was dancing in a temple yesterday. Only cost me eight annas each!"

Smith sat at attention while McIntyre made a low gargling noise in his throat that warned he would not send for constables to have me removed, but might well do it himself.

In a more reasonable tone, I said, "The witness, Dutta, is bunkum. Complete codswallop. Fellow never set eyes on Satya. *Or* Adi Framji!"

McIntyre snarled, "And I'm to take *your* word for it?"

"Please. Release Adi. You've got to."

His reply was to curl his lip and sniff. I had never liked him less.

I cried, "You don't have the slightest wisp of evidence against him!"

McIntyre stiffened. "The trial has begun, Mr. Agnihotri. If he's acquitted, he'll be released. Not an hour before."

"Surely you can release him on bail? You *know* the Framjis."

"And have him hop the next boat to Canada? Not a chance 'a that, laddie."

I glared at him, then groaned. Adi would have to undergo the trial after all. They had no case against him, but I'd tossed pie in their face, so the court would doggedly continue its work. The only glimmer of hope was that once exonerated, the double indemnity rule would prevent Adi from being tried again for the crime.

* * *

I returned to Framji Mansion in a blue funk. The family had gathered in the morning room where Diana perched on a corner of the couch.

Mrs. Framji lay back, supported by pillows. Eyes closed, she pressed a kerchief to her temples.

Diana was explaining to her parents what the law clerk had announced in his monotonous drone. "There's no jury selection, Papa, because there will be no jury. Since an Indian was accused, the judge determined that a native jury could not be trusted to deliver a fair verdict. That's what the announcement was about. This trial will be handled in a different manner—Jim, can you find out about the judge, his reputation? Does he dislike Indians?"

Feeling grim, I said, "He ruled on the communal riots, last year. Seems a fair man. Tough on both Hindus and Muslims, so he's got a reputation for being racially unbiased."

She said, "All those legal terms, ugh! Anyway, as long as there's no evidence incriminating Adi there's a good chance he'll get off. There's no witness that he did it."

"Acquitted for lack of proof," Burjor growled. "Like Manek. And what's happened to *him,* since then? No one will employ him. Can't show his face at the temple, not even for his uncle's funeral."

Diana said, "Jim, thank heaven you got rid of that lying witness, that *worm.*" She gave a strangled laugh though worry etched her tight face. Dabbing a cloth in the bowl nearby, she leaned over to place it on her mother's forehead.

"It's eau de cologne. Mama has a terrible headache," Diana whispered, adjusting the satin *rajai* around her mother.

"Can I help?" I asked, matching her low tone. "Carry her upstairs, if she wants?"

"No, *beta,*" said Mrs. Framji in a faint, rasping voice. "I will be all right, in time."

Diana bent and replied, then rose to her feet with a finger on her lips. With a few words to me, she went to attend the children, so I took out my notebook and studied it. Burjor's lawyers had asked to speak with me in the morning.

Jiji-bai brought a platter of small chutney sandwiches. Since no one had any appetite, she left them on the table. At ten that night, they were still sitting there, Burjor hunched in his chair, his great shoulders bowed, staring at his slippered feet, his wife buried under a satin blanket like an insubstantial bird in layers of plumage.

Diana was quiet as we prepared for bed. In silence she turned down the lamp. Later, gazing up at the darkness, I knew she was awake. And I knew with conviction that she did not want me to speak.

What would I have said, if emotion had not closed my lips? That I had tried to get Adi released, and failed? That surely he must be acquitted, for no one who knew him would believe for a moment in his guilt? All that had been said.

Adi would now face a verdict from a man who did not know him, but who would put such things aside, even if he did. Justice Sargent would decide purely on the circumstances of the case—the employees' testimony and the mali's translated statement. The bank manager would testify about Adi's visit that morning. Would that be enough of an alibi?

Adi had brought Diana and me together. Yet when he needed me most, I'd made a mess of it.

The night was long. I'd learned during my years in the army to confront what loomed over me, to stare my fears in the eye, though my heart might be cowering inside. I'd learned to give it words, to acknowledge the worst. And it was this: Diana was losing faith in me, perhaps even regretting her daring choices.

CHAPTER 34

A MOTHER'S LIES

The trial proceeded slowly, while for two days I demanded access to Dutta, insisting that he, or whoever had hired him, was likely behind Satya's murder. It was no good. Smith and McIntyre had both questioned him. He denied taking payment, but described the lawyer he met as a slender, well-dressed man. Dutta claimed he did not know his name or where he practiced.

"Bosh!" I cried. "Bunkum! How can seasoned investigators believe this?"

McIntyre said that I'd be arrested if I went near Dutta again.

I grumbled to Diana at teatime. "Back to square one. Still got nothing on Adi's employees. Nor some thin, well-dressed blighter who bribed that witness!"

"Jim, dear," said Diana, "about that key you're trying to identify. You went all over to find what it unlocks, so I wonder, why not try a locksmith?"

I paused, my knife over the bowl of gooseberry jam. "Damn."

"Oh?"

"Should have thought of it," I grumbled, heaping the golden confection into the gash I'd cut in the side of a crusty, sweet-scented *brun-pav*.

"You would have, in time," she assured me, which only made it worse.

I visited three locksmiths after court that very afternoon. "I can only tell you it is new, a modern design," said the last of them, with the air of making a weighty pronouncement.

Disheartened, I returned to my traps, like a lobsterman checking empty cages. Outside Adi's factory, my trusty *chanawala* sat on a low wall overlooking the crossroad.

I offered him a coin and my well-worn question. "Seen anyone going in?"

"*Adab,* sahib!" he greeted me, handing me a twist of peanuts. "For days there was no one. But yesterday, a woman entered."

Afraid to hope for a break in my case, I asked, "How long was she inside?"

He scratched his chin. "One hour, perhaps more. It was noon and I wanted some food. But I stayed, sahib, and waited for her to leave."

"Young? Old?"

He shrugged. "She was wearing a shawl. A brown chador over her head."

"Did you see her face?"

"No, sahib. She came that way." He pointed across the lane. "I saw her back."

I handed him the agreed sum. "How did you know it was a woman?"

He grinned at me. "Her sari, sahib. And the way she walked."

This was new. A woman visiting the factory? Looking for what? Could a woman have struck the old mali? It seemed unlikely, yet it was possible. There was an unknown player in this game—why couldn't it be a woman?

I'd met only one related to this case, so I took myself off to question her.

* * *

All my life, I'd wanted siblings. Brothers with whom to race or leap into pools, sisters to bring me samples of cooking and wait expectantly for my verdict. Above all, I envied sepoys for their families, and sourly watched those who were careless of a proud pater or their mother's embrace. Yet Satya had had a family and he could not get away from it fast enough. How could he squander such a gift? Descending from the bicycle tonga, I paid the sweating driver and approached Satya's home.

Through the metal gate, I demanded an audience with Meera, Satya's mother, and was shown into the rear courtyard. This time, I did not fold my hands in greeting but held her gaze.

She straightened, raised her chin and dismissed the waiting *darwan*.

After he'd passed out of earshot, I asked in Hindustani, "What have you to tell me?"

She raised an eyebrow in silence. I admired it—she had an investigator's patience. Let the blighter blab, in time you'll get what you seek.

But now I had no time for her parlor games. I said in a flat tone, "You came to the factory yesterday. Looking for something."

She moved her head an inch. There was no give in this lady.

"My guard recognized you."

My long shot struck true. Satya's mother drew an audible breath.

I asked, "What were you searching for?"

Still she made no reply. I puzzled over it. She was a *sonar*, after all, daughter of a respectable goldsmith and matriarch of the clan.

"Were you looking for Satya's things?"

She glanced away, her expression remote. Yet I did not think I was too far from the truth; she was still standing with me in the courtyard. Why hadn't she sent someone to the Framjis to retrieve whatever it was? Ah. I guessed the answer: she did not want them to know.

"Did you find what you wanted?"

Her glance was dismissive. So no, then. She had not. Was she looking for Satya's key or his statuette? Or was she party to his plans?

On a chance, I went on, "But that's not the only time you were there."

She jerked, her dark eyes shocked.

One blunder and I'd blow my advantage. Masking my surprise, I tiptoed into unknown terrain. "You knew the way, and that the entrance is on the side street."

If a bluff is to succeed, it must be advanced boldly. There can be no caution, no testing the waters, no finding one's way. One either struck true or went wide. The risk was egg on one's face; I'd had my share and it hadn't killed me yet. Still, it wasn't my neck awaiting the noose, but Adi's. I could not fail him.

"Satya took something with him, yes? Something that belonged to you, to the family. So, the first time, you went to demand its return. Did he deny it, refuse to listen? He wasn't a child anymore. You had no control over him. Did he laugh at you?"

She shook her head. One foot rubbed the instep of the other.

I pushed harder. "No longer obedient. Toying with his scalpel—was he showing you what he'd made? Or . . . did he ignore you, as though your words were of no account. You picked up a blade and thrust it into his throat."

She delicately wiped her mouth with the end of her sari. Her husky voice wobbled as she asked, "What proof do you have?"

I gave her a long look. "The innocent say, 'I didn't do it.' The guilty say, 'You can't prove it.'" I sighed at strands of grey that laced her hair. "And here you are, asking for evidence."

Tears welling, she pulled her sari over her face.

Smoke from the cooking fire blew around us. My palms tingled, some old memory trying to push forward, bringing restlessness. Not now, I thought, swallowing the sour tang in my mouth.

In a weary voice, she said, "He did not come home that night. So often in recent months. He had come the previous day. After he left a theft was discovered. Such a *hangama*! The men wanted to confront him, beat him! But *mistri* forbade it."

"What did he take?"

She flicked away my question. "At dawn that day, after *pooja*, I went to his phac-ta-ry."

"That day? August twenty-fifth?" The day Satya was killed.

"He was making tea. In pajamas and a torn undershirt. I begged him to come home. Living like a pauper, looking like a drunk, what will people think? Consider our name, our reputation. It was no use. So I left."

I would have probed further, but some implacable quality had entered her face.

"And yesterday?"

"I remembered him, so I went. Now go."

She pointed me at the gate, scrubbing a hand over her face. What did a mother feel, I wondered? Was a child an extension of oneself, a font of surprise and wonder, or a source of dismay, a constant stabbing at the heart? As I turned from her grief, a shout caught my attention.

I glanced around—a worker ran through the courtyard in his undershirt, crying out. Others took up the din in the floors above.

"What is it? What's wrong?" I called.

Satya's mother was staring upward, her mouth open.

I followed her gaze, sniffing the air. What was that?

Smoke wisped from a window above.

CHAPTER 35

FIRE

Fire spreads quickly in an old wooden structure. I could hear it above us, cracking and popping like someone tearing paper, snapping twigs. The acrid smell grew stronger as smoke clouded the air and embers floated down like dying stars.

Were the upper floors already consumed? I rounded the corner to the forecourt at a run. Workmen clustered around the staircase from which others emerged coughing. Tansen stood in the courtyard, feet planted wide, shouting orders like a demented quartermaster.

Buckets were found, men hurrying to and from the well in the garden, yet the crowd blocked the stairs. Few ventured inside.

Some unwrapped turbans to soak and wind them about their faces. Following suit, I covered the lower part of my face, then grabbed a bucket of water from someone and pushed upstairs.

I passed along a murky corridor where women carried children past. The wet cloth over my nose allowed me to breathe, but my eyes stung as I entered an open door where the acrid fumes were thickest. A blast of heat singed the hair on my arms, so I tossed the contents of my bucket in a wide arc.

A hiss followed, oddly alive, like something sentient in the murky chamber. A cloud billowed over me.

"Soak towels, cloth, saris. Soak them!" I cried. Muffled by my wrappings, my voice was lost in the creaks and hiss, the stamp of feet, questions and shouts.

As I retreated, others passed bearing buckets, then I heard a cry. Holding a cloth to her face, a woman in the passage gestured frantically. Together, we dragged a *charpoy* away from the sparks at the window, then I flipped the string bed sideways and hoisted it onto my shoulder. Others joined me to carry out containers or drag them to safety.

In the courtyard below buckets of water were passed along a chain to avoid spillage. Someone said the fire had started in the larger workshops. Others carted out boxes.

When I tried to enter, Tansen blocked my way. "No, sahib!"

Ah! They crafted gold in that workshop. Even in an emergency, Tansen kept it secure. As I stepped back, a boy carrying a crate careened into me.

While Tansen yelped, "Pandu!" I caught myself against a wall and grabbed the teenager's arm, but the carton tumbled, spilling its contents.

Circlets of gold shone like jewels on the stairs. Crying out, the thin lad scrambled to collect them. Tansen spread his arms to hold back the barrage of oncoming bodies as the youth and I scooped up the delicate bangles.

Never had I seen such craftsmanship. Each filigreed circlet was adorned in facets that fractured light into myriad sparks. Yet the intricate work was smooth to the touch, admitting no sharp edges. With my palms trayed like a devotee offering flowers, I returned the delicate ornaments.

Eventually the blaze was put out. Had it been an hour, or longer? Daylight had turned smoky grey while we moved furniture and bundles. Men slumped against the outer wall while the thin youth who'd crashed into me doled out water.

A piece of twine looped over one of the boy's protruding shoulder blades and wound around his waist. I glanced at it, puzzled. What did it remind me of? Then I remembered—the prayer thread that Diana donned after morning ablutions. Curious, I thought—Persians and Hindus had similar religious symbols.

The lad dipped into an earthen pot and offered me the metal tumbler. Sweat beaded on his skin, but the growth on his upper lip and chest showed he was no child. My singed fingers tingled as I unwound the cloth over my face.

He pulled back in surprise, then offered his water again. I drank. As the cool liquid trickled down my chin and throat, I chuckled in relief. Others grinned. Some spoke of when and how they'd noticed the blaze.

I asked an old man slumped beside me, "The fire. Has it happened before?"

He wobbled his head, considering this. "Yes, but not so bad. Sparks fly from the forge—heating the metal, to pull the wire . . ." He launched into complex terms I did not understand.

Some were washing faces and hands by the well. I followed suit, earning smiles and puzzled looks. Someone passed me a wedge of lemon to use in lieu of soap.

Tansen arrived with women carrying bowls of food. In the forecourt, workers sat cross-legged in parallel rows. Tansen beckoned me, saying, "Agnihotri. He was known to Satya."

As a woman laid metal plates before us, I asked, "Was Satya a craftsman?"

Tansen nodded. "From an early age. No one could match him at working gold thread. A genius." He went on in a tone of pride, naming Satya's talents.

Abruptly, the youth who'd brought water cried, "He chose working with silver! He *stole* our gold! And you would have made him *karta*?"

A piece of the puzzle clicked into place. Satya had stolen some of the precious element that was their lifeblood. As betrayals go, it took the cake. Was this why the clan threw him out?

The boy's outrage drew stares. Others ducked their gaze. So, some members disliked Satya, others were disturbed by this. It was an opportunity, but a delicate one.

I broke the awkward silence. "What is—*karta*?"

Satya's mother was serving a gruel of dal onto the plates. She blinked as though she'd forgotten who I was. With an impatient motion, she served me, saying, "Hindu joint families are very large. Many children, many generations. The *karta* makes decisions, assigns work."

She gestured down the row with a spoon. "We live together, uncles and their families, brothers and their wives and children. *Mistri* is the *karta*." She did not use her husband's name, but his role. Curious, I thought. Did Hindu women not speak their husband's given name?

The pause had eased some of the disgruntled looks. I counted more than twenty men, all related by blood. How did it feel to stand beside such an army?

"Ah . . . how is the *karta* chosen?" I asked.

Meera continued serving down the row. Since her husband Tansen sat across from me, he answered, "By tradition, it is the oldest son. When he cannot perform his duties, often his own son takes his place."

Primogeniture, I thought, like English peers. A tradition that had no place for illegitimate offspring, oldest or otherwise.

"Satya would have been the new leader?"

No one answered. But in Meera's eye I glimpsed an ache.

Taking charge, she said, "Do you know how our caste came to be? Each caste has its own story. We Daivadnyas are descended from Lord Vishwakarma, the craftsman who made the chariots and weapons of the gods!

"When Portuguese brought ships and guns and people to convert people to their religion, our ancestors left Konkan and spread far and wide. However, we knew each other, so our caste also became like a bank to help pilgrims. People going to Haridwar could not carry cash because of bandits. So, they would carry a special *chitti* from a Daivadnya family. With this they could visit other Daivadnya houses, as honored guests. Over the centuries we gained reputation, made temple ornaments and became goldsmiths."

On previous visits to temples, I'd heard Sanskrit recitations of the scriptures, mythological stories with fantastic feats of magic and battle, intrigue and heroism. Buried in the stories were the origins of castes, their lineage. Devotees weren't just enjoying a tale, they were hearing of their own origins. Perhaps man's search for belonging transcended all cultures.

Turmoil forgotten, my companions discussed plans, tasks still undone. Some were washing their hands by the well, while others returned to the workshop. Absorbing what I'd learned, I scooped up

spiced vegetables with pieces of fried puri and ate. Satya was to head
the family but rejected his birthright by leaving. What wasn't I seeing?
I needed to speak with his mother again.

Sometime later, Tansen expressed his gratitude as I took my leave. I
asked, "May I thank Meera-ji for the food?"

He asked someone to fetch her.

When Satya's mother arrived, I praised her meal and hospitality,
while assessing her carefully. Just then someone called from the floor
above, and Tansen hurried away.

Using the formal form *aap*, I asked, "Meera-ji, have you lied to me?"

She waved off my question as though it were a curious fly. That flick
of the wrist carried a world of meaning: who was I to demand her hon-
esty?

I said, "Satya stole some gold. You should have told me."

She inhaled, then faced me directly. "Why did he need it? What was
he doing?"

"You didn't ask him?"

She shook her head, worry lurking in her eyes.

"He plated silver statues and sold them as gold."

"*Apshagun!*" An ill omen. She covered her mouth. Lowering trembling fingers, she asked, "Sold them? To whom?"

Her eyes were deep wells of terror, quickly hidden like a tarp pulled
over an open pit. I tried to fathom her reaction, but it was gone. Could
she have murdered Satya? I did not think so—but did she know who
had?

* * *

Diana was not pleased to see the state of my clothes. My hands were
already scabbed from my last mishap. At the sight of my reddened forearms, she cut off her rebuke to rush away for ointments.

Disregarding my assurances, she fussed over the bandages, her
voice low. "You were questioning Satya's mother when the place caught
fire?"

The salve numbed my stinging palms. "I smelled smoke. Thought it
was from the kitchen."

She frowned, putting away bottles. "But why *then*? I don't believe in coincidence." She bit her lip. "Could someone see you with her?"

"Anyone. We were standing below the windows."

She shook her head, misgivings writ large on her face.

I said, "Would someone set a fire to stop us speaking? Bit far-fetched, don't you think? Cutting off one's foot to cure a blister."

Her eyes blazed. "Not if you got too close! It was a perfect diversion. You're playing with fire!"

I held up my bandaged arms and attempted a grin. Did one of the cousins fear Meera might spill the beans? Perhaps their "little diversion" had got out of control.

Then Diana said, "Keep going, Jim. You will get to the bottom of this."

CHAPTER 36

SONA

Diana's ointment relieved my burns as she narrated the day's events at court. Since I'd set the Gurkhas to watching Adi's staff, Diana sent me to Adi with his meal. I was glad to go, for I could not stop thinking of neat, fastidious Adi in that dank place.

When I arrived, a barber was shaving Adi as he perched on a stool. In lockup one could scarcely see sunlight, so any shave was a luxury. The books I'd brought lay beside Adi's bed. Two stacks, almost equal in height. I said, "Hullo? Brought you some dinner."

Adi looked away. I added, "Diana and your mother send their love."

He mumbled, "Di usually brings meals."

That did not surprise me. The barber stepped back, smiling. I handed him a coin as Adi mopped his face, apparently fascinated by the tiled floor.

After the barber gathered up his things, salaamed, and departed, we discussed the medical examiner's testimony, which seemed to neither help nor harm Adi. Then I took out Satya's mysterious little key and frowned at it. "This damn thing is the key to everything. If I knew what it unlocks, we'd know why Satya was doing all this."

On a whim I went to the barred door and tried the key, fumbling because of my bandages. The guard standing just outside watched, incredulous. The key was far too small. Clicking my tongue, I tucked it away.

Adi looked up with an awkward expression. I met his gaze and shrugged.

He gave a slow nod, receiving my message, *Being here is nothing to be ashamed of.*

I went on. "I've been thinking about Satya's dying words. Was there a pause, after he said 'sona'?"

Adi dropped the cloth and gasped. "A century ago, you'd be burned at the stake for a witch. *Yes.* How did you know? Satya struggled, frothing. It was awful, Jim. His mouth full of blood."

A rhythmic thump sounded in the corridor beyond, ending in a clank. Somewhere outside, a peanut vendor called, *"Chana-sing, chana-sing!"* On Caskine Road, the day's market was closing. We were in Bombay and yet not, for the jail was a world unto its own.

In Adi's murky cell I found the quiet that eluded me elsewhere. In Framji Mansion, Burjor's anxiety and grief filled every chamber. Mrs. Framji constantly hushed the little ones, until the atmosphere was as thick as a funeral held underwater. Even in my "little slum hideaway," as Diana called the Dockyard Road warehouse, I had the urge to hurry, to be out *doing* things, as though any moment spent thinking was a shocking disservice to Adi.

Here, naphthalene's odor overlaid the stench from the corner commode—covered of course, with what Adi had at hand, a towel. Despite that, here, at last, I could think.

I leaned my forearms on my knees, working through the snippets I'd collected. "If you were taking your last breath, and you knew it—as Satya surely did—what would you think of? Would you waste that moment on worldly things? Doubt it. I wouldn't."

Adi scrunched his face. "What then?"

"You'd name some important task—'Take care of Diana,' or 'Look after Mother,' yes? So why didn't Satya do that? Maybe sona doesn't refer to gold, as we imagine."

An elusive discomfort filtered into me, the feeling that I'd missed something blatantly obvious. "When Allie and Diana speak—they use diminutives for their friends. Cornelia is Nelia, while someone called Monali is Mona. Ergo, possibly sona is—"

"Sonali." Adi's eyes were wide. "It's a common name. Satya's lips were moving. He could have been trying to complete the word. But, then he said, 'Don't let them sell it.' That's why I thought it was an object!"

"*Na beych-ney doh* does not imply an object," I reminded him. "More like 'don't let them sell.' What else do you recall? Any little thing could be useful."

He frowned, eyes unfocused. "Nothing I can tell you."

"You're not unobservant," I protested.

His mouth twisted in a rueful smile. "You mean, I'm not a dolt?"

"No, but it's a good act," I chided. "I will find out. If there's something, tell me now."

"Perhaps it's no act!" He gave a mournful laugh. "I wish . . ." Shaking his head he got off his stool but there was nowhere to go. Moving some clothes, I scooted to the end of his bunk so he had somewhere to sit. Instead, he began to pace. Three steps up, three down.

"Adi?"

He stopped at the bars. I asked, "What? What do you wish?"

"Uh, that I . . ." Still that negation, that oscillation of his head. His voice went up a half octave. "That I'd *seen* what was going on!"

"Did you suspect?"

He stared at me. "That Satya forged a vast amount on Papa's note? I didn't even know he had it!" Returning to his stool, he dropped his head into his hands.

I had no words to reassure him, so I patted his shoulder and left, saying, "Back soon."

In earlier days, he'd seemed removed from my immediate investigation. How wrong I was. He'd been rebuking himself.

* * *

When I told Diana that evening, she covered her lips. "A *girl*!" she blurted out. "But he said, 'Don't sell!'"

"Not exactly. And the two phrases may not be related," I said. "Such as, 'Diana. Almost dinnertime.'"

She glanced at the clock and made a face, then slipped a purple dress over her head and turned her back to me, saying, "But those *are* related. 'Diana—dinner.' Directing me toward something."

I began latching a long row of tiny hooks down her back. "True, but when a man's dying, he might want to get something out quickly. If Sona was his girl, say, and in trouble, wouldn't he say, 'Help Sona' or 'Find Sona'? Was he saying, 'Don't let *them* sell,' or 'Don't let Sona sell something'?"

Diana twisted around, lips parted. "Sell what? Sell Sona herself?"

Trust her to instantly get to the heart of it. She brooded while I completed the troublesome row of hooks, then faced me, biting her lip. "Jim, what if we've got everything wrong? What if Satya did this underhand business, not willingly, but under duress? I met him, you know."

"You *what*?" I gaped at her, stumped at this revelation.

"In London. Adi brought him to visit while I was staying at the Channings'. He was a shy, quiet sort. Dark-skinned, receding hair, that awful birthmark."

"Hmm?"

"The butterfly shape on his forehead—oh. You didn't see him. He was awfully self-conscious. Older than other students, so they probably made jokes about it."

I struggled to remember the notes in McIntyre's file, but all I could see was the photograph of Satya on a slab, long lashes nearly reaching his thin cheeks, his Adam's apple prominent over the deep gash that had ended his life. Was there a birthmark? Yes, I recalled a misshapen grey mark on his forehead. It hadn't been prominent.

"Older? How old would you say?"

Diana said, "Probably about your age. Maybe thirty?"

Thirty and unmarried. No wonder his mother had been furious.

Diana was saying, "If he had a sweetheart or lover, who would know?"

"Not his parents," I replied. "They're extremely traditional. He'd never tell them."

"He said nothing to Adi, or the staff?"

"An illicit affair? Doubt he'd speak of it. I pushed Adi's employees quite hard. If they knew, it would have leaked out."

Diana pressed her thumb to her lip. "He'd need someone to cover for him. A relative or servant?"

"And put himself in their power? Not a chance. That's why he lived at the factory, to escape vigilant monitors."

Her voice was wistful. "He had no friends?"

"Only Howard Banner, I suppose. Played cards with him. It's a good bet Satya wouldn't tell an Englishman. But . . . Banner did say Satya had no head for drink. Might have said something in an unguarded moment."

The Gurkhas, Ganju and Gurung, were absent, watching the employees' homes in turns with Bhim, the new groom. Jiji-bai had placed platters of food on the table. Burjor handed our dishes to Mrs. Framji, who served. Neither seemed keen to sup.

Burjor asked, his tone wistful, "Any progress?"

I apprised them of our latest conjecture.

"Then Sona may refer to his wife?" said Mrs. Framji, a hand flying to her chest.

"It's possible he was secretly married. Doesn't appear he mentioned her to anyone." On that desultory note, we dined.

Little Shirin was particularly truculent this evening. She pushed her food around in circles until it dropped off her plate. Pleased with this success, she proceeded to follow it with another piece, and then a series of peas that rolled across the tablecloth.

The rest of us tried to behave as though it were an ordinary day.

Diana bit her lip and frowned so I said, "My dear?"

"Sona. There are two options: she may come from a caste that's higher than Satya's, or she's from a lower caste."

"If she were equal, there would be no objection, is that what you mean?"

"Castes are subdivided into hierarchies or ranked by wealth, property, and assets. There is no 'equal,' Jim. If she's high caste, then Satya's family would balk at first, but they'd be secretly pleased. What caste did Satya belong to?"

I thought back to my first conversation with his mother. She'd been proud, defiant. "Brahmin, I believe, a sect from the Konkan, near Goa."

Diana knotted her forehead. "So that's not it, then. Sona would be from a lower caste. That would send them into a tizzy. No wonder Satya left the house!"

I lowered my fork. "Wait. You're saying they'd be furious."

"Well, if she married down, her family would be outraged. There's your motive for murder; but if she's lower caste, then Satya's family would . . . forbid it."

Forbid Satya. Like me, I thought, remembering Burjor's initial refusal to let me court Diana. I skewered a chunk of sweet potato and ate.

What did it all matter—caste and class. Just more ways to let some feel superior, so they could exclude the rest of us poor bastards.

"Oh dear!" Diana's hand shot out, but it was too late. Shirin's chubby arms flew apart, her glass toppled. Yellow sherbet streaked over the white tablecloth.

"Shirin!" cried Mrs. Framji and delivered the gentlest scolding I'd ever heard.

Baby Tehmina promptly drew a large breath and bawled. Shirin glowered at her mother and tossed her fork on the maligned tablecloth.

Nodding apologies, I beat a hasty retreat. I'd face an armed group of grumpy Afghans over a pair of pocket angels with lungs like bellows.

* * *

Since Satya's key was a bust, I focused my energies on the idol we'd found in the mali's hut. Adi said it was made of silver, so as soon as the markets opened that warm October morning, I headed for an address Burjor provided, Jussawalla's store in Byculla. It turned out to be a window-fronted establishment on a busy street. Jussawalla was weathering the heat in a thin cotton shirt that hung over white trousers, his religious thread wound about his waist, like Burjor in his casual at-home clothes.

Tossing his polishing cloth over a shoulder, at first Jussawalla refused to attend me, citing a duty to his customers. When I pointed out that the store was empty, he grudgingly conceded a few minutes.

Gazing around at the artifacts on his shelves, I expressed my admiration, pointed, and asked questions. Gradually he warmed and grew animated as he talked about his craft. Pointing at a row of intricate goblets, he said, "It takes three weeks to make each one. First the base is cast. Then I do the bowl and handle, and join them. Lastly, the etching."

He reached out and hoisted a heavy candelabra, turned it upside down to show it was hollow in the center. "They have to cool before I remove the clay shell. Then the designs are etched. Take this Ganesh for example." He brought down a silver statuette from a shelf.

"The ears, trunk, necklace, arms, fingers—I cast each one, then attach it in place like a puzzle. It's a sequence. Put the ear on first and the trunk will not fit. One wrong move and I lose days of work. The sequence is secret. Took me years to develop."

I stared. It was identical to the one from the mali's hut, except for the sheath of gold.

"Is this what you sold Satya?"

He started, then admitted it, his lips an inverted crescent.

"You told Adi it was ingots. Forty kilos!"

He put up a hand. "I did not say ingots. Satya said a South Indian temple wanted them."

"And you kept that from Adi. How many statues did Satya buy?"

"Ten," said the merchant. "Five hundred rupees each. A good price."

My pulse gave a jump and began to canter. I'd found the craftsman who made Satya's statuettes. There were nine more statues somewhere.

Satya's family were goldsmiths, so he could well have learned gold plating. He'd stolen gold from his kin. But why had Jussawalla been so irate with Adi?

I peered at his broad face. "You spotted your statue someplace, didn't you? Except it wasn't in silver, but gold! Where did you see it?"

"I don't remember where."

So he had found one. I grabbed his shoulder. "I think you do recall. You recognized your work, dressed in gold. You were furious."

Jussawalla twisted, trying to yank free. Shoving at his bitterness, I said, "Did you confront Satya, demand to be cut in? After all, it was your work. Did he mock you?"

Abrupt color flooded his face. "You're accusing *me*?" he bellowed. "Get out!"

"A man's life is at stake! Was the statue in Bombay?"

He locked gazes with me, then nodded a resentful chin.

I released him. "Here, in the city?"

"Yes. Now leave!"

When I gave him my best imitation of McIntyre losing patience, he finally answered, "In Cammattipoora, but I don't know where! It was in a procession!"

So! Jussawalla had visited Bombay's infamous red-light district. It explained his reticence. If I found Satya's customer, I might reach his network and whoever was behind it. Adi did not believe Satya had engineered this mess. I was beginning to believe him.

CHAPTER 37

SATYA'S CODE

Banner seemed unhappy when I was admitted to his parlor. He got up and shook hands reluctantly, as though I were a tax collector making an unannounced call. We spoke of inconsequential matters, then I asked, "You said that Satya couldn't hold his drink. Did he say anything unusual?"

When he hesitated, I said, "Must have been peculiar, since you remember it?"

"Uh, not peculiar exactly," he stammered, "just . . . not what one might expect."

"What did he say?"

"You can't expect me to recall . . . it was just idle talk, really."

"Details matter. Minor things can add up."

He fussed with his immaculate cuffs and lapels, then said, "We'd had some drinks and he said . . . I couldn't swear to this, all right? He said, 'Can a child despise their parent?' Just out of the blue. It threw me, I mean, thing like that, how's a bloke to answer? I said, 'I suppose,' but he wasn't listening."

I leaned closer, elbows on my knees. "Who did he mean?"

"Couldn't tell you. Perhaps his parent—the pater, what? It's always the father, isn't it? I'd been grumbling about mine . . ."

I covered my fist with my palm and pressed my lips to my knuckles.

Can a child despise their parent? It felt significant, but what the devil did it mean?

Banner went on, "After that, he seemed embarrassed, so I let it alone. Bad form to press him, eh?"

"He say anything else?"

"N . . . no, we were swapping stories. Traditions, Hindu culture, up-bringing. Did you know, when he got back from Oxford, his family couldn't touch him? He underwent some sort of ceremony to become pure again. Oh! I remember—before that, he asked whether it was un-natural. To hate a parent. I was in my cups, I'm afraid, not sure what I answered. Probably said, 'Depends upon the parent!' Been so long, I really can't recall."

"Hate. He used that exact word?"

Banner scratched his eyebrow. "Think so."

This put a new cast on things. Did Satya really despise his father? Thinking of Tansen, the quiet man who had so ably marshaled his troops, I could scarcely conceive it. Was it unnatural?—a strange way to put it. As though he felt guilt for his feelings. Yet this too did not satisfy. It left me feeling uneasy, as though I'd seen something from the corner of my eye, which when I turned to look, wasn't there.

I dug out the dratted key and showed it to Banner. "Seen this before?"

He blinked, took it, then handed it back with a grin. "Sorry, old chap. You know, you are the most interesting guest I've had all week."

* * *

Next, I visited Adi and learned that the Bank Manager's alibi had withstood cross examination. It was still light, so I took myself off to Jameson's infirmary. Accustomed to seeing me at all hours, the orderly admitted me without question.

"Is the mali asleep?" I asked.

He jerked his chin at the ward.

The beds contained few patients, just long shapes covered by thin blankets. I sat in the bedside chair beside Bala Mali and slumped.

God, I was tired. The previous day's excitement from battling the Ras-togis' fire had worn off, and I felt worn to a crisp. I leaned my forearms on my thighs and gazed at the wizened figure swaddled in bedclothes.

A machine whirred at the back of the quiet infirmary. The smell of phenol was mixed with medicinal odors, not unpleasant. Memories of my year in hospital flickered past, a year when, like Bala Mali, I'd been barely conscious.

Bala sniffed. Blinking, he rubbed his face. "Sahib?" he said in a thin voice.

"How are you?" I asked, pitching my voice low.

Lifting his thin hand, he turned it over in a hopeless gesture. "Satya is dead," he whispered. "There's no one left."

No one left. No one for whom he had any affection, no one who cared whether he lived or died. My throat tightened. When I covered his cold, bony hand, he made no reply.

Why had I come, I wondered? He'd given me the statuette hidden in his hut. Satya was unlikely to have confided anything of import. But was that all there was? Was this my life, then, to demand, cajole, bribe or threaten? I wanted to rescue Adi, but that made my motive no less selfish, from the mali's view.

"You fed Satya," I said. "He had no one to care for him. You brought him food."

The mali's eyes flickered as I went on. "You saw how hard he worked."

His thin chest rose with a breath. "Night and day. He was skilled. Such an intelligence, but . . . there was no pride in him. A quiet child. A silent youth."

"Did he have, ah, an affection for someone?"

Bala dropped his chin and silence enveloped us. Satya had grown apart from his family, his clan. Was that why he'd lived in self-imposed exile? In his youth, or even earlier, he'd found he was no longer aligned with his family, his lineage. A cog out of place. Trained to fit into the machine, yet somewhere along the way he had outgrown that role. Perhaps when he'd met and loved Sona, it made him a pariah to his kin.

Pity spurted in me for a lad I had never known, because I had been more fortunate. Our circumstances were the opposite of each other: in meeting Diana, I had also found my life's path.

To the mali I said, "You knew him as a child, comforted him. And when he was weary, you brought him *vadas* or *puris*. For that, you have earned thanks."

To my surprise, his face crumpled and shook with silent sobs. Tears slipped down the hollows of his face, but he did not notice. Here was a father, I thought, a father bereft.

Did he know Satya was plating statues at night?

I said, "He hid his work from Adi. Bala, what was he doing in the factory?"

Silence answered.

"Why did he work so hard?" I asked. "What did he want?"

To my surprise, the mali covered his face with his hands. I caught some words, which ended with ". . . promise."

"I also made him a promise," I said. "He was trying desperately to do something. I saw his office, wire baskets, chemicals, forms and molds. I swore I would give him justice, give him peace." I drew a slow breath and waited.

A touch on my forearm. The mali said, "He sent me with messages."

"Where?"

My question disturbed him. Pained, he mumbled and rubbed his forehead, his scrawny hand like a crow's foot. "Cammattipoora."

My heart lurched and kicked into a gallop. The red-light district of Bombay where women were sold for an hour's pleasure? Jussawalla had seen his Ganesh statue there.

In an urgent whisper I asked, "Which house?"

He shook his head. "They will not admit you. There is a way . . . Satya reminded me each time, 'Take two *boondi laddoos*. Don't forget.' I would buy them from the market and offer them at the door."

Boondi? Those sweets were available on most streets. "Who did you ask for?"

He shook his head. "No one. Just gave the *laddoos*, and the message."

"Written?"

"Very short messages. Just few words."

"Could you read them?"

Bala smiled a toothless grin, shaking his head.

"Who received the messages?"

He said, "A girl. And one time"—he squeezed up his face with effort. "Sahib, one time there were no *laddoos* to be had. I bought *jalebi*, but at the door, they turned me away!"

I breathed, my pulse racing. "Only *boondi laddoo* would do. That was the code."

In Cammattipoora I might find Satya's girl, or his coconspirator, the wellspring of this plot. I was so close!

Bala said, "One time he sent me to buy four *laddoos*. In a box. He was very clear about that. In a box. But he didn't send me to Cammattipoora!"

I stiffened. "No?"

"Sahib, he was wearing his best kurta. He went himself, carrying the box!"

There were two codes. Two *laddoos* for a message; four, to visit in person.

"What color was the box?"

"Red and white, sahib. The sweets have a thin gold covering."

Gold leaf on the sweets. Gold. Sona. That was the "open sesame" to this lair.

"Where would you present those *laddoos*?" I asked. My voice sounded rough as I tamped down my excitement. If a door was cracked open, I must push my way in and discover Satya's secret.

Bala named a street. "After the lamppost, it is the ninth door, sahib."

"From which side? Falkland Road, or Byculla?"

He repeated the directions, left after the garbage pile, right at the cowshed.

Before I left, I told Bala, "Do not fear, you will be cared for. Adi sahib must give up the factory and the garden, but you will be safe. I will find you a suitable place."

Folding his hands, he assured me that he was strong and knew about plants. All he wanted, he said, was the shade of a few trees, and one roti a day. He would work for it, he said, and not be a burden. I swallowed hard and told him to eat and get stronger. Then, with a clumsy pat on his shoulder, I prepared to visit the brothel.

As I exited the infirmary, two native constables approached, huffing.

"Stop!" a harsh voice cried. "Agnihotri, you're under arrest!"

CHAPTER 38

A PLAN GOES AWRY

There's something you're not telling me," said Chief Superintendent McIntyre.

I shrugged. It was always difficult to lie to him.

"Humph." He gave me a long stare. As light faded from the window, I'd spent an hour and a half describing my investigation. As promised, I'd omitted Padamji's problems at the Bombay mint and any mention of Vishal's brother, the mint worker.

McIntyre took out his pipe and tapped the bowl over his knuckles. In the patient tone of one starting over at the beginning, he said, "You visited a slew of banks. Every major banking house in the city, actually. You were at the mint. Won't say why . . ."

"The key—"

"So you say," he growled. "Two days ago a man was run over by a tram, did you know? Worked at the mint. The foundry, I'm told."

My pulse jumped. *He knows. He knows!* I kept my face immobile. Tap, tap went the pipe, slapping against his palm. I let him play it out, knowing there was no hiding from it. Blast. I had to protect Padamji.

He said, "Fellow hadn't shown up for work in days. Know anything about that?"

When I made no reply, he reached over and grabbed my hand.

Before I could react, he turned it over. My scrapes were healing, but a few were still painful. My fingertips were singed pink, skin peeling.

He snapped, "You're not invisible, you know, when you traipse round like a native. Fellow your height! Grey eyes, long black hair. Yes, yes, even wearing a turban. And you limp."

He turned his head and beckoned someone behind me. An English officer entered. I glanced up and felt as though he'd dumped a bucket of cold water over me. It was the officer from the tramway accident.

I met his gaze with a look of inquiry but did not try to shake hands. It wouldn't do. I was dressed as an Indian.

McIntyre was saying, "Is this him?"

The inspector frowned. Had I been dressed in Western clothing he would have been named, even introduced. British administrators were mighty democratic like that; a bloke in pipes might be dark as coal, but a neat well-cut suit earned him a hearing.

The Englishman seemed taken aback by my frank gaze.

"Yes," I said gently. "I am Anglo-Indian. Eurasian, if you like." I gave him half a smile.

McIntyre's brogue thickened as he said, "Fellow at the tramway, with blood on his hands—that him? Stand up, Agnihotri," His face was ruddier than the weather allowed; he cleared his throat as I climbed to my feet.

While I waited at parade rest, McIntyre said, "Medical discharge with military honors. Medal and all. A bloody war hero." Meaning me, meaning my history. Meaning Karachi.

I swallowed and cast my gaze to the floor.

The officer fumbled. "Yes, sir . . . but I don't think . . ."

"All right. That will be all," said McIntyre.

When we were alone again, he dropped his pipe on his desk. "What are you doing, Jim?"

"Sir?"

"How will it help if you're in the clink too? What will old Framji do then, hmm? Goddamn it boy, why can't you leave things alone?"

If I told him about following the mint worker, I'd have to break my word to Padamji. Knowing McIntyre's absolute loyalty to the Crown, asking him to turn Nelson's eye was pointless. Leave it alone? His words stung like nettles scraping my skin.

Across the vast expanse of his blotter I asked, "Is it so important to wrap up Rastogi's murder quickly? Anyone will do, as long as you've got someone for it? You know Adi's innocent."

He looked at me with something akin to pity. "So. Those blinders are coming off."

I had no reply.

"The tram. Did you kill the chap from the foundry?"

I jerked. "What? No!"

He grunted and peered again at his pipe. When he spoke, his voice was heavy with regret. "You're not telling me something. I can smell it." He raised his head toward the door and barked, "Havildar! Arrest this man."

"No," I said, with splayed hands. "Not today. Arrest me tomorrow. There's something I need to do today."

I turned to brush past the burly guard bringing McIntyre's tea. With a strangled shout, the havildar saved his wobbling tray.

"Stop him!" barked McIntyre.

Three blokes blocked my way. Blast. I turned and glared at McIntyre.

"Lock him up," said the superintendent, adding to me, "Do you good to cool your heels a bit. Do that knee some good too." He beckoned to his inspector and growled instructions while someone shoved me from behind.

They led me through the maze and into a bank of cells. I cursed softly, until I recognized the place.

"Jim!" Adi cried, leaping to his feet.

I grinned. "Hullo."

The havildar pulled open the door of the cell beside Adi. I entered and thanked him formally. He mumbled something about mealtimes, then I asked whether Major Smith had left for the day. He had.

Sitting on the metal plank that passed for a bed, I met Adi's stunned gaze.

"I would have brought your supplies, but I didn't expect to return just yet."

Adi chuckled in surprise. Over the next few hours, lying on the bunk, I brought Adi fully into the picture. Cross-legged on the floor of the adjoining cell, he laid out the prosecution's case, and plied me with questions. More than anything, he seemed hungry for conversation—what did it matter if the jail's electric lights blinked out? I had much to tell.

When the talk wound down, Adi asked, "Jim, what exactly did you do for Jeejeebhoy?"

"Mmm. Adi, some other time, yes?" I yawned, stretching it out. I would not put it past McIntyre to tuck an assistant nearby, scribbling in shorthand to record our conversation.

Adi did not want to say good night. "The baronet's a brilliant man, Jim. Someday I want to build a business like that—not just a factory, but an entire industry. Something I can be proud of, that my staff tell their families and friends about. Something to make Indians stand tall."

"Give it time. If anyone can do it, you can."

From beyond came the clang of a door closing.

"Tell me about the army, Jim."

The lad was lonely. He'd been cooped up for days—was it two weeks already?

I said, "I lived and breathed the army for fifteen years, Adi. Thought I'd seen life bare of fripperies and politeness. Stripped to the unvarnished truth. I've seen men sweat in the flurry of preparation, quick glances before an action, saying without words, 'This is madness! But if you're going in, I will too. I can't be the one to cave.' It's a different world. Feels like a different lifetime."

Adi spoke quietly. "It took . . . courage."

Did McIntyre in fact have a bloke writing down our words? He wouldn't have much luck in the dark. It was strange, speaking into the night like this, knowing Adi was listening, and would understand. It brought a deep sense of peace.

I told him, "During a skirmish, there's sometimes a moment when things get out of hand. Something goes wrong, something we didn't expect. A surge of panic, training forgotten, blokes flee. I learned to tell when it was near, and threw my weight against it, yelling orders, calling out names to avert it. Men who break and run can scarce look themselves in the mirror."

Adi sighed. "You've seen a lot."

"Didn't know anything about civilian life. All I knew of women were bawdy songs and anecdotes told after a trek. And sometimes, with the curry on our mess plates licked clean, I'd sit under a jacaranda tree and hear about some other bloke's romantic adventures. Never someone in our company, 'course, always one company over.

"I'd been chuckling over some lewd rubbish when my commander, Colonel Sutton, overheard. The others he sent to dig latrines. To me he said, 'You're coming with me. Quickly now, *jaldi, jaldi!*' I must have been eighteen perhaps, or nineteen.

"He took me to his quarters and presented me to his wife and daughters. I was so embarrassed, I didn't know how to greet them! Then in his study I got a tongue-lashing that made me feel like a week-old banana peel left out in the sun. 'If you speak of women or to them, you speak with respect or I'll have your hide for a pillowcase,' he said.

"Before dismissing me, he handed me a book. Ordered me to read and return the next week to discuss it. You could have knocked me down with a puff!"

"What was the book?"

"*Oliver Twist.* He asked what I thought of poor Nancy."

A long pause. Adi asked, "You've seen . . . death?"

"Mmm. Odd, now, remembering it. I read that book just before our ambush. I turned in Dickens after drill and went out on a sortie. Then we took fire. Just a few shots, really. Came from a nearby thicket. We scurried, took cover, but one of the lads was cut down. I knew the bloke. Shot in the gut."

Adi said nothing, so I went on. "What could I do? Put an arm around him. He was weeping. From pain? Shock? Fear? I gripped his hand, spoke to him the way Father Thomas talked, gently, with certainty. The bloke watched me for the half hour it took him to die. Chaps started to call me 'Padre' after that, yet I had no vocation for it. Books, now—reading was my vocation. In books I was not a mixed-blood urchin with horseshit in my hair, but an explorer, a conqueror, or a gentleman."

Adi chuckled. "First book I loved was *Robinson Crusoe.* And then *The Count of Monte Cristo.* Snuck it into my room at night. Did you read a lot?"

"Whenever I could lay my hands on a book. Most afternoons, while furloughed in Simla, or Lucknow. Each day was much like the last. Bugle calls at the same time, ate meals, boxed, drilled—loading and unloading the guns. Carried supplies, set watches, slept. It was a blessed change when some message had to be delivered, or volunteers needed to fetch the mail. Got my pick of the horses then. Usually made good time."

"No fun, no parties at all?"

I thought about those years. "Oh, we sang aplenty. But most places we had no female company. Few single women, mostly officers' wives who'd followed from England. They organized card games and dances, but a fellow without prospects isn't invited. Instead, I plowed through Shakespeare with the aid of a tattered Oxford dictionary. The women in those pages! Juliet, just fourteen, running away for love. Wise Portia, ill-fated Desdemona!"

Adi chuckled at my pronunciations.

In those days I'd thought of a wife as a delicate ornament, a prize to be won and set up in costly finery. I'd considered them fragile. How wrong I was. Diana had saved my life several times. Would she know where I was? God, I hadn't sent any word to her. She'd be ruddy furious.

* * *

In the morning, a guard brought me a small metal tumbler of tea and a rusk that would have left a sparrow hungry.

"Mmm! Such posh fare! They spoil us here, don't they," I said, sipping the steaming liquid while holding the glass on end, a thumb on the rim, my fingertips on the bottom.

"Oh, it's the Ritz," called Adi. "Best chai on the western ghats. On the continent!"

I spotted a familiar set of shoulders at the end of the corridor and hailed him. "Smith! Dammit, man! Major Stephen Smith!"

He spun around. "Bloody hell, Jim? You sent the jailor to get me?" He strode over and peered as though I'd done a magic trick, and not a particularly nice one. "What the devil you doing in there?"

I joined him at the bars. "It's a mistake. Mac sent me to cool my heels. I need to get out, Stephen."

His mouth opened and closed.

I could have wept for impatience. Somewhere in Cammattipoora,

Sona was waiting to meet her sweetheart. But Satya wouldn't come, would he?

Voice rough, I said, "It's me, Smith. I'll explain everything. Sign me out, now!"

"Ah—" He seemed flustered.

I groaned and used my last chip. "You said you owe me."

His pupils dark, he gaped at me. I'd saved his life in Karachi; I was demanding repayment. I grimaced in apology, hoping he'd understand I had no recourse. If there was any other path, I'd take it.

"Right," he said and turned on his heel, leaving me with a sour taste in my mouth. Yes, I was a heel. And no, I had no alternative.

Sometime later, the guard keyed my cell, saying in Hindustani, "You are released. You can go."

Straightening my rumpled clothes, I snapped a salute to Adi and hurried after my erstwhile captor. Damn and blast. How much time had I lost?

A box of sweetmeats in hand, I entered Cammattipoora. In the heat, the stench of rotting vegetables and urine heralded the garbage pile at the corner of Banpura Lane where tenements bordered the street. Hindus and Muslim families had commingled in most suburbs when I left Bombay two years ago. But last year's riots over cows had separated Muslim *mohallas* from Hindu enclaves.

As the lane narrowed, the bicycle rut in the middle served double duty as a sewer, so that one had to straddle it with each step, or walk aslant on one side, ducking to avoid the overhanging wooden windows. These dismal hovels were crowded with occupants, men of all ages leaning in open doors or squatting to defecate in the street.

In my army years, I had a fair tolerance for bodily odors. Blokes living in close proximity ignore flatulence or turn it into fodder for limericks. Sweat smells no worse than vomit, and one can become inured to the stench. But I was out of practice. Assailed by these, I strode quickly. At the cowshed, the clean smell of manure was a welcome change.

Mouth dry, I counted the ninth door and hurried up the stairs.

I knocked. Nothing. Not a whisper within, no footstep, no murmur. I thumped the door, but it remained uncooperative. The shuttered windows were dumb.

"Gone, sahib," said a voice behind me.

A plump fellow in a dirty black vest brushed his trousers to smooth them.

"Where have they gone, the women?"

He shrugged. "All gone here and there . . ." He spread his hands to either side.

"And who are you?"

"I live there, sahib! Come." He pointed to a structure down the street and invited me, eyebrows wriggling. I quizzed him for a few minutes, then turned my attention to the neighbors.

When I approached, two of them got to their feet and advanced, eyes narrow in the universal sign of a challenge. Both wore belts. Both bore knives.

I asked about the boarded windows. The pair answered with suspicious looks.

"Who owns the place?"

They did not know or would not say. Yet the furtive glances that passed between them spoke another tale. I tried other doors, but the residents stayed mum. It was almost . . . as though they feared someone. Someone who might be watching, even now.

CHAPTER 39

JAMESON'S QUEST

I'd reached a dead end. I had little chance of finding Sona without questioning every woman in the Cammattipoora *kothas*. Then again, was Sona a private name for a favorite girl, or her given name? Did these women remember their names, or shed them when their families discarded them? Were they bitter or reconciled to their fate? Each likely hid a tragic tale, I thought. Eroded by the years, did they take new, exciting names to render them desirable? The name Sona—gold—in this light, it seemed a dismal means to gain value.

At Framji Mansion, Diana cried, "Jim! Where have you been?"

Her cry brought the rest of the family. I'd greeted them with a brief explanation, when five-year-old Shirin glowered at me.

Gosh, did I look that bad? Brushing a hand through my hair, I asked, "Is something wrong, *rajkumari*?"

The princess pouted and said, *"Tu maneh malyo bhi nai!"* You didn't even greet me.

I crouched before her in abject remorse. "Oh, princess! Forgive me. Will you not say hello?"

She softened, then reached out. "Hello."

Her tiny hands felt cool against my skin, still raw from the blaze at Satya's home. Little arms went around my neck and squeezed as she said, sotto voce, "You must take a bath soon!"

Burjor bellowed a laugh, while Diana doubled over, shaking.

Before I could dash upstairs, Mrs. Framji called, "*Beta,* wait."

She took in my rumpled state and asked, "You did not come home for dinner. Where were you last night?" It was the first time she'd called me to account.

"Ah . . ." I glanced at Burjor, and thought, what the heck, his son's in jail too.

I shrugged. "In the nick. Next door to Adi."

She drew back, astonished. Burjor's mouth opened, then he chortled. "Got yourself locked up to speak with Adi? Brilliant!"

Much as I enjoyed this interpretation, I couldn't have him gaze at me with such delight, not for an untruth. "N-no. I couldn't tell McIntyre much, so he tossed me in the clink. But yes, Adi and I did speak at length."

Diana asked, "Any leads?"

"Satya used to visit a house in Cammattipoora."

Diana made an O with her lips. "Is Satya's sweetheart a *nautch* girl, a dancer? It would explain why he was ashamed."

He had more cause than that, I thought, if Sona was in a *kotha.* "Sona may be on the verge of being sold—possibly to someone in another city. Satya must have been desperate. The poor sod was trying to buy his girl's freedom."

Diana's eyes clouded. "Oh, *Khodai!* Now that he's dead . . . Jim, we've got to help her. It's what Adi would do. Satya was his friend!"

"Easier said, my dear," I grumbled, dropping into a chair. "The place is rough and self-contained. How do we find her without checking every house?"

"Every house?" A curious look crept over Diana's face as she tilted her head. Her eyes narrowed, then dimples deepened in her cheeks. "What if there *is* a way to search every house?"

I glanced over in surprise. "As a gas meter man? Would take too long . . ."

"Not that way." Her gurgling laugh spilled over and found a place inside me. "Go see Jameson, will you? I've got an idea."

* * *

Dr. Patrick Jameson welcomed me with a wave of his hand. "Sit, sit!" and then finished giving instructions to a pair of orderlies.

Setting his stethoscope on his desk, he pulled out a bottle and two small glasses. "Drink," he said, handing it to me. "You look like you need it."

I pawed at my hair, remembered that I'd spent the night in the clink and barely washed my face and hands at Framji Mansion. Once Diana explained her proposal, I could not wait to put it into motion.

"Need your help," I said, and downed the fiery liquid.

"Certainly, my boy! What can I do for you?"

I blinked, trying to clear my head. His brandy was potent stuff.

"Help me get into a brothel."

I should have waited. Jameson had raised his glass to his lips and now he choked and coughed violently. It was some time before I could explain Diana's plan.

"And she'll come too?" he said, rubbing his eyebrow. He poured some water and sipped it, then cleared his throat. "To the—red-light district. Miss Framji. In the . . ." He shook his head as though questioning my sanity, but it was Diana's idea and she'd have a conniption if I excluded her.

I used her trump card. "Half a million died from cholera in 1891."

That carried the round. It took longer to convince him to act immediately. Many phone calls later, he persuaded the necessary municipal authorities and called in favors at the Public Health Department. I returned to tell Diana that her faith in him was vindicated, and to prepare for our expedition.

* * *

It was late morning by the time we'd marshaled the necessary troops. Diana wore a neat grey sari, wrapped modestly and tucked in at the waist. A white triangle over her head was vaguely reminiscent of army nurses I'd seen in Poona. Then it came to me. Of course!—Diana had visited the Florence Nightingale school in London. She'd imitated their uniform, albeit in a modified form for the tropics.

Our plan was simple. Jameson would conduct the usual "health checks"—weeks early, this time. He'd collected a motley group of orderlies to batten down the inmates and measure temperatures. Jameson had raided every hospital ward to equip each of us with a stoppered vial of alcohol and a thermometer. Between "patients" we were to clean the thermometers by inserting them into these vials. Once fouled, I only hoped that our public health conscripts would not imbibe the potent stuff!

Face grave, Diana asked Jameson, "Are we looking for cholera, or typhoid?"

He blushed for the umpteenth time. "And ah, other, ailments."

"Diseases of the flesh trade?" Diana inquired, which set him off into a paroxysm of coughing. She went on, "Originally, *nautch* girls were dancers and singers, you know. The ban on public performances forced them into *kothas* to make a living. The result of Victorian morality!"

"Are you quite certain you wish to—" He motioned to the street where he'd marshaled orderlies at every door.

"Quite. Wouldn't dream of letting Jim in there without me." She smiled. "His reputation, you see. Mine's shot already, but I shall do my best by his."

Leaving us gents to absorb this convoluted logic, she trotted up the steps and knocked, setting our plan into motion. When the door opened, she made her announcement. "Health department check!"

It caused a tumult. A wave of customers exited in all manner of dress and undress, brushing past in an ignoble hurry. Jameson had mustered twenty men from nearby hospitals, but they weren't nearly enough to stem the tide. A dozen got away in the very first rush. These were not our quarry, so a troop of havildars securing the street, we stepped through an archway.

In the courtyard, a half dozen women sat around a pile of blooms, tying them into strings. Some in small *choli* blouses or *dupattas* flung over bare chests sat up with startled questions. Nose rings and hair ornaments. Multicolored skirts crowded scalloped archways in walls so faded one could not tell what color they had once been. Heavily garlanded frames, in which buxom goddesses held petals and weapons. The main chamber had the air of a durbar hall gone to seed.

"Yes, I mean everyone," Diana said to a large protesting woman in an orange kaftan. "What is your name?"

Now I saw the virtue of heading the expedition with a female vanguard. Diana wrote down the woman's name, drew the attention of an orderly to check for fever and went on to the next, a youngish creature, no more than twelve.

"Where is Sona? Is she around today?" Diana asked casually as she cleaned off the thermometer.

I paused to hear the girl's puzzled answer, then went on to the next room.

Here, an irate, thick-waisted madam was arguing with Jameson, who had run out of Hindustani and was exhorting her in English.

After assisting him as translator, I continued to an inner chamber piled with pillows and bolsters in a riot of color. At night, lanterns might have cast a mysterious glow, but now the place had all the allure of laundry ravaged by tipsy monkeys.

A shriek stopped me in my tracks. Swearing bitterly, a young fellow dashed past me in a state of undress, while a pair of young things snatched up their clothing and berated me.

"Health department," I repeated, brandishing my thermometer. Loud protests ensued.

When they perceived the instrument was to be placed under their armpits, they quieted. Inventing quickly, I said, "Sona wanted medicine for a wart. Do you know her?"

They did not, but showed their elbows and knees, complaining of boils, calluses, and an ingrown toenail. Sending them back to Jameson, I made the notations required and continued through the house.

As I emerged through a gaudy curtained doorway, Diana said, "Have you checked the cupboards?"

"Hmm?"

She floated past and pulled open the largest almirah. Crowded together inside were two little boys, barely six years old. Shrugging at my dismay, she said, "Check cabinet drawers and almirahs—we don't want babies to suffocate!" She crouched to help the boys out, saying in Hindustani, "Hello, and who are you?"

Giggling happily, they gave their names. After writing these down, she sent the lads downstairs to their mothers.

Since our health department conscripts did not know the raid was a subterfuge, they proceeded at the usual plodding pace, which served me well. I went through, asking my question, "Have you seen Sona?" but it brought forth only shrugs.

The next building was a *chawl* where rooms led off the front-facing balconies. Alerted by the hubbub, the occupants peered downward, murmuring.

The tenement had an inner courtyard. Stepping through the main archway, I glanced up at a cluster of girls in brightly colored clothing, yellow and orange skirts twinkling with tiny mirrors. A man at the entrance gave a wordless shout that thrust them out of sight. There were women in the courtyard too, sweeping, tending a meager garden and hanging clothes on a line. Faces inscrutable, they watched as I shooed in the health department conscripts.

In the courtyard a woman sat cross-legged on the floor. She rose, scowling, her hair in an untidy bun. Her round face must once have been handsome, but now bore an expression of distaste.

Her lips oranged by betel leaf, she demanded, "What do you want?" and spat at my feet.

I'd seldom seen a more disgusting exhibition. Yet here I might find the elusive Sona, so I folded my hands in greeting. *"Pranam."*

Her eyebrows shot up at this politeness. Squeezing her eyes she asked, *"Angrez ho?"* Are you an Englishman?

I chuckled in reply. This puzzled her even more.

"Health department," I said, showing Jameson's document.

She glowered and stalked off, so I hailed the people at windows and balconies. "Come down. The health department is here!"

Women turned to each other in consternation. Were they captives? I saw no sign of chains but that did not mean they were here by choice. Some pressed their foreheads to balcony grilles, faces hidden. It reminded me of a squad of soldiers, waiting out the hottest part of the day, attempting to sleep. Ah, I thought, this market functioned at night, we had arrived during their afternoon nap.

The madam returned to puncturing blooms for her garland as the hospital folk took down clotheslines to set up their table. This caused the madam of the *kotha* to holler at them, "My clothes! *Hai hai!*" as she was beating her palms against her head.

Once the place was secure, I climbed the stairs with an orderly and began the usual drill, sending the complicated cases out to Jameson, who'd set up shop in the street. The afternoon wore on. As we flung open windows in the small, unaired rooms, I began to fear our efforts were misguided. Were we too late? Was Sona already on her way to some other house of ill repute?

Diana proceeded to the next chamber, and stooped before a small door. It seemed to lead to a small, windowless cubby. Stooping, she called, "It's all right, come out."

A girl, about twelve years old, came crouching through the opening. I hunkered down and asked in Hindustani, "What's your name?"

Her kohled eyes were enormous in a pointed face. "Sona."

Cold shock ran through me. My God, Satya wasn't trying to save his wife or lover, but his child! Skin tingling, I said, "Did you say Sona? That's your name?"

She nodded with a grave expression, so I added, "We are friends of Satya."

Her gaze flashed to me, then her face crumpled.

Casting a look of rebuke at me, Diana comforted her. "We've been looking for you, Sona. Hush, child."

As I retreated to negotiate her release from the madam, my feet faltered, for Sona looked as bereft as my little sister Chutki, who had given her life for me two years ago.

CHAPTER 40

ANGRY WOMEN

In the carriage, Sona peeked often at Diana, her worried eyes searching Diana's oval face. She was silent all the way to Malabar Hill, while Diana and I spoke English.

Diana said, "Poor little mite. Jim, she reminds me of little Chutki!"

We had negotiated a modest sum to secure Sona's release. Since I didn't carry enough, Jameson supplemented my funds. The madam of the *kotha* claimed Sona had no blood relatives. She did not mention the child's father, although Sona had recognized Satya's name. Now, eyes round with enchantment, Sona gazed at the palm trees speeding by.

With a sideways glance to check that Sona did not understand us, Diana said, "Wonder why that madam let the child go so easily. She hardly bargained at all."

I shrugged. "Once she admitted the child wasn't related to her, she could hardly demand more. All those uniforms, Jameson glowering at her. Probably thought I was an Englishman."

"But . . . who was Sona's mother? She said the woman died, but she didn't give us her name!"

I shrugged. "Perhaps she didn't know. The child had recently come to that house. An orphan, another mouth to feed. The madam said she was stubborn—that could mean anything—that's why she locked her in the closet."

"Satya used to visit her with sweets. His death was in every news-paper. Is that why Sona was sent to another *kotha*? There are so many unanswered questions!"

"Doesn't explain why the place was abandoned."

Diana had come with the intention to recover Sona. Now she wor-ried about who might raise the child, asking could *we* foster her? This was news—I'd only hoped Sona could reveal Satya's secrets. Diana's interest in her was quite different. She'd expected a woman, abandoned much as my mother had been. It was sobering to consider which of us had the nobler motive.

* * *

Around five that evening, we rattled through the gates of Framji Man-sion.

Sona asked in a thin voice, "What is this place?"

Diana assured her that she would be safe, and could even learn to read if she wanted. "Would you like that?" Diana asked.

"I want to work," the youngster said in a plaintive tone. "I can sew designs on clothes and make chai." They spoke of household chores as we climbed from the carriage, Diana carrying the child's box.

Gazing up at the sweep of stairs leading to Framji Mansion, Sona said, "I asked Satya-ji to take me from that place. So many times I begged him."

Diana's glance caught mine, then I asked, "Satya? You knew him?"

Her dark gaze darted around. "My papa. Is he here?"

How did one tell the child? All along I'd been certain that solving the riddle of Satya's last words would unveil his killer. But here was the answer, a girl with an untidy braid, face smeared with soot, who hesitated to set foot on the white marble steps of Framji Mansion. How could I say that her father was dead?

Fortunately, I didn't need to. Giving me a meaningful look, Diana touched the child's shoulder and said, "Shall we see the garden? There are houses behind there. Let's go by the banana trees."

She pointed out a squirrel, and the two started off toward Jiji-bai's quarters. Since Diana had the matter in hand, I went up to tell Burjor and Mrs. Framji of our success. We had Sona, but would Satya have told the child anything of import?

As I hung my hat on the stand, Burjor barreled toward me. He wore a white suit, gleaming shoes, and the shiny formal *pugree* hat he'd worn to Diana's birthday ball.

Mrs. Framji cried, "Thank heaven you've come! Do you have Shirin?"

I stared. "Baby Shirin?"

Mrs. Framji gave a keening wail and staggered. Burjor helped her into a chair.

I searched his jowly face. "Something's happened?"

His voice crusty as a *brun-pav,* he said, "I was on my way to meet Adi's lawyers. Mama stopped me just in time. Shirin was outside playing, but . . . now she's not there!"

Mrs. Framji pointed to young Fali and baby Tehmina sitting on a couch. "The children were climbing trees by the servants' quarters. But when I called them at teatime, no one knew where she'd gone. We searched the garden, rooms, godowns. Where could she go?"

Burjor mopped his forehead. "The well is closed with a metal grille. Shirin could not have pushed off the cover." He glanced around. "Diana's not with you?"

"We found Sona, Satya's daughter," I said, and quickly described our progress. I had the sinking sensation of having gone down a blind alley while a crisis loomed at home. When I assigned the Gurkha guards to watch Adi's employees, it left Framji Mansion vulnerable.

"What's the matter?" Diana asked, coming up with Jiji-bai and Sona in tow. Hearing of Shirin's disappearance, she covered her mouth, aghast.

Jiji-bai hurried Sona into the kitchen as Diana clutched my arm. "We found Sona, and someone grabbed my sister? On the same day!"

"You think this was planned?" My mind spun at the implication. "How could they even connect little Shirin with us?"

Diana grimaced. "Jim—they knew because . . . oh God, because of me!" She ran to the morning room where teacups had been abandoned and biscuits half consumed.

Reaching into a cabinet, she unwrapped the gold-plated Ganesh. "You asked us to find out where the other statues were, yes? To whom Satya Rastogi sold them? I've been taking this around to our friends and neighbors. I asked their entire households, men, women, children. But Shirin has grown so attached to me, some mornings she wailed when I left. So, I took her with me."

My heart gave a jerk like a mule's kick. "Took her where?" Diana had risked being rebuffed by her neighbors and other families? All to further our investigation.

Color leached from her face. In that pale oval her eyes blazed, black with fury, though she answered calmly enough.

"Our last trip was to Bandera. My aunt who lives there knows everyone around. We showed the Ganesh in her home and asked all her neighbors. We even went to Chuim village and asked the fisherfolk. Shirin was with me . . . she thought it such a lark," she said, her voice breaking.

I felt as though I was falling into a whirlpool. "Each time we get closer, the killer moves. We have Sona, but he's snatched your sister. Why? It makes no sense!"

CHAPTER 41

ON THE SCENT

In one of Conan Doyle's stories, Holmes had said, "The most diffi-cult crime to track is the one which is purposeless." What was the purpose here? No one had been on guard when little Shirin was abducted. I blamed myself for that carelessness. After consulting Burjor, I sent the new boy Bhim to bring back the Gurkha guards, then hurried to the Teen Batti crossroad nearby.

Victorias lined up at the corner, the drivers awaiting fares. Most watched passersby or played idle card games. One by one I asked them who had passed by that afternoon.

Within an hour I learned that three men in a cart had come through the crossing and been seen near Framji Mansion. Last week a Victoria had lost a wheel nearby, but the same cartmen refused the customer. An ekka driver who'd seen the incident warned me to steer clear of the trio.

"One was a bad man, sahib." The *ekkawala* shuddered. "He had the eyes of a cobra. Do not anger him." Head wobbling in dismay, he sa-laamed and took his leave.

The three had been observing Framji Mansion, but what was their game? If Diana was right, someone had noticed the gold idol in her possession. Satya had stolen from his kin, so could the Rastogis be re-sponsible? I paused in the shade of a jambul tree to reflect. Perhaps Satya's clan considered the statuette theirs by right. We had received no

demands, but that meant little. One could hardly admit openly to ab-
ducting a child. If a ransom note was on its way, I could make provision
to trap the messenger.

However, I could not reconcile myself to wait for such a missive. Returning to Framji Mansion, I gave instructions to detain any messenger
who brought a note.

"... have you left your revolver, Jim?" Diana was asking.

I jerked my attention back to the company. "The Webley? Ah ..."

"It's here," she said, lifting a box from the sideboard and setting it
before me. "Why don't you carry it?"

I shook my head. "I'm a lousy shot." At the back of my mind, a memory wafted, like tendrils of smoke. A glance between Satya's parents,
Meera and Tansen. Meera's fear, the knowledge in her eyes, some truth
she did not want to acknowledge.

Diana was persistent. "It's because of ... what you've seen, isn't it?
You know what bullets can do."

"Leave it be, sweet," I said. "There are other ways to solve an argument."

"Fists, and knives." She gave an impatient wave. "I think ... you're
not afraid you'll miss. You're afraid you *won't* miss."

"Put that away safely." I gestured at the golden statue, then laid
Satya's little key beside it. "This too. I'm going to Satya's home." Yanking on the bellpull, I sent Gurung for the carriage.

Ganju brought the coach, riding atop. Giving him directions to
Lohar Chawl, I stepped into it. Diana insisted I take Gurung along, so
he climbed in too. As the carriage rattled along, I warned him we could
be heading into a bit of unpleasantness.

He leaned forward. "Life is dull without you, sahib," he said, cracking his knuckles, then muttered a foul word. "To take a child—cowards!
If only I'd been there."

At the Teen Batti intersection, we passed a posse of carriages hurrying the other way. Alarm spurting, I pulled away from the window.

Police coaches! I could not afford to be tossed in the clink again.
Then I realized Burjor had likely called McIntyre on the phone and
summoned the force himself.

When my carriage halted outside the *sonar kholi,* the gatekeeper was nowhere around, and the building seemed deserted. A tingle of warning ran down my spine. Where would they take little Shirin? It seemed a rash, improbable risk, unlike anything Tansen would undertake.

I called out and shook the wrought-iron gate, but there was no answer, so Gurung gave me a leg up and I clambered over. The chain was padlocked from the inside. I looked around and called again in the mournful silence.

Although sturdy, both Gurung and Ganju had the short stature of most Nepalis. While they worked out how to climb over the gate, I made my way around to the kitchen.

A loud sniff startled me—but not as much as I shocked Satya's mother with my appearance.

"*Heh bhagvan!*" she cried, snatching up a kitchen knife. "Cap-tin sahib?"

"*Pranam.* Where is everyone?"

She slumped on the top stair and shook her head. "Gone. Great shame has come upon us. Satya has ruined us."

"What's happened?"

"My nephew Pandu was betrothed . . . but the girl's family has broken it off. They will not say why . . . we know it is because of Satya. How I prayed for a son, all those years ago. But Satya has brought us nothing but trouble."

"Where have the men gone?"

She looked down at her knife, her voice dull. "It is hopeless, now. Hopeless."

An aged woman peered from an upstairs window, her white hair braided over a shoulder. She called down to Meera, who answered in the vernacular. The joint family took care of both children and the aged, I thought. No disabled or troubled individual was abandoned. Yet all must bend to the will of the *karta*. What did that do to their feeling of self, their independence?

Even in the army, where I'd been chained to routine through law, tradition and military discipline, I'd had some say over my time, and my interests. Here, each decision was made by "elders." A man was bound to a craft; his wife chosen for him. Each interaction with others was ruled by their status, every purchase controlled by the head of the family. It must stifle the very soul. No wonder Satya had rebelled.

I said, "Meera-ji, I need your help. Where is your kin?"

Dabbing with her sari *palloo,* Meera said, "My husband cannot control Pandu. The others are angry too. To refuse the match after gifts were exchanged, it is an insult. A stain. No one will marry into our family."

"Tell me about this boy Pandu."

"He is not the oldest, but he is smart. Customers ask for him. He learned our craft very early. It is in his blood. Designs spin from his hand like music."

When I made no reply, her chin rose. "Why did you come? What's happened?"

I said, "Someone has abducted a child."

"You think we did it?" She pulled back, disbelieving.

I sighed. Did she know about Satya's criminal dealings? To jar her off balance I said, "Because of Sona. Satya . . . cared for her."

She sucked on her teeth. "He did all this for a woman? For love?"

"Satya has a daughter," I said.

When she reared back, her nose pinched, I lost patience. Spreading my arms, I swung around. "Where is everyone?"

"I don't know." The rasp of truth was in her voice.

Was that fear lurking at the back of her eyes? In a moment it was gone. I was reminded of the madam who'd conceded Sona without much of a fight. Remembering her flat, watchful look sent a warning shiver over my skin. She would have liked to sink her little knife into me, I thought. Did we have more than one enemy?

Dusk had settled around the city. Shopkeepers closed their doors and vendors carted away their wares as I returned to Cammattipoora. The coach could not enter its narrow, twisted streets, so I sent it back with the Gurkhas.

At the first intersection, I passed a thickly bearded man. He avoided my glance and spat a stream of red betel into the lane. On a whim, I followed the rude cove. He glanced back and flinched. Hitching up his baggy trousers, he hurried away.

This sudden agitation gave me a spurt of unease. Had he been sitting there, or just exited one of the houses on the street? I strode faster, keeping him in sight.

And then it came to me—I'd seen him just as I left the carriage. Had he followed me? My random movements must have jolted him, especially when suddenly I was behind him.

Pain exploded at the back of my head.

I fell, the world all atilt. Darkness overcame me.

CHAPTER 42

BOUND

Consciousness came slowly, with the drumbeat of a headache. Some part of me observed that the itch on my face had worsened. It grew sharp as I came awake. When I moved to escape the burning, my shoulder stabbed a protest. What the devil? I straightened. Something tightened, sending up a flash of pain. It bit into my wrists.

I could not move my arms.

Damn. I was bound. Sweat trickled down my skin like a track of acid. I clenched my jaw against a moan and turned to see my prison.

It was bright. Blinking against the glare, I realized I lay directly in the sun. Sunlight streamed down, slowly cooking my skin. An oversight? Or a clever torture? If my body was found in such a state, it could be presumed I'd succumbed to the heat. Perhaps Jameson would notice a lump on my head, which now throbbed incessantly.

I studied the small, dirty room with patches on the walls. A thread of ants trailed from a high window. Peeling paint on the green door. I smelled onions, garlic, spice, woodsmoke. A kitchen was nearby.

Groaning, I slid into the shade. There I pulled up my knees, shifted sideways, and took some of my weight on my forehead. My skin stung, but with small movements, I struggled to my knees.

Footsteps tapped outside my chamber, soft padding steps. The door opened.

A boy came into sight. With a startled yelp, he dashed away.

He'd left the door open. Breathing hard, I leaned into the wall and tried to rise. A mistake. My elbow shrieked a warning, and my vision swam. My head throbbed like I'd lost a boxing match. Blast. In a way, I had.

But my feet were not bound, so I would make for the kitchen. Could I get there before the boy brought help?

I remembered entering Cammattipoora, when something had struck me. Bollocks. The gang was bold to assault and cart me away. It had been evening then, so they might have been seen. An angry carpenter was sawing away inside my head. As I inched forward, I heard no temple bells, no rattle of carriages outside the window. In all of bustling Bombay, could there be an enclave without the jingle of ekka bells, the wailing call of street hawkers? My heart skipped a beat, then made up the omission double time. Where the devil was I?

Cammattipoora was between the crowded areas of Grant Road and Byculla. In most of the city I would be able to hear trains, but now that low rumble was missing. From outside the window came a bleat, followed by the flutter of pigeons. Cool air brushed my skin. Was that the hiss of surf breaking over rocks? I was near the sea.

Since Bombay is an island, this did not offer much to pin my location. It only meant that my captors had a convenient way to dispose of me. Ocean currents could drag my body far out. With any luck, in a week or two I'd be found by an unhappy fisherman.

My mouth too dry to salivate, I swallowed and pushed to my feet. The pounding in my head drowned out faraway sounds as I swayed, trying to steady myself, when footsteps clattered to the door and a gang poured in.

Most were scrawny, clothed in a mix of dhotis and shirts, sleeves rolled up, glaring from under grimy turbans. Workingmen, six or seven, perhaps. One barked to another, who replied roughly, with a shrug. *You said he was unconscious?*

I grasped some words, though it was a dialect unlike the Gujarati spoken by the Framjis. It was broader, flatter in sound. Clearing my throat, I asked in my rudimentary Gujarati, *"Kon Cho?"* Who are you?

This caused a stir. The leading two jabbered back and forth, then sent the boy away.

I leaned against the wall, weary and overheated, sweat dripping and no way to swipe it off. I watched the two deputies, for surely they had sent word to their leader. I was awake, therefore the task of polishing me off would not be easy. Both men were armed, the hilts of daggers jutting above their belts, but neither reached for his weapon. On alert, they waited, dark gazes impenetrable.

The door swung open to admit an affluent, round-bellied man. He was dressed like a merchant, a chain of gold glinting around his neck as he said in thickly accented English, "So the mountain must come to Mohammed, it seems!"

I did not return his smile. "Are you a Mohammedan?"

He seemed surprised. "Certainly not. It's just a saying. The boys were to bring you to me, instead I must come to you. But no matter. You are awake."

"*Tameh kon cho?*" I asked again. Who are you?

He blinked. "That's what puzzled them," he said. "You asked so politely. A rough man would demand, *Tu kon che?* But you used a term of respect. An Englishman who speaks thus, what are we to make of you?"

"You know who I am," I said, tiring of his games. "Or you would not bring me here and steal my property."

He gestured to his men and stepped aside. In no time, two chairs were brought into the room. A pair of hoodlums shoved me into one.

The ringleader sat and gave more softly worded commands. A frisson ran down my spine, for this was no unmannered crook. An underling produced a cloth-wrapped parcel and held it out to me. The covering was gingerly peeled back to reveal my pocketbook and my grandfather's watch.

All courtesy now, the leader asked, "As you say, your property. How did you learn about the golden Ganesh?"

I blinked. Was that what this was about? I'd been so worried for Shirin, it had faded from my mind. The idol's weight. I'd written it in my notebook. Had the hoodlums taken that too?

The leader was waiting for my answer. I said, "From a friend. It's part of an investigation."

His eyebrows shot up. "You are police?"

"A private investigator."

He blinked, his face blank. I added, "A detective. Who are you?"

He smiled. "Dee-fective sahib, you may call me—Rai Chand. Which friend?"

I frowned. "Why?"

He rubbed his clean-shaven upper lip, then said, "Come now. To gain something you must give something, yes?"

"What can *you* tell me?"

He chuckled. "You don't ask for food or water? To be freed?"

I heaved a breath. "Water would be nice. And these . . ." I turned slightly, showing my hands.

"Tsk-tsk." He flicked a finger at the door. A boy came forward with a metal glass.

He carried it toward me and carefully put it to my lips. I drank it all, begrudging the drops that trailed down my chin.

"Better?" said my cheerful captor.

I did feel more hopeful. If he'd wanted to do away with me, he had no need for this piece of theater. No, he wanted something from me, therefore I was determined to get every last bit of intelligence from him.

I said, "Thank you, Mr. Chand. Why did you bring me here?"

He sighed. "The English always want the upper hand. You are the one whose hands are bound, and yet you are asking questions? Come now, Agnihotri."

He knew my name. Damn.

His face grew curious. "Anyway, how does an Englishman come by that name? It is, ah, *nakli*? A false name?"

Catching sight of my look, he said, "All right, all right. We both know why you are here."

I held his dark gaze. "Indulge me."

At this, he frowned "You went to Ghanshyam, the goldsmith. With a golden statue, a *murti*, yes?"

I recalled the store I'd visited in Kolaba. Was that a week ago? It seemed longer. If Rai knew about it then he'd had me followed for some time. "The storekeeper," I said. "He put you up to this?"

"Mr. Agnihotri, please. Answer the question."

I frowned, recalling the curious undercurrent at the goldsmith's shop. Squinting at Rai, I asked, "Where is my book?"

He exhaled, his mouth grim, then flicked a finger without looking away. A man placed my notebook on my knee.

This, more than anything, puzzled me. They had my notes, watch, and wallet. Did they intend to return them? For thieves, they were not behaving to form. Unless they believed I had access to more gold statuettes. My fingers were almost numb, so I wiggled against my burning wrists. "D'you mind?"

Rai tilted his head, his mouth drooping. The boy stepped around me like a frightened crab, and worked at my bonds, flinching when I grunted in discomfort. My little book slipped off my knee and fell between my feet. Untied at last, I rubbed my raw wrists with tender, swollen hands the color of cooked lobster.

One of Rai's men loosened his blade. Another was carrying a rod. They were afraid.

Rai watched me with a pained expression. "Why did you weigh the *murti*?"

The statue. When I caught his gaze, the knowledge was in his eyes.

I said, "The Ganesh is fake."

He sat up. "Not fake, Mr. Agnihotri. Pure silver, with a veneer of gold. *Where* did you get it?"

I scoffed. "Hoping to acquire more?"

A series of facts fell into place. He knew it wasn't gold, only plated. Therefore, he knew about Satya. Rai was Satya's accomplice. "You know that no more can be made, because you know the craftsman is dead."

"Wait." Rai showed me his palms. "Detective-ji, think. If I killed him, why would I tell you all this?"

I dragged in a breath. "You were working with Satya. You admit it?"

He leaned forward, his manner intent. "A lucrative business. We sold a lot during festivals, for weddings, and to those giving to temples. This is our *karkhana*, the workshop where we built the wooden base, the housing. We are his craftsmen."

He'd just admitted to selling forgeries but seemed eager to convince me he was quite legitimate. "What was Satya's part?"

"His family is well known for generations. Satya went to the customers, offered them the Ganesh-ji. He was quite willing! He got a nice commission."

"Until he changed his mind. Then you silenced him."

Rai reared back. "Think, Detective sahib! Why would I kill him? His death hurts me. It hurts my business! It brings police, a detective to weigh the gold! Our business is kept safe, *as long as no one weighs the gold.* And why should they? It comes from a reputed *karigar* from a notable goldsmith family. If he wished to leave, I could have bought his silence; we did not need to kill him!"

The truth in his voice was unmistakable. I stared at him in consternation.

Sparrows chittered outside the window as I asked, "So who put an end to your windfall?"

Rai's shoulders relaxed. His men stirred, releasing their tense stance. Two of them dropped to their haunches to watch the conclusion of our pantomime.

Rai's voice was low. "It was not us. You must look elsewhere."

If I didn't believe him, would he set his hoods upon me? I demanded, "And that's why you knocked me out and tied me?"

He spread his hands. "I apologize. I am a businessman. Not a killer."

This was too smooth to be believed. "And now that I know your business, what do you plan?"

"You are after Satya's killer. I also want him caught."

"If it's one of your hoods?" I used the word *goonda*, implying his was a gang of crooks.

He pulled back. "My workmen do not defy me. Without me they would starve."

I gave each of his men a good look, but none struck me as shiftier than the others. Two of them touched their foreheads, perhaps in apology for my rough treatment. What would Rai make of Satya's dying words? Would he know who Sona was? I watched him closely. "This has something to do with you. It must."

He pulled back. "But why?"

"Satya's last words."

Rai sat very still as I said, "He was still alive when he was found."

He leaned forward. "What did he say?"

The moment of truth, I watched for the flicker of awareness, of knowledge. "*Sona. Na beych-ney doh.*" I quoted the elusive fragment.

Rai blinked, frowning. "Gold. Don't sell the gold."

He'd translated it differently, as though it was addressed to *him*.

As he squinted upward, his lips silently repeated the words. Blast it, he didn't know.

"So where is it? Where is Satya's *poonji*?" he demanded.

He thought I had Satya's stash!

When I just gaped at him, he blustered, "If you want the child back, give it to us. It is ours. Satya stole it. Return it, and you will have your child."

He'd seen Shirin with Diana and decided she was my daughter! He saw my face and hurried to add, "She is unharmed! We have no wish to hurt her. Return our property."

Panic stabbed me. "Return it? Don't you understand? I don't have Satya's gold!"

Cocking his head, he drew back. "You have the Ganesh, so you have everything. You don't want your child?"

"Of course I do! But I can't trade what I haven't got!"

He took out and studied a piece of paper, mouthing the words in silence. Frowning, he slowly read them aloud.

"Then you must get gold bars from the mint. At dawn on Thursday they will be taken on English ships. Bring us that gold and you will have the child."

Yesterday was Monday. Thursday was the day after tomorrow. I snapped my jaw shut and swallowed, feeling as though I'd downed a walnut, shell and all. "The transfer of taxes from the Imperial Mint. You want me to steal the Queen's bullion?"

He nodded, mouth grim. The page he held quivered as he read, "Steal the carriage, once it's loaded."

"It will be guarded."

"You were a soldier."

I was to overcome the guards. Commit grand larceny and possibly murder. I felt detached, as though watching myself prepare for the firing squad and admiring my posture.

He continued reading in a measured tone, "You will drive the carriage with the gold bars. You will see a man with a red flag. You will take him up and hand over the reins. He will take you to the rendezvous." Rai Chand labored over the last word, parsing out the syllables.

He met my gaze, then read the words again. "Then you must get gold bars from the mint . . ." The repeated phrases sent a shiver over me. Who was it that spoke thus? It seemed the hallmark of a strange mind, a devious, detailed mind that had already mapped out the route I would take. This plan had been in motion for days, I thought, ever since I'd solved Padamji's problem and confronted his missing worker.

That mint worker who ran when I approached him. A flash of wild panic had filled his eyes—what could make a man so afraid?

Rai Chand's hand had trembled as he held the paper.

I squinted at him. "Who gives you orders?"

He folded the page into his sleeve. "We each answer to someone, mister detective. Now I leave you to think it over."

"Wait! How do I know the child is well?"

His face drooped. "You don't."

He began to turn away, then stopped in the doorway. He made as though to speak but shook his head. Shoulders slumped, he left. The men shuffled out behind him, the last stepping backward. The door clanged. Frustration churning, I heard the lock click.

CHAPTER 43

BREAKING OUT

Despite my exhaustion, that last glimpse of Rai Chand both puzzled and disturbed me. He'd looked like a man with no good choices. I did not for a moment think that would work in my favor.

The Framjis did not know where I was, so Diana would be frantic. How long had I been unconscious? I did not even know what day it was.

After dropping that assignment on me, Rai Chand had not set me free. Why not? Was he planning to dispose of me after all? Perhaps demanding that I steal the Queen's gold was a blind—but why go to the trouble of such theater?

My knee almost buckled when I groaned to my feet. When I bent to pocket my notebook and watch, my head swam. I blinked, feeling weak. The room tilted, then righted itself. I could not recall when last I'd eaten. Ignoring my churning gut, I examined my prison.

For all its peeling paint, the locked door was sturdy. A narrow window hung high in the outer wall, slightly above my head. I ran my fingers over the stones. The mortar between was riddled with holes and cracks. An old stone building, ill kept.

Sweat stung my eyes. I mopped it away with a cuff and blinked, but my sight was still blurred. *The water.* It had been waiting at the door. The group had silently watched me drink.

My gut tightened as awareness dawned. I had less time than I imagined. They had not set me free because they were waiting for me to pass out. I tasted the sour tinge of bile as I understood. Whatever they had in store, it was something I would not accept while conscious.

I dragged the chair to the window and propped my foot on it, then dug out the little blade from the heel of my boot. Just inches long, the rounded wood handle fit snugly in my palm. With this I made a series of gouges in the wall, loosening the already crumbling mortar into footholds.

My injured knee shrieked at the first step onto the seat. The second was easier, since I'd got my hands over the window ledge. The third brought my elbow over the ledge, so I ducked my head through into the fresh air. If the window had been barred, I'd have been stumped. My boot slid around, scraping the wall. Then my shoulders scraped painfully through, barely fitting.

I was on the second floor—too high to drop to the ground. I'd only save the gang the trouble of killing me. To my left was another window, to my right, a water pipe bolted to the stones. All I needed was somewhere to sleep, a place I would not be found. I blinked and tried to clear my vision. Time to choose. Left or right?

By shoving the toe of my boot at the wall, I found purchase and pushed upward. Clinging to the window jamb, my hips squeezed through. I stifled a grunt, but the pain helped. My vision cleared and my mind.

The only safe course was the roof.

* * *

The sun was at the horizon when my bicycle tonga stopped at the gate of Framji Mansion. I'd waited on the roof of Rai Chand's lair, wedged by the chimney, its shadow sheltering me from the heat. Perhaps I'd even slept. Eventually the hubbub below had ceased.

Gurung hauled open the grille, crying, "Captain Sahib has come!" Ganju ran to aid me up the stairs.

"Jim!" Diana yelped. "Are you all right? Your face!"

Burjor came from his office, his bulk fairly bouncing toward us.

Her arm guiding me, Diana asked, "Where on earth have you been?"

I recalled hiding from the searchers with jocular relief. "Rolling in ditches, I'm afraid."

Mrs. Framji arrived with baby Tehmina on her hip, exclaiming, "Did you find Shirin? Oh! What happened to you?"

Someone propelled me to a long chair and pulled out the leg rests so I could recline. Mrs. Framji gave orders. ". . . sunburnt. Smash up two raw potatoes and bring the pulp!"

Little Tehmina appeared near my elbow, peering. Diana poured water from a glass jug whose beaded mesh tinkled softly. "God, Jim, what happened?"

Someone applied a cool cloth to my face. Lightheaded, I closed my eyes, speechless, my arm curved around Tehmina's birdlike frame. I was home.

If only I could have brought Shirin with me, I might have been able to rest.

CHAPTER 44

BREAKING AND ENTERING

There was a strange smell in the darkness. I remembered Rai Chand. I'd hid, slid down a water pipe. The rattle of carts—returning! I'd tripped, tumbled into a ditch. Had they taken me again? My memory cleared, bringing the touch of Diana, the softness of baby Tehmina. My body unclenched. I sniffed my hands but could find no explanation for the powder that crumbled off my skin.

Dried potato pulp! Mrs. Framji's remedy—I brushed the same poultice from my face. The grandfather clock dinged five just then, a doleful resonance that rang through the dark hallways of Framji Mansion like a sentinel. They'd let me sleep in the morning room.

I got up, biting back a groan. My body ached as though I'd gone rounds with an angry heavyweight and lost. To spare Diana the disturbance, I dragged myself into Adi's room. His long oval mirror showed a wild, rumpled bloke, hair standing on end. I had the mottled face of a drunk, but not the rowdy memories to show for it. Though the backs of my hands were a patchwork of peeling skin, the dreadful itching had subsided.

What had I told Diana? I staggered to the washroom to get decent. Paramount in my mind was baby Shirin. But what I had to do was insane. And impossible. Wasn't it?

By daybreak, I had assembled my thoughts, a kaleidoscope of

speculation with monstrous gaps. My mind churning, I cut into a small mountain of poached eggs that Diana plated.

Diana listened without interruption as I described what I intended. To her credit, she flinched twice and clutched her book to her chest, but held back her protests.

"The part I'm most concerned about," I said, "is afterward. What if they open the boxes? If they find Adi's scalpels instead of gold . . ." I trailed off, unable to say it out loud. Shirin's life could be forfeit for such a betrayal.

Diana said, "It's likely they'll open the crates?"

"Any crook worth his salt would check the goods before handing over the prize."

"Hmm." She had a faraway look. "Can you prevent them from touching the gold bars?"

"I could manage that," I said, hardly daring to hope.

"The police will give chase, of course. So you need a distraction." She put aside her book and got up. "The Imperial Mint is quite close to the pound where they've been collecting stray animals. Come, we need Mama and Papa for this."

I protested, "Diana, wait! You can't involve them . . ." but Diana was already swishing down the verandah corridor.

Despite the early hour, both her parents answered Diana's tap on their door. She whisked into their bedchamber, waving me in.

I hesitated at the doorstep, reluctant to invade their intimate space. Burjor beckoned, seated at the edge of a wide four-poster in his pajamas and muslin undershirt. The prayer cap on his head showed that we'd interrupted his morning devotions.

In a booming voice, he said, "Don't stand on ceremony, Captain! Come in!"

Her head wrapped in a pink flowered scarf, Mrs. Framji was speaking with Diana. "Get Shirin back? How?"

Diana explained. "Jim will do it. But we need a diversion, Mama. Remember the dogs they're killing every day, how upset Mrs. Wadia was?" She turned to me. "The Wadias' poodle was snatched by a dogcatcher. Soli's mother was so upset she collapsed. Here's what I propose."

She laid out her plan, concluding, "Papa, you can call Banaji, Byram, and Mr. Mehta. In the meantime, I'll start with the Wadias. They have a telephone too—we could speak to all the main families this morning!"

Diana had not been so animated in weeks—her eyes shone, and her voice!

She asked, "What say you, Papa? Should we not oppose cruelty? Parsis are peace-loving, yes, but we're not cowards. Shall we do it? Shall we riot?"

I had protested Diana's decision to bring Burjor into our plan—but she was right. He leapt to it with gusto, making a host of arrangements that would have been far beyond me. And all without explaining why he wanted things just so. Mrs. Framji too rose to the occasion, her eyes red-rimmed with fatigue.

After shaving and dressing neatly, I scarpered off to the Bombay Jail. I was a wanted man, but so long as I did not venture through police headquarters, it was the last place anyone would look for me.

Clad in a nice brown suit, I entered my name, CPT AGNIHOTRI, and signed, then turned the ledger back to the guard. Glancing over the guard's shoulder, the English supervisor said, "Fellow of this name was wanted . . ."

I said idly, "I'd hardly be visiting, would I?" and emptied my pockets into the metal tub as usual.

He grunted and poked through my things, wallet, watch, notebook, pencil stub, and Satya's key which I'd retrieved this morning.

"All good," he said to the *thanedar* who opened the gate.

No guard accompanied me this time, so I assumed I was to find my own way. I'd been through the maze of corridors often enough, so I headed for Adi's cell.

"Jim!" Adi shuffled over from his bed. "Good of you to come," he said, shaking hands through the bars. Never mind that his cheeks were hollow in his thin face, or that his clothes hung as though two sizes too large, he was invariably courteous, and today was no different. Yet I was in a fever to consult him, so belaying the usual pleasantries, I launched into it.

"I've got bad news," I said, and told him about little Shirin's abduction.

"She's five," he said in a choked voice. After a moment, "What happened to your face?"

As he heard about my assault, he pressed a fist to his mouth.

I asked, "Are you going to be sick?"

He shook his head. "Go on. They let you go?"

"I escaped. They drugged me, and I had no wish to wake up in the middle of the bazaar or in a dung heap."

His mouth smiled as I made light of the affair, but lines crowded tight around his eyes.

"Why, Jim?" Knuckles white, he clenched the bars. "Why did they take my sister?"

"They think you were in it with Satya. That you've got his loot."

"Give them the gold Ganesh," he cried. "Exchange it for Shirin!"

"That's not all they want. The Imperial Mint. I'm to hand them the taxes."

His breath rasped as he absorbed the fullness of my predicament. "You can't do it, Jim. I won't let you."

I smiled. "I was rather hoping you'd help. Satya was swindling the swindlers, wasn't he? Let's take a page from his book."

His eyes flashed, then his thin shoulders pulsed as he huffed out a chuckle. For three shaking breaths he pressed his forehead to the metal bars between us.

Voice low, he said, "Gold is heavy, but few know how much it weighs. And I've got plenty of heavy metal pieces in the factory."

"Where would I get wooden boxes?"

"You need crates?" He grinned and told me.

* * *

All day we worked to assemble the plan. Gradually it took shape. Padamji balked at first, then, reminded of his debt to me, acceded. Diana immediately rushed away with Gurung and Ganju to Adi's factory.

I could not be a part of that, since I was likely being watched. So Mrs. Framji sent me to make urgent purchases from the market. This done, I returned to the mint and walked the possible routes radiating in each direction. Where would Rai Chand's message reach me? Where would it send me? How did he plan to exchange boxes of bullion for one small child? Or was this all to lead me a merry chase? Perhaps he had no intention of returning baby Shirin at all!

Was she even still alive? Diana's worn face told me she shared that gnawing fear. At dinner, no one could eat. Burjor persuaded Mrs. Framji to take a sleeping draft.

***

Taking extra precautions to dislodge anyone following me, I began the final step of my preparations. While Gurung drove the carriage about town as a decoy, I broke into McIntyre's home after dark. It posed little difficulty to slip over the backyard wall and duck into the well-tended shrubbery.

However, Mrs. McIntyre had company in the room overlooking the formal garden, which caused a short delay. Slouching between the bushes I mimicked a gardener's low walk.

Taking my time, I plodded to the side of the house where Mac had his smoking room, jimmied the window, and settled into a chair. It was the only chamber where his missus was unlikely to venture—I had no desire to terrify her.

For my nocturnal visit, I'd worn my usual journalist's garb, dark vest over long kurta and baggy trousers. Gazing in the mirror over the dumbwaiter, I winced. I'd had no time to clean up into a gentleman before breaking into the chief superintendent's home.

The clock chimed in high, merry notes while I waited, reminding me that it was past eleven. I had no way to judge how long McIntyre's dinner companions would stay. If I heard visitors at the door, I'd have to dash over the windowsill, so I kept myself in readiness.

Despite my anxiety, as the minutes inched past in the quiet chamber, my limbs sank into the comfortable chair and my eyelids begged a short rest. Rising, I browsed McIntyre's library, fingering the books' leather spines. And there it was. A beautiful bound copy of *The Memoirs of Sherlock Holmes*.

This I took down and opened to "The Adventure of the Crooked Man." Turning the book to the lamplight, in moments I was absorbed in Mr. Holmes's case about an English soldier during the Indian Mutiny. A suspicion began to form—he was deformed, but had been unusually handsome in features . . . I had just got to the crux of it, where Watson and Holmes were to question the poor twisted creature, when the door opened, and Mac turned up the gaslight.

He stopped as though turned to stone, then growled under his breath, and shut the door firmly behind him.

"Evening," I said, setting down the book with regret as I rose to my feet. One of these days, I hoped I'd get to read the end of a story.

"I've got a warrant out for you. Why are you here?"

"Sorry to intrude like this . . ." I said, thinking that was a nice, polite opening, then noticed his clenched jaw and got to the point. "Thought you should know. I'm, ah, going to steal the bullion."

He didn't move.

Wondering whether he'd understood, I went on, "From the mint. You saw me there, remember? The Imperial Mint?"

"I know what the bloody mint is," he snarled, then pointed with the stem of his pipe. "Sit. Spit it out. It's what you're here for."

He came around his desk, sat, and put his pipe down. He laid his forearms to either side of it like the sphinx at Giza, peering at me without expression. My admiration swelled when he didn't even look at the fine whiskey bottles on the sideboard.

He listened without interruption as I told him about Shirin's abduction, and the price I was asked to pay, in exchange for her life.

"I'm sorry," he said, his voice low. "The Framjis lost two children before."

"And you've locked up their son for murder," I reminded him. "They cannot lose this baby. Not like this."

He stared at his pipe as the grandfather clock ticked away the seconds.

Then he said, "We had a daughter. Died of cholera in '83." When he looked up, his gaze was a rapier. "The gunships arrived an hour ago. How did you know?"

"I didn't," I replied. Blast. The escort was here. Little Shirin's abduction was well timed.

He cleared his throat, then said, "I will not have you obstructing the transfer of taxes."

I tried a half grin. "How 'bout a decoy? A load of fake bullion. The staff at the mint will cooperate." As his eyes snapped up, I added, "Close-knit Parsis, I'm kin to them now."

He squinted, weighing my tone as much as my words.

Every hour's delay could cost little Shirin her life. Losing patience,

I said, "If you think I'm up to something, call the baronet, Sir Jamsetji. Ask him about me. Ask him if he'll stand guarantor!"

McIntyre reared back at this outrageous statement. I bore the mammoth weight of his icy gaze as long as I could stand it, then spread my hands in silent beseeching.

"It's madness," he said. "What d'you want from me?"

It took over an hour to work through, but with the preparations Adi offered, McIntyre grudgingly agreed I had just the slightest, slimmest chance of success.

"My sentries, they'll fire," he said, his Scots accent rough. "No blank cartridges, you say, else word gets out. They'll shoot lead, you understand?"

I nodded. If it got that far I would already have failed.

I left McIntyre sitting with bloodshot eyes, making a low gurgling noise that telegraphed the curses he'd love to hurl at my head. I'd insisted that no one else was to know, because Rai Chand would surely be watching from the moment I left Framji Mansion.

That left only one part, in truth, the piece of this daft business that worried me the most. Would Chand fall for our ruse? Nursing my anxiety like a dog with an injured paw, I returned from McIntyre's with my cloak over my head and part of my face, walking in a peculiar doubled-over fashion that would be starkly memorable. *The safest disguise is to be very visible.* Was that from Holmes? I could not recall him saying so.

Entering the midnight bazaar at Charni Road I slipped into a narrow alley to shed my guise, exiting the other end with long strides to hail a passing Victoria.

* * *

That night sleep deserted me. In the wee hours, our preparations made, we finally sought our beds. Yet I kept hearing Rai Chand's instructions.

"You will drive the carriage with the gold bars.

You will see a man with a red flag.

You will take him up and hand over the reins.

He will take you to the rendezvous."

How did he know when the bullion would be moved? I feared that the mind who'd written that knew all I'd done, where I'd been, and how

I'd retrieved Satya's child, Sona, now safely ensconced in the Framji nursery.

But little Shirin's bed lay empty. How was she treated by her abductors? Those chubby little arms around my neck, that bold little face! God, her trusting eyes peering at me, her little fingers patting my cheeks. Someone had watched the Framji household and struck at the very heart of it.

I lay awake for a time, listening to Diana's soft breathing, then eased away from her warm softness, picked up my book from the nightstand and stole away to read.

Turning up a lamp in the morning room, I settled into the easy chair beside and turned the crisp pages. Should I try to finish "The Adventure of the Crooked Man" or "The Adventure of the Naval Treaty"? My eye fell on the title of the last story: "The Final Problem."

If things went wrong tomorrow, I'd never get to read it. Did I want to?

I'd heard the talk in Boston. In this tale, my hero, Sherlock Holmes, that scything intellect, would die. Could I bear to lose him, even if only in fiction?

Why had Conan Doyle destroyed his magnificent creation? What devilish business had Holmes faced that ended so badly? Again I heard Rai Chand's voice, saw the tremor in his hand as he read out my instructions. That measured meter, those repeated phrases were indicative of a strange intellect. A cold hand closed around my insides.

Holmes had lost his battle, then. Would I lose mine?

How did he lose? Was he ambushed? Or was it a sacrifice to achieve some greater purpose? It mattered to me *how* he died.

I began to read.

CHAPTER 45

GRAND LARCENY

Lord Cornwallis's statue stood high atop a plinth in front of the Imperial Mint. The square around it was paved—I'd find no shelter from a rain of bullets there, but the dense bushes encircling the base would hold me until sunrise.

I got there in the wee hours, stooping in a sweeper's doubled-over pose as I swept my way closer. When the sentry turned the corner, I crawled into the foliage. Sitting cross-legged in the hydrangeas with leaves brushing my face, I prepared to commit grand larceny.

All's hushed as midnight yet, I thought, Shakespeare's *Tempest* running through my mind. If this adventure mimicked that tale, who was I? Angry, twisted Caliban, servant of Prospero? Was Burjor the magician? What he lacked in Prospero's magic he made up with his vast influence. Diana would be Ariel, a creature of air and sunbeams. Shirin's abduction was a tempest in our lives that might blow our newfound togetherness to shreds. Losing her would cut her parents to the heart and leave Diana and Adi ravaged by guilt. And me? For good or ill, my very soul hung in the balance.

Hours yet to dawn. I recalled lines of the play: *The dropsy drown this fool! Let it alone, and do the murder first.* I was but a tool now, so my mind had called up Shakespeare's varlets. I'd begged McIntyre to keep our plan close, lest someone leak the details to that strange intellect

pulling the strings. Who was the spider at the center of the web, working his plans through others, like Professor Moriarty himself?

A bird fluttered and shook the foliage, calling out a high-pitched
song. Fingers of dawn touched the horizon. I'd need to play the thug
with sufficient force to be believable. The face of old Father Thomas
came to mind, his sad, watery eyes peering deep into me. Perhaps most
criminals believe they have reason to break the law. Convinced I had
the right of it, was I crossing into that murky realm? I prayed the day
would not end in murder.

Wheels rattled in the courtyard, waking my pulse to their rhythm.
I felt that strange ether rise, as though the bile in my belly now ran
through my veins. With the snort of horses, McIntyre and his cohort
of havildars arrived. Of the three wagons, the first was my target. I had
not told Mac everything, nor Diana, because this risky business would
ruin her sleep.

From the shrubbery I watched four havildars carry out a wooden
crate, grunting under its weight.

Burjor had telephoned Padamji, forge master of the Imperial Mint, to
admit our decoys through the back door. Sealed with imperial wax, these
were loaded. Having stashed the last crate, two policemen descended
from the lead wagon and began on the next. My limbs tensed as I hauled
in deep breaths, preparing to move quickly. My hand fisted around my
weapon, the only one that would not give alarm, a broom of dried palms.

Stealing the Queen's taxes involved a tricky sequence, all of which
I needed to time precisely. A slip at any step would cascade into disaster. First, I had to evade the guards at the perimeter. Then I needed to
startle the horses into moving and take charge of the wagon. Its route
was down the Eastern Boulevard with its row of coconut palms, past
the Town Hall to Government Docks. Instead, at Elphinstone Circle I
would swerve away. Trouble was, I had no idea where I was supposed to
drive the stolen goods.

"Rank foolishness!" McIntyre had cried. "They're trained for this,
Jim! You'll be shot!"

But the memory of little Shirin stung me—if this was the only way
to get her back, then the law be damned. Was that how Satya began his
career of crime?

In for a penny, I thought, as the guards ceremoniously turned to salute a group of British officers, their white gloves stark in the pale gleam of dawn. I scurried, crouching low, so that I'd passed two sentries before the third caught sight of me.

Time slowed. His mouth opened in an O of surprise as I swiped the broomstick at his face. When he threw up an arm to block it, I darted to the nearest horse.

I struck its rump with the broom, giving the poor creature a nasty fright. While it reared, I struck the second mare, crying, "Hiy! Hiy!" to get them moving.

The carthorses charged forward while I was still between them, so it was by the barest chance I caught the harness and swung my legs up to the wagon seat.

Unfortunately, it wasn't empty.

Something slammed my ear. Another blow glanced off my eyebrow. I caught a fist and gripped for dear life. While my feet scrabbled for purchase, I hauled on the arm and levered myself up onto the seat. The wagon jolted about as the horses dashed ahead.

More blows came in rapid succession, so I lashed out and socked the fellow, then trapped his arm. We struggled, the wagon jostling us to slide on the precarious seat. Throwing my elbow around his neck I yanked him backward into an embrace. Only then did I recognize my opponent, one with whom I'd boxed time and again in the ring.

Damn. It was Smith wriggling out of my grasp.

"Stephen! Stop!" I cried into his ear, throwing him around to left and right. His body clenched tight in horror.

The thunder of hooves in my ears, I glanced back. A police carriage was close behind, with two fellows on horseback rapidly gaining. Ahead, near Town Hall, swelled a sea of white coats protesting the killing of stray animals.

"Ask Mac! He knows. Ask Mac!" Desperate to time it well, I caught sight of Burjor, and shoved Smith off the seat.

"Aargh!" He clung to me, feet dangling. As our carriage passed, Burjor hooked an arm around Smith and the pair was swallowed by the crowd filling the street.

Unencumbered, I slid to the footrest and scooped up the reins, then flicked them at the horses. Behind me the mob chanted, "Down with dogcatchers! Down with cruelty!"

Burjor and Soli Wadia had labored for hours to set this into motion. They'd found a willing audience, since most Parsis deplored the slaughter of strays.

Urging the horses, I rode on to Elphinstone Circle. What should I do? Rai Chand had recited, *You will see a man with a red flag. You will take him up and hand over the reins.*

And lo! A figure stood at the circle waving a red cloth.

Pulling on the reins, I peered at the scrawny youth knotting the fabric at his waist. As the wagon neared, he caught the footrest and vaulted up beside me.

It was Pandu, Satya's cousin and rival. Without a word, he reached to grab the reins from me. I yanked away, which upset the horses and set them into an uneven canter.

"Why are you here?" I demanded.

He reared back, his mouth open. "Cap-tin sahib! *Hei ram!*" Then he hissed, "Don't speak! Don't talk to me! I must do as I am told."

"And what is that?"

The whites of his eyes showed large as he glanced about helplessly. "Take the reins. Drive fast to . . ."

"Where?" I held the reins away from him. We were now careening north toward the *Bombay Gazette* newspaper office.

Desperately he reached around me. "You will kill us both! Give it to me!"

"Where?" I held him off with an elbow.

He groaned, then cried, "Tulsidas Mandir."

I released the reins to him, then pulled notebook and pencil stub from my vest.

Jostled, bumping along, I wrote. He cried, "He will kill us all! Oh God. We are not to speak of him. Take the reins, ride fast to Tulsidas Mandir. Do not speak."

Driving the horses with lashes and shouts, he whispered the words in a litany.

Do not speak? Something dark coiled inside me. I timed my throw to toss my notebook at the foot of the largest tree we passed. Now I could only hope that Burjor would follow and find my missive. Either way, today I would retrieve Shirin, even if I must bloody my hands again.

CHAPTER 46

WHERE IS SHIRIN?

Pandu whipped the reins over the horses with both hands. We bounced and rattled over cobbles, while under my bravado swam a deep fear. Shirin's captor had taken her to a temple intending to trade her for my bullion. Tulsidas Mandir—where the devil was it? If they discovered my subterfuge, what would become of her? And who had the reach to terrify a man like Rai Chand? A cold-eyed murderer? A master of the underworld?

Was it the gunships' approach that set this villain's plan in motion? He knew to the hour when they would load India's taxes. I was his puppet, and baby Shirin, my string. I rubbed my wrists, remembering the burn of ropes, and felt a low growl push at the back of my throat.

The sun twinkled off the waves as our wagon climbed the road toward a promontory. A familiar stretch of sandy beach stretched in the distance. Could it be . . . ?

Through the palms, the shape of a broken wall was familiar, piles of stone tumbled along its base. Snatches of memory returned. I'd tripped into a ditch, crawled over a knot of roots . . . a palm grove, husks of coconuts broken open . . . Rai Chand's den!

Our coach flew past clustered shanties, overturned fishing boats and nets stretched over bamboo poles. Here and there children squatted among the rocks, hunting for crabs. On the beach, women crouched over red piles of tiny shrimp, sweeping them into semicircles to dry. The smell of fish, earth, and salt hit my nostrils, as though it was an ordinary day.

Passing a mango grove, the wagon followed a curved path. Stone-built houses stepped up the cliff in various states of disrepair. I spotted Rai Chand's two-story dwelling. Had I really climbed onto that roof? I stared as we swept past, shaken by my foolhardiness.

Tulsidas temple was built on a cliffside. The approach wound upward, bounded on one side by a steep drop. Here sunsets would color the sky with wonder, lovers join hands and watch the day retire. It was a holy place too, an ancient place, now neglected, with twisted banyan trees bowed under the weight of centuries.

Outlined against the sky, a white-limbed statue of the elephant god Ganesh gazed down over a wide courtyard. Over ten feet high and seated on a plinth against a verdant background, this was a peaceful god.

Under an ornamented crown, his serpentine trunk was perfectly proportioned. Two hands held embellished weapons, a third curved over a round belly, while a palm was raised in blessing. I caught glimpses of a low shed, its terra-cotta tile roof likely a recent addition.

If I'd been less irate, I might have thought better of barging unarmed into Rai Chand's grasp. But my blood was up; urgency drove me on. If only I wasn't too late.

Our carriage clattered into an open terrace bounded by a low, curved wall. At the center, the mammoth Ganesh statue was flanked by a triangular temple. Pandu hauled on the reins, his scrawny frame arched backward. Once the wagon rolled to a halt beside a few wide steps, he swiped a forearm across his perspiring forehead, wilting in relief. His part of this foul business was done; mine was still underway.

A group of men came from between the temple pillars. Catching sight of my erstwhile captor, I hollered, "Rai Chand, you coward!"

If my gaze could have scorched him, he'd have burst into a pile of cinders.

He folded his hands to me. "Sahib, we are not what you think. We would not have harmed you."

"No? You drugged me. Easier to handle an unconscious man, huh?"

He showed his palms. "We put medicine in the water. Only to return you to the street."

"Now you hide behind a small child? Bring her out."

In the silence, a faint clatter of wheels grew louder. One of Chand's men shouted, "Seth-ji, police coming! Three carriages!"

"What have you done?" he cried, then waved his men forward. "Open the wagon!"

Vaulting down from the seat, I elbowed my way to the wagon's rear. A pair of Chand's men unhooked the plank and climbed in. Aided by others at the open end, they slid out one of the heavy, flat crates Diana had prepared.

I yelled to Chand, "I've done what you asked. Where is the child?"

He flicked a hand to send a man hurrying away.

As I feared, one of his henchmen lowered a crowbar onto the crate and began to pry the top open. Chand hurried over, his eyes bulging. Once the crate's lid was loosened, the man squatted and worked it off.

Under a thin layer of straw, gold gleamed bright in the noonday sun.

When Rai Chand reached toward it, I knocked his hand away with a growl. "Touch one bar and I will break your arm."

Grimacing, he motioned to me. "Take her! Take the girl!"

"Captain Jim!" wailed a high voice behind me. I felt a small tug on my clothes.

My breath jolting like a runaway train, I scooped up little Shirin, tucked her in my arms, and glared over her head at Chand.

"I have ransomed the child in full. Steal one bar, and you will regret it."

He recoiled as though I'd struck him. Backing away, he gestured to his men to close up the crate.

The toddler's arms tight around my neck, I strode from the gang to the open courtyard where the Framjis' carriage had just arrived. However, the terrace was no longer empty. How did Chand imagine he'd get the wagon and its heavy boxes away?

Then I did not care, for Diana stepped down and ran toward us. People spilled out of other carriages too, some dressed in saffron, others in the white garb of devotees.

With a squeal, Shirin yanked forward and tumbled into Diana's waiting arms.

Diana hugged her close. "Thank you, thank you," she cried, burying her face in little Shirin's mass of curls.

I propelled them on, hoping to be gone before Rai Chand discovered Adi's steel implements and Mrs. Framji's gold-leaf-wrapped sweetmeats layered under the thin cover of hay.

CHAPTER 47

DEADLY INTENTIONS

Burjor descended from the carriage to hoist Shirin into his arms. Mrs. Framji peered from a window, then cried out with joy, reaching for her child.

Fresh from the protest rally, Soli Wadia grinned from the driver's seat. "All Parsi businesses are closed today. We've shut down the city!"

I chuckled, remembering the flurry of fervent phone calls. "Where did everyone go, after the Town Hall?"

"To bar the barracks gates, so the cantonment will get no food or water!"

That would keep McIntyre busy. I laughed, preparing to hoist myself up beside him as soon as Diana and Burjor were seated.

More devotees arrived. This high, overlooking the Arabian Sea, the wind fluttered their clothing. The morning air was cool despite the mid-November sun. The aroma of incense wafted from joss sticks at the temple.

Behind me, a woman called out to someone. "*Arrey ji!* Why is everyone here?"

I knew that voice. Satya's mother. What the devil?

Satya's father separated from a group. "Meera?"

My pulse gave a jerk and began a familiar warning rat-tat. I'd missed something. Those devotees—were all of them Satya's family? Meera asked Tansen something that was plucked away by the wind.

He replied, "Breaking customs destroys society. We have come to atone." Recognizing me, he started. "Captain?"

Meera caught his arm. "Where is the girl? Satya's child?"

Tansen pointed toward the temple entrance, where their nephew dragged someone along. My stomach lurched as I recognized the thin figure. Pandu had her by the elbow, handling her so roughly she might have been a doll.

Goddamn it, she should have been safe in Jiji-bai's care. I called, "Sona?"

The girl turned toward me, her fingers reaching, fluttering, too far away. One side of her face was marked. A red splotch covered her cheek—had someone slapped her? Pandu turned, glaring. Sona whimpered.

When I cried, "Stop! She's Satya's child!" Pandu hauled the girl to the side and yelled something in their dialect.

I dashed forward but a group blocked my path, his clansmen. One shoved me in the chest. Glowering, two sturdy blokes faced me, their faces dark with warning.

Pandu was headed to the stone parapet overlooking the ocean. I saw a sliver of surf and froze in disbelief. My God! Was he going to toss her over?

"Halt!" I yelled, biting off the word in a military tone.

Pandu snarled, "Satya ruined our name, our livelihood! No one will trust us, no one will believe us. We have to do this!"

Around me, voices rumbled in angry confusion. Spotting Tansen, I pleaded, "You are the *karta*. Stop him!"

Pulling farther away, Pandu cried, "It is our forefathers' trade. We are sonars for a thousand years!"

Desperate to stop him, I dug into my pockets for some way to distract him.

Holding aloft Satya's key, I cried, "Here—see this key? Do you know what it is?"

He sent an impatient glance toward me. "What of it? Pah!"

My gut clenched in frustration. "Take it! In exchange for her, take Satya's hoard!"

He scoffed and spat to one side, but the men murmured to one another. Tansen hurried forward, exhorting them. Order resumed as they deferred to him. He motioned to Pandu to return, but the youth protested in rapid-fire Gujarati. I pulled back, searching for Sona's scrawny shape.

Distant notes shrilled over the terrace stones, growing louder. Police whistles. Constables appeared on the terrace and advanced with batons waving. In their midst would be McIntyre and Smith, I thought, just in time.

The crowd was looking upward, some covering their lips, pointing. The devil?

On the temple roof. Pandu held Sona with an arm around her neck. The thought of Chutki stabbed me. *Not again.* Not another innocent caught in the crossfire. Pandu's vengeance was aimed at Satya's twelve-year-old.

"What are you doing? You cannot escape," I shouted. "Look! Thirty witnesses!"

He yelled, "What do I care? My life is over! Because of this filth!"

Emotion glittered in Pandu's wretched face. A chill ran over my skin. Distraught, he might toss Sona into the treacherous waters below, or drag her with him.

I called, "What's damaged can be repaired. Let her go."

"Aargh!" he screamed. "My *rishta* is broken off! Because Satya was a cheat!"

"*You* are not Satya. You are your own man."

"Englishman, that is not how it works." He groaned, looking over the shocked company. His voice rose as he cried, "She must die! Only then can we show people our faces again. I do not matter. Our family honor, our *khaandan* will go on."

He took another step back.

A shot cracked out. People turned, a tremor rippling through the crowd, the terrace a mosaic of movement.

Diana stood atop an urn, leveling her revolver. She'd fired the warning shot. Panic spiking, I cried, "Diana! Don't shoot!"

Turning, I hollered, "Pandu, release the child! My wife won't miss!"

For a moment he froze, glaring at Diana in her riding skirt, outlined against the sky. Then he whirled at Sona.

"Don't!" I yelled, even as Diana fired.

Pandu clutched his thigh. He doubled over and slumped on the tiles. In the ensuing hullabaloo, Tansen and others crowded to the roof to help him.

Where was Sona? I craned my neck, trying to get through the crowd. She had disappeared in the uproar. I scoured the melee, feeling helpless.

Long moments later, I spotted her higher on the shed's roof, and now crouched on the shingled overhang. Her back to me, she gazed out over the water.

After working my way to the terra-cotta edge, I called in Hindustani, "Sona. It's over, child. Come down now."

She glanced over a shoulder, then away. When my entreaties failed, I tried to hoist myself up on the shingles, but they rattled and moved, and some broke away. After a few attempts I took my weight on my arms and got a knee on to the roof, then the other.

Pausing there, I cajoled, "Come, you've had enough for one day. We can't stay here."

Her voice worn with disappointment, Sona said, "Why should I? Why can't I fly with them?" She pointed to the horizon, where a wedge of geese soared homeward.

To draw her attention I called, "Sona, your father Satya—he was trying to help you."

She looked away, uninterested. A shot of pique rammed me. "Everything he did—*everything* was for you. And someone jammed a knife in his neck. Don't you want to know who? Don't you care?"

"No!" she yelled.

She got up quickly and darted off. Shingles clattered and rolled as she ran.

"Sona!" I cried. "Be careful!"

She turned and flung something at me.

Blast! I dodged it, calling, "I won't hurt you, child. You are safe now!"

The temple overlooked a bay that bled into the Arabian Sea. High above, an arrow of geese turned, honking their way north. They curved, great wings beating mighty strokes. Sona followed their progress, stepping lightly across the terra-cotta roof.

Once I had her, we could go home. Back to Framji Mansion, where they'd prepare *dhan daar* rice with yellow lentils to celebrate Shirin's return. I tried to stand on the uneven tiles, but my wobbling knees would not obey.

Sliding on my backside, I saw what had been hidden from the terrace. Rocks, far below. Waves breaking into splinters of foam. The line of geese circled overhead, their wingspans wide as they descended, making long shadows over the jagged tapestry.

Looking outward, Sona said, "He was sending me back."

She was too far from me. "Who?"

"Papa! I hate the *kotha*! They beat me! So I climbed down a drainpipe and ran away. I walked and walked. I asked the way to his *karkhana* and rode on a cart. But he wasn't happy to see me. He asked me, 'Where is your box?'"

She was too close to the edge. I slid closer on the broken tiles. "Sona, it's not safe there."

Her high voice shrilled, "He scolded me. *He sent me back!* He didn't want me, only the box!" Her mouth in a wide grimace, she sobbed. "He was packing things, shiny knives, cleaning them. I took one and hit him. It went right in!"

I had no words. Closing my mouth, I winced at the irony.

She hiccupped, swaying her head in torment. "Silly box! He cared more for it than me. What did I do!" Her voice ended on a keening wail.

Satya had lied, stolen, and sold fakes, all to buy his daughter a future, to spare her the life her mother had suffered. But he had not told her of his plans—how could he? And so, he paid the price.

All those weeks of searching had led me to this place of ancient prayers, of centuries of bargaining with the Almighty. Sona stepped back.

"Stop, child," I called, feeling my years weigh like an anvil around my neck.

It was the wrong thing to say.

Her voice shredded as she whirled away. "I'm not a child! I killed . . . I'm dirty."

I grasped for a way to reassure her. "So am I, Sona," I said. "Look—"

I pointed toward the wide, smooth curve of the Ganesh's trunk where the peaceful stone god gazed down on us. "Only the gods are clean. The rest of us must keep trying."

It didn't work. Her little forehead puckered.

Meera called from nearby. "Sona, come down, *beta*! I am Satya's mother!"

Sona startled. Her feet slid out from under her as she dropped backward.

Now! I grabbed my chance, unfolding my length to reach, arms outstretched. I slammed on to broken shingles that stabbed my side. Pain filled my mind.

But I felt cloth clenched in my fists, Sona's orange and green skirt.

Out of sight, the child wailed, her cries strangely distant to my stunned ears. When I tried to haul her up, she shrieked.

I stopped, fear choking me. She was stuck, scraping against something jagged below the overhang. Then I heard the tear of cloth ripping.

Meera crawled beside me, reached below the roof's edge, and came up holding Sona's little hands.

"*Chup, beta!*" she hushed the child. "I am your grandmother. No one will harm you."

Someone else was beside me. Tansen's calm, steady voice gave instructions. Between them, they lifted and pulled Sona back into their world.

The broken tiles pressed against my face as I lay prone, gasping. It was a while before I peeled myself off the shingles. When I eased down to the terrace, holding my aching side, Diana was near, her arms around my waist. Her hands touched my side, my chest, checking for wounds. How good it felt to lean and rest my face against the top of her head.

Clouds filtered the sunlight, and a playful breeze snatched at my clothes. Concern writ large on their faces, Burjor and Mrs. Framji waited beside their carriage with Shirin. Seeing uniformed constables everywhere, I staggered toward them.

"Did you hear her?" Diana asked McIntyre, an ache in her voice. "The child, Sayta's daughter, killed him. She didn't know what she was doing."

"That so?" he said in his low baritone. "We'll decide if it was an accident, miss."

Diana swung to him. "Can't you release Adi? Surely he need not spend another night in custody."

"All in good time," said McIntyre and ordered constables to secure the area. He squinted at me. "Can you talk yet, laddie?"

CHAPTER 48

SUCCESS AND FAILURE

Pandu was carted away to hospital. Rai Chand and his men had disappeared. Diana examined my bruises and pronounced me "tolerable." Constables were taking statements from bystanders, so I sent the Framjis home when their part was done.

McIntyre questioned Satya's family, while I stood by to translate. Sandwiched between grandparents Meera and Tansen, sobbing, Sona joined her hands to the great stone Ganesh.

Under that peaceful gaze, she told Mac how a moment's outrage had led to tragedy. "I did not know. I did not know the knife would go in like that." Shaking, she dove into Meera's embrace.

Once McIntyre was satisfied, Tansen said, "Sonali was alone, but we will raise her now."

Satya had shown little faith in them, so I objected. "Did you know Satya had a child?"

Tansen hesitated. "He said there was a child by a *rundi*. We are respectable people! How could we accept this? But the girl is orphaned . . ."

Behind him, their heads close together, Sona nestled against Meera's bosom.

I asked, "Will she be safe with you? Pandu almost killed her!"

Tansen spread his hands. "Pandu is hotheaded. But this child is our own blood. We will protect her. I swear it." With a parting *pranam*, he gathered Sona and his wife and retreated into his clan. The afternoon drew on as McIntyre insisted I repeat my own part for the record.

The search for the culprits found a pulley behind the temple, fitted into the stone above a cliff. Hemp ropes led to a sandy beach below where Chand and his men had likely escaped with the crates of fake bullion.

As lanterns cast long shadows on the courtyard, McIntyre and I climbed into a carriage and headed to Bombay Jail. The court session had ended for the day, so with a gruff word to me, McIntyre signed papers for Adi's release and went off to astonish the prosecution with our new evidence.

In his cell Adi saw me and got to his feet. My throat clenched. After all that had happened, I could not find words to tell him. I tried to smile. It seemed to alarm him.

I managed to mutter, "Time to go."

The guard pulled open his door, waiting for Adi, who looked around at his books and clothes.

Did he understand? I wrapped my arms about him, learning again how to breathe. Gradually his thin body relaxed. I felt him return my embrace.

Voice muffled, he asked, "I'm free?"

"You bet," I choked out.

When I told him little Shirin was safe, his body shook with sobs. I tightened my grip, then pulled back in distress only to find that he was laughing. He didn't seem to know his face was wet.

The carriage ride was short and without conversation. Adi poked his head out the window, hair flying wild in the open air.

I should have been relieved. I should have been able to close my eyes in the soft darkness of the coach and rest. Yet all the while a distant suspicion whirled in the recesses of my mind, something off-kilter, something not quite right.

We didn't know who was in charge, who'd snatched baby Shirin. I filled my lungs with the cool air blowing through the open window and watched Adi's hair flicker around his head, making haloes each time we passed a streetlamp.

His welcome at Framji Mansion was all he could have wanted. Adi sat sandwiched between Burjor and Mrs. Framji on a couch that was not meant for three. Burjor's arm lay along the back. Now and again, he squeezed Adi's shoulder with a massive hand.

Mrs. Framji had no such inhibitions. She'd wept openly to see Adi, kissed and garlanded him, blessing him with a red mark on his forehead, while Diana clung to him.

He grinned through it all, answering in bursts, half sentences of wit and rueful sarcasm.

Now, emotion choking his voice, Burjor asked me, "How can we thank you?"

I waved it away, hoping he would not try to pay me. It would sting too much, and I did not want to pretend it was all right. One does not pay family.

Diana cast me a quick glance, and said in a warning tone. "Papa . . ."

Burjor blinked. "Of course," he said, "Captain—I mean Jim, is one of us . . ."

Mrs. Framji came to his rescue. "We are grateful, son. Is there anything we can do?"

"Ah." I thought of the decrepit old mali, weeping because I had touched his hand. He needed a kind place to live, and then to die. "Could you take on an old servant? Not sure he's good for much. Would mean a lot to me . . ."

Adi asked, "Bala Mali? Of course! Papa, it's Satya's gardener."

"Certainly!" Burjor rumbled. At that moment, I think he would have given away his last penny. "Bring him to us. He can do as much, or as little as he wants."

* * *

While the family rested the next day, I recovered Sona's box from the nursery upstairs. It was Satya's old traveling case, still carrying his name tag from the SS *Carpathia*.

So after dinner, I pulled Sona's valise on my lap. Deep scratches around the clasp showed numerous efforts to break it, but the sleek metal lock had held.

Was this what Satya tried so hard to hide?

Diana said, "I can't understand why Satya did this. When Sona came to him, why did he send her back to the kotha? For this valise? What could it possibly contain?"

On that fateful noon, Satya's words must have seemed to reject Sona—a betrayal which cut so deep it almost drove her to suicide. I palmed the silver key, recalling Banner's prescient words. Satya feared that his child hated him. Perhaps she did. He may have thought he deserved it for abandoning her mother. This was conjecture, but Satya's last words, "Don't let them sell her," revealed remorse for sending Sona back for this case.

I said, "What's in it? One way to find out!"

Satya's key slid easily into the valise's keyhole. The clasp opened without a sound. I heard Diana gasp as I pulled clumps of crumpled paper onto the low coffee table.

They were wrinkled banknotes, rolls of rupee notes tied with yellow rubber bands. Satya's hoard tumbled onto the dark wooden table—the funds he'd gathered to rescue Sona and start a new life. I felt a pulse of pity for Satya, who'd got so close to his goal, and lost.

Adi started counting the cash. I told Burjor, "That's yours. The five grand he stole."

The valise contained a tattered chemistry book and a dog-eared primer, Satya's treasures, I thought, as I flicked through pages with a single letter imprinted at the top. A wobbly scrawl replicated it in rows. At the letter P, Sona had given up.

Satya's visits must have ceased about then.

He'd been teaching Sona to write. I felt as though I'd entered a parade ground at dawn and found it empty when it should have been teeming.

"Wait," I blurted. "The mali carried messages for Satya. But Sona can't read."

Diana looked up. "They were for someone *else*. Someone keeping Sona there."

The case was still heavy, so I upturned it over the table. A small gold brick thunked onto the rosewood. When I picked it up with my fingertips, it was heavy, smooth, and cold. A row of numbers and the imperial crest gleamed, identical to those at the Bombay mint.

The Framjis stared at it.

I said, "Satya held on to one—a fail-safe, should he need to run." I turned the bar on its side. "I can't see where he sliced off the bottom and replaced it with silver."

Taking it carefully, Adi examined it. "Plated in gold, it would be almost invisible."

Diana reached for the bar, then pulled back. "Jim! If this is fake . . . it's an unexploded bomb! This could cause more damage than the bank panic!"

What the devil? I gaped at her. "Why?"

"The gold standard! Currency is backed by gold. It's the ultimate safety for savings. If it becomes known that there are fakes at the Imperial Mint, why, it could cause chaos! How could one trust theirs was genuine?"

The grandfather clock ticked off the seconds while I tried to imagine such a world. Something moved in my mind, a ripple in a dark curtain.

Adi said, "Gold is the ultimate currency. This could devalue everything. If it was known that the Bank of England dealt in fake bars, the value of gold would drop. It could ruin Great Britain!"

My mouth dry as paper, I asked him, "Could Satya have intended this? Striking a blow from within, to knock out Britain's financial system, sow mistrust of its very currency?"

In a wondering tone, he said, "Blow everything up, like an anarchist?" His face was pale against his dark jacket. "I wouldn't believe it of him . . ."

Diana said, "Silver prices tumbled last year. The proponents of 'Free Silver' wanted to reinstate the dollar coin. But the price of silver is so volatile, well, it ruins their argument."

Silver had been dethroned as a currency because it was unstable. But the rupee was still pegged to silver, wasn't it? Diana was saying, "Jim, how did Satya get this?"

This I could answer. "Vishal's brother worked at the mint. It was a neat plan. He smuggles out a gold bar stuck to the bottom of a trolley. Satya slices off a part of the bar, replaces it with silver, and plates it again in gold. The empty carts are stacked on the road. Disguised as a sweeper, one of the gang attaches the fake when no one's around. A guard rolls it back inside, and Vishal's brother simply adds it to the stack."

Adi whispered, "An endless supply, as long as Vishal's brother co-operated."

"And didn't get caught."

Diana motioned to the bar on the rosewood table. "So is this real, or fake?"

"He'd have kept an untampered one for himself, don't you think?"

She frowned. "Can Padamji return it?"

Burjor shook his head. "He would have to explain how he got it."

Diana slumped. "Then what do we do with it?"

Adi put up his hands. "Nothing! Can't sell it, can't even be seen with it. If we gave it to a jeweler to melt down, he'd ask all sorts of questions!" He mopped his forehead. "Questions I can do without!"

I grinned at Burjor. "Lock it up as safeguard against a rainy day."

Brows ridged, Burjor shook his head. "I'll have the funds I'm owed, no more. Why not give it to Satya's family? He stole from them, no?"

Adi spoke slowly. "They'd rejoice, but . . . how do we explain it? And if we ask them to keep it quiet, well, they'd have a hold over us. I don't like it, Papa."

Diana frowned. "So, then what? You don't expect Jim and me to keep it!"

Burjor spread his hands. "Why not? The captain's worked hard to free Adi. Why not take that?" He pointed with his chin.

Diana shook her head. "It . . . feels strange to say this. Satya cheated so many people." She grimaced. "Out of desperation, it's true. But . . . it feels wrong, somehow."

"As though there's blood on it," I said softly.

She came alongside and dropped a kiss on my forehead.

"Right," I said, turning to Burjor. "Your family priest, the Ervad? Could you invite him to the house?"

"Dastoor Kukadaru? I can . . . but why?"

I smiled. "He's building a cathedral. A big temple of sorts?"

Burjor sucked in an audible breath. "The Atash Behram. But if we donate this, it will bring the taxman to our door!"

I chuckled. "Your priest is a holy man, isn't he? Ask him to pray on it."

CHAPTER 49

A LOW PROFILE

When Dastoor Kukadaru heard our proposal, he refused point-blank and stalked from the house, his mouth downturned. Three days later, however, I received a note with specific instructions. It ended: "Take this knowledge to the grave."

I fed the message to Jiji-bai's kitchen fire and planned how it might be done.

A week later, newspapers reported "the Miracle of the Gold Bar." After praying in full view for three days, Dastur Kukadaru had requested the head priest of the Parsis to visit. Still seated on the porch swing, Kukadaru bade him enter and take as a donation whatever he found in his room. The gold bar was duly discovered on a table near the window, examined for finger marks and found to have none but the head priest's!

Burjor's dark eyes crinkled at the corners as he read aloud from the morning papers. "Construction on the Atash Behram has resumed. It is funded by the miraculous gold bar which sold for the princely sum of ten thousand rupees."

Adi choked, set down his cup, and let loose a guffaw.

"It will delight Parsis for decades," Diana said, grinning. "Our very own miracle!"

I glanced from Burjor to Adi. "It *is* a miracle. Who would believe sensible people could turn down a gift like that!"

"Hush," Diana scolded, but her cheeks were flushed with pride.

* * *

Later that evening, when Diana breezed into the morning room, she smiled to see the company. Soli Wadia stood up to offer his chair and his parents beamed a welcome.

Diana waved Soli back into his place and swooshed over to me. Before I could rise, she plunked herself down across my lap.

I chuckled, moving my arm to make a backrest while Adi hooted. "Diana, really!"

"Whatever's the matter? We *are* married!"

"Well, one doesn't realize how small you are until you're next to that giant. And likewise, one forgets Jim's size until you are together."

I grinned and told her, "That compliments you, my dear, and smacks my face nicely."

"Adi does everything beautifully," Diana said, like a regent bestowing a knighthood.

"Except spill what he knows," I grumbled. "You suspected Satya was in trouble."

Adi's eyes grew mournful. "Jim, I didn't want to bias you against him. He was my friend. Once, he talked about . . . a girl, then clammed up. Wouldn't share any sordid details, 'course."

"Christ, Adi. Perhaps he was asking for help."

Adi winced. "I regret it. Now, it seems cold, unfeeling. I . . . I was embarrassed."

"Embarrassed!" cried Burjor. "You were accused of murder!"

Adi touched his ears as though the blast might have injured his hearing. I chuckled, pressing my jaw to Diana's hair. She gurgled a laugh, and then the others joined in. It was a while before, gasping and choking, we wound down.

In the soft silence, I suspect, each of us recalled a different aspect of Satya Rastogi. A man can be different things to different people.

Diana pulled in her lower lip and nibbled on it. "Satya made one mistake and gave his life to rectify it."

I agreed. "I think he left for Oxford not knowing he had fathered a child. When he returned, he probably learned his lover was dying. He was willing to do anything, cheat anyone, to save Sona. You have to admire him for that."

"Do I?" she said. "He was completely immoral. He used everyone."

I shrugged. "What choice did he have? His family controlled every decision. They would have had him walk away from his child. Sona would be sold into a horrendous life. How else could he rescue her?"

Diana rounded on me. "So who, then? Who's to blame?"

Cartloads of bullion left India, shiploads, while millions lacked drinking water, food, housing, and electricity. It was easy to blame the colonizer. Yet the administrators I knew were hardworking competent men, determined to do right by their responsibilities. Someday, would I be forced to choose a side?

Thinking aloud, I said, "What sort of society allows girls to be sold? What sort of family demands blind devotion? It is easy to blame the 'haves,' call them looters, exploiters. But there's cruelty all around."

The curtain in my mind twitched. I frowned, grasping at an elusive thought.

Diana stirred, "What is it, Jim? You've gone stiff."

I glanced at the creamy oval of Diana's face. "Satya had so much cash—why didn't he take the child and run?"

She shrugged. "Perhaps he was afraid, like that mint worker. And Satya *was* leaving. His final step would have been to take Adi's funds."

I said, "Chand's gang escaped in the confusion, when Satya's cousin Pandu grabbed hold of Sona. What if . . ." My mouth felt dry. "What if that was planned?"

Diana's eyebrows shot up. "You think he was in on it?"

"No." I recalled his frenzy as he whipped the horses. "He kept repeating his instructions. That's all he knew. Ah!" The mist cleared as I said, "*That's* why he was chosen. Yes, he was dispatched to bring me to the temple, but . . . the message ensured *he'd* come too."

Diana frowned, sitting up. "He was—called there to cause a ruckus when he spotted Sona? A diversion so Rai Chand could escape?"

I shook my head, seeing a shape behind that curtain in my mind. "Chand is a puppet. McIntyre telephoned this morning, said that when they raided his place, it was deserted. Perhaps one of these days his body will wash up on some beach. Chand failed, you see. When those boxes are opened, his life won't be worth much."

I remembered his hand trembling as he read aloud. He knew the rhythm of those words.

Diana began to pace. "But Sona? How could someone know I'd bring her? Papa got your notebook as we planned, and telephoned us from a store nearby. McIntyre was expecting my message. But when we were getting into the carriage, Sona clung to me. How could anyone know we'd bring her?"

I rubbed my forehead. "Drive fast to Tulsidas Mandir. Those were Pandu's instructions. How could anyone know I'd tell you our destination?"

Adi's voice wobbled as he said, "Someone . . . knew you would. And that Diana would bring Sona. *And* that Sona would leave the carriage and be snatched by Pandu. It seems incredible. But it explains why Satya was so quiet, so secretive, and so terrified."

I nodded slowly, seeing a face behind the curtain in my mind. A face that seemed to turn and look at me.

CHAPTER 50

FAREWELL?

Diana descended the stairs in a lavender sari, one hand on the banister.

Gazing upward, I said, "But soft, what light from yonder window breaks? It is the east, and Diana is the sun."

She stopped, a smile tugging the corners of her mouth. "*Romeo and Juliet* again!"

"Act two, scene one."

"I wish you wouldn't, Jim. That play's a tragedy. Doesn't end well for them."

"You're not superstitious."

"Tosh!" she scoffed, resuming her descent, a hand clasping folds of shimmering silk. "Fellows will think you're trumpeting how well-read you are."

"Can't a bloke romance his wife?" I asked, raising her hand to my lips.

"Oh you," she chuckled, eyes twinkling. "When shall we buy our steamer tickets? I want to stay for Adi's birthday. That's in three weeks. What d'you think, Jim? Will Dupree mind?"

As she spoke, I thought I had never seen anything so magnificent. She glowed with health and vitality, her smile as tender as any man could hope. If only she'd remain this content in Boston! But what if her glow came from being in the bosom of her family, her reunited family, now that Adi was back? Were *they* what she needed, even more than me? She spoke with matter-of-fact anticipation, yet I wasn't as complacent. She'd faced rejection and disgrace, yet she'd gone house to house asking about Satya's statue. She'd braved a Cammattipoora brothel, and got the Parsis to riot, to aid me. In time she might rebuild her close friendships in Bombay. Yet she seemed determined to leave.

"You're certain?"

"Mmm. Last time I left, I was running away. But I'm not afraid anymore. I'll probably still get nasty looks and condescending smiles. What's it matter if they cut me? When we needed them, most dropped that nonsense and helped."

Two years ago, she'd been a society heiress. Now she was far more.

"Steamer tickets," she said quietly. "Let's go home, Jim."

I blinked, trying to remember what time the shipping office opened. But last night we'd inferred the presence of someone working behind the scenes, someone that hardened crooks feared. Was Diana trying to get me away from him?

Sure, we'd won this round. But wouldn't our fake bullion enrage him? No, I thought. This was an intellect in complete control of his emotions. The Framjis would be safe only as long as he had no use for them. Little Shirin had been returned, unharmed, and said she'd wandered through an enormous house—a palace—and dined with an old man who took snuff. The rest of her tale seemed muddled with some bedtime story: libraries that smelled of old books, a hall of maps, books stacked along an endless stairway, Chinese vases as tall as the ceiling. Young Fali could have identified the place, but not a five-year-old.

I asked, "Think I'll get to see the London sights this time? I'd dearly like to take a look at Baker Street."

Diana smiled her relief.

❊ ❊ ❊

At breakfast, I asked Burjor, "Do you trust Byram the editor?"

He set his paper aside and said, "He helped us to protest the dog-catchers."

I buttered a slice, smiling. "Not what I asked."

Pushing away his plate, he leaned on his forearms. "A year ago, two, I would have said of course! But Jim . . ."

I waited. Had he ever used my name before?

He said, "I trust him, but there's a lot I don't know about him. He's very well connected, too. I tried for a seat on the Governor's Council, but they chose Byram."

"That caused a distance between you?"

"Political envy? No." He sighed. "No, that was me. You don't know . . . Mama, Rati was a famous beauty in her time."

I grinned. "Diana has her looks."

"Diana has some of me too!" He chuckled, pointing at his sagging jawline. "Rati was a catch! Gentle, beautiful . . . so poised. Byram wanted to marry her."

"But she chose you."

"Yes!" He marveled.

I chuckled. "I know the feeling. So about Byram?"

"He's so . . ." He struggled for a word. "So urbane! And I'm . . ." He laughed and turned a palm toward his girth.

I asked, "Should I trust him?"

Burjor's face cleared. "He admires you. Told me you are an honorable man. He will never harm Mama or the children. So yes, you can."

That very morning, I visited the *Chronicle,* where I navigated through the reporters' hall, having worked there briefly two years ago. Beyond was Byram's glass-walled office. I stepped to the open door and rapped the glass. "Good morning!"

"Good Lord!" Byram took off a narrow pair of glasses and came around to embrace me.

The scent of good tobacco, soap, and old leather enveloped me. He'd grown thinner, his skin sagging at the throat. His lined cheeks split in a delighted smile. I grinned back.

"Have you forgiven me?" he asked.

"For what?"

"For whatever Burjor said I've done. I interfered. There, I admit it. He was being a boor, and I told Diana to force his hand. She's very dear to me . . . Now, how can I help?"

He waved me to a seat, which I took. "Perhaps I'm just here to say hello."

"Nonsense, nonsense!" He poured two glasses of pink sherry and handed me one. "You are a busy man. A useful one." He smiled. "Padamji is grateful."

I twitched in surprise. "What did he tell you?"

Byram chuckled, leaning back in his tall chair. "Who do you think sent Burjor to Dastoor Kukadaru in the first place? And why *him*, when there are a dozen priests of greater influence? No. You see, Padamji from the mint had begged Kukadaru for help and he came to me!"

"I see." Staring at the old conniver who'd schemed for my benefit without a qualm, I made a decision. "I do need your help. Someone kidnapped Shirin, the Framjis' five-year-old."

Eyes bulging, Byram's mouth dropped open. With a strangled sound he pushed away the sherry and shot up. "My God! Let's go. Let's go to them."

"Wait." I stayed him. "She's all right. I got her back."

He dropped into his seat, gasping, as I said, "I need to know who did it. He's a danger to them."

Breathing hard through his nose, he quaffed the sherry, then sputtered and coughed. "You had better tell me everything."

Swearing him to secrecy, I described the kidnapping and my own abduction. When I mentioned stealing the fake bullion, he gave a strangled laugh. However, he grew silent as I described the scene at the temple. When I finished he sat still, looking inward.

"You have an enemy," he said. "All right. What do you know about him?"

"Not much." I enumerated on my fingertips. "He has a network of loyal men—one with cold eyes like a cobra. Rai Chand worked for him and feared him. The mint worker was terrified of him. He has a large empty house in the city. We think he's thin and tall and can appear to be a senior lawyer."

"Indian?"

I'd begun to say, "Yes, of course," but stopped short. "He held Sona prisoner and hired a false witness, but those could be managed through others."

Agreeing, Byram helped himself to more sherry. When he'd downed it, he said, "Shirin saw his home, saw him?"

"She said he was pretty like Diana, but old."

Byram stifled a laugh. "That could mean anyone over twenty. She's your only witness?"

"And the false witness at the trial, Pritam Dutta. Trouble is, Dutta's missing."

"Ah." Byram looked sad.

"Pandu said Rai Chand was his go-between. And Rai Chand's on the run."

"A large empty house in the city—that's your only lead." He went to a cabinet and rummaged, returning with a file.

He said, "For many years I've known of a hand behind the scenes, moving funds, controlling markets. This recent spate of burglaries, it's not random, you know."

I raised a hand for the file but he withheld it, pages wobbling.

He sat, shoulders curling forward. "There are whispers in the underworld. They call him Yama, god of death, because anyone taken to him is usually found dead."

I tilted my head for the file. He sighed, his hand covering it. "My boy, think about it. A large empty house."

Who'd own a vast, empty mansion somewhere in the city? My throat dry, I said, "You think he's British."

* * *

Chief Superintendent McIntyre summoned me the next day, so I went in my best tropical suit. However, when I arrived in front of the constabulary I had a surprise. The first inkling was when two constables snapped me salutes.

I glanced down at my white linen suit, feeling glum. Did it make such a difference? Joining my hands I said, *"Namaskar."*

They replied with wide, knowing smiles. Huh. Something was wrong.

Perplexed, I hurried along the outer perimeter of the bullpen toward McIntyre's office. Just as the door opened, I heard a stamping noise.

I swung around. Every officer, native and British, was at attention. I glanced at McIntyre, expecting him to let them stand down, but he stood there puffing away at his pipe. With an amused look, he raised an eyebrow.

Me? They were at attention for *me*?

Ignoring that I was not in uniform, I returned the salute and gave the order, "At ease!"

First one bloke, then another came up and shook my hand. Smith's bruised face was the color of mottled tomatoes still on the vine. "What the devil have you been telling them?"

He shook with silent laugher, then said, "The truth, Jim, nothing but."

I was aghast. "All of it?"

Mighty pleased with himself, he cracked a wide smile. "Oh, yes. Every little bit."

Later, lounging in his office, McIntyre and I made small talk. Then he cleared his throat and said, "There aren't many natives, ah, Indians I trust, laddie." He glanced over to see whether I resented this description. I did not.

"Care to stay a bit longer? Knotty problem we've got . . ."

I straightened in surprise. "You know we're going back to Boston?"

McIntyre harrumphed and picked up his pipe. "Won't always be like this, you know," he said, waving the thing around. "Natives are doing better, some even in Civil Service! Justice Satyen-dra-nath Tagore holds court in Satara district. Too late for you, 'course."

The civil service exam was closed to those over nineteen, an age I barely recalled. McIntyre grinned a sour smile, poured whiskey into two glasses and slid one over.

"Here. Take a look." He pushed a page toward me. "Show it to that wife of yours. That there's a decent salary. More 'n I made, when I started."

Christ. I cast a glance over the paper, then took a swig and agreed it was fine stuff, best I'd ever tasted. We spoke about my investigation, as much as I could divulge; I danced around the rest on tiptoe, while he watched with crooked eyebrows.

He sipped, then said, "Quite a chance you took to retrieve the Framjis' child. Could have been shot. Really think Rai Chand had someone watching? The whole street's closed, you know, when we're moving taxes."

I shrugged. "There were a dozen Indians there."

When his eyebrows knotted in a question, I said, "The guards."

"Humph." He gazed at his glass as though it puzzled him. "We found Mr. Chand, or rather, his body. Wife identified him this morning."

My breath rasped. "How did he die?"

"Hanged. On a tree near that temple. Old priest found him at dawn."

I sighed. "I don't think Chand was behind everything. Someone was holding Satya's child in that brothel. Chand didn't know anything about her."

"I can help you there," he said. "Seems Satya visited the *kotha* in '82. A little rebellion, perhaps, or on a lark. The woman bore his child just before he left for England. She died of cholera in '91." He took in my astonishment and gave a wry smile. "We record everything, you know. Births, deaths, occupations, it's all there."

I absorbed that. "So who was blackmailing Satya? And who hired Dutta to frame Adi?"

McIntyre looked out of his window, frowning. "Any theories?"

I grimaced. "Only speculation. Byram and I tried out some ideas. A thin, tall man with international connections." McIntyre didn't know about Padamji's problem, so I hurried on. "His network has men who'd die rather than be taken alive." The terror in that mint worker's face before he bolted still haunted me.

"Lives in a large mansion—baby Shirin was clear on that front. And he's got a henchman with, um, cold eyes."

McIntyre tilted his head at me. He didn't laugh.

I said, "And what about the old mali? Who assaulted him?"

McIntyre grunted. "Satya's cousin. Looking for the gold Satya stole from them."

I understood. "The mali wouldn't point the finger at Pandu because he's loyal to the family. What about the two thousand Satya withdrew? Ever find it?"

McIntyre chuckled. "Same boy. He said Satya had a habit of hiding things in his shoes. He took the cash, and the shoes, as it happens. We have it all. We can send him up for theft, if young Framji presses charges?"

Adi sue Satya's bereaved family? "I doubt that."

I leaned back as the puzzle pieces fell into place. Satya had glimpsed someone behind Burjor. He'd probably expected Pandu, so he'd palmed off his key to a more amenable ally. Burjor and Adi would be relieved to know that Pandu had recovered some funds for Satya's kin.

The talk moved to general topics. When we'd said what needed to be said, I set down my empty glass. McIntyre looked somber, his gaze on the offer I'd left on his blotter.

The quiet seeped into me, a comfortable quiet, which a year ago I would not have imagined was possible in McIntyre's volatile presence. The smooth burn of the Glenturret spread through me like a blanket. Perhaps that was why the question slipped past my lips.

"You were in Poona, in the '60s, weren't you?"

His eyelids flickered. "After the mutiny? We went all over. A foul time."

"Where'd you furlough?"

"Lucknow. Mysore . . ."

"Poona?"

He gave me an odd look. "'Course."

"In '60? '61?"

"Possibly. Wouldn't know dates, 'course. The missus might . . . she got here about then. Looking for someone?" Was that a glint in his eyes?

So close now. Should I stop before I went too far? *Thus conscience doth make cowards of us all*, I thought. *And makes us rather bear those ills we have, than fly to others that we know not of*. Hamlet was a namby-pamby bloke, I thought, feeling rebellious. I'd waited so long to know! McIntyre had his head back against the chair, his eyes closed to narrow slits.

I plunged ahead. "Did you know a woman named Shanti? Aged sixteen or so."

He blinked, eyebrows jerking upward. "Who's she?"

"Dead, now," I said. *Whether 'tis nobler in the mind to suffer the slings and arrows of outrageous fortune, Or to take arms against a sea of troubles, and by opposing, end them.*

My next words might quash our new amity, I thought, this delicate balance, so hard won. Some might even call it friendship. But I had lost friends before, some to death or disrepute, others to disdain and sudden anger. I could survive it. So I would take up arms, come what will.

"Shanti was my mother. She died when I was two."

My question sank in, causing ripples in his demeanor. "Did I *know* her? Is that a . . . ? Good Lord!"

His shocked eyebrows were answer enough.

"Right," I said, and stood up to leave.

His mouth closed, he clambered slowly to his feet. "Why'd you think . . . ?"

I stuck out a hand, locked gazes; we were the same height, of similar build, our linked hands equally browned by the Indian sun.

"Perhaps I'll always look for him," I said. "Thank you for the whiskey. Good night."

He didn't release me. "About that," he said. "Sit down a minute."

He dropped my hand and waved at the chair, then, when I remained standing, he eased into his seat and leaned back.

"Remember your commander, Colonel Sutton, from Poona? 'Fraid the bloke went up north on Shikar. 'I'll bag me a tiger,' he said. Well, tiger or not, he's gone missing."

Toying with his pipe, he watched my astonishment, my worry, my confusion. Why now? Why had he waited until now to say this?

He cupped the bowl of his pipe in his palm, covered it with his hand. "You know those frontier foothills, don't you? Care to go find him?"

AUTHOR'S NOTE

At the end of *Murder in Old Bombay,* when Captain Jim and Lady Diana left India, I knew they would return only under the direst circumstances. And yet, I knew they *would* return. Adi is Diana's beloved brother, almost her twin. He's also Jim's closest and dearest friend, "as near to blood as I could have." What could be more dire than saving Adi from the gallows?

I wrote *Murder in Old Bombay* after being inspired by the real-world tragedy of the Godrej girls, Bacha and Pilloo, two young ladies who fell to their deaths from Bombay University's Rajabai Tower in 1891. A widower at just twenty-two, Ardeshir Godrej mourned his wife Bacha deeply. He went on to found Godrej Enterprises, now a vast multinational conglomerate. This real-life hero's resilience, fortitude, and devotion moved me deeply.

However, Godrej's first business venture failed. As a young man, he'd invested in a factory making steel scalpels and other surgical equipment. In those days, no one believed that high-quality goods could be made in India, so he was asked to stamp "Made in UK" on his products. He refused and the business failed. This prompted me to write an adventure about my character Adi's venture, making surgical equipment. The real-life hit play *Charley's Aunt* with a cross-dressing rascal is real enough, though the rest is fiction: Adi finding himself in terrible trouble, facing the noose.

It occurred to me that a surgical scalpel is a perfect murder weapon, one that could be wielded by anyone in a moment of rage, thus offering a wide range of potential suspects, each with a different motive. This setup gave me the opportunity to explore India's caste system and the possible impact upon bold young men. An elderly Indian friend once told me that all the important decisions in his life had been made by his parents: his career, the selection of his wife, where he'd live, and much more. It was expected that he would comply and be grateful. The traditional structure offers clarity and purpose. Duty grips with a strong hold. But oh, how he longed to make his own decisions!

While there is much to admire about a social structure that protects children, seniors, and disabled and mentally ill individuals within the joint family system, few have counted the cost to an individual's psyche. What toll does it take to be constantly told what one must do, must like, must buy? Does it chafe, to be limited by the expectations and demands of the clan's leader, the *karta*?

I've long been fascinated with crime and how we rarely know where the story begins. There are grey boundaries: awful deeds may come from a moral cause. Here I studied a man desperate to save his child from a terrible fate; a father willing to risk anything—lie, cheat, and steal to rescue his daughter. Is he a crook? Certainly! But if we grasp the whole story, that verdict isn't as easy. Compare Satya with Burjor—another man trying to help his daughter, who seeks to negotiate his way out of difficulty. Diana's actions place her family in social jeopardy, but they do not abandon her. Fifty years later, in 1940, the late Sir Dinshaw Petit is said to have deserted his twenty-two-year-old daughter Ruttie Petit as punishment for eloping with Mohammed Ali Jinnah, the future founder of Pakistan.

Captain Jim's adventure at the end of this book also parallels Satya's. Both are faced with the need to commit crimes to rescue a child. However, Jim possesses assets that Satya lacked: resourceful allies in the Parsi family, relationships within the constabulary and an inventive wife, Diana.

As I worked through this mystery, it became clear that murder victim Satya had a dark secret. Each person saw a different aspect of him. But which of the many people he cheated had actually killed him?

The poignant answer stunned me; everything he had done was for Sona, his child, but he had told *her* none of it. In the end, his secrecy is his undoing, and hers, too.

Many individuals and events in this book are sourced from history. During the 1890s, a Parsi, Bomanji Dorabji Padamji, had charge of the Bombay mint. In 1903, he was awarded the title of Khan Bahadur for decades of faithful service. His son was, in fact, a crack shot and won many rifle competitions.

Diana being expelled from the fire temple also has a precedent in history. The 1903 lawsuit *Petit* v. *Jeejeebhoy* was initiated after Suzanne Tata (mother of J. R. D. Tata), the twenty-three-year-old Frenchwoman who married forty-six-year-old widower Ratanji Tata, was denied entry into a Parsi temple. Interestingly, she took the name Soona (pet name Sooni, or "Golden"), which reflected her blond hair.

In 1898, Mlle. Delphine Menant published a book in French, *Les Parsis,* based on her association with Parsi visitors to France. The Indian lawyer M. M. Murzban, who had corresponded with her, then undertook an English-language version. Imagine my surprise when I read about Rata-bai and Mehr-bai, daughters of Parsi lawyer Ardesir Framji Vakil. While Mehr-bai was a Glasgow-trained physician, her younger sister Rata-bai translated chapters of Menant's book into English. Sadly, in 1896, she died at the age of twenty-six, probably of bubonic plague. M. M. Murzban published an English version of Menant's book in 1917. I devoured the reprint from 1995 and decided that the two sisters should feature in my story as Diana's new girlfriends.

My own history is referenced in this book, too. My family name was Parakh, given to those with the hereditary occupation of testing the purity of gold. It comes from the Hindi verb *parakhna,* to perceive. Dara Parakh is fictional, but I could well imagine him wrestling with a quandary, to call out the fake bar or spare his friend's reputation.

About the Miracle of the Gold Brick—it happened too! Dastoor Jamshed Sorab Kukadaru is revered by many orthodox Parsis for miracles attributed to him. And this priest was extremely liberal! In 1882 he performed the (first-ever) *navjotes* (initiation into the Zoroastrian faith) of the "Mazagaon eleven," who were mixed-race adults and children. At the time, this caused great tumult in the Parsi community.

Ervad Kukadaru is said to have conjured a gold brick that funded the 1897 completion of the glorious Anjuman Atash Behram (fire temple) in Mumbai. How I enjoyed writing the scene where he grills Captain Jim and recruits him to defend a fellow Parsi's reputation! Of course, my story is a fictional explanation for the Miracle of the Gold Brick.

The Bombay dog riot was real as well, although I moved it six decades to fit into this tale. In 1832 a group of Parsis protested the overzealous dogcatchers who were killing stray dogs for their bounties. The Parsis then marched to the City Court, went on strike, closed their businesses, and paralyzed the city. When word reached them that the army garrison would be called out, the Parsis crowded the cantonment gates to prevent deliveries of food and water to the army! The Riot Act was then read out and their leaders arrested. These were released when the court determined they had rioted for the sake of dogs and not for political gain. Although it happened in 1832, I could not resist using this as the diversion to aid Captain Jim's escape during his fake embezzlement of bullion from the Bombay mint. I hope readers enjoy this as much as I did while writing it!

The *aachu meechu* ceremony is just as described. It is likely a remnant of a time when each journey might be one's last, so farewells took on a poignant significance. My grandma blessed us this way each time we came to spend the summer in Poona with her and my uncles. She repeated the ceremony when we departed, gifting me a little envelope of cash even at six years old! On the envelope she scrawled blessings in auspicious red ink. As children we loved to be made a fuss of, with the red *teeli* on our foreheads and grains of rice clinging to it. The words of blessing mentioned are directly from my beloved mum-in-law, Roda. We always giggled at the end, as she exhorted the recipient, even toddlers, to "become old and ancient!" In North America we maintain the practice on birthdays, weddings and ceremonies during pregnancy and babyhood. I hope they continue.

False testimony was indeed offered for sale during the Raj. Superintendent of Police C. J. Forgett's book describes the payment for a false witness who could stand cross-examination as one rupee (sixteen annas) but only half that if he was less skilled a liar. Little knots of candidates for the witness box could be found sitting around a banyan tree inside the court compound, being coached what to say in pending cases!

"You didn't even greet me!" That complaint comes from a favorite family story that was retold to much laughter at reunions. Apparently, I was the three-year-old who felt neglected and growled at my urbane six-foot uncle Jamshed. He and his wife hold a special place in my heart, so it seemed only right to preserve that moment in my novel. The temple at the climax of this book does exist at Surya Arghya statue near Bunker Muscum, Malabar Hill, but the mammoth white stone Ganesh is elsewhere.

I am indebted to Jay Langley, retired executive editor of the *Hunterdon County Democrat* newspaper. My writing partner and co-conspirator, he offered developmental and line edits for this manuscript that elevated it to be one I am truly proud of. I'm grateful to Sumi Mehta, who offered insights into the functioning of the joint-family system and sonar communities. I'd like to thank the team at Minotaur: Kelley Ragland, Katie Holt, Hector DeJean, and Stephen Erikson. Thank you to the fun team on the board of the New York chapter of Mystery Writers of America. My writing group, Elissa Matthews, Kathleen Schumar, Pamela Hagerty, Mary Olmstead, J. R. Bale, thanks for the delightful craft talks and support.

To my family members, who offer quiet support and encouragement: You are my reason for being.

And thank you dear readers, for your warmth and loyalty as we discover the adventures of Captain Jim and Lady Diana!

ABOUT THE AUTHOR

H. Merchant

Nev March is the first Indian-born writer to win the Minotaur Books/Mystery Writers of America First Crime Novel Award for her Edgar-finalist debut, *Murder in Old Bombay*. After a long career in business analysis, she returned to her passion, writing fiction. Nev sits on the board of the New York chapter of Mystery Writers of America and is a member of Crime Writers of Color. A Parsi Zoroastrian, she lives with her family in New Jersey and teaches occasionally at the Rutgers University Osher Institute.